WHITE LIES

ones who make it out and they do it by climbing over everybody else. They do what it takes to survive."

"You can't blame them for that," said Bell.

"No, you can't. But the sort of ruthlessness that got them this far is the sort of ruthlessness that could lead to them knifing me when we're out at sea and throwing me overboard so that they get my money and my boat. That's why we search them before we put them on board and why I carry a big gun. Got it?"

"Got it," said Bell.

"It's for protection."

Bell held up his hands. "I hear you, Ally. It's not a problem."

"Good man. Now let's get this cargo delivered."

"When are you going to tell me where we're going?" said Bell.

"I've given the GPS coordinates to Frankie," said Coatsworth. "Don't take it personal, mate. I'm the only one who knows the drop-off point."

"Keeping your cards close to your chest? I can understand that."

Coatsworth slapped him on the back. "I've been doing this for a while and never come close to being caught," he said. "I want to keep it that way. Look, you'll see it on the GPS anyway. We're heading north, up to the Suffolk coast. Near a place called Southwold. It's a quiet beach. I've used it before."

"That's a long trip," said Bell. "Close to a hundred miles."

"A couple of hours," said Coatsworth. "The water's quieter up there and there's almost no Border Force activity. Not that it matters that much, our boats can outrun anything the government has. The only thing that can keep up with us is a helicopter and there's almost zero chance of us coming across one." He slapped Bell on the back again and led him down the stairs. A thick chain had been fixed to the sea wall to give them something to hold on to as they made their way down.

Coatsworth climbed into the rib with Mercier. All the passengers were on board and Mercier was checking that they had all fastened their seat belts. Their luggage was lying on the floor, close to their feet.

Bell carefully climbed into his rib. It was a few feet longer than Coatsworth's and the seats were laid out slightly differently in four rows of two. His passengers were already strapped in. The Iraqi woman was sitting in the front row with her son on her lap. Her daughter was in the seat next to her.

Bell walked over to her and held on to the back of her seat for balance. "Your boy needs to be in a seat," he said.

She shook her head fiercely. "He is too small. He will fall out."

Bell looked at the boy and realised she had a point. He turned to Rainey. "Frankie, there's a cupboard under your wheel with some life jackets in it. There's a kid's one there."

Rainey bent down, pulled open a hatch, then straightened up with an orange life jacket in his hand. He tossed it to Bell and Bell handed it to the woman. "Put that on your boy, just in case."

He went up to the bow and knelt down to reach into the storage bay. He pulled out another seven life jackets.

"Ally never bothers," said Rainey.

"Yeah, well, I'm the skipper of this boat and I'm bothering," said Bell.

He went back down the rib, distributing the life jackets. When all his passengers were wearing them, he undid the ropes that kept the rib tethered to the jetty, sat down in the left-hand seat and started the engine. Rainey slid on to the right-hand seat. "Frankie, you're not carrying a gun, are you?" asked Bell.

Ahead of them, Coatsworth started his engine. Rainey frowned. "Why?"

"Why? Because I want to know if you're sitting there with a loaded gun in your pocket, that's why."

Rainey grinned. "Yeah, the look on your face when Ally pulled out that gun. I thought you were going to piss yourself."

"Nobody told me there'd be guns," said Bell. Coatsworth turned and gave Bell a thumbs-up. Bell grinned and returned the gesture.

"Guns don't kill people, people kill people," said Rainey.

"People with guns kill people without guns, that's generally how it works," said Bell. "Now do you have one or not?"

Rainey shook his head, then reached behind his back and pulled out a large hunting knife with a black handle. "No gun, but I've got this little beauty if we have any problems."

"Bloody hell, Frankie. Be careful you don't cut yourself with that." Rainey grinned and put the knife away.

Coatsworth gunned his engine and his rib moved away from the jetty. Bell looked over his shoulder and checked that all his passengers were strapped in. He noticed that the young Iraqi boy's belt was loose so he waved at the mother and mimed for her to tighten it. She did as she was told, then put up the hood of the boy's anorak. Bell nudged the throttle forward and steered the rib to starboard to move away from the jetty. There was a quarter-moon and the sky was virtually cloudless so visibility was good even at that late hour. Bell pulled a pair of protective goggles from his pocket and put them on. At the speed the rib would be travelling, even a small insect could potentially blind him. Rainey entered the GPS coordinates into the onboard computer. After a few seconds a dotted line appeared on the display, connecting their current position to their destination on the Suffolk coast. Rainey pulled on his own goggles and flashed Bell a thumbs-up. "Chocks away!" he shouted. "And don't spare the horses!"

Sea spray splattered across his goggles and Bell used his sleeve to wipe them clean. There was some traffic around — the English Channel was the busiest waterway in the world — but not enough to cause them any problems. There were freighters and container ships and a few miles away was a massive cross-Channel ferry heading towards the French coast. Bell was on his feet,

WHITE LIES

STEPHEN LEATHER

LARGE PRINT
Oxford

First published in Great Britain 2014
by
Hodder & Stoughton

Published in Large Print 2015 by ISIS Publishing Ltd.,
7 Centremead, Osney Mead, Oxford OX2 0ES
by arrangement with
Hodder & Stoughton, an Hachette UK Company

CIP data is available for this title from the British Library

ISBN 978–1–4450–9972–9 (hb)
ISBN 978–1–4450–9973–6 (pb)

Printed and bound in Great Britain by
T. J. International Ltd., Padstow, Cornwall

For Marie

"It's the ultimate earner, mate, better than drugs, better than guns, better than anything." The speaker was a dark-haired man in a black pea-coat. Alistair Coatsworth, Ally to his friends. He was forty-nine years old but looked a decade older. "People pay thousands to get into the UK. Thousands." His nose and cheeks were flecked with broken blood vessels, the result of years at sea and a taste for strong liquor.

There were three men sitting at the table listening intently as they finished off their plates of steak and chips. They were on their second bottle of red wine and a third had already been opened. They were in a small restaurant in a coastal village between Calais and Dunkirk, close to the border with Belgium. They had a table by a roaring fire that had shadows flickering over the roughly plastered walls.

Coatsworth waved his knife in the air for emphasis. "It's the Wild West over here, mate. You can make money hand over fist if you know what you doing. I've got a pal who smuggles them on to trucks for a grand a go. He pays the driver two hundred of that and keeps eight hundred for himself. Gets maybe five on a truck. He makes four grand and the driver gets one. They almost never get caught but, if they do, the driver just says they snuck on and he knows nothing."

"Sounds good," said the man sitting opposite him. His name was Andy Bell. He was a few years younger than Coatsworth, his face burned from exposure to the sun. He was wearing a heavy green polo-necked jumper, combat trousers and Timberland boots.

"He's got an even better deal with trucks that have been built with secret compartments. Usually when the driver owns his own rig. You can build a compartment that holds three or four and they'll never be found. He can charge four grand a go for that and the driver takes half. So that's two grand a person, six grand a run."

"Why the fifty-fifty split?" asked Bell.

"It's obvious," said another of the men at the table. Bruno Mercier was an Algerian, short and stocky with a crew cut and a diamond stud in his left ear. "Because if they get caught in a secret compartment, the driver can't say he didn't know."

"But most trucks aren't checked, right?" asked Bell.

"They don't have time," said Coatsworth. "Dover would grind to a halt if they searched every vehicle. The only problem is finding the right driver. That's not easy. At least doing what we're doing, we're not beholden to anyone. No one can let us down. And more importantly, no one can grass us up."

Bell nodded and popped another piece of steak into his mouth. Coatsworth emptied his glass and refilled it. He tried to pour more into Bell's glass but Bell put his hand over the top. "It'll help keep out the cold," said Coatsworth. "The English Channel gets bitter at night."

"Go on, then," said Bell, taking away his hand.

Coatsworth topped up Bell's glass. "I'll have some of that," said the fourth man at the table. Frankie Rainey was in his late twenties. He'd hung his fleece jacket over the back of his chair and had rolled up the sleeves of his denim shirt to reveal a tattoo on each forearm: a galleon in full sail and a dagger with a snake wound around it. One of his front teeth had gone black and the rest were stained from coffee and cigarettes. Coatsworth filled his glass.

"Business is good, yeah?" said Bell.

"That's why we need you," said Coatsworth, putting the bottle back on the table. "I was getting backed up."

"Where are you getting them from?" asked Bell. "It's not as if you can advertise smuggling runs to the UK, is it?"

"I pay some middlemen to cruise around Calais and the other jumping-off ports," said Coatsworth. "We need a particular sort of refugee. Ideally some government official or army guy from Iraq or Afghanistan or Syria who's managed to grab a decent wad before running away with his family. We're looking for the happy medium. We don't want the ones with no money. And if the guy's got megabucks he can just buy his way into the UK by paying for passports."

"What, real ones? Real passports?"

"Depends," said Coatsworth. "The really rich ones get the red-carpet treatment; invest a million quid in the UK and you and your family can all get passports. But twenty grand or so will get you a genuine passport, probably from some UK-born Asian who's never left

3

the country. He applies for a passport then sells it and forgets about travelling for ten years. But passports aren't easy to get and we offer a cheaper way in. The trick is to find the ones with cash. It's just a matter of separating the wheat from the chaff."

"The chaff being what?"

Coatsworth laughed. "The chaff being the morons with nothing, the ones who climb into refrigerated vans and freeze to death. My middlemen make sure that the clients have the cash to pay."

"Always cash?"

"Mostly," said Coatsworth. "Dollars, euros or pounds, no funny Arab money, though. So long as it adds up to three grand sterling, I'm happy. But I've taken gold in the past. And jewellery." He pushed the sleeve of his jacket up his arm and showed Bell the watch on his wrist. It was a gold Rolex. "Got this off an Iraqi doctor. It's the real thing, it'd cost you twenty grand in a jeweller's."

"It's genuine, right?"

Coatsworth scowled and held the watch under Bell's chin. "Of course it's bloody genuine. I'm not stupid. You can tell by the way the second hand moves. If it's jerky it's a fake. If it moves smoothly, it's real."

Bell looked at the watch and pulled a face. "I thought it was the other way around," he said.

Coatsworth frowned and pulled back his arm. He stared at the second hand and his frown deepened.

Rainey and Mercier burst out laughing but stopped when Coatsworth glared at them. "I'm yanking your chain," said Bell. "It's kosher. You can tell just by looking at it. Quality."

"Yeah," said Coatsworth. He tapped the watch. "We should be heading out soon," he said. "We've got to meet the van in ten minutes."

Bell sipped his wine. "So you think this is good money, long-term?" he asked.

"Best you'll ever see," said Coatsworth. He leaned across the table. "I've been doing this for eighteen months now. During the summer the weather's good enough for maybe twenty-five days. Less during spring and autumn. I've not done a winter yet but even then there'll be days when I can do a run. The summer months, I was doing two runs a day. Eight customers each trip, that's sixteen a day. Sixteen a day is forty-eight grand. OK, I've got costs. I pay the middlemen in France and I pay a guy to handle transport in the UK, and there's fuel and expenses, but I can still clear forty-five grand a day. A day, mate. In August alone I pulled in more than a million quid."

"So what do you do with all the money, that's too much cash to hide under the bed."

"I've got a guy who does my laundry," said Coatsworth. "He lives on Jersey, I take a run out to see him every month and leave the cash with him. He gets it into the banking system for a fee of ten per cent." He nodded at Rainey. "Frankie uses the same guy."

"That's a lot, ten per cent," said Bell. He put his knife and fork down and belched. "Better out than in," he said.

Coatsworth shook his head. "It's cheap as chips, mate. If you ever do get done the first thing they do is to go looking for the money and take it off you. My money's in shell companies and trusts all around the world, safe from their grubby little hands. It's worth paying ten per cent for. Trust me." He frowned. "What do you do with your money, then?"

"Spend it," said Bell. His face broke into a grin. "But then I haven't been earning a million quid a month. Running tourists out to the Holy Island doesn't bring in the big bucks."

"Yeah, well, now you're with me that'll change. And you need to start thinking about what you're going to do with the money you earn. The reason I brought you in is because I'm getting more customers than I can handle myself. It's a growing market, mate, and you'll grow with it." He looked at his watch again, drained his glass and stood up. "Time to go," he said, dropping a fifty-euro note on to the table and waving at the waiter, a grey-haired man in his fifties who doubled as the restaurant's barman.

"I need the toilet," said Bell.

"Bladder like a marble," said Rainey.

"Be quick about it," said Coatsworth. "We'll be in the car."

Bell hurried off to the toilet while Coatsworth, Rainey and Mercier headed outside and climbed into a large Mercedes. Rainey got into the driving seat and Coatsworth sat next to him. "Your mate's not in there throwing up I hope," said Coatsworth.

"He'll be fine," said Rainey. He lit a cigarette and then offered the pack to Coatsworth. Coatsworth took one and handed the pack back to Mercier. "He's short of a bob or two," Rainey continued. "He borrowed from the bank to buy his boat and he's having trouble with the payments. Did you see the look on his face when you asked him what he did with his money? He was thinking about selling his boat, things were that bad."

"I hope it works out with him," said Coatsworth. "With two boats we make twice as much money."

"Amen to that," said Rainey. He started the engine.

The door to the restaurant opened and Bell jogged over to the car and climbed in the back next to Mercier. "Sorry," he said. "Better to do it here than at sea, right?"

Rainey edged the car out of the car park and on to the main road to Dunkirk. Bell wound down the window and let the breeze play over his face.

"You've never been a smoker, Andy?" asked Mercier.

"Nah," said Bell.

"You should take it up, now you're on this crew. We smoke like chimneys."

"I think I'm getting a nicotine high from the secondary smoke," said Bell.

They drove to a garage that had closed for the night and parked behind it. "Where the fuck are they?" asked Coatsworth. He looked at his watch and scowled.

"I'll call him," said Rainey. He pulled out his mobile phone but before he could make the call a large white Renault van pulled on to the garage forecourt and switched off its lights. It drove slowly around the garage and stopped next to the Mercedes.

Coatsworth climbed out, dropped what was left of his cigarette on to the tarmac and ground it out with his boot. Mercier and Bell joined him.

The driver of the van was a middle-aged Frenchman wrapped up in a sheepskin jacket and a thick red wool scarf wound several times around his neck. He climbed out of the cab and hugged Coatsworth, his breath reeking of garlic and brandy. "We have a problem," said the Frenchman as he broke away.

"I pay you so I don't have any problems," said Coatsworth.

The Frenchman looked pained. "One of them, he didn't come up with the money."

"He's in the van?"

The Frenchman nodded.

"Why the hell's he in the van? You know the deal, Alain. No money, no passage. If he doesn't have the cash, he doesn't get in the van."

"It's complicated," said the Frenchman. "He's with his family."

"Do I give a shit?"

"He said he wanted to talk to you. I didn't see the harm."

"You mean you want me to do your job, is that it? Well, how about you give me back the commission for the whole family? How about that?"

"Ally, my friend, come on . . ."

"Don't give me that, you fat French fuck. I pay you to make sure that everything goes smoothly, not to bring the problems to me." He shook his head. "This ain't right, Alain."

"He's got kids."

"Yeah? You've got kids and I've got kids, we've all got kids. Having kids doesn't get you a free pass in life."

The Frenchman held up his hands. "I'm sorry. You're right."

"I know I'm right," said Coatsworth. He gestured at the van. "OK, get them out." He turned to Bell and Mercier. "You need to search them. No weapons and no drugs. One bag each. They know that's the deal so don't take any shit from them."

The Frenchman pulled open the rear doors. There were sixteen people sitting on the floor of the van: men, women and children. "Sortez!" he said. "Get out!"

The first man out was a young Somalian, tall and with a wicked scar running down his left cheek. He was carrying a Manchester United holdall.

"Over there," said Coatsworth, pointing to the front of the van.

Three Middle Eastern men were next out, all in jeans and pullovers and wearing heavy overcoats. "Where is the boat?" asked one in a thick accent.

"We search you, you pay, then we go to the boat," said Coatsworth.

"We want to see the boat first," said the man.

"No, you pay me first. Or you can fuck off. I don't care which."

The three men talked among themselves as they walked towards the front of the van. The one who had

9

done the talking looked over his shoulder but looked away when he saw that Coatsworth was glaring at him.

A man and a woman climbed out of the van with a small boy who couldn't have been more than six or seven years old. The boy was holding a toy dog and looking around excitedly as if he were on his way to a fairground. The woman had a black headscarf and the man was wearing a Muslim skullcap. The man was carrying two suitcases and the woman held the boy's free hand.

"Come on, come on," said Coatsworth. "We haven't got all night."

Three Somalian teenagers climbed out and stood looking around. They were carrying supermarket carrier bags stuffed with clothes. They were all tall and gangly, well over six feet. "What's their story?" Coatsworth asked the Frenchman.

"Their father's already in London. He sent them the money to come over. They're OK. Good kids."

Coatsworth pointed for the teenagers to go to the front of the van where Bell was patting down the three in the big coats. Mercier was on his knees, going through a suitcase.

"This is the guy," said the Frenchman. "He's Iraqi."

A middle-aged man in a heavy leather jacket climbed out of the van. He held up his arms to lift down a small boy, then offered his hand to help down a teenage girl. His wife then handed him three large blue nylon holdalls and one by one he placed them on the ground before helping her down. The wife and daughter were wearing long coats and headscarves.

"Does he speak English?" Coatsworth asked the Frenchman. The Frenchman nodded.

Coatsworth pointed at the man. "I want a word with you," he said. The man hesitated so Coatsworth grabbed him by the arm and frogmarched him over to the Mercedes. "Where's my money?" he asked.

The Iraqi reached into his jacket pocket and pulled out an envelope. Coatsworth snatched it from him. It contained hundred-euro notes and Coatsworth flicked through them. "There's only fifteen thousand euros here," he shouted. "That's not what we agreed. You have to pay twenty thousand. What game are you fucking playing?"

The man's wife was looking at them anxiously. Her son began to cry and she picked him up and whispered into his ear. The young girl slipped her arm through the woman's and bit down on her lower lip as she watched Coatsworth argue with her father.

"I gave him the deposit," said the Iraqi, gesturing at Alain. "Five hundred euros each. Two thousand euros."

"The deposit gets you on the list," said Coatsworth, waving the envelope in the man's face. "The real money gets you on the boat. The fee is four grand a head. Four thousand pounds. Or five thousand euros. That's the fee and you were told that before you signed on for this."

"My son is only three years old," protested the man. "He is a child."

"Four thousand pounds a head," said Coatsworth. "He's got a head, hasn't he? Four heads, sixteen thousand pounds. Or twenty thousand euros."

The man held out his hands, palms up. "I don't have twenty thousand euros. I have fifteen thousand. That's all I have." There were tears in his eyes and his hands were trembling.

"Bollocks," said Coatsworth. "You've got money, you're just trying to cheat me and I'll tell you now that's not going to work."

The man's wife shouted something in Arabic and the man turned and shouted back at her.

Coatsworth put a hand on the man's shoulder. "Don't talk to her, talk to me," he snarled.

"I don't have twenty thousand euros," he said. "Not in cash. It's in a bank. I can pay you when we get to England."

"Yeah, my cheque'll be in the post and you won't come in my mouth," said Coatsworth.

The Iraqi frowned. "I don't understand," he said.

"Then understand this. No money, no trip. You've enough for three people so I'll take three of you. One of you will have to stay behind." He looked at the watch on the man's wrist. It was a cheap Casio. "Does your wife have any jewellery? Any gold?"

The man shook his head. "We were robbed when we were in Turkey." The man's wife walked towards them, the boy in her arms, and said something in Arabic to the man. He replied, and she started talking faster, her free arm waving in the air.

"Bruno, get over here!" Coatsworth called to Mercier. Mercier closed the suitcase he was searching and jogged over.

The Iraqi was speaking to his wife in Arabic. Coatsworth turned to Mercier. "What's he saying?"

Mercier moved closer to Coatsworth. "She's saying she thinks they should wait. And find another way to England. Says she doesn't like you."

Coatsworth laughed harshly. "Doesn't like me? Doesn't fucking like me?" He pointed his finger at the woman. "You can fuck off back to Arab-land for all I care," he shouted. "There are plenty of people more than happy to pay me. You and your whole family can just fuck off and I'll get someone else to take your place."

The woman glared at him defiantly. Her husband stepped in front of her and began talking animatedly.

"What's he saying now?" Coatsworth asked Mercier.

"He's calming her down," said the Algerian. "He says they're to go ahead and he'll follow once he's got the cash." He listened for a few seconds and then nodded. "They've got family in Milton Keynes. Her uncle and her aunt. He wants her to stay with them until he gets over. Says he'll get the money from the bank and come on the next run."

Coatsworth nodded. "Finally he sees sense." A small group of men and women were still inside the van, watching what was going on. Coatsworth pointed at them. "Get the hell out now and bring your bags with you."

The Iraqi man finished talking to his wife and came over to Coatsworth.

"My wife, she is very upset," he said. "You have to understand, her brother and her cousin were killed this year. Her brother worked for the Ministry of the Interior and the Taliban weren't happy about what he was doing with border controls. Her cousin was a teacher and she was killed because she taught a lesson about female political leaders. The Taliban shot her in the face. We had to leave, you understand?"

"I hear sob stories like yours all the time, mate," said Coatsworth. "I'm not a charity, I'm a business. You pay, you go, you don't, you stay. When you've got the extra five thousand euros I'll take you." He gestured at the road. "Now on your bike."

"My bike?" The Iraqi frowned. "My bike? I have no bike."

"Get lost," said Coatsworth.

"But how do I get back to Calais?"

"That's not my problem," said Coatsworth.

"You have to help me," pleaded the Iraqi.

Coatsworth reached inside his coat and pulled out a gun, a small semi-automatic. He pointed it in the Iraqi's face. "I don't have to do anything," he said. "Now fuck off."

The Iraqi looked over at Bell but Bell just folded his arms and stared back at him. Mercier said something to the Iraqi in Arabic and the Iraqi opened his mouth to say something back but then he had a change of heart and walked away, his head down. Coatsworth turned to look at the woman. She put her arms around the two children. "Up to you, you can go with him or you can come to England. I don't care either way."

The woman nodded slowly. "We will go with you," she said. There was no disguising the hatred in her eyes, but she managed to force a smile. "Thank you, for what you are doing. We do not want to cause you any trouble."

Coatsworth nodded curtly and put his gun away. "Finish searching them," he said to Mercier. As the Algerian went over to the refugees, Coatsworth turned to watch the Iraqi walking down the road towards Calais. "Stupid bastard," he muttered under his breath.

Bell and Mercier finished searching the refugees. They had found two kitchen knives in the suitcase of one of the Arab men and all the Somalians had been carrying knives. Bell tossed the knives into the boot of the Mercedes.

"Line them up and tell them to get their money out," Coatsworth said.

Mercier shouted at the group in rapid Arabic, French and English. "Line up and get your money out now!"

The refugees did as they were told. Coatsworth walked along the line, taking the money from them and checking it. Once it was checked, he handed the notes to Mercier, who put them in a black backpack. When he reached the Iraqi woman and her two children, Coatsworth grunted and waved at the van. One of the Somalian teenagers helped her up.

When he reached the three Iraqi men, the one who had asked about the boat the first time had his chin up defiantly. "We want to see boat," he said.

"Do you see any water here?" asked Coatsworth.

The man frowned. "Water?" he repeated.

"The sea? Do you see the fucking sea? We're two miles from the coast. When we get to the coast you'll

15

see the bloody boat." He held out his hand. "Now give me the money or you can walk back to Calais with that other prick."

The man frowned, clearly not understanding what he was saying, so Coatsworth gestured at Mercier. "Tell him what I said and get them in the van." He took the backpack from Mercier, thrust in the last of the cash and took it over to the Mercedes. He tossed the backpack on top of the confiscated weapons and slammed the boot shut.

He got back into the Mercedes and watched the refugees climb into the van. The Frenchman slammed the doors shut and got back into the cab. Rainey offered him a cigarette and he took it. Rainey lit it and then lit one for himself.

Bell and Mercier got into the back of the Mercedes. Rainey gave Mercier a cigarette and then put the car in gear and followed the van down the road. There was no traffic and they reached the small harbour in just five minutes. The van pulled up next to a line of fisherman's huts that had been locked up for the night. Rainey brought the Mercedes to a stop behind the van and switched off the headlights.

Two teenagers in heavy jackets and wool beanies walked over. Mercier wound down the window and spoke to them in rapid French. They answered. "All good," Mercier said to Coatsworth.

"Let's do it, then," said Coatsworth. "Open the boot, Frankie."

Coatsworth climbed out of the car and went around to the back. He pulled out the backpack containing the money. Bell and Mercier joined him and retrieved their own bags.

Rainey got out and tossed the keys to one of the teenagers.

Coatsworth gestured at Mercier with his chin. "Tell them no joyriding and they'd better be here when we get back."

As Mercier translated Coatsworth's instructions, Rainey went around to the boot to get his bag, a Nike holdall. He slammed the boot shut.

The Frenchman had opened the van doors and the refugees climbed out and gathered together in a tight group like worried sheep.

"Right, get them on to the boats, now," said Coatsworth. He waved goodbye to the Frenchman, who climbed into the van and drove off.

There was a gap in the sea wall leading to a flight of stone steps. At the bottom of the steps was a wooden jetty where two high-performance rigid inflatable boats were bobbing in the swell. Rainey and Mercier ushered the men, women and children down the stone stairs to the waiting ribs. Each was about twenty feet long with a solid hull surrounded by a flexible inflatable collar that allowed the vessel to stay afloat even if swamped in rough seas. Each had a single massive Yamaha engine at the stern. There were few faster boats around, and these were certainly faster than anything owned by the UK's Border Force or HM Revenue and Customs. The boats were also virtually invisible to radar, making them the perfect smuggler's boat. Each had dual controls at the bow and a double bench seat in the centre with spaces for eight people and nylon seat belts to keep them securely in place.

Mercier and Rainey dumped their bags in the bow and helped the refugees into the boats.

"You didn't say anything about guns," Bell muttered to Coatsworth.

"What, you think I'm gonna be wandering around in the dark with thirty grand in my bag without some way of protecting myself?" sneered Coatsworth. He pointed down at the Somalians who were fastening their seat belts. "For all we know they could be bloody pirates. You think I'm going out to sea with people I don't know without a gun?" He gestured at the group, who were giving him anxious looks and muttering among themselves. "Look, mate, the meek don't inherit the earth and they sure as hell don't get out of shitholes like Iraq and Afghanistan or those African countries where they chop off each other's arms. Anyone who has made it this far has had to lie, cheat, steal and probably done a lot worse. Thieves, warlords and murderers, the odd torturer or two, they're the ones who get this far."

"She's a teacher, the wife of that guy you sent packing," said Bell.

"Yeah, well, she's the exception," said Coatsworth. "And how do we know she's telling the truth? For all we know her husband could have been Saddam Hussein's torturer-in-chief. Do you think teachers and farmers and bus drivers can get the money to escape from Iraq and get here? Do you think nice smiley people with a song in their hearts claw their way out?" He shook his head. "No, mate. The bastards are the

leaning against the white plastic bucket seat behind him. He held the wheel with his right hand and gripped the throttle lever with his left. They were doing just under fifteen knots and the throttle wasn't even at the halfway point. The rib's single outboard engine, the biggest on the market, cost upwards of fifteen thousand pounds and was capable of generating three hundred horsepower. At close to its top speed of sixty knots the engine burned through eleven gallons an hour and the fifty-five gallons in the tank were more than enough to get them across the Channel and back.

Rainey was standing to Bell's right. He had a matching set of controls but he kept his hands away from them and held on to a grab rail for balance. Both men scanned the waves ahead of them, not just for other boats but for anything floating in the water that could rupture the hull or smash the propeller.

Coatsworth and Mercier were off on his port side, about a hundred yards away and slightly ahead of them. Mercier waved. Bell didn't want to take his hands off the controls so he shouted over at Rainey to wave back. Coatsworth pushed the throttle forward and the rib began to pull away. Bell took a look over his shoulder to check that his passengers were OK. They were huddled together in the middle of the boat, hanging on to the guide ropes. "Hold on tight!" he shouted. The Iraqi woman hugged her son and whispered something into his ear.

Bell turned back to look ahead of the rib. The boat was smashing into the crests of the waves as it powered through the water. He had to grip the wheel tightly and his hand was vibrating on the throttle.

Coatsworth had already got close to full speed and his rib was planing over the tops of the waves, cutting across them like a knife. The rib was designed to lift above the waves once it reached fifteen or sixteen knots. There was a tilt lever on the steering wheel that changed the angle of the propeller relative to the hull and Bell adjusted it before pushing on the throttle. The massive engine roared behind him and the boat leapt forward. The moment it passed sixteen knots the juddering stopped and the boat planed across the top of the waves. Bell continued to move the throttle forward — twenty knots, thirty knots, forty knots. The night vision glasses protected his eyes from the slipstream but the wind was bitterly cold against his exposed skin.

Coatsworth's rib was several hundred yards ahead of him already and by the look of it had reached full speed. He wasn't worried about losing sight of the other rib as the GPS display was guaranteed to keep him on course. All he had to do was follow the dotted line on the display and it would take him straight to their destination on the Suffolk coast.

Bell pushed the throttle as far as it would go and the vessel's speed steadily increased. Fifty knots. Fifty-five. Sixty. Rainey shouted something but his words were lost in the slipstream. He shouted again and then pointed ahead. Bell saw what he was pointing at, a clump of something, rubbish or vegetation, about eighty yards ahead of them. The rib would probably cut through whatever it was but Bell didn't want to risk damaging the hull or the propeller so he steered the boat hard to port and missed whatever it was by yards before straightening up again.

The throttle was in the full-on position and Bell placed both hands on the wheel. It kicked and bucked as if it had a life of its own.

After almost two hours skimming the tops of the waves, Bell finally saw the coastline ahead of them. Rainey was handling the steering. They had taken it in turns; the wheel bucked and kicked constantly and steering was so tiring they rarely managed fifteen minutes before having to hand over control.

"Can you see the other boat?" shouted Bell above the roar of the outboard engine.

Rainey shook his head.

Bell wiped his goggles with his sleeve and looked at the GPS screen. They were bang on the dotted line that led to their landing point. He looked up again and scanned the sea ahead of them but there was no sign of Coatsworth's boat. He took a quick look over his shoulder. The passengers were all shivering. The Iraqi woman was clutching her son to her chest. Tears were streaming down her face but Bell couldn't tell whether they were the result of the cold wind or whether she was crying.

"I see him!" shouted Rainey, pointing off to the starboard side. Spray splashed across Bell's goggles and he pushed them up on to the top of his head and squinted into the wind. With no navigation lights,

Coatsworth's rib was just a black smudge in the water and it took Bell several seconds to see it.

"He's stopped," said Rainey.

"Cut the engine," said Bell. He took out his mobile phone as Rainey brought the throttle back to neutral. The rib slowed and began to toss and turn in the waves. They were close enough to land to get a signal and he called Coatsworth. "Where are you, I can't see you?" growled Coatsworth as soon as he answered.

"About four hundred yards on your port side, behind you," said Bell. "Is everything OK?"

"I don't see any lights on shore, I'm going to call my guy. You stay put."

Coatsworth ended the call. Rainey looked across at Bell. "What's happening?"

"He's waiting for the guy on shore."

"Can you take over the driving, I'm knackered," said Rainey.

"No problem." Bell's phone vibrated in his hand. He'd received a text message from Coatsworth. "TALLY HO!"

"We're on," said Bell, pushing the throttle forward. He took the rib up to ten knots. Coatsworth was already moving towards the shore.

A light flashed on the beach. Three short flashes. "That's them!" shouted Rainey.

"Do you think?" said Bell.

The shore was close now, a couple of hundred yards at most. The rib was perfect for smuggling operations, it could go into shallow water where most other boats would run aground. But where it really proved its worth was when it came to landing on beaches. The propeller could be lifted out of the water and the boat could run right up on to the beach. It didn't need a harbour or a dock, any flat stretch of sand or pebbles would do. And once the boat had been unloaded it was a simple matter to push it back into the water and head off again.

Rainey moved to the stern, ready to lift the outboard. On Coatsworth's rib, Mercier was doing the same. The light flashed again, about halfway up the beach.

The rib was rocking from side to side, making it hard to control, so Bell increased the power. Ahead of him Coatsworth gunned his engine and the rib leapt towards the shore. Mercier pulled the outboard towards him, lifting the propeller out of the water as the prow of the rib touched the sand. The rib's momentum carried it on to the beach. Mercier leapt out, ran to the prow and tugged at a rope there. Coatsworth started urging his passengers to get on to the beach. A man in a Barbour jacket and green wellington boots hurried over, and once the passengers were all on the sand he helped Mercier drag the rib on to the beach.

Bell twisted around. "Here we go!" he shouted at Rainey, and Rainey flashed him a thumbs-up. Bell pushed the throttle to the halfway position. The engine roared and the rib surged towards the beach. A wave broke under the hull just as the boat began to move and the prow pointed up at the stars and then just as quickly dipped down. Bell pulled the power for a second until the bow was back in the water and then he blipped it again. The propeller bit and the rib rode another wave. When the prow was ten feet from the water's edge he pulled the power and put both hands on the wheel and concentrated on keeping the rib facing head-on.

The rib hit the sand and almost immediately Rainey was by Bell's side. He jumped on to the beach and grabbed the rope at the prow. "Right, everybody off!" shouted Bell.

His passengers undid their seat belts, took off their life jackets and clambered over the side. The Iraqi woman was struggling with her son so Bell held the boy while she jumped over the side. He handed the boy to her and then helped the woman's daughter.

The man in the Barbour jacket jogged over to help Rainey pull the rib farther up the beach.

The passengers gathered together on the beach, splitting into nationalities. Bell climbed out and joined Mercier and the man in the Barbour jacket. The three of them gave the rib a final tug up the beach. "What happens now?" Bell asked the man.

"He's new," Rainey said to the man in the Barbour jacket. He was in his sixties with long grey hair tied back in a ponytail. "This is Derek, he handles the transport to London," said Rainey.

Derek held out a gloved hand and Bell shook it. "Andy," said Bell. "He's right, it's my first run."

"First of many, hopefully," said Derek. He gestured up the beach. "I've parked the coach on the other side of the dunes there. Any problems, Frankie?"

"Sweet as a nut," said Rainey. "I'll get my bag."

"Good man," said Derek. He walked over to the passengers and held out his arms like a shepherd trying to control his flock. "Everyone, please move up the beach, the coach is waiting for you."

Mercier walked across the sand, repeating Derek's instructions in French and Arabic.

Coatsworth jogged over to Bell and Rainey. "Frankie, give them a hand getting them on the coach," he said.

"I was just going to get my bag," said Rainey.

"Get them on the coach first, I don't want to hang about."

"OK, OK." Rainey walked over to the Iraqi woman, who was struggling with her son and her suitcase. He grabbed the case from her and headed after Derek, muttering under his breath.

Coatsworth grinned at Bell. "How easy was that?" he said.

Bell nodded. "Is it always plain sailing? No pun intended."

Coatsworth slapped him on the back. "Always," he said. "It's a milk run, every time. You see how easy it is, now? We can do two runs a night without breaking a sweat."

A beam of light blinded Coatsworth and he threw up his hands to shield his eyes. "What the fuck?" he shouted.

They heard shouts from the dunes and more beams of white light cut through the night sky. "Border Force!" shouted a man. "Stay where you are!"

Bell heard a woman scream but his eyes were blinded by the lights and he couldn't see who it was. He ducked down, blinking. More than a dozen figures in black overalls and yellow fluorescent jackets were running towards them.

Two of the Somalian lads started to run down the beach, their feet kicking up sprays of sand behind them. Five of the men in fluorescent jackets ran after them. Bell couldn't help but smile as the pursuers were overweight and didn't have a hope in hell of catching the Somalians.

A group of passengers had almost reached the dunes and they were surrounded by Border Force staff. More men in fluorescent jackets were heading their way. Off to Bell's right, a woman screamed.

Coatsworth reached inside his jacket but Bell put a hand on his arm. "Don't even think about it, Ally," he said. "You fire that thing and they'll throw away the key. Same as shooting a cop."

Coatsworth glared at Bell, but then nodded. "Aye. You're right. Worst I'll get is a few years for trafficking, maybe not even that." He tossed the gun into the rib behind him and raised his hands.

The woman screamed again off to their right. Bell used his hands to shield his eyes. Rainey had picked up the Iraqi woman's child and was holding his knife to the boy's throat. Three big men in fluorescent jackets were advancing towards him but they stopped when he pressed the knife harder under the boy's chin. "One more step and I'll kill him!" Rainey shouted.

"Shit," hissed Bell. He looked around. While there were more than two dozen Border Force staff on the beach, he couldn't see any police and more importantly he couldn't see any police with guns.

Mercier turned and ran, heading for the dunes, but he was quickly brought down by two big men. One of them straddled him and used plastic ties to bind his wrists as Mercier cursed them in French.

Bell hurried over the sand towards Rainey. The three Border Force men were standing about ten feet away from him, clearly unsure what to do. Bell looked around but there was no one obviously in charge.

"Frankie, don't be stupid, mate!" Bell shouted.

Rainey kept his eyes on the men in front of him. The boy's mother charged towards him, her hands splayed like claws, screaming like a banshee. He kicked her in the stomach and she fell back on to the sand. One of the Border Force men knelt down next to her. A blond woman in a fluorescent jacket ran over and put up her hands in an attempt to placate Rainey. "Come on, there's no need for this," she said. "Just put the boy down before you hurt him."

"Hurt him? You stupid cow, if you come one step closer to me I'll slit his throat. Now keep your distance, all of you!" He backed slowly towards Coatsworth's rib. "Ally, come on, get in the rib, we're getting the hell out of here."

"Don't do it, Ally," said Bell. "It's an immigration bust, it's no big deal."

"Ally!" shouted Rainey. "Get a move on."

Bell reached out for Coatsworth's arm but Coatsworth shook him off and hurried across the sand towards his rib.

There were more than a dozen Border Force staff gathered on the beach around Rainey but they were unwilling to move in. The boy had gone still, his eyes wide and staring, his face wet with tears. Three searchlight beams illuminated Rainey and the boy and threw elongated shadows across the sand and into the waves.

"Get me my bag, Andy!" shouted Rainey.

"What?" Bell shouted back.

"Get my bag, it's in the hold."

Coatsworth pushed his rib back into the water.

"What do you need your bag for?" asked Bell.

Coatsworth climbed into the rib and made his way to the stern so that he could drop the propeller back into the water.

"Just get it," shouted Rainey. He pressed the knife tighter against the boy's throat. "I'll cut him!" he shouted at the Border Force team. "Stay back!"

"This isn't helping anyone," said the Border Force woman. She had the clipped tones of a headmistress addressing an unruly child and Bell could see that she was only inflaming the situation.

"You, shut the fuck up!" shouted Rainey.

The Iraqi woman struggled to sit up and began to scream at Rainey. One of the Border Force men knelt down and tried to quieten her but she turned her venom on him, spat in his face and continued to scream.

Bell climbed on to the rib and retrieved Rainey's backpack from the storage hold in the bow. He straightened up and unzipped it. Inside were six plastic-wrapped packages, each the size of a house brick.

"What are you doing?" shouted Rainey. "I said bring it here, I didn't say open it."

"What is it, Frankie? Cocaine or heroin?"

"Get over here, Andy. Don't fuck about."

"You brought drugs with you?" shouted Coatsworth. "What the hell were you thinking?"

"Fuck off, Ally," shouted Rainey. "The pittance you've been paying me, you can't blame me. Andy, get over here, now."

Coatsworth's gun was by Bell's foot. Bell bent down and picked it up.

"Andy, come on! We've got to go, now!"

Bell climbed out of the rib and walked along the beach, carrying the bag in his left hand and the semi-automatic in his right.

"Get a move on!" shouted Rainey. The child began to scream and Rainey shook him. "Shut the fuck up!" he shouted.

"He's scared," said Bell.

"Throw the bag in the boat," said Rainey. He shook the boy again, then changed his grip so that his hand was over his mouth, muffling his cries.

Bell did as he was told.

"Where did you get the gun from?" Rainey asked.

"It's Ally's."

"Well, point it at them," said Rainey, gesturing at the Border Force people.

"I'm not pointing a loaded gun at anybody," said Bell.

There was a roaring sound from the dunes and then a blindingly bright light shone in their eyes. Bell heard the whoop-whoop-whoop of a helicopter's rotor blades. He shielded his eyes with the flat of his hand but the light was still too bright for him to see the helicopter.

"Andy, give me the bloody gun, come on!" shouted Rainey, his voice barely audible over the roar of the helicopter's turbine.

Bell walked over the sand towards Rainey. "You've got a knife and the kid, how are you gonna hold a gun?"

"Just give it to me."

Bell tossed the gun at Rainey and it fell at his feet. "What are you playing at?" shouted Rainey.

"If you want the bloody gun you can have it, but I'm having nothing to do with it."

The boy was still struggling in Rainey's grasp. "Be still, will you," hissed Rainey, pressing the knife even harder against the boy's throat. He took a step towards the gun. "I'll cut him if you even think of moving!" he shouted at the line of fluorescent jackets.

The helicopter banked to the side and the huge beam lost Rainey for a few seconds and then swung back to capture him once more. Rainey bent down, dropped the knife and picked up the gun. He pointed it at the Border Force woman and grinned. "This changes things, doesn't it," he shouted. "Now back up the beach, all of you!"

The woman held up her hands. "There's no need for any of this," she said, then flinched as Rainey jerked the gun as if he was about to pull the trigger. "OK, OK!" she shouted. "Everybody back!"

The fluorescent jackets started backing away.

"That's more like it!" shouted Rainey.

"Let the boy go, Frankie," shouted Bell. "You've got the only gun on the beach."

"There could be armed cops in the helicopter!"

"It's a Border Force chopper, they're not armed," said Bell. "They're too stupid to be trusted with guns." He nodded at the Border Force woman, who seemed to be running the show. "No offence."

"Just push the boat out," shouted Rainey, his words almost lost in the roar of the helicopter's turbine. He took a quick look over his shoulder. "Ally, get the propeller in the water as soon as you can." He looked back at Bell. "Come on, come on, we've got to get out of here."

One of the Border Force men took a step forward and Rainey screamed, "Stay where you are!" and pointed the gun at him.

"Frankie, mate, it's over," shouted Bell.

"Over? It's not over until we're back in France!"

"The gun's not loaded."

Rainey looked at the gun in his hand. "Bollocks."

"It's loaded," shouted Coatsworth from the stern of the rib. "I loaded it myself."

Bell shook his head. "Give it up, Frankie. Let the boy go."

Rainey pointed the gun at Bell, his finger tightening on the trigger. One of the Border Force men moved forward and Rainey swung the bag towards the rank of fluorescent jackets. "Get the hell back or I'll shoot!" he yelled.

"Andy, push the boat out and get in!" shouted Coatsworth. "Let's get the hell out of here!"

The helicopter was directly overhead now, the rotor wash buffeting them and sending sea spray over the boat.

"It's over, Frankie!" shouted Bell.

"Like hell it is," shouted Rainey. "I'm not going to prison again!" He aimed the gun over the heads of the Border Force team and pulled the trigger. Nothing happened. Rainey's jaw dropped. He pulled the trigger and again nothing happened.

Rainey looked over at Bell, his mouth wide open. The young boy slipped from his grip and ran towards his mother.

Bell reached into his pocket with his right hand. He held up the ammunition clip from the gun.

Rainey cursed and almost immediately disappeared under a scrum of fluorescent jackets.

Bell looked over at Coatsworth, who was holding on to the outboard motor to keep his balance as the downdraught from the helicopter rocked the rib from side to side. Coatsworth frowned as he tried to work out what had just happened. He looked up at the helicopter and was immediately blinded by its searchlight. He put his hands up to shield his eyes, lost his balance and fell over the side into the water. It was only waist deep so he was soon on his feet and staggering through the waves to the shore.

Three large figures ran over to Bell. One of them was the woman who had tried to talk to Rainey. She was as tall and heavyset as the men on either side of her. They were both holding big Magnalite torches. The man on her left was ginger-haired and had a crop of freckles across his nose and cheeks. "Hands behind your back," he growled in a West Country accent.

"I'm on your side, pal," said Bell. "I'm with MI5."

"Yeah? And I'm James bloody Bond," said the man. He brought his flashlight crashing down on Bell's head and he dropped like a stone.

"Spider? Can you hear me?" The voice sounded muffled, and far away. Dan "Spider" Shepherd groaned and opened his eyes. The voice was that of a woman but the face looking down at him had a greying goatee. It was a paramedic in a fluorescent jacket. "Thank goodness for that, you had me worried for a moment." The voice was definitely female and the paramedic's lips hadn't moved.

Shepherd realised that Charlotte Button was standing behind the paramedic. She was wearing a wool beanie hat and a North Face fleece-lined jacket. "Charlie?"

The paramedic shone a small torch into Shepherd's eyes and he flinched. "You're not going to hit me with that as well, are you?" he said.

"You'll be all right," he said. "It's superficial."

"Superficial enough to knock me out cold," said Shepherd.

"I can take you in for an MRI if you want," said the paramedic.

"It's OK," said Shepherd. "It's not the first time I've been hit and I'm sure it won't be the last." He put his hand up to his head and felt a dressing just above his right ear.

"There was some bleeding and some swelling," said the paramedic. "Are you allergic to aspirin?"

"No, I've got no allergies, but I'm not partial to Magnalites at the moment."

"He'll be fine," said Button, patting the paramedic on the shoulder. "He's got a thick skull. Can you do me a favour and give me a minute or two?"

The paramedic nodded and climbed out of the back of the ambulance. Shepherd struggled to sit up. "How long was I out?"

"Fifteen minutes or so," she said.

"He could have killed me."

"I think that's a slight exaggeration," she said.

"Why the hell did he hit me?" asked Shepherd, touching the dressing again. "Didn't he know who I was?"

"He was a late addition, a replacement for a guy who called in sick," said Button. "Seems there was a breakdown in communication and he wasn't told that you'd be on one of the boats."

"And why was no one there armed?"

"They didn't tell the police. I gather they were worried that they'd take the credit."

"You're joking."

"I wish I was. I understand it was discussed but there'd been no indication from you that anyone in

Coatsworth's gang was armed so they decided to do it without an armed police presence."

"They're blaming me? Are you serious?"

"Not exactly blaming you, just pointing out that you hadn't mentioned firearms so they didn't consider it necessary to ask for armed police support." She grimaced. "But I think you know as well as I do that it's probably more that they wanted to keep the arrests in-house. Once they call in the armed police it becomes a police operation."

"Yeah, well, there's a reason they call it Border Farce," said Shepherd. "You know, these days it's more likely that it'll be law enforcement hurting me than villains. It wasn't that long ago that I was tasered by cops, remember?"

"I remember. It was regrettable. As was what happened tonight."

"Regrettable? Armed cops tasered me while I was doused in petrol. I could have gone up like a Roman candle. And tonight I got walloped over the head when I was in the process of surrendering."

"Luckily you've got a thick skull." She smiled. "I'm sorry, I know it's not a laughing matter."

"Damn right it's not. Charlie, even if I was a bad guy, he was still out of order belting me the way he did. I had my hands up. I was no threat to him."

"You can make an official complaint if you want," said Button.

"What's the point?"

"Exactly," she said. She looked at her watch. "Look, I'm sure you're tired. I've got us rooms booked at a local hotel.

Nothing fancy but I'm told they do a good breakfast. You should get some sleep and we'll do a debrief later."

The hotel was surprisingly good considering it was well away from any main road and had only a dozen rooms. Shepherd showered and then slipped naked under a duvet and was asleep within seconds. He woke to the sound of the phone ringing next to the bed. He groped for it. "It's a quarter to ten and they stop serving breakfast at ten," said Button. "What would you like?"

"Coffee. Eggs and bacon." He ran a hand through his hair and winced as he touched the dressing.

"They do a wonderful full English, I'm told."

"OK, fine. Thanks."

"I'll order it now," she said.

Shepherd rolled out of bed and pulled on his clothes from the previous night. There was a small washbag by the sink containing a toothbrush, a tube of toothpaste, a disposable razor and a small can of shaving foam. He shaved, brushed his teeth and hurried downstairs. Button was sitting at a table by the window. Two other tables were occupied — a suited businessman reading the *FT* sat at one and a middle-aged couple sat silently at another. Button had changed into a grey suit and had her chestnut hair clipped up at the back, and she smiled at him over her cup of tea. "Sleep well?"

He dropped down on to the seat opposite her and picked up his coffee. "I was dog-tired," he said.

"Can't be easy, driving one of those ribs." She raised her cup in salute. "Anyway, job well done. You've closed down a people-trafficking route and a drug-trafficking route in one fell swoop. Two birds with one stone, to complete the avian theme. Plus you saved that young boy's life."

"Rainey was panicking, I don't think he would've killed the kid."

"Spider, he held a knife to the boy's throat. Anyway, you didn't give him the chance. How's the head?"

"Still hurts," said Shepherd.

"Worse than before? Do you want to swing by the hospital?"

"It'll be OK," said Shepherd. "Like I said, I've been hit before."

A waitress arrived and put a plate of eggs, bacon, sausage, tomato, black pudding and beans in front of Shepherd, along with a full toast rack, before serving Button with a small portion of scrambled eggs and smoked salmon. She caught him looking at her food and smiled. "I'm on a bit of a diet," she said.

"You don't need to be," he said. He laughed and picked up his knife and fork. "And I'm not just saying that."

"I'm on that eat for five days, fast for two days," she said. She picked up her fork. "Not a real fast, I just have to cut back to five hundred calories on a fast day." She nodded at her plate. "This is about it, I'm afraid."

Shepherd tucked into his breakfast while Button took small mouthfuls and chewed slowly.

"That turned out to be one of your longer cases, didn't it," she asked. It was a statement rather than a question.

"Four months, on and off," he said, as he buttered a slice of toast. "It wasn't easy getting them to approach me. Softly, softly. I had to get close to Rainey and then wait for him to introduce me to Coatsworth. It took time. And a lot of trips on the boat." He sipped his coffee. "You know, I was on a similar case seven years ago, when I was with the cops. That's when I learned to drive a rib."

Button nodded. "That's what made you the perfect choice for this job."

"Yeah, but here's the thing. Seven years ago they were using ribs to dash across the Channel. My case back then was counterfeit currency, but it was clear the same boats were being used for drugs and for people. Seven years later nothing has changed."

"Your point being?"

Shepherd smiled thinly. "I'm not sure there is a point," he said. "In fact the whole exercise seems pointless. Anyone can go out and buy a rib and a GPS and set themselves up as a smuggler."

"And we stop them. That's how it works."

"But we're not stopping them, are we? We stopped Coatsworth, sure. But how many others are there?"

"You're saying that because so many people are breaking the law we should just stop what we're doing? That's like saying we should let everyone drive at ninety miles an hour because so many people break the speed limit."

Shepherd shook his head. "I just think there has to be a more efficient way of handling it. Make ribs harder to buy, for instance. Or have them all chipped so that

42

they can be tracked by satellite. That way if one keeps running back and forth to the Continent, someone can knock on the captain's door and ask him what he's up to. How hard would that be?"

"Fitting a tracker would be easy enough, but so would disabling it. But it's a good idea, I'll raise it with the relevant authorities."

"Not Border Farce, please."

Button chuckled. "You really must stop calling them that. I'll end up picking up the habit and that really won't do."

"Charlie, with the best will in the world, their incompetence nearly got me killed last night."

"You got a bump on the head."

"No, I had a Magnalite torch smashed down on my skull. If he'd hit my temple, I could have died. And that whole business with the kid wouldn't have happened if there had been armed cops to take care of the situation."

"As I said last night, there had been no mentions of a gun so the Border Force commander didn't think an armed response was necessary."

"The commander would be that woman who was on the beach, right? She seemed to be running things. Though by the size of her, I doubt she does much actual running."

"Spider! Please. That's uncalled for."

"OK, I take it back. But you can understand why she's not my flavour of the month just now." He gestured with his knife at the dressing on his head.

"Anyway, she wasn't the commander. The commander wasn't on the scene, but she was his number two. She's very experienced, Spider, she was ten years with Revenue and Customs investigations."

"She let the situation get out of control, way out of control." He buttered another piece of toast.

"And you rescued it," said Button. "She knows that, and I will take it up with her commander. But really, all's well that ends well." She refilled her cup from a white pot. "Now, let's look ahead. I've nothing pressing for you and you put in more than enough hours on the Coatsworth case, so why not take a couple of weeks off. Have a holiday."

"I'm not a great one for beaches or swimming pools. But yeah, I could do with some downtime." He put down his knife and fork. He hadn't realised how hungry he was but he'd cleaned his plate and eaten half the toast in the rack. He looked over at Button's plate. She'd barely touched her scrambled eggs and salmon. "I'll head back to Hereford, if that's OK with you. I'll need transport."

"There's a car and driver outside ready to take you wherever you want to go," she said. "Where's the Andy Bell vehicle?"

"Up north. In the Seahouses harbour car park. I left it there when I took the rib over to France."

"I'll get it collected," said Button. "And I'll arrange for the cottage in Seahouses to be cleared. Is there anything there you need?"

"It's all legend stuff," said Shepherd. He took off his wristwatch, a battered TAG Heuer, and put it down in front of her. "That has to go back, too." He reached for another slice of toast, buttered it and covered it with marmalade.

"Do you always eat like that?" she asked.

"Only when I'm ravenous," he said.

"You must have a high metabolic rate."

"Piloting the rib takes a lot of energy," said Shepherd. "You're on your feet all the time and fighting the wheel. What's happening with Coatsworth and the rest?"

"They'll all be charged with human trafficking, and the importation of Class A drugs. There were eight kilos of high-grade Afghan heroin in Rainey's backpack. We'll try to get him to tell us where the drugs were headed."

"And cut him a deal?"

"That's how it works."

"But no deal for Coatsworth?"

"Not on the drugs. He's denying all knowledge of the heroin."

"I don't think he knew, Charlie. He never mentioned drugs to me."

"Why would he, you're the new guy on the team." She leaned towards him. "Seriously, Spider, you did well. Coatsworth's operation has brought over hundreds of illegals and heaven knows how much heroin."

"Ally always said the great thing about smuggling people was the penalties were so much lower."

"Ally?" She raised her eyebrows.

"Just because I use his first name . . ."

"The drugs were on his boat, Spider."

"No argument there, I'm just saying that he probably didn't know what Rainey was doing. It was just a backpack. We all had gear with us."

"Yes, but you didn't have eight kilos of almost pure heroin in your backpack, did you?"

"So Coatsworth is going to be charged with drugs smuggling as well?"

"That'll be a CPS decision," she said.

"That's not fair." He held up his hands. "I know, life's not fair."

"Spider, he ran a smuggling operation and the day we busted him there were eight kilos of heroin on his boat. If Rainey wants to stand up in court and say that Coatsworth didn't know about the drugs, then that's all well and good. But it's not your problem." She picked up the TAG Heuer and put it in her handbag, then looked at her own watch, a slim gold Cartier. "Right, I've got a debrief with the Border Force commander at noon. I'll be sure to bring up the matter of you being belted over the head. Let me know what you decide holiday-wise. Oh, and your biannual is due. Caroline Stockmann will be in touch."

"My favourite psychologist," he said. Six-monthly psychological evaluations were a nuisance but he liked Stockmann as she had the knack of making them seem like friendly conversations.

"You love your little chats with her, you know you do." Button laughed. "And she can check that the torch didn't do any lasting damage."

The instructor's name was Hammad. He was thirty-seven years old, a former captain in the Afghan National Army, and a jihad warrior who believed with all his heart that his mission in life was to kill those who did not agree that Allah was the only God and that Muhammad was his prophet. Hammad knew the Qur'an by heart and his favourite verse was "I will cast terror into the hearts of those who disbelieve. Therefore strike off their heads and strike off every fingertip of them".

Hammad fervently believed that Muslims who didn't join the fight against the infidel were hypocrites that Allah would surely send to Hell. He had joined the Taliban as a teenager and six years later had cheered and praised Allah when the Twin Towers had been attacked and destroyed. Like many of his compatriots he had gone to ground when the Americans had invaded Afghanistan, dumping his weapons and passing as a struggling farmer until the Americans had decided to rebuild the Afghan army. Hammad had joined using a false name and had been trained by the Third Special Forces Group in a Soviet-built camp on the eastern side of Kabul. In 2004 he was promoted to captain and three months later he left his barracks with an M-16 and half a dozen grenades and killed three Americans and twenty-three Afghan soldiers before disappearing over the border into the badlands of Pakistan.

He was a short, stocky man, his skin dark brown and leathery from a lifetime lived mainly outdoors. There was a jagged scar on his left cheek, a hearing aid in his left ear and he was missing two fingers on his left hand, the result of an improvised IED exploding prematurely. He was wearing a grey salwar kameez — a long shirt over baggy trousers that flapped in the wind and stirred up the dust around his sandals. On the table in front of him was a ground-to-air missile and standing around him were six men, all in their twenties, who were hanging on his every word. They had been up since dawn. After a breakfast of circular sweet flatbreads, dried apricots, yogurt and green tea flavoured with cardamom, the men had been taken for a two-kilometre run followed by an hour of physical exercises and unarmed combat training.

Three of them were wearing salwar kameez and one was wearing an ankle-length thawb of rough cotton. The other two wore combat trousers, T-shirts and Nike trainers. There was no dress code at the training camp, it was the quality of the men that mattered, not their clothing. At just before midday they had all retreated to a goatherd's cottage. An American spy satellite was due to pass overhead and would be photographing the area for at least twenty minutes before it passed out of range. Hammad had a notebook that contained the dates and times that satellites passed overhead and several times each day training had to be interrupted. There was now a five-hour window before the next satellite was due and Hammad planned to use the time to introduce the young jihadists to the ground-to-air-missile that was central to al-Qaeda's plan to unleash havoc in the United Kingdom.

The missile had been delivered in the back of an old pick-up truck, packed in a wooden crate. Now it sat on a wooden trestle table. It was a practice model, coloured blue. The live version was green, but it would be some time before the jihadists would be shown the real thing. It was a little over five feet long, the firing unit at the front with most of the barrel behind it. Hammad let the jihadists stare at the weapon for more than a minute. One of them, overweight and dark skinned, said something to the man on his left. The other man laughed and replied but Hammad had no idea what they were saying. They both had Bangladeshi parents but had been born in Glasgow and had accents so impenetrable that whenever possible he tried to avoid talking to them. They were both wearing ill-fitting salwar kameez. The fat one — his name was Sami — had a knitted Muslim cap on his head, and his chest strained at the material of his shirt. The other, Labib, was always pulling up his trousers as if he feared they were about to drop around his knees.

Labib reached out to touch the missile but then pulled his hand back as if he feared it would somehow hurt him. Hammad smiled. "The weapon is called an Igla, and has the designation 9K38. You are never to refer to it that way. In all communication it is to be called 'the parcel'. That applies not only to phone and email conversations, but even when you think you are talking to a brother in a secure location. Do you all understand that?"

The six men nodded. One of them raised a hand to ask a question. His name was Rafiq, a British-born Pakistani who had proved himself an enthusiastic and diligent student. He was one of the men wearing Western clothing. The men who ran the training camp had high hopes for Rafiq, and the other jihadist who had come from Bradford, a twenty-year-old mechanic called Naseem. Like Rafiq, Naseem dressed in Western clothing and was of Pakistani heritage. Naseem was clean shaven but Rafiq had a thick, neatly trimmed beard.

"Why is it blue?" asked Rafiq.

"It is a practice model, it cannot be fired and there is no warhead," said Hammad. "We will be using this practice model so that you can familiarise yourself with the components. Tomorrow you will be shown a working version and eventually we will be conducting live firings."

"Will we be shooting at a plane?" asked Naseem.

"Let's leave the questions until the end," said Hammad. "Now, you will hear it called by several names. The Russians call it Igla, which means needle. The Americans call it the Grouse. There is an earlier version the Americans call Gimlet. And a new version, introduced to the Russian army in 2004, is called the Grinch by the Americans. The versions we have are all the Igla. You train on this and when we are ready, you will be firing one."

"Wicked," said one of the Birmingham men. He was known as "KC" or "Casey", Hammad wasn't sure which. His parents were Kenyan but KC had been born in England and had a strong Birmingham accent. In contrast to his problems with the Glaswegians, though, Hammad had no trouble understanding KC. KC was enthusiastic, perhaps too much so. He was the fittest of the group, and a fast runner, but he tended to speak without thinking, and while there was no doubting his devotion to Islam he was not a good student of the Qur'an.

Hammad's jaw tensed and he gave KC a hard look but didn't say anything. KC looked away, realising his mistake. "Sorry," he muttered under his breath.

Hammad made a soft snorting sound through his nose as he stared at KC, then addressed the group again. "This version of the Igla has been around for more than thirty years, and is tried and tested," he said. "It has a probability-of-kill ratio of between 0.3 and 0.5 against unprotected moving targets. That means that when fired at a fast-moving plane, the missile will miss at least half the time. That ratio falls to one-in-four if the target is able to employ countermeasures."

Rafiq frowned. "You mean, most of the time it misses its target?"

"When fired at military jets or helicopters, yes," said Hammad. "But at static targets, it is much more accurate. Also, planes landing or taking off are much easier to hit." He smiled. "Sitting ducks, as they say."

He ran his finger down the barrel. "There is a lot of technical information that you don't really need to know, but I will run through it with you now," he said. "The missile has an operational range of a little more than three miles and can hit planes as high as eleven thousand feet after travelling at twice the speed of sound. Once fired the missile heads for the heat signature of the target, usually an engine. The missile uses a two-colour infrared guidance system which improves accuracy. The missile is designed to alter its course at the last second so that it hits the fuselage rather than the engine, which is guaranteed to do more damage. The warhead weighs two and a half pounds but the missile also incorporates a delayed-impact fuse and an extra charge that ignites any remaining fuel." He smiled. "One direct hit is virtually guaranteed to destroy a 747 or any other passenger jet." He patted the tube. "It has an optional friend-or-foe system so that it cannot accidentally shoot a friendly plane." His smile widened. "Not that we will be needing that function, of course." Several of the men chuckled. "The missile system is also equipped to combat infrared countermeasures and to minimise the effect of decoy flares and jammers, though generally such things are not fitted to passenger aircraft."

"Will that be our target, back in England?" asked Rafiq.

Hammad looked at him for several seconds before replying. "Your targets will be given to you nearer the time," he said. "All you need to concern yourself with now is how to use the equipment."

"Sure," said Rafiq. "It's just that you keep talking about planes. I thought . . ." He left the sentence unfinished and looked away.

"Brother, you are a jihad warrior, there is no need for you to think," said Hammad. "The thinking will be done for you so that you can best serve Allah. Plans are being laid and you will play your part. That is what this training is about, to prepare you so that you can fulfil your role."

"I understand," said Rafiq.

Hammad surveyed the group. "I realise that you all have questions, that you all want to know what lies ahead." He put his hand over his heart. "Brothers, I too would like to know the future, but my part is to train you, nothing more and nothing less. That is my role and I will do what is asked of me. You in turn have your roles to play. It is as if we are all pieces in a giant jigsaw puzzle. As individual pieces none of us can see the complete picture, but I can assure you it will be glorious."

The men gathered around him nodded.

"*Allahu akbar*," said Rafiq. "God is great."

"*Allahu akbar*," said Hammad.

"*Allahu akbar*," repeated the others, in unison.

Hammad bent over the missile and waved his hand over it. "The system comes in four parts," he said. "There is a ground power supply source, a launching tube, the launching mechanism and the missile itself. I shall explain to you first how to aim the weapon, then we shall practise."

A small transceiver on the table burst into life and Hammad picked it up. It was one of the spotters in the hills to the west. "A bird is on the wing," said the spotter. "With twenty feathers."

"Understood," said Hammad. He slid the transceiver inside his man-dress. "There is a drone on its way, brothers. Coming this way at twenty thousand feet. Help me take everything inside."

Hammad picked up the missile launcher and took it over to the goatherd's cottage. Rafiq picked up one end of the table. One of the Somalians — a lanky six-footer called Asad — took the other end and together they carried it over to the cottage. KC grabbed the whiteboard and hurried after them.

The cottage stank of goats. There was a bare concrete floor and the walls were made of clay bricks that had been covered with a layer of brown plaster. The ceiling was flat planks of wood with earth piled up on top.

Hammad sat down cross-legged and motioned for the men to do the same. The transceiver crackled again. "The bird with twenty feathers is flying east."

"Is it a Predator?" asked Rafiq. The Predator was one of the most feared American unmanned aircraft. It was usually fitted with two Hellfire missiles with more than enough firepower to destroy the cottage they were huddled in. The United States Air Force operated most of the Predators in Afghanistan and Iraq, but the CIA had also been flying them across the border to attack targets in Pakistan's federally administered tribal areas.

"If it was a Predator, the spotter would say eagle, not bird," said Hammad. "Bird means it is a surveillance drone. It is nothing to worry about, the Americans fly them over the border all the time. We simply have to wait until it passes and then we can continue. You are from Bradford?"

Rafiq nodded. "I was studying to be a dentist." He smiled. "I suppose I still am. I've got another year to go."

"It is a good profession," said Hammad. "My uncle, he is a dentist. So which team do you support?"

"Team?"

"Football. I support Chelsea. Chelsea are a great team."

Rafiq smiled. "Arsenal," he said, scratching his beard.

"Arsenal? You're from Bradford."

"Bradford are shit," said Rafiq. "My dad was an Arsenal fan. Don't ask me why."

The others began to shout out the names of their favourite teams as six thousand feet overhead the unmanned drone continued on its way, beaming footage of the countryside up to a satellite and from there to Creech Air Force Base in Nevada, where a team of three operators stared at a bank of screens. One of the operators was handling the controls, keeping the drone on a steady course to the east. It was a routine patrol and the operators weren't expecting to see anything. They kept a watchful eye on the screens but spent the time discussing the merits of various blackjack strategies. The base was an hour's drive from Las Vegas and the operators were planning to hit the casinos at the weekend. As they argued over what to do with a pair of eights, they saw the roof of the goatherd's cottage and the thirty or so goats walking listlessly in the afternoon sun as they searched for scrub to sustain themselves, but that was all.

The doorbell rang and Shepherd went to answer it. It was Caroline Stockmann, wearing a beige trenchcoat and a woolly hat that looked as if it might double as a tea cosy. She was carrying a battered leather briefcase and a rolled-up copy of *The Economist*. "Hope I'm not too early," she said. "I thought it would take longer to get here from the station but there was a minicab waiting."

"I've got nothing else on today," said Shepherd. "Maybe a run later on."

He took her coat and put it on a hook by the door before showing her through to the sitting room. "Can I get you a coffee?"

"Lovely," said the psychologist.

Shepherd went through to the kitchen and made two coffees. When he took them back to the sitting room, Stockmann was sitting on the sofa with a notebook on her lap. She was wearing a pair of square-rimmed glasses and she looked over the top of them as she took the mug of coffee.

"So how is everything?" she asked as he sat down.

"All good," said Shepherd, crossing his legs. He remembered that she was an expert at reading body language and she might take the leg-crossing as being defensive so he uncrossed them and smiled.

"So you're forty this year?"

Shepherd shrugged, figuring that the question was rhetorical and that there would be a follow-up whether he answered or not.

"Any thoughts on that?"

"Planning on buying me a gift, Caroline?"

"I could certainly run to a bottle of Jameson's," said the psychologist. "The reason I was asking is that forty is often seen as a milestone. People often set themselves targets that they want to have achieved by that age."

Shepherd shrugged. "I'm not a great one for setting targets," he said.

"I find that strange," she said. "I doubt that you would have got into the SAS if you were worried about testing yourself."

"I wanted to join the Regiment, but I wasn't concerned at how old I was when I did it. I would have been just as happy if I'd joined at twenty-seven as I was getting in at twenty-two."

"Is there anything you haven't done yet that you wished you had done by forty?"

"A threesome with Angelina Jolie and Jessica Alba would have been nice," he said. He grinned. "Joking," he added. "Career-wise, no, I'm all good. I've been lucky. I've been in the SAS, been a cop, worked for SOCA and now I work for MI5. Barely a dull moment."

"For much of that time you've worked undercover," she said. "How have you found the stress?"

Shepherd shrugged. "It's never been a problem."

"I'm sure you've seen undercover agents who have had problems, over the years," she said.

"Sure."

"Alcohol, drugs, sex, pretty much every crutch available gets used at some time or another."

"You're not going to ask me to pee in a cup, are you?"

Stockmann waved her hand. "Perish the thought," she said. "The point I'm trying to make is that you have performed one of the most stressful jobs imaginable for more than ten years. Almost twelve, in fact."

"And I still have all my own hair and I'm not smoking crack? Is that what you mean?"

"Is the stress manifesting itself in any other way perhaps?"

Shepherd shrugged. "I sleep like a baby. My blood pressure is as steady as a rock and my appetite is just fine."

"Well, that's good to hear," said the psychologist. "This latest case you were working on. Any problems?"

"I was belted over the head by an immigration officer, but other than that it went OK, I guess."

"You were undercover quite a long time."

"Three months or so. But it was on and off. I wasn't in character twenty-four-seven."

"How do you find long-term operations?"

Shepherd shrugged. "It can get boring pretending to be someone else. But no big issues."

"You know that a lot of agents who work undercover start taking risks, to spice things up?" She took a sip of her coffee and Shepherd could feel her assessing his reaction over the top of her mug.

"I've seen it happen," he said. "Not recently, but when I was with the police undercover unit I worked with a couple of guys who were heading that way."

"Specifically?"

"One had started carrying his warrant card in his wallet. I flipped when I found out. The other started to talk about undercover cops all the time. He'd raise the subject for no reason. It was weird, as if he wanted to draw attention to himself."

"You know why, of course?" she said. She picked up her coffee mug and took a sip.

"Because they know that lying is wrong and subconsciously they think they deserve to be punished," said Shepherd. "It's the same force that drives murderers to confess. Or at least to tell someone what they've done."

"And you've never felt that compulsion?" asked the psychologist.

"The sort of work that I do, that'd be tantamount to a death wish," said Shepherd. "I'm lucky, I seem to be able to compartmentalise things quite easily."

"That's something sociopaths are adept at doing," she said. She put her mug down. "Just an observation."

"I don't think I'm a sociopath," said Shepherd. "In fact the big problem I have is that sometimes I find it too easy to empathise."

"With the people you're working against?"

Shepherd nodded. "When you're undercover on a long-term case, you get to know everything there is to know about a person. You get to understand them but sometimes you can grow to like them. That's the bit you have to control."

"Was that a problem with this recent case, the people smugglers?"

"Not really," said Shepherd. He took a slow drink of coffee, using the time to get his thoughts in order. "The main guy wasn't particularly likeable, but he was only in it for the money. And to be honest, at the end of the day, what he was doing wasn't that bad. He was helping refugees to get into the UK. In some parts of the world he'd be regarded as a hero. The problem was that when we busted him, one of the guys he was working with had several kilos of heroin on him."

"Ouch," said Stockmann.

"Exactly. Now he's facing ten years or so for drug smuggling." He forced a smile. "Mind you, he was carrying a gun so he really only has himself to blame."

"But you think it's unfair that he'll be charged with the drugs."

Shepherd nodded. "I guess so."

"That's always been important to you, hasn't it? A sense of fairness."

"Sure. Isn't that what everyone wants?"

"It depends on what you mean by fair," said Stockmann. "Fairness and justice aren't always the same thing, of course. Back in the bad old days, the police were often as bad as the villains they were chasing. The police would sometimes lie and cheat to get their man, and weren't averse to getting physical if it meant a confession was forthcoming."

"That was well before my time," said Shepherd. "I've always had to do everything by the book."

"And is that frustrating sometimes?" She took another sip of coffee, her eyes watching him closely.

Shepherd smiled at her. She really was a first-class interrogator. Chat, chat, chat, all smiles and chuckles, then suddenly she'd slip in a question that required very careful handling. But if she caught him self-editing then she'd see that as significant, too. "Rules have to be followed," he said. "Short cuts are all well and good, but you wouldn't want a case thrown out of court because of a legal technicality."

"So you never break the rules?"

Shepherd laughed. "I know you won't let me take the Fifth, so let's just say I might very occasionally bend them."

"Because the ends justifies the means?"

"Because when I'm undercover I have to be flexible. If I wasn't, I'd stand out straight away."

"And I'm guessing that as time goes by, your wriggle room is being continually reduced."

"It's the way of the world, isn't it? Every year there are more rules and regulations, more paperwork, more boxes to be ticked. Regular policing has become a bureaucratic nightmare but it's starting to happen at Five, too."

Stockmann nodded sympathetically. "Have you ever heard of Pournelle's Iron Law of Bureaucracy?" she asked.

Shepherd shook his head.

"A writer and journalist by the name of Jerry Pournelle came up with it. It states that in any bureaucratic organisation there will be two kinds of people: on one hand you have those who are devoted to the goals of the organisation. That's how I always see you, Dan. You believe in what you do, often passionately."

Shepherd grinned. "I can't argue with that."

"But the other sort of people are those who are dedicated to the organisation itself. They're usually the administrators, the middle management."

"Yeah, well, I've met my fair share of those," agreed Shepherd.

"Well, the Iron Law states that in every case the second group will gain control of the organisation and will set down the rules that govern the way the organisation acts, and decide who gets promoted within it."

"That was SOCA in a nutshell," said Shepherd. "It was full of middle managers and all they seemed to do was to generate paperwork and hold meetings."

"Do you think it applies equally to MI5?" asked Stockmann.

Shepherd chuckled. "Do you expect me to badmouth my employer?"

"I'm interested in what motivates you," said Stockmann. "As I said, I think you want to achieve the objectives of the organisation and are less concerned about the organisation itself."

"I don't plan to climb the slippery pole, that's true," said Shepherd. "I prefer to stay at the sharp end."

"So you'd turn down a promotion if it was offered?"

"It would depend on the job. I don't want to be behind a desk. And I'm not sure how good I would be at motivating or managing people."

"You were never an officer, in the army?"

"Never wanted to be," said Shepherd. "Not that it was ever offered."

"But in the SAS, being an officer generally means being away from the sharp end, doesn't it?"

"It does in most jobs," said Shepherd. "Let me ask you something. Am I being sounded out for a promotion here?"

Stockmann laughed. "No, I have no ulterior motive here other than finding out what makes you tick. Are you happy with the way that Five functions?"

"I've had no problems with it," said Shepherd. "There are fewer restrictions than there were with the police, and with SOCA. Generally the people working at Five are there because they believe in what they're doing."

The psychologist nodded. "I suppose that is the main difference between law enforcement agencies and bureaucratic organisations in general — it's clear where the moral — and legal — high ground lies. Generally you know who is wearing the white hat and who's wearing black so there is always a sense that you are doing the right thing." She sipped her coffee and smacked her lips appreciatively, then smiled at him as she put her mug down. "How's your boy? Liam?"

"He's a teenager," said Shepherd. "Going through what all teenagers go through."

"Those were the days," said Stockmann. "The spots, the anxieties, the mood swings. He's at boarding school, still?"

Shepherd nodded. "It's working out well. Lots of sport, he gets on well with his classmates. Best thing for him, especially with me being away so often."

"It's been ten years since his mother died, hasn't it?"

Shepherd nodded but didn't say anything. He never felt comfortable talking about Sue.

"We haven't really discussed it, have we?"

"It's not an issue. For Liam, or for me."

"It can cause a lot of problems, a child losing a mother at a young age."

"Sue's parents were very good. And we've had Katra for many years. She's sort of become a mother figure for Liam."

"The au pair?"

"She was hired as an au pair but she's one of the family now." The kitchen door opened. Shepherd grinned. "Speak of the devil."

They heard the sound of laden carrier bags being dumped on the kitchen table and then footsteps in the hallway. She appeared at the door, wearing a long leather jacket over tight blue jeans and purple Ugg boots. She had tied her dark brown hair back into a ponytail.

"Sorry, I didn't know you were expecting a guest," she said. "Do you want something to eat? Sandwiches? Coffee?" There was the faintest of Slovenian accents but she sounded more Australian than East European after years of watching Australian soap operas.

"We're fine, thanks," said Shepherd.

"I got lamb chops for tonight."

"Excellent." He gestured at Stockmann. "This is a friend from work, Caroline."

Katra flashed her a smile. "Pleased to meet you."

"And you," said Stockmann. "Dan tells me what a great help you are."

Katra's smile widened, then she gave Shepherd a small wave and went back to the kitchen. Shepherd turned to see Stockmann was smiling at him. "What?" he said.

"She's very pretty."

Shepherd pulled a face. "I hadn't noticed."

Stockmann raised an eyebrow.

"Seriously, she's like a member of the family." He shrugged. "I don't know what you want me to say."

Stockmann chuckled softly. "Dan, I was simply pointing out how pretty she is."

"You think I'm being defensive?"

"Now don't you go putting words into my mouth," she said. "But I wouldn't mind exploring the fact that you never remarried."

"I haven't met the right person yet."

"So you are looking?"

"Not actively, no. I haven't joined 'find me a new wife dot com' if that's what you're implying." He threw up his hands and immediately regretted it because he knew how good Stockmann was at reading body language. "I'm not sure how relevant my personal situation is."

"Generally I'm interested because the nature of undercover work is such that it can impinge on the family. As you're no doubt aware, the job has a much higher divorce rate than average."

"So maybe it's a plus that I don't have a wife."

"That's one way of looking at it," said the psychologist. "The other way is that a secure family life can be an asset. It can bring some stability to what is a very unsettling career."

"Most undercover agents I know are single or divorced," said Shepherd.

"True," said Stockmann. "But not many work undercover for more than a decade."

"Caroline, what are you getting at?"

"I'm not getting at anything. I'm just getting a feel for your situation. That's what these biannuals are all about. Assessment." She sipped her coffee. "You don't feel lonely?"

"Lonely? Are you serious?"

"You're a single man in a line of business that doesn't lend itself to forming stable relationships."

"I've got friends." Stockmann smiled but didn't say anything. "You mean girlfriends?" The psychologist continued to stay quiet, but her smile widened.

Shepherd shook his head. "Caroline, I'm not a monk. I do have my moments, it's just that I don't shout it from the rooftops."

"That's good to know. Look, don't read too much into what I'm asking. I just want to make sure that you're socialising outside work, because when you're working more often than not you're not yourself. You need time to be Dan Shepherd among regular people."

Shepherd pulled a pained face. "There's a problem with that, of course. I work for MI5, and that fact can't be public knowledge. So any relationship I have with anyone has to be based on a lie."

"True," said the psychologist.

"That's the problem, and always will be. No matter who I meet, one of the first things that comes out of my mouth is a lie, and there's no taking that back."

"What do you tell people, civilians?"

"That I work for the Home Office. Boring administrative stuff."

"And they buy that? With your physique?"

Shepherd laughed. "My physique?"

"You don't look like a man who spends his day driving a desk," said Stockmann. "That's what I meant."

"I tell them I run, which is true."

"You still do that thing with the rucksack of telephone directories?"

"Bricks," he said. "Wrapped in bubble wrap. Do they still make telephone directories?"

Stockmann laughed. "You're right. It wouldn't be the same with a couple of CDs, would it." She sighed. "I should exercise more," she said. "My blood pressure is creeping up. Ditto my blood sugar levels. But you're disgustingly healthy, I gather."

Shepherd smiled, noting that she had obviously seen his last medical.

"So, I think I've pretty much run out of questions."

"And I'm good?"

"I wish everyone I saw was as well balanced as you, Dan." She bent down, picked up her briefcase and put away her notepad. She looked at her watch. "Is there any way you could run me back to the station, there's a train to London in half an hour."

"Happy to," said Shepherd. "Just promise not to ask me any more questions about my love life."

"The food could be better, couldn't it?" whispered KC. He glanced over his shoulder to make sure that

Hammad was out of earshot. KC was sitting with Rafiq, Sami and Labib, cross-legged around a rough wooden table placed on a grubby green and red *dastarkhwan* that had been spread across the rock floor. They were in a large cave halfway up a hill that overlooked the goatherd's cottage where they did a lot of their training. Hammad had explained that the drones that flew overhead were equipped with thermal imaging equipment that would show up their bodies in any normal structure, but in the cave they were safe. It was where they ate, slept and prayed, and bathed from water stored in large earthenware jars. The food was filling but not particularly tasty and was brought in each morning in the back of a battered pick-up truck, along with fresh water.

They were eating in traditional style, using their right hands to dip their naan bread into bowls of lentil curry or watery chicken korma and picking up cubes of lamb from kebabs that had been cooked on a small fire at the entrance to the cave. The fire had also been used to heat a kettle for the tea they were drinking. The fire had been quickly extinguished once the meal had been prepared. There was a very low risk of the smoke being spotted but even so the fire was used only for cooking. To keep themselves warm during the cold desert night the men either snuggled into sleeping bags they had brought with them from the UK or wrapped themselves in rough blankets.

"We're not here for the food, brother," said Rafiq, brushing crumbs from his beard.

"No, but would it hurt them to give us a decent curry?" asked Sami, gesturing with contempt at the bowl of korma.

"And that lamb tastes more like dog to me," said Labib.

Labib and Sami spent most of their time outside training with Rafiq and KC because everyone else had problems understanding their near-impenetrable Glaswegian accents.

"You've eaten dog, have you?" asked KC.

"You know what I mean," said Labib. "My dad owns a curry house in Maryhill and he'd be disgusted with this."

"Well, Sami seems to be doing all right on it," said KC, gesturing at his colleague's tight-fitting shirt and the buttons that seemed in danger of popping off.

"I've dropped five kilos since I came here," said Sami, patting his stomach.

"How would you know that, brother?" asked KC. "There are no scales here."

"I can feel the weight falling off me," said Labib.

"You're Bangladeshi, right?" asked Rafiq. "They make the best cooks. That's what my dad always says. Go into any Indian restaurant and you'll find a Bangladeshi chef in the kitchen."

Labib laughed. "That's no lie, laddie," he said.

"You're not a chef, though?"

"Me, nah, computers. I've got two brothers working with my dad, though. It's good money, a curry house. Pretty much a cash business, too." He dabbed a chunk of naan in the lentils, but scowled at it instead of eating it. "My dad always says that his father invented chicken tikka masala."

"Get away with you," said Rafiq.

"Nah, true. Back in the fifties."

"So you're third-generation?" asked Rafiq.

"Yeah, my grandad came over in the early fifties, back when anyone from the Commonwealth could come. He came on his own and started cooking in one of the first curry houses in Glasgow. Earned enough to get his wife over and then brought her whole family."

"And he invented chicken tikka masala?" said Rafiq. "Seriously?"

"That's what my dad says. Grandad died not long after I was born so I never got the chance to ask him. But the family swear it's true. He was in the kitchen and a punter sent back his chicken tikka saying that it was too dry."

"Chicken tikka is supposed to be dry," said Rafiq.

"Yeah, you know that and I know that but back then punters knew nothing about Indian food. He thought that all dishes were wet curries so assumed that the cook — my grandad — had screwed up. Anyway, Grandad was a nice guy so instead of going and giving the punter what for, he decides to give him what he wanted. He chucked in some tomato soup, yogurt and spices and the rest is history."

"That's awesome," said Rafiq. "You know it's the most popular dish in the UK, right? Outsells meat pies, fish and chips, outsells everything."

Sami nodded. "And yet no one out here has ever heard of it."

"By here you mean the middle of nowhere?" said KC.

"Asia, I mean. No one in India or Bangladesh or Pakistan would know what the hell it was. It's a completely British dish. And my grandad invented it."

Rafiq raised his glass of tea. "Kudos," he said. "And God bless your grandad."

Sami groaned and stretched out his legs. "I hate this sitting on the floor business," he said. "Would it be too much to ask for a table and chairs?" He stood up and stretched.

"It's character-building," said KC. "Makes us hard."

"I'm from Glasgow, don't forget," said Sami. "I was born hard." His companions laughed and Sami scowled. "Carry on laughing and I'll introduce you to the Glasgow handshake."

"What's that?" asked KC.

"Stand up and I'll show you," said Sami. He beckoned at KC. "Come on."

"Stay where you are, KC," said Rafiq. "It's a head-butt. Aka a Glasgow kiss."

Sami laughed. "Damn right," he said. He stretched his arms above his head and twisted from side to side. "Sitting on the floor wouldn't be so bad if we at least had cushions. Seriously, I don't get this sitting on the floor. They did that because they didn't have furniture. Same as they wiped their arse with their left hand because they didn't have toilet paper. Now we do have toilet paper that left-hand business is just nonsense."

"Keep your voice down," hissed Rafiq. "You don't want Hammad hearing you talk like that. He'll have your balls off."

71

"He's right," said KC. "Remember, this isn't just about weapons training, it's about making us good jihadists."

"And good jihadists wipe their arses with their hands, do they?" said Sami.

"Seriously, Sami, you need to be careful," whispered Rafiq. "These guys don't fuck about."

Sami opened his mouth as if he was about to argue, but then he shrugged and sat down again.

KC reached for his tea and leaned towards Rafiq. "This is the real thing, isn't it?" he said.

Rafiq chuckled. "You think this is a game, brother?"

"You know what I mean," said KC. "I spent years planning stuff, stuff that would never happen. Crazy stuff."

"Like what?"

"You know. Checking the internet to see how to make ricin, that poison stuff. And botulism, from mussels."

Rafiq frowned and massaged his forearm. "Muscles?" He knew exactly what KC meant but sometimes it was better to play stupid because that tended to encourage people to talk. His MI6 handler had taught him that.

"Nah, the shellfish. You can bury them in the ground and they go off and they produce botulism. One drop can kill like a million people or something. We tried it but couldn't get it to work." He laughed. "We tried to test it on a cat and the thing went ballistic, biting and scratching." He shook his head, still laughing. "My mate almost lost an eye. Cats can fight, I tell you." He popped a piece of meat into his mouth. "I drew up a list of kaffirs I wanted to kill. Cameron, Beckham, Prince Harry, had all their pictures on the walls of my bedroom. My mum got a bit worried, thought maybe I was getting a thing for older white guys."

"Beckham?"

KC shrugged. "I hate the twat, him and that stick insect wife of his."

"Yeah, but a footballer, KC? Come on. Politicians, sure. And I get the point of random kaffirs. But targeting the former England captain, that's bizarre."

"If you want to talk about bizarre, what about the Father Ted guy?" said Sami.

"Father Ted?" repeated Rafiq.

"The guy that wrote the Father Ted thing. Irish but he lives in London. He took the piss out of Bin Laden after the Americans murdered him. You didn't hear about that?"

Rafiq shook his head.

"He wrote the *IT Crowd* thing as well," said Labib. "Bloody hilarious that was."

"Yeah, well, he tweeted that Bin Laden was a big fan of one of his shows and that he was watching an episode when the Americans killed him. Took the piss out of the Sheikh something rotten. Seemed to think it was funny. There was a piece in the *Guardian* with him laughing about it. Me and a group of brothers went down to London. Turns out he'd moved to Norwich but we found where he lived and we were already to make a YouTube video of us cutting his head off when I got the call."

"The call?"

"A friend of a friend of a friend pulled me to one side and told me that I was wasting my time, that no one would care about a dead comedy writer. That's when I started on this path." Sami picked up another piece of meat and chewed on it. "What about you? What did you want to do? After they invaded Afghanistan and Iraq, we all wanted to do something, right?"

"I thought about attacking a shopping mall," said Rafiq. "I saw what they did in Kenya, when those guys shot the place up. But I couldn't get a gun."

"You're from London, right?"

Rafiq shook his head. "Bradford."

"You should have driven to Birmingham," said KC. "You wouldn't have any problem picking up a gun in Birmingham, same as Glasgow. Pop into any pub and you'll find someone to fix you up. Did you ever think about taking out a plane?"

Rafiq nodded. "Sure. But these days they check you too carefully, right? You can't even get nail-clippers on a plane."

"A friend of mine had this idea where we get twenty brothers on a plane. Then as the plane is taking off or landing they all get up and move to one side of the plane, then run to and fro. He reckoned it would definitely make it crash."

Rafiq laughed. "And kill twenty brothers at the same time."

"Yeah, he hadn't really thought it through."

"I tell you what would work, though," said Rafiq. "They still let you on with duty-free and cigarette lighters. Two or three brothers with a couple of bottles of brandy each could set fire to a plane mid-flight with no bother. I put together a plan to do that. That's when I got recruited to this. One of the imams got to hear about me and he hooked me up. Said that I was too valuable to become a *shahid*, that there were better ways to serve Allah."

"He's right," said KC. He picked up a piece of naan, dipped it in the korma, and popped it into his mouth. "These MANPADS are the dog's bollocks. We can bring down a whole plane and be away before the wreckage hits the ground. This is what jihad is about, all right."

Rafiq nodded. "I can't wait. I wish they'd let us know where our targets are."

"I reckon we'll be used locally. I'm a Brummie so they'll have me at Birmingham Airport. You'll be at Leeds, maybe."

"You're sure it'll be a plane?"

"That's what the MANPADS are for," said KC. "You can fire them at buildings, sure, but for the real damage you want a plane. Having said that, it'd be something to fire one at 10 Downing Street, wouldn't it?"

"Hell, yeah," said Rafiq. "I'd be up for it. *Inshallah*." *Inshallah*. God willing. Even though he knew that pretty much every word that passed his lips was a lie.

Charlotte Button was on her second glass of Pinot Grigio when Caroline Stockmann hurried through the door of the wine bar and over to her table, apologising profusely. "I was stuck on the Tube," said the psychologist, popping her briefcase under the table.

"Wine?" asked Button.

"Wine? A long profanity-laced moan would be more like it." She grinned. "I'd prefer a beer."

A sleek blond waitress came over carrying a tray and Stockmann asked what beers they had, listened intently as the waitress rattled off a number of brands. "Nothing draught?" asked Stockmann. "A Peroni, then. Thanks."

The waitress headed towards the bar and Stockmann sighed. "It was a body on the line," she said.

"I'm sorry?" said Button.

"The reason the train was held up. They didn't say suicide, though. They never do. An incident, they called it. I've never understood why anyone would choose to end their life by throwing themselves under a train. For one thing, half the time it doesn't work and you end up crippled and disfigured. But does no one think about the effect it has on the driver?" She shuddered, then smiled brightly. "So, how are you?"

"I hope that's not a professional question because we know each other too well for you to be giving me a psychiatric evaluation."

Stockmann laughed. "Perish the thought," she said.

Button sipped her wine. "So how is Dan?"

Stockmann shrugged. "I've been wondering how to answer that question," she said.

"Is there a problem?"

"Not as such, no. No real red flags. Just a feeling."

Button said nothing. She knew that Stockmann would explain what was troubling her in her own good time. The waitress came over and put a bottle of beer and a glass in front of Stockmann. Stockmann smiled her thanks, ignored the glass and picked up the bottle. "You know I like Dan," she said.

"We all do," said Button.

"And there's no question that he's a good operator."

"One of the best," agreed Button.

"He's very centred, he doesn't seem to have any vices, he enjoys his work, clearly. If it was the first time I'd given him a biannual I'd probably give him full marks and not give it a second thought. But I've been meeting with him for a few years now so I've had been able to establish a baseline. That's my worry, Charlie. The Dan Shepherd I met this week is different. Not hugely different, and to be honest I'm not sure if it's something to worry about, but he has changed."

"We're all getting older," said Button.

"And not necessarily wiser," said Stockmann. "What I can say about Dan is that he seemed to be taking more care with his choice of words than he used to." She took a sip of beer. "It was as if he was telling me what he thought I wanted to hear rather than what he was actually thinking."

"You think he was lying?"

Stockmann shook her head. "Not lying, no. More as if he was running everything he said through a filter. That suggests to me that he perhaps has something to hide."

"Do you have any idea what that might be?"

Stockmann chuckled. "I was only with him for an hour. It would take a lot longer than that and ideally with him connected to a lie detector to get any sense of what he might be worrying about. But seriously, it might be nothing. He's had a rough few years, he might just be becoming more cautious with age. The young tend to speak without thinking; as you get older you learn to control your impulses. I just got the feeling that this time he was being a little more careful about the answers he gave."

"You think perhaps he was worried that you might ask him something specific? Something that he might lie about?"

Stockmann nodded. "Exactly. But I didn't see any of the physical signs that suggest apprehension. No lip-licking or difficulty swallowing caused by a dry mouth. There was no avoiding of eye contact, no rubbing of hands."

"You wouldn't, though, would you? Dan has spent most of his life lying to some of the most dangerous criminals and terrorists in the country. He's an expert at controlling his body language."

"Exactly," said Stockmann. "All I have to go on is the fact that he seemed to be taking a fraction of a second longer to answer each question than I seem to remember from our previous chats." She shrugged. "It's probably nothing. I just thought you should know, that's all."

"I'll feel him out when I get the chance. See if there's something on his mind. Did you ask him about his thoughts on promotion?"

"I did, and he's not keen. He's happy doing what he's doing."

"That's interesting," said Button.

"Is he in line for a promotion?"

"It has been discussed," said Button. "It would be a question of the right slot opening up."

"I did notice one sensitive area," said Stockmann. "He's definitely uneasy talking about relationships."

"I didn't realise he had any," said Button.

"That's what I said," said Stockmann.

"Don't tell me his masculinity was threatened? Not Spider, not in a million years."

Stockmann chuckled. "No, he was just a bit defensive, that's all. I think he felt that his relationship status had no bearing on his ability to do the job."

"Which is probably true, up to a point. Is he seeing anyone at the moment?"

Stockmann smiled at her over the top of her spectacles. "Now that's an interesting question."

"You know as well as I do that a stable family life makes the job we do much easier. I do worry about him bringing up his boy on his own."

"Well, to be fair, you're a single mother yourself."

Button laughed out loud. "You're not analysing me, are you, Caroline?"

Stockmann grinned. "Perish the thought."

"Or playing the matchmaker?"

"Well, he is a very attractive guy. And close to your age."

"Oh my God, you are matchmaking." She shook her head and then took a long drink of wine.

"That wasn't my intention, but I don't recall that you were seeing anyone."

"I'm a single mother with a job that pretty much takes up my every waking moment," said Button, putting down her glass. "But even if I had the time, and if I had the inclination, the last person I'd consider dating would be someone from the office. I can't believe you've switched this around to me."

"Well now, to be fair, there are similarities in your situations," said the psychologist. "You've both had very successful careers in law enforcement, you both lost your spouses and are now single parents with teenage children at boarding school."

"You mean we'd have a lot to talk about over dinner?" said Button. "You're terrible, Caroline."

"Now you're reading too much into what I'm saying," said Stockmann. "I simply meant that career-wise and family-wise, in many ways you're dealing with similar situations. I wondered if that might give you an insight into what he's going through."

"He's as professional as he's ever been," said Button. "He's reliable, he's loyal, he gets the job done. He does tend to complain when others aren't as professional as he is, but I'm just as guilty on that front."

Stockmann nodded. "Neither of you suffer fools, gladly or otherwise," she said. "Of course, he prefers to be at the sharp end, as he calls it."

"He's never been one for sitting at a desk," agreed Button.

"Well, we both know that Dan is attracted to situations where he finds himself under pressure."

"He's an adrenalin junkie, you mean?" Button nodded. "That's what makes him so good at his job."

"So long as the risk-taking itself doesn't become his *raison d'être*," said Stockmann.

"You think that's happening?"

"Dan has been working undercover for a long time. More than ten years. You know how stressful that is. And that most undercover agents do it for two or three years and then move on to more routine duties. Of those that continue with undercover work, more than half end up with stress-related problems. Drug or alcohol addiction, gambling, domestic violence."

"Which is why we have the biannuals," said Button, running her finger around the edge of her glass.

"Indeed. And hopefully we manage to nip any problems in the bud. But sometimes the adrenalin addiction can be just as dangerous. There have been cases of agents deliberately jeopardising operations to increase the risk factor, to make the work more exciting, if you like."

Button frowned. "Are you saying that he's reached that stage?"

Stockmann put up a hand. "No, absolutely not. I've no evidence of that. But Dan is very clued up on the dangers of long-term undercover work and it might be that he is becoming more aware of his addiction to the adrenalin rush and he is trying to downplay it in conversation with me. That would explain why he was being extra careful during our chat."

"And this is new, is that what you're saying?"

Stockmann nodded. "It's the first time I've noticed it, yes. Which suggests that something has happened to make him behave that way." She shrugged. "Mind you, as you said, we're all getting older. It could just be that hitting forty has given him food for thought and he's just being a bit more careful in conversation."

"He's forty this year?"

Stockmann smiled. "You didn't know?"

"I haven't bought him a card, if that's what you're suggesting," said Button. "Perhaps that's it. He's turning forty, which is a time for reassessing one's life. That's made him a bit more careful. Does that sound possible?"

"It's as good an explanation as anything I've been able to come up with," Stockmann said. "And of course it might be a one-off. Next time he might be back on track. Anyway, it's not a serious red flag, but I felt you ought to be aware of it, that's all."

"Duly noted, Caroline," said Button. She finished her wine and wiggled her empty glass. "One for the road, do you think?"

Rafiq woke with a start and realised immediately that he'd been slapped, and slapped hard. He put his hands up to protect himself but he was too slow and he was slapped again. His cheeks were burning and he thrashed around, trying to avoid more blows, wondering whether he'd overslept and was being rudely awoken for missing morning prayers. "What the fuck?" he shouted.

He was slapped again and this time he tasted blood in his mouth. It was still dark and all he could make out was shapes standing over him.

"What's wrong?" he shouted.

A foul-smelling sack was thrust over his head and he panicked. He clawed at the rough material but then he was yanked to his feet and his arms twisted up behind his back.

He heard voices, muffled by the sacking, then he was roughly pulled across the floor of the cave. He lost his footing but they held him firmly by the arms and half pulled, half dragged him outside. There he was thrown against a large boulder and he felt his hands being tied.

"Would someone tell me what's going on?" he shouted. He shook his head, trying to clear his thoughts. He hoped and prayed that it was part of his training and that he was just being tested.

Once his hands were bound he was pulled away from the boulder and pushed down a slope. He felt the stony ground beneath his bare feet, then he heard a car door being opened.

"What do you want?" he asked.

Something pushed him in the small of his back and he staggered forward. A hand pushed his head down and his knees banged against something and he realised they were pushing him into the vehicle.

"Where are you taking me?" he shouted.

He was shoved into the car, then roughly put into a sitting position. Someone climbed in next to him. Then the door slammed and the engine started.

Rafiq was panting like a sick dog and he forced himself to calm down. No matter how bad his situation was, nothing would happen to him while he was in the car. He took a big breath, held it, then slowly exhaled. It was probably just a test, he told himself. They'd take him somewhere and ask him a few questions and then they'd laugh and tell him that he'd passed with flying colours and they'd go back to the camp and carry on with his training. He closed his eyes, trying to quell the panic that kept threatening to rise up and overwhelm him. It had to be a test. It had to be.

Katra had just put a plate of steak and kidney pie and chips in front of Shepherd when his mobile rang. It was Charlotte Button. "Where are you?" she asked.

"In my kitchen," he said.

"Hereford?"

He could tell from her tone that something was wrong. "Yes. What's up?"

"Remember Raj? Manraj Chaudhry?"

"Of course."

"He's in trouble. In Pakistan."

"What sort of trouble?"

"Not over the phone," she said. "I need you in London. Do you want to drive or shall I send you a car? The trains aren't great, I gather."

"It's a three-hour drive even if the traffic's good," said Shepherd. "Sending a car will take for ever. I'll drive." He looked at his watch. It was six o'clock in the evening. "I should be there by nine. Ten at the latest."

"Call me when you're an hour outside London," she said, and ended the call.

Shepherd stood up. "Is something wrong?" asked Katra, standing by the sink.

"I've got to go to London," he said.

"Now?"

He nodded. "Now. I'm sorry about dinner."

"Shall I make you a sandwich? You could eat it on the way."

"Good idea," he said. "But quick as you can, I have to leave now."

"Cheese and ham?"

"Perfect." Shepherd hurried upstairs. He always kept a packed holdall in his wardrobe containing two changes of clothes, a washbag and his passport. He grabbed a jacket and the holdall and a spare mobile phone and headed back downstairs. Katra had done him two rounds of sandwiches and put them in a Ziploc bag. "You're an angel," he said.

"When will you be back?"

"No idea," he said, picking up the keys to his BMW X5. "I'll phone you from London."

"Be careful," she said.

Shepherd frowned. "Why do you say that?" In all the years she'd worked for him he didn't remember her ever telling him to take care.

Her cheeks reddened. "I don't know," she said. "Just a feeling."

Rafiq could barely breathe, the sack over his head was stifling and he was close to passing out. He had lost track of time. He'd been in the car or truck for an hour, maybe longer, and they'd driven across rough ground for most of the way. Eventually they'd stopped and he'd been dragged inside and tied to a chair. He'd begged for water but his pleas had been ignored. He had no idea whether or not he was alone in the room, the sack muffled most sounds, though at some point he had heard another vehicle drive up outside.

He slumped in the chair and tried to slow his breathing. He tried to think calming thoughts but he wasn't able to do that for more than a few minutes before the panic would set in again and he would start panting and crying out.

Eventually he heard footsteps behind him. Something touched the sack behind his head and he flinched, expecting a blow, but then the sack was ripped off and he blinked as the sun shone into his face. He was facing a window, the glass streaked with dirt. There was a man standing to the left of the window. Rafiq blinked again and narrowed his eyes as he struggled to focus.

"What is your name?" asked the man, and Rafiq realised it was Hammad, the instructor.

He felt relief wash over him. It was a test. Hammad was testing him. And if it was a test, all he had to do was hold firm and eventually it would end.

"What is your name?" asked Hammad.

"Rafiq. You know my name. Rafiq Mahar."

"Your real name."

Rafiq frowned. "My real name? Rafiq Mahar is my real name. I gave your people my passport when I arrived in Pakistan."

"Your British passport?"

Rafiq nodded. "I was born in Britain."

"In Leeds, that's what your passport says."

"Yes, in Leeds." Sweat was running down his face but his hands were still tied behind his back so he shook his head but that didn't help. "There has been some mistake. Whatever you think has happened, there is a mistake."

"Your parents were from Pakistan?"

"Yes. From Lahore. They moved to Bradford in the sixties and I was born there. What is this, why are you doing this to me?"

Hammad ignored his questions. "You have siblings?"

Rafiq shook his head. "I'm an only child. My mother was almost forty when I was born and she couldn't have any more children."

"That is a shame," said Hammad. "It is the duty of every Muslim sister to have as many children as possible."

"She married late," said Rafiq. "And I was a difficult birth. So I was their only child. Please can I have some water. My mouth, it's so dry. It hurts to swallow."

"They are still in Bradford, your mother and father?"

Rafiq shook his head. "They died, seven years ago."

"I am sorry to hear that, brother. To lose a parent is an awful thing. To lose both, to be an orphan, that is terrible."

"It was a long time ago." Rafiq heard a noise behind him, the sound of a sandal scraping across the floor and he turned to see who it was.

"Do not look at them, look at me," said Hammad.

Rafiq turned back to look at Hammad. "Please, this is crazy," he said. "You know who I am and you know why I'm here."

"Do you think I'm stupid, Rafiq?"

Rafiq stared at him, confused. "What?"

"It is a simple question. Do you think I am stupid?"

"I don't know who you are," said Rafiq. "But I don't think you're stupid. Why would you think that? Have I been disrespectful?"

Hammad nodded slowly. "You have, brother. Yes, you have been extremely disrespectful."

"Then I apologise, brother. It was never my intention to be disrespectful."

Hammad stared at Rafiq with cold, black eyes.

"There has been a mistake," said Rafiq. "Tell me what you think I have done so that I can put this right."

Hammad smiled. "You want to put this right?"

Rafiq nodded enthusiastically. "Of course."

"All you need to do to put this right is to tell me the truth."

"I'm telling you the truth. As Allah is my judge."

Hammad took a long, deep breath as he stared at Rafiq, and then exhaled slowly. "You must be very careful in your choice of words, brother," he said. "Lying to me is one thing, it is quite another to lie to God."

"Brother, I swear to you, I am telling the truth. Ask me anything and I will answer you honestly."

"Anything?"

"Anything," repeated Rafiq.

Hammad nodded slowly. "Then tell me your name," he said. "Tell me who you really are."

"Why are you doing this to me, brother?"

Hammad stepped forward and slapped Rafiq across the face, so hard that the breath exploded from his mouth and saliva sprayed across the room. Before he had time to cry out Hammad backhanded him on the other side of the face, the slap echoing around the room like a pistol shot.

"Brother, what is it you want from me?"

Hammad slapped him again, then he screamed, drew back his fist and punched him in the face so hard that the chair fell back and Rafiq's head slammed into the ground.

"Be careful, brother," said one of the men who had been standing behind Rafiq. "We don't want him to die. Not yet, anyway."

Shepherd phoned Button when he was an hour away from central London. "Best you drive direct to Vauxhall Bridge, the SIS building," she said. Shepherd frowned. The SIS building was the headquarters of MI6, jokingly referred to by the intelligence community as Babylon-on-Thames, and sometimes as Legoland because of its distinctive modular shape.

"How is Six involved?" asked Shepherd.

"Raj was working for them," said Button.

"What?"

"I've only just found out," said Button.

"He went out to Pakistan for Six? In what universe was that a good idea?"

"I'm as stunned as you are. When you get there, ask for Jeremy Willoughby-Brown. He was handling Raj."

"Was?"

"Was, is."

"Is Raj OK?"

"No, he's not OK, but I don't have the full details. Willoughby-Brown will brief you."

"Is there anything else you can tell me?" asked Shepherd.

"I'm afraid not. Even if I had any intel it's not the sort of information I'd want shared over an open line. Call me after you've seen Willoughby-Brown." She ended the call.

Shepherd cursed under his breath. Raj Chaudhry was a medical student who had penetrated an al-Qaeda cell in London two years earlier. Shepherd had been his handler, as well as overseeing another student, Harvey Malik. Both lads had been virgins at the intelligence game and Shepherd had held their hands from start to finish. Their operation had been a success, though Harvey almost lost his life to an al-Qaeda assassin. The last time they'd met, Raj had said he was going back to his studies and he'd barely given him any thought over the past two years.

He realised that he'd been pressing down harder on the accelerator and just as he braked there was a flash of light from what was almost certainly a speed camera and he cursed under his breath. He slowed to the speed limit.

Shepherd wasn't sure whether Button had arranged car parking for him at MI6 so he left this SUV parked on a meter. He walked in through the main entrance, showed his MI5 credentials at reception and was asked to wait on a low grey sofa. After ten minutes a young woman in a dark green suit came over and asked whether he was Dan Shepherd, even though he was the only person in reception. He stood up and said yes, and she asked him to go with her. She took him through a metal detector arch and into a lift up to the fifth floor.

They stepped out of the lift into a corridor lined with identical doors, identified only by a number. She took him along to a door at the far end, knocked twice and opened it. The man inside was standing with his back to the door, looking out of the window. "Mr Shepherd is here for you, sir," said the woman. The man turned as Shepherd stepped into the office. The woman left, pulling the door shut behind her.

Shepherd's jaw dropped as he recognised the man. It had been almost twenty years since he'd last set eyes on him in the Middle East, not long after Shepherd had joined the SAS. They'd also worked together in Sierra Leone, and it hadn't been an experience that Shepherd had enjoyed. Back then Jonathan Parker had favoured a linen suit, an MCC tie and a panama hat. He'd put on quite a bit of weight and lost a fair amount of hair, but there was the same supercilious smile on his thin lips and a cold calculating look in his hazel eyes that reminded Shepherd of a vulture eyeing up its next meal. The linen suit had gone, replaced by a dark blue pinstripe that looked as if it had come from Savile Row, and the tie was yellow with blue anchors on it.

"Small world, Shepherd," said the man, holding out his hand.

Shepherd had half a mind to refuse to shake hands as they hadn't parted on the best of terms, but realised that would be churlish. The two men shook. Shepherd had to resist the urge to wipe his hand on his trousers and he forced a smile. "Willoughby-Brown? What happened to Jonathan Parker?"

The man smiled. "We never use our real names in the field, Shepherd. You know that."

"So is Willoughby-Brown your real name?"

He tapped the side of his nose. "Need to know, old lad." He waved a languid hand at a chair on the far side of his desk. "Please, sit."

"You don't look like a Jeremy," said Shepherd as he sat down.

Willoughby-Brown smiled without warmth. "Did I look like a Jonathan?"

Shepherd wrinkled his nose as he considered the question. "Yeah, actually you did."

"You can call me Jonathan, then, if that makes you feel better." He dropped down into a high-backed executive chair that squeaked as if it were made of real leather.

"It won't," said Shepherd. "I'd just like to know who I'm dealing with, that's all."

"We never use our real names, you know that."

"I'm Dan Shepherd."

Willoughby-Brown nodded. "True. But when you're undercover, you use legends. And even when you're running agents at Five, you use assumed names."

Shepherd waited. If the MI6 man was ever going to tell him his real name, now would be the time to do it. But Willoughby-Brown, or whatever his name was, just smiled. "I see you've dropped the MCC tie," said Shepherd eventually.

"That was always an affectation," said Willoughby-Brown.

"Were you ever a member?"

Willoughby-Brown smiled. "What do you think?"

"I think not."

Willoughby-Brown's face broke into a broad grin. "Damn, you were always a good judge of character, Shepherd." He patted Shepherd on the back. "Sierra Leone was interesting, wasn't it?"

"It was a hellhole," said Shepherd. "I don't have too many fond memories." He wanted to talk about Raj but the MI6 man seemed to be taking pleasure in talking around the houses.

"It had its moments. Have you been back?"

"Been back? Why would I go back?"

"There's quite a tourist industry now."

"I think I'll give it a miss," said Shepherd.

"Beautiful beaches," said Willoughby-Brown. "By the way, we never talked about the diamonds you took back from the mercenaries."

"Didn't we?"

Willoughby-Brown took out a small cigar and studied it as if it was the first time he'd seen it. "You remember Laurence Beltran, the lovely French lady at Medicaid International?"

"Sure. She was an angel."

"She seemed to have come into quite a lot of additional funds, not long after you came back with the diamonds."

"Really?"

"Really," said Willoughby-Brown. "And once, over a drink, she referred to you as her white knight. Said you'd ridden to her rescue just when she needed rescuing."

"That was nice of her."

"You've never kept in touch?"

"We were shunted out at short notice, so I never really got the chance to say goodbye."

"Well, it was all very strange. Before you came on the scene she was forever complaining about being short of funds, but after that mercenary business, well . . ." He shrugged and looked up from his cigar. "Let's just say that funding didn't seem to be a problem. And she became quite pally with that Lebanese diamond merchant. What was his name again?"

Shepherd shrugged. "I forget."

Willoughby-Brown jabbed the unlit cigar at him. "Now we both know that's not true," he said. "You've got one of those eidetic memories. You never forget anything."

Shepherd frowned. "It was a long time ago, Jeremy."

"Farid, his name was. Big Lebanese guy. Always sweating."

Shepherd nodded. "I remember."

"Of course you do. Well, he got very close to Laurence. Makes you wonder, doesn't it?"

"Not really," said Shepherd.

"I mean, God forbid you might have put a few of those blood diamonds her way."

"What did happen to those diamonds?" asked Shepherd.

Willoughby-Brown tapped the side of his nose again. "Need to know," he said. His face broke into a grin. "Anyway, enough of this chit-chat. Do you mind if we go outside? I really do feel like a smoke and it's going to take some time to explain what's happened." Willoughby-Brown led Shepherd out of his office, along a corridor, into another room and through a set of French windows on to a small terrace overlooking the Thames. "Strictly speaking I can't even smoke here."

"Place of work," said Shepherd.

"Exactly," said Willoughby-Brown, lighting his cigar. He blew smoke over the river. "Can't smoke, can't drink, can't have fun with the ladies. Who would've thought the world would have ended up like this? PC madness, that's what it is." He took another long drag on his cigar and then exhaled slowly. "You did one hell of a job with young Manraj," he said.

"Not that great a job, obviously. What the hell has happened?"

"In a nutshell, young Manraj has been captured by a group of Islamic extremists in Pakistan."

"What the fuck was he doing in Pakistan?"

"Working for us, obviously. Infiltrating a group of British-born Muslims who were being trained over there."

"How did that become an MI6 operation?"

"We had a number of al-Qaeda operatives under surveillance in Pakistan. There was communications traffic between them and several imams in the UK."

"So why didn't you pass that intel on to Five?"

Willoughby-Brown looked at him, frowning. "What's that got to do with anything?"

"Raj should never have been sent to Pakistan. He was almost certainly exposed during the operation we ran."

"His friend was attacked. There's no evidence that Raj had been compromised."

"Bollocks," said Shepherd. "Raj and Harvey were peas in a pod. They were recruited together and they were trained together and they were both taken to see Bin Laden. If Harvey was blown then so was Raj."

"We had no evidence that he had been compromised. We had him under constant surveillance the whole time he was in Bradford and we would have pulled him out if there had been the slightest hint that he was having problems. He was accepted by the mosque and eventually approached by the imam. They would have checked him out before approaching him, so we knew his legend was good."

"Bradford isn't Pakistan," said Shepherd.

"I know some members of the English Defence League who might disagree," said Willoughby-Brown. He put up his hand. "OK, bad joke," he said. "But if his cover wasn't watertight it would have shown up long before he went to Pakistan."

"Then you explain to me what went wrong," said Shepherd.

"We don't know," said Willoughby-Brown. "Maybe he slipped up."

"He wasn't the sort to make a mistake," said Shepherd. "He was a quick learner."

"And he always spoke highly of you. Or rather John Whitehill." Willoughby-Brown flashed his cold smile. "In fact young Manraj thinks the sun shines out of your arse. He was a virgin before you took him under your wing, wasn't he?"

Shepherd nodded. "He was a medical student. He was infiltrating a radical group in London and he needed some guidance. Surveillance and counter-surveillance, undercover techniques and the rest."

Willoughby-Brown blew smoke and sighed contentedly. "What was it Churchill said? A woman is just a woman but a good cigar is a smoke?"

"It was Kipling."

"The baker?"

"The poet."

"But he did make exceedingly good cakes, didn't he?" said Willoughby-Brown before chuckling at his own joke.

"What was Raj doing in Pakistan?" asked Shepherd. "And how did he end up working for Six?"

"Second question first, he was too good an asset to waste. Five were going to let him go back to his studies. We realised that there was a lot more he could do."

"We?"

"My boss, as it happens. He has a contact in Five and they chatted at their club."

"Not Charlie?"

"The lovely Miss Button?" He shook his head. "Above her pay grade."

"Did she know?"

"Why does that matter?" asked Willoughby-Brown, narrowing his eyes.

"I'd just like to know."

"Curious?"

"I guess."

Willoughby-Brown smiled thinly. "You know what curiosity did to the cat."

"It's a fair question," said Shepherd. "I was Raj's handler. I was told he was going back to his studies. If she had known that he was remaining active then she should have told me."

Willoughby-Brown looked at him levelly. "She didn't know," he said.

"So he was approached by Six?"

"By me."

"You were his handler?"

Willoughby-Brown nodded. "But not in Pakistan, obviously. Pasty white face like mine would stand out a mile and not do him any favours."

"Please don't tell me you sent him to Pakistan on his own?"

"We had a handler for him over there. A Pakistani."

"A local?"

"No, one of ours. British-born, bit of a rising star, actually. Double first at Oxford, fluent in Urdu and Arabic and a smattering of Pashto."

"How old is this wonder kid?"

"Why does that matter?"

"It matters."

Willoughby-Brown sighed. "Twenty-seven."

Shepherd groaned. "You handed Raj over to a kid?"

"Taz is an experienced operative. Tazam Bashir. His father's a QC, his mother's on the boards of several charities."

"So young Taz is being fast-tracked, is he?"

"You say that as if it was a bad thing," said Willoughby-Brown. He blew smoke over the river and flicked ash over the balcony. "He's bright, he's articulate, and he can think on his feet."

"Undercover experience?"

"He's been a handler for almost five years and never put a foot wrong."

"Until he managed to lose Raj?"

"That was just bad luck," said Willoughby-Brown.

Shepherd folded his arms. "You had a twenty-seven-year-old handler running a twenty-two-year-old. You don't think there's anything wrong with that?"

"How old were you when I met you in Sierra Leone?"

"That's not the same thing."

"Sierra Leone in 1997 was a hell of a lot more dangerous than present-day Pakistan. And you were what? Twenty-three?"

"I was in the SAS."

"Exactly. You were doing stuff a hell of a lot more dangerous than we asked of Manraj. You took out a group of mercenaries. You were chased by drugged-up AK-47-toting child soldiers. And I'd barely turned thirty."

"You weren't handling me, Jeremy."

Willoughby-Brown laughed. "Yes, I was."

Shepherd shook his head emphatically. "We did a few things for you to kill time. You weren't involved in the planning or the execution."

"If that makes you feel better, you carry on believing it," said Willoughby-Brown. He took a long pull on his cigar and held the smoke deep in his lungs. He stared at Shepherd, a slight smile on his face.

Shepherd considered what the MI6 man had said. Was it true? Had he been played when he was in Sierra Leone? Had he been following Willoughby-Brown's lead the whole time? He scratched the back of his neck. He'd been a relative youngster when he'd been in Sierra Leone with the SAS, but he hadn't been stupid. Had Willoughby-Brown been manipulating him? He could see the sparkle of amusement in the MI6 man's eyes so he forced a smile. "It's not worth arguing about," he said. "We did what needed to be done, it doesn't matter who was or wasn't calling the shots."

Willoughby-Brown blew smoke. "Exactly," he said.

"But that doesn't make this Taz any less culpable," said Shepherd.

"You're going to have to treat that as water under the bridge," said Willoughby-Brown. "The mission at hand is to rescue Manraj, not to apportion blame."

"Was Taz working for you?"

"The decision to put Manraj with Taz wasn't mine. I knew of Taz but I hadn't worked with him. Just between you and me, he wouldn't have been my first choice but it was felt that he was ready and able to take on the task."

"Yeah, well that was clearly an error of judgement."

"No arguments there," said Willoughby-Brown. "But as I said, we need to put that behind us. What matters is where we go from here."

"You have a plan?"

Willoughby-Brown smiled thinly. "I have an aim. I want to bring Manraj home. So far as a plan's concerned, well, that's why you're here, isn't it?"

Rafiq heard footsteps outside the door to his cell, then the sound of two bolts being pulled back. He was lying on his side, facing the door, his hands still bound behind his back. The cuts in his mouth had stopped bleeding but he still tasted blood each time he swallowed. The door opened and a big man in a dark green shalwar kameez and a white skullcap appeared. Rafiq blinked up at him. "Brother, I have done nothing wrong," he said.

The man ignored him. He took a plastic bottle of water and a rough clay bowl from an unseen figure and carried them into the cell. He knelt down and put them on the floor by Rafiq's head. There was cooked rice in the bowl, topped with a splash of brown liquid that might have been a curry of some sort. He lifted Rafiq into a sitting position and then pulled a curved knife from his belt. Rafiq flinched and the man smiled savagely, then he knelt down and cut the rope that was binding Rafiq's wrists. A second man appeared in the doorway, squat and well muscled, holding a pistol in his right hand.

"Thank you," said Rafiq. He picked up the bottle of water, twisted off the cap and drank greedily. He gulped down half the bottle and then wiped his mouth with his sleeve. "Where am I, brother?" he asked.

The man folded his arms but said nothing. He had a long beard, twice the length of Rafiq's, dark brown at the end but white close to his skin. His eyebrows were jet black and his hair was only flecked with grey.

Rafiq put down the bottle and reached for the bowl of rice. He scooped some up with his fingers and pushed it into his mouth before chewing slowly. "Brother, if I am to be held here for much longer I will need to pray," said Rafiq. "Can you get me a prayer mat and a copy of the Qur'an? And water so that I may bathe."

"Praying won't help you, brother," said the man.

"Praying always helps, brother," said Rafiq.

"You are a liar and a traitor and Allah will not listen to your prayers," said the man. He pointed a yellowed fingernail at Rafiq's nose. "You will burn in hell and all the prayers in the world will not save your lying soul."

"You have to believe me, brother, I am not lying. I am a good Muslim and a committed jihadist. I would not be here if that were not so."

The man cursed and slapped the bowl out of Rafiq's hands. It shattered and the rice scattered over the ground. Rafiq stared up at him in surprise. The man kicked him in the chest and Rafiq fell back, banging his head against the wall so hard that he lay there stunned as the man left the cell and bolted the door.

After a few minutes Rafiq rolled on to his stomach, crawled across the floor to the shattered bowl and began to lick up the spilled rice.

Willoughby-Brown walked over to a large map that had been pinned to the wall opposite his desk. It covered the Middle East and most of Asia. "This is where Manraj was being trained," he said, tapping the north-eastern part of Pakistan. "He and the five men he was with flew to Islamabad about a week ago. From there they went overland, close to the border with Afghanistan." He had taken off his jacket and rolled up his shirtsleeves.

"You don't have an exact location?"

"They move their training camps around, they're never more than temporary," said Willoughby-Brown. "The Yanks are forever flying drones over and that whole area is regularly looked at by their satellites."

"So what intel were you hoping to get from him?" said Shepherd. "If they're temporary, there'd be no point in attacking them."

"To be honest, we were more concerned about what they were planning here in the UK," said Willoughby-Brown. "He only knew one of the men he was flying out with, a chap he'd met at the mosque in Bradford where he was recruited. The operation was to identify the rest of the men who were being trained so that we could put them under surveillance back in the UK."

"Wouldn't that have been a job for Five?"

"Possibly, yes," said Willoughby-Brown. "But we were interested in the funding and the logistics of whatever attacks they were being trained for. Once we knew who was involved in the UK, we could follow the money trail and hopefully identify the paymasters."

Shepherd nodded. What the man was saying made sense, but it would have made even more sense for there to have been a joint operation.

"He really shouldn't have gone," said Shepherd. "He should have backed out and you could have followed the other guy to Pakistan and seen who he met up with."

"We didn't see there'd be any real risk," said Willoughby-Brown. "They were due to be away for a month and his legend was rock solid."

"Well, something went wrong, obviously."

"And hindsight is always twenty-twenty. If I had known that this was going to happen then I wouldn't have allowed him to go. But at the time, with the information I had at hand, it was the right call."

"Do you have any surveillance photographs of the area?" asked Shepherd.

"They wouldn't help. He's been moved."

Shepherd frowned. "How do you know that?"

"The Pakistanis have told me."

"Who specifically? Where is your intel coming from?

"It's from the Pakistani Secret Service," said Willoughby-Brown.

"That's awkward because there's no such thing," said Shepherd.

"I was using shorthand," said Willoughby-Brown tersely. "Of course I mean the Directorate for Inter-Services Intelligence. ISI."

Shepherd nodded. The ISI was the country's main intelligence agency, the others being the Intelligence Bureau and Military Intelligence. He had little confidence in any of them as sources of intelligence. During the Russian occupation of Afghanistan the ISI had actively helped the mujahedin, albeit with the assistance of the CIA, and they had supported the Afghan Taliban during the country's civil war in the 1990s. Now they were supposedly on the side of the West but Shepherd doubted that old allegiances could be so easily forgotten. "From what I've heard, the ISI leaks like a sieve," he said.

"There is a lot of idle gossip in the intelligence world, as I'm sure you know," said Willoughby-Brown.

"It's more than gossip. The Afghans have been complaining for years that the ISI is financing and helping to train Taliban insurgents and tipping them off whenever the Yanks are firing missiles into the tribal areas."

"I think there're two sides to every story," said Willoughby-Brown. "I'm sure there were close connections between MI5 and agents and sources within the IRA, but that doesn't mean security was compromised. I've no doubt the Pakistanis would argue that they need to be in contact with the Taliban in order to gain intelligence. I can assure you that in this case the intel is good."

"So which division has supplied the intel?"

"Which division?"

Shepherd frowned. "You are a Pakistan expert, right?"

"I'm more of an al-Qaeda expert, to be honest."

Shepherd smiled but he was far from happy about the way the conversation was going. "There's the Covert Action Division that's in charge of covert operations, there's the Joint Intelligence Bureau that's mainly concerned with political intelligence, there's the Joint Signal Intelligence Bureau that handles electronic intelligence, there's the SS Directorate that monitors terrorist groups in Pakistan. And there's another five or six divisions, all separate fiefdoms. Some are trustworthy and some aren't, so your source matters."

"I know it's human intel," said Willoughby-Brown.

"So the ISI has an inside man?"

"That I'm not sure of," said Willoughby-Brown.

"You don't seem sure of much," said Shepherd.

"The ISI are as protective of their sources as we are of ours. But I can tell you that Raj has been exposed and is being interrogated. And if we don't do something, they'll kill him."

"How much does he know?"

"Raj?"

Shepherd suppressed a sudden urge to grab the MI6 man and hurl him off the balcony, but instead he forced a smile. "Yes, Raj."

"Other than his own operation, not much," said Willoughby-Brown. "We did some training with him, but mostly we were debriefing him."

"How much does he know about you?"

"Next to nothing. Same with Taz. He doesn't know our real names."

"But he knew you were with Six?"

Willoughby-Brown nodded.

"What about other assets? Does he have any names he can give them?"

"No. He was a stand-alone."

106

"So he doesn't have any solid information to give them?"

"Nothing that can damage any ongoing operations."

Shepherd sighed. Whether or not Raj had any useful information on MI6 investigations wouldn't matter to his interrogators. They would know that his handlers would act quickly to render useless any information that he had. What would be of much more interest to them would be what Willoughby-Brown had asked Raj to find out. That would show up the gaps in MI6's knowledge as well as indicating the direction the investigation had been taking. "Had he had any counter-interrogation training?"

"It wasn't thought necessary. Raj was well trusted, he'd already been out to Pakistan when you were running him. The last thing we expected was for his cover to be blown."

"So he's no idea what to do? How to act?"

"We're assuming he'll deny everything at first."

"Until they torture him, then he'll crack."

Shepherd gritted his teeth. Willoughby-Brown's offhand attitude was seriously starting to annoy him. Raj had risked his life to penetrate an al-Qaeda cell in London and now he was being tortured in some Pakistani hellhole while Willoughby-Brown preened himself and smoked his ridiculous tiny cigars.

"So what's the plan? What are we going to do?"

"The Pakistanis are going to go in and rescue him."

"The army?"

"The SSG. Special Services Group. They're equivalent to the SAS."

"Do you have any operational details? Are they using helicopters? A ground approach?"

Willoughby-Brown shook his head. "They've not been forthcoming on that front, I'm afraid."

"But they're happy to allow me to go in with them?"

"Apparently they feel it would be helpful if someone who knows Manraj was there. You were the obvious choice because you know the man and you've got SAS experience."

"Can you do me a favour and stop calling him Manraj?" said Shepherd. "Everyone calls him Raj."

"Are you serious?"

"Yeah, I am. His name's Raj. Calling him anything else just seems disrespectful."

"You're a funny bugger, Shepherd."

"Yeah, well, I'm the funny bugger that's going to be risking his life in Pakistan to rescue the guy you put at risk, so you're going to have live with it."

Willoughby-Brown's eyes narrowed, but then he nodded. "No problem," he said. "Raj it is." He went back to his desk and pulled open a drawer. He took out a manila folder, sat down and opened it. It contained several dozen photographs, most of which appeared to have been taken from CCTV cameras. Willoughby-Brown flicked through them and then slid one across the desk towards Shepherd. "You should know that Raj's appearance has changed a bit."

Shepherd looked at the photograph. It was split in two, a full head-on shot and a side view. He frowned. The profile was markedly different from the Raj he remembered. He looked back at Willoughby-Brown and found him grinning. "We gave him the scars, lengthened the nose and added to his chin. On top of that, he's grown quite a respectable beard."

"So that he couldn't be recognised? So you knew there was a risk?"

"A calculated risk."

Shepherd glared at him. "A calculated risk when the downside is torture and beheading? Who the hell made that call?"

"Raj was OK with it."

"Raj is a kid. He's easily led, as I'm sure you know."

"He wanted to go. He was insistent."

Shepherd shook his head in disgust.

"He believes in what he's doing. He's a patriot. Proud to be British."

"And you played on that, I bet?"

"He wants to serve his country, I helped him to do that."

"And now he's being tortured in the bloody desert," said Shepherd. He tossed the photograph on to the desk. "What about his parents?"

"His parents?"

"Have they been told?"

"Of course not."

"They need to know what's happened," said Shepherd.

"I'm not sure there's any advantage in keeping them in the loop until we have a clearer idea of where we stand."

"Do they know he's in Pakistan?"

"He told them he was going there for a friend's wedding and to do some travelling. A few white lies. It's no big deal." Willoughby-Brown passed him another photograph, a surveillance picture of a young Asian leaving a mosque. "Naseem Naeem," he said. "He's the one who flew out with Raj. He's a mechanic, Bradford born and bred. Third-generation, his grandparents came over in the fifties to work in the mills."

Shepherd studied the photograph. The man looked younger than his age and could easily have passed for a schoolboy. Willoughby-Brown pushed the file towards Shepherd. "The rest of the pictures are young men who flew on the same flight, and on other Pakistan flights the day before and the day after. We've weeded out the ones who were working or who went to Pakistan for genuine family reasons."

Shepherd flicked through the photographs. There were more than fifty. "That's a lot."

"You're telling me. And that's just three days. It's a lot of needles in a bloody enormous haystack, which is why we needed Raj there. If we can get him back, he'll be able to tell us who the naughty boys are."

"Was Raj able to communicate with you or anybody while he was at the camp?"

Willoughby-Brown shook his head. "We couldn't take the risk of him taking any sort of communication device with him. He had a mobile with GPS but they took it off him when he arrived in Pakistan. We were able to get a look at him from an American spy satellite."

Shepherd frowned. "Run that by me."

"We spoke to the Yanks and they gave us access to the feeds of satellites moving over that general area of north-west Pakistan. Most of the scans showed nothing. The Yanks tell me that al-Qaeda know the times and orbits of most of their long-standing surveillance satellites, but there's one that they don't seem to know about."

He went back into the drawer and pulled out a couple of photographs, grainy and with the colour washed out. One showed a group of men doing some sort of exercise. Press-ups or planks, it was hard to see. Willoughby-Brown tapped one of the figures. "We're pretty sure this is Raj."

Shepherd peered at the picture. The faces of most of the figures were hidden and he wouldn't have been able to recognise anyone from the grainy photograph. Willoughby-Brown pushed over the second photograph. The men were on their feet, facing a bearded man dressed in white. The figure that Willoughby-Brown said was Raj was still blurred.

"We've had them enhanced, and we're reasonably sure it's him."

"When were these taken?"

"The time and date and map reference are on the back," said Willoughby-Brown.

Shepherd turned the photograph over. It had been taken four days earlier. His mobile phone beeped. He'd received a message. He took a quick look at it. It was Charlotte Button.

"Anything important?" asked Willoughby-Brown.

"Not really," said Shepherd.

★ ★ ★

Shepherd left the MI6 building and walked back to his car, deep in thought. A black Lexus was parked behind his SUV. As he reached his car the rear door of the Lexus opened and Charlotte Button climbed out. She was wearing a Barbour jacket and dark green corduroy trousers and she thrust her hands into her pockets as she walked towards him, her shoulder-length chestnut hair blowing in the wind. "How did it go?" she asked.

"As well as can be expected, I suppose," said Shepherd.

He climbed into the front seat of his BMW as Button walked around to the passenger door. He left the engine switched off but sat with his hands on the steering wheel. "How much do you know about what's going on?" he asked as she sat down and pulled the door shut.

"Very little," said Button. "Just that there's a problem with Raj and that your expertise was required."

"But you're my boss, why wouldn't you be in the picture?"

Button shrugged. "Five and Six are separate entities and their operations do tend to be more secretive than ours."

"How well do you know Willoughby-Brown? If that is his name."

Button frowned. "By reputation only. Is there a problem?"

Shepherd's hands tightened on the steering wheel. "I don't know if it's a problem. But I'm being asked to do something above and beyond the call of duty and I'm getting a bad feeling about it."

112

"They're putting you in harm's way?"

Shepherd nodded. "Very much so. If it was you asking me to do it, that'd be fine. But Willoughby-Brown and I have a history."

"I didn't know that."

"Yeah, I ran into him in Sierra Leone. He used me and a few mates on a couple of operations, which was fair enough, but I never really trusted him."

"He was with MI6 back then?"

"Yeah. Strutted around in an MCC tie as if he owned the place. Have you met him?"

"No. I haven't even spoken to him. There's surprisingly little mixing between the two agencies."

"And they've told you nothing about what they're asking me to do?"

Button shook her head. "If you're not happy, you can always turn it down."

"I can't. Raj's life is on the line." He turned to look at her. "I need to talk this through with you."

Button looked pained. "I can't, Spider. I'm sorry. This is a Six operation, it's nothing to do with Five. I shouldn't even be here."

"That's not good enough. I need your advice, if not your help."

"I can't do that, Spider. I'm sorry."

"So I'm on my own?"

"You're not on your own. You're attached to Six." She folded her arms. "I need a drink."

"You and me both."

She flashed him a tight smile. "Find us a bar," she said. "You're buying."

Shepherd parked outside a pub in Battersea. There were two bars either side of the main door. There was a pub quiz going on in the bar on the left so they turned right. Button went to a table in the corner while Shepherd went to the bar and paid for a glass of white wine and a Jameson's whiskey with ice and soda. He went over to the table, gave Button the wine and sat down. He toasted her and sipped his whiskey.

"What is it you want, Spider?" she said.

"I want someone watching my back," said Shepherd, leaning towards her. "I want someone who knows what I'm doing and why so that if the shit hits the fan I'm not out on a limb." He smiled. "Forgive the clichés."

"I told you, it's not my operation. If it was . . ." She shrugged. "There's no point in my finishing that sentence because if it had been any operation of mine I wouldn't have involved Raj." She ran a hand through her hair. "I was told to put you in touch with Willoughby-Brown and facilitate your secondment to Six. The actual details of the Six operation are need-to-know." She stared at him for several seconds, then took a long drink of wine. She raised her eyebrows appreciatively. "Good choice."

"The barman recommended it."

She took another sip then put her glass back down on the table. "Officially I can't know anything," she said. "And officially we never had this conversation."

"Understood," said Shepherd.

"This is putting me in a very difficult position, you realise that?"

Shepherd nodded. "Not half as difficult as the position I'm being put in, believe me."

"And you have a problem with this Willoughby-Brown?"

"I don't trust him," said Shepherd. "And if it was you asking me to go to Pakistan, of course I'd do it, no questions asked."

She smiled. "That's good to know," she said. "OK, tell me everything."

Shepherd quickly laid out what it was that Willoughby-Brown wanted him to do. Button listened, her face a blank mask, until he'd finished. "I can see why you'd be uneasy," she said eventually.

"That's an understatement," he said. "The thing is, Raj is in danger so I can't not help. But joint operations are never a good idea at the best of times and the Pakistani special forces don't have the best reputation."

"They've had their moments," said Button.

"There's no way that this could be an off-the-books operation, is there?"

Button's eyes narrowed. "What makes you think that?"

"This whole need-to-know business worries me. You're my boss so it seems only right that they'd want to keep you in the loop. In Sierra Leone, Willoughby-Brown seemed to be doing things off his own bat. I got the feeling that back then he was on a very long leash, getting us to do stuff without clearing it with the office. In fact some of the stuff he got us to do, I'm pretty sure he wouldn't have got official approval."

"But you did it anyway."

Shepherd grinned. "We were SAS, we were bloody invincible. A lot of the time we had nothing to do so it helped relieve the boredom." He took a sip of whiskey. "So that's why alarm bells are ringing now. He's screwed up, obviously. He was running Raj and Raj has been caught. I wonder if he's using the SAS again to save his own skin."

"Without clearing it? I think that's very unlikely."

"Unlikely or impossible?"

"Nothing's ever impossible," said Button. "But sure, it's highly improbable, especially these days. What's your main concern?"

Shepherd shrugged. "Where do I start? He wants me to go in with a team that I have zero experience with. He's promised me a few rehearsals when I get to Pakistan, but storming a building with armed targets is a bloody dangerous business. Before I went with the SEALs to get Bin Laden I spent a week rehearsing entries in North Carolina and another week in Nevada practising helicopter assaults. And despite all that it ended up as a cock-up on the night; they crashed a helicopter and ended up having to blast their way in through the front door."

"Helicopters crash, they're inherently unstable," said Button.

"Agreed. But that's more of a reason to be with a team you can depend on," said Shepherd. "When I was in the SAS, you knew everyone, you knew what they'd do in every possible situation. Most of the time you'd know where they were without looking. Once you start bringing new faces in, the risk goes up exponentially. A stray bullet in the back can seriously ruin your day. Happened in Sierra Leone, a warrant officer I knew got shot by a Para. He was wearing body armour so he was OK, but even so."

"They want you on the operation so that Raj will see a friendly face, presumably?"

Shepherd nodded. "That's the plan."

"So you can hang back, take more of an observer's role, same as you did on Neptune Spear."

"Sure. And I'll do that. But the picture worries me. What if something goes wrong? I'm out there on my own. What if Willoughby-Brown denies all knowledge of me?"

"You think he'd throw you to the wolves?"

"It wouldn't be the first time that MI6 had abandoned an agent," said Shepherd.

She sipped her wine. "What do you think I'll be able to do?" she asked.

"Like I said, watch my back."

"From here? Thousands of miles away? What can I do?"

Shepherd rubbed the back of his neck. He could feel the tendons there, as taut as steel wires. "Keep an eye on the operation. Listen to the chatter. I don't think Willoughby-Brown is telling me everything."

Button smiled. "You're asking me to spy on spies?"

"Pretty much, yes."

Button drained her glass. "Tell you what, get me another drink and it's a deal."

"Thank you," said Shepherd.

"Don't thank me," said Button. "You're one of my best men, I don't want anything to happen to you."

Rafiq didn't know how many men were keeping him prisoner, but he knew how many had beaten him. Four so far: all Pakistanis, all in their thirties or forties, and all intent on causing him as much pain as they could without actually killing him. They tended to work in pairs, one carrying out the beating while the other one stood at the door holding a weapon, sometimes a handgun, sometimes an AK-47. The gun was unnecessary because Rafiq didn't have the strength to fight back. All he could do was curl up and pray for the beating to stop. There were no questions and when he asked them what they wanted from him, they remained silent. They slapped him, they punched him and they kicked him. And once one of the men used a cane and whipped Rafiq's legs and backside so hard that the welts bled. Sometimes Rafiq would pass out, but the men seemed skilled at what they were doing and would pull back just before his consciousness faded, waiting for him to recover, before starting again. Rafiq soon lost all sense of time. He wasn't aware of the hours passing, he didn't even know if it was day or night. He was either being beaten, or he was lying on the floor waiting for the next beating to start. That was his life now. There was nothing else. Just the pain. And the anticipation of the pain. They would kill him eventually, he was sure of that. He didn't want to die. Nobody wanted to die. But he didn't think he could take the pain for much longer.

Shepherd spent the night at the Premier Inn, part of the massive riverside building that had once been County Hall. He caught a black cab to the MI6 building at eight o'clock the following morning. "So are you James Bond, then?" asked the driver as they drove to Vauxhall Bridge.

"Yeah, that's me," said Shepherd. "Licensed to kill."

"But you work there?"

"Just visiting," said Shepherd.

"Weird, innit?" said the driver. "They're spies, right? They do secret stuff. So why would they tell everyone where they're based?"

"That's a good question," said Shepherd. "It makes no sense to me, either."

"And if you were really spies, why would you want to be in a building by the river where anyone can take a potshot at it? Like the IRA did back in 2000. I was working in Battersea when they did it, fired a bazooka from across the river. Bang!"

Shepherd nodded. In fact it was a Russian-built Mark 22 anti-tank weapon and it was never likely to do any serious damage to the building. But the driver was right. Open government was a wonderful idea in theory, but when it came to spies it made no sense to have them or their headquarters on public display. Far better to have them in a secluded location surrounded by high walls and barbed wire. Which is exactly where he'd like to have Willoughby-Brown billeted.

The cab dropped him outside the building and Shepherd headed inside. This time it was Willoughby-Brown himself who came down to take him upstairs.

He was wearing the same clothes he'd had on the previous day and he didn't seem to have shaved. His shirtsleeves were still rolled up and there were dark sweat stains under the armpits. "Have you had breakfast?" he asked as they rode up in the lift to the fifth floor.

Shepherd shook his head.

"Me neither. Let me have a smoke and then we'll have a bite." Willoughby-Brown took him along to the terrace where he took out his cigar case and lit one of his small cigars and flicked the match away. "So, the good news is that the Pakistanis are getting ready to go in and they've approved your involvement."

"When?"

"A couple of days. They're getting their ducks in a row as we speak."

"What ducks?"

"The personnel. The equipment. Logistics."

"The longer they leave it, the more pain Raj is going through."

"They know that."

"But do they care?" asked Shepherd. "If they know where he is, why don't they just go in?"

"They don't want to rush it," said Willoughby-Brown. "Softly-softly, catchee monkey. On the plus side, it gives you time to get out there."

"I'd like to go to Hereford first, to get in some practice. It's been a while since I've held anything bigger than a handgun."

"Can you get there and back by tomorrow?"

"With your help, sure."

"I'll fix that up after breakfast."

Shepherd nodded. "You still haven't told me what Raj was doing in Pakistan."

"Does it matter?" asked Willoughby-Brown.

"Don't pull that need-to-know bullshit," snapped Shepherd. "I need to know everything there is to know."

The MI6 man blew bluish smoke into the sky before speaking. "MANPADS," he said. "You know what a MANPAD is, of course."

Shepherd nodded. "Man-portable air-defence systems. Shoulder-launched surface-to-air-missiles. Weapon of choice for taking out a low-flying aircraft or a helicopter. And just so you know, there's no such thing as a MANPAD. It's always MANPADS. The S stands for system."

"I stand corrected," said Willoughby-Brown. "They're the perfect terrorist's weapon, portable, relatively cheap and damn effective. They've been used in South Africa, Georgia, Sri Lanka, Mombasa, Mogadishu, and of course Iraq and Afghanistan." He took a long pull on his cigar and blew smoke before continuing. "Manraj was being trained in the use of MANPADS. Him and other British-born Asians." He held up a hand. "Sorry. I mean Raj was being trained in the use of MANPADS. Anyway, they told him they wanted him in Pakistan to train him in the use of the 9K38 Igla. You're familiar with it?"

Shepherd nodded. Igla was Russian for "needle" and the ground-to-air missile had been used by the Russian

121

army since the eighties. "NATO calls it the Grouse, right?"

"That's the one. What makes it especially nasty is that the propellant acts as a high explosive once detonated by the warhead's secondary charge. The whole thing, ready to fire, weighs less than forty pounds. Maximum range seventeen thousand feet and can hit anything travelling at less than seven hundred miles per hour." Willoughby-Brown took another pull on his cigar. "Just between you and me, Manraj — sorry, I mean Raj — wasn't overly happy about making the trip. But he was told by his al-Qaeda handler that it was imperative that he went."

"Because?"

"Because they are in the process of shipping a consignment of Iglas to the UK. They want people trained to use them ready and waiting for when they arrive."

"To attack what?" asked Shepherd.

"To attack whatever the hell they want to attack," said Willoughby-Brown. "They could shoot civilian airliners at any of the major airports, they could do a lot of damage to pretty much any London landmark. Remember when the IRA fired an RPG at MI6 headquarters back in 2000? That's nothing compared to what the Igla can do."

"Totally different piece of kit," said Shepherd. "And you're saying that al-Qaeda is bringing Iglas into the UK?"

"I'm not saying that, Raj's handlers said as much. And not just one or two. Raj was one of six they took out training, and there's every chance his wasn't the only group."

"All Brits?"

"So far as we know, yes. The idea seems to have been to take them to Pakistan for intensive training and then to get them back to the UK. Two were from London, two from Bradford and two from Birmingham."

"So multiple attacks."

"That's what we were assuming. The hope was that Raj would come back and we could do a full debrief." He took another long pull on his cigar.

"Where did al-Qaeda get the missiles from?" asked Shepherd.

"They've been around for years," said Willoughby-Brown. "Most of them were looted from Saddam Hussein's arsenals after the Gulf War."

"So why is it becoming an issue now?"

"We think this particular consignment were in a US-controlled area and while the Yanks were there in force the missiles had to stay put. Now that the American troops are being wound down, the bad guys have been able to retrieve them."

"Do we know how many?"

Willoughby-Brown shook his head. "We were depending on Raj coming back. They could be using two-man teams, they could be trained as individual shooters."

"Sounds to me you don't know much," said Shepherd sourly.

"It was an ongoing operation," said Willoughby-Brown. "We had no idea it was going to go so badly wrong."

123

"And what about the other groups?"

"We're checking flight manifests to and from Pakistan and comparing them with MI5 watch lists, we've increased surveillance at troublesome mosques, we're listening to internet chatter . . ."

"You're clutching at straws is what you're doing," said Shepherd. "This is bad, right? For all you know the MANPADS could be here already, and so could the operators. You could be behind the curve in every way possible."

"It's not good, no. I'm under no illusions. But the one thing we have in our favour is that they don't know how much we know."

"You know nothing."

"Yes, but they don't know that. They don't know whether we know who their people are or if we know the location of the missiles."

"So they'll be torturing Raj, is that what you're saying?"

"They'll be trying to find out how much he's told us. How much we already know."

Shepherd shook his head. "Shit, shit, shit."

"The good news is that they won't be in a rush to kill him," said Willoughby-Brown.

"And the bad news is that they'll be torturing him? You're a piece of work, you really are."

"I'm just telling you the way it is," said Willoughby-Brown.

"Raj isn't a professional, he's not been trained in interrogation resistance techniques."

"He's young, he's fit, he can take pain."

124

"Have you ever been tortured?" asked Shepherd.

"Not as such."

"Then maybe you should keep your opinions to yourself on that score," said Shepherd.

Willoughby-Brown shrugged and flicked away what was left of his cigar. "The sooner you're in Pakistan, the sooner we can get him out of there," he said.

Shepherd nodded. "Amen to that."

"Come on, let's eat."

Willoughby-Brown took Shepherd down to the third floor to a canteen, where they picked up trays and joined a queue mainly composed of young men and women in suits. Shepherd loaded his plate with bacon, eggs and mushrooms while Willoughby-Brown took two croissants and a bowl of fruit. "Trying to get my cholesterol down," he said. He patted his ample stomach. "I've put on a few pounds since Sierra Leone."

"I guess sitting at a desk every day doesn't help," said Shepherd.

"You work out?" asked Willoughby-Brown, helping himself to tea while Shepherd poured himself a coffee.

"I run," said Shepherd.

"Never fancied running," said Willoughby-Brown. "Feet pounding on pavements, never been my thing."

They carried their trays over to a table by a window overlooking the Thames. "I always knew you'd end up with one of the agencies," said Willoughby-Brown as they sat down.

"It was more by accident than design," said Shepherd.

"You were perfect. You always thought like a spook, even back in Sierra Leone, and that trick memory of yours is one hell of an asset."

"I didn't plan it this way," said Shepherd.

"Oh, I know exactly how it happened," said Willoughby-Brown. "In fact we almost made an approach when you left the cops, but it was felt it would be bad form stealing you away from the lovely Charlotte."

Shepherd frowned. "You were watching me?"

"Monitoring your progress," said Willoughby-Brown. "We were a tad worried that the Yanks might steal you away, but that turned out for the best."

"You know Richard Yokely?"

"Tricky Dicky? I know of him. And there were big sighs of relief all around when you didn't go and work for him." He took a bite of croissant and washed it down with tea. "How do you find Five?"

"It has its ups and downs."

"And the lovely Charlotte?"

"She's OK. We've got a history."

"SOCA? What a fiasco that was."

"We had our successes."

"Precious few. You wonder whoever thought that you could put together cops, customs officers and tax inspectors and end up with a cohesive unit. It was doomed to failure and its replacement isn't going to do any better."

"Five is a more professional set-up, that's for sure," said Shepherd.

"And what about job satisfaction?"

Shepherd shrugged. "It has its moments."

"You could always move to Six."

"And work for you?" Shepherd chuckled. "I'll pass."

"Not necessarily for me," said Willoughby-Brown. "There are plenty of options. And the work's challenging. Plenty of travel, too."

"I'm a single parent, travel's not high on my agenda these days."

"Yes, but Liam's at boarding school now, you don't have to be home at night to tuck him in."

Shepherd's eyes narrowed. "You're still looking at my files, then?"

Willoughby-Brown grinned with no trace of embarrassment. "I'm a spook, old lad. It's what I do. Look, you have a good life at Five, I can see that. But that's because Charlotte shields you from a lot of the crap that goes on. And she's not going to be there for ever."

"Do you know something?"

"I know lots of things, Shepherd."

"About Charlie?"

"Let's just say she's not going to be in her current position for ever and the time might come when you're not as happy there as you are at the moment. If the situation changes, I'd just like you to bear Six in mind. I said it back in Sierra Leone and I'll say it again — you're a perfect fit. If you'd been with Six and not Five it would have been you handling Raj and not Taz and maybe we wouldn't be in the position we're in."

"Is that you admitting that Taz was a mistake?"

Willoughby-Brown smiled amicably. "I'm just saying that things might have worked out differently," he said. "Look, the beauty of Six is that our mandate is overseas so we don't get caught up in all the domestic politics here. We make a real difference. Yes, we've got a problem with home-grown terrorists, but the major threats are overseas. They're the ones pulling the strings and they're the ones we need to take down." He ripped into his second croissant. "Anyway, I won't press it," he said. "The offer stands and you know where to find me."

Shepherd pushed a forkful of egg and bacon into his mouth. There would be more chance of Hell freezing over than taking a job with Willoughby-Brown, but he thought it best not to say as much.

Rafiq had no idea what time it was when he was taken from his cell. The door had been thrown open and two of his captors had stood for a moment in the doorway with savage grins on their faces. Rafiq had curled up into a foetal ball and waited for the beating, but it never came. They grabbed him by the arms and dragged him out of the cell and down a dusty corridor. Rafiq was sure that they were going to kill him and he tried to focus on the people he loved. His mother and father and his sister. If he was going to die, he wanted to be thinking about them. He tried to block out the horror of what was happening to him. Death would be painful but it wouldn't take long. A few seconds. A minute at most. He had been beaten and tortured for hours, he was sure he could get through a few seconds of pain.

128

He heard a door opening and he was dragged through to another room. There was a table and a man sitting behind it. A bearded man in a long cotton dishdasha, with a white knitted skullcap atop a mop of curly black hair. Rafiq blinked, trying to focus. There was a brass teapot on the table, and plates of food: some fruit, some cubes of meat, slices of cheese and a stack of naan bread. There was a window behind the man and there was a halo of light around him, making it hard to make out his features. His two captors pushed him down on the chair. Rafiq slumped forward, his head in his hands.

"You may eat," said the man.

Rafiq didn't react, wondering whether he had misheard the man.

"There is food for you. Please, eat."

Rafiq heard tea being poured. He looked up. The man was holding the teapot.

Rafiq closed his eyes and hugged himself. It was a trap. He was sure it was a trap.

"Rafiq, you will need your strength if you are to get through this," said the man quietly.

Rafiq opened his eyes. He blinked and focused on the plate of fruit. There were slices of orange, chunks of pineapple, and green grapes. He slowly reached out with his right hand, picked up a grape and pushed it between his cracked and bleeding lips. He bit down on it and the grape popped and his mouth was filled with sweetness. He swallowed and felt the soft flesh slide down his throat. He grabbed a handful of the grapes and began pushing them between his lips, biting once and swallowing.

"Take your time," said the man. "Don't eat too quickly." He had a hooked nose and his eyes were deep set, giving him the look of a bird of prey.

Rafiq's hands were shaking as he reached for a piece of goat's cheese. He slotted it into his mouth and sighed as the rich creaminess of the cheese mixed with the sweetness of the grapes. He was certain that he had never tasted anything so delicious in his entire life.

He reached for a chunk of lamb, knowing that it would be hard to digest but also knowing that he needed protein. His jaw ached as he chewed. He tried to eat quickly, fearful that the platter would be taken away from him, but his mouth had gone dry and he almost gagged.

The man seemed to sense his discomfort and pushed a beaker of tea across the table towards Rafiq. Rafiq pushed the rest of the lamb into his mouth and then took a swallow of tea. It was sweet and minty, lukewarm rather than hot. He drained the beaker and the man refilled it for him.

"My name is Mahmud," said the man. "And yours is Manraj Chaudhry." He smiled. "You see, Raj, I do not insult you by pretending not to know who you are. You are a man and I am a man, and men should be known by their true names."

Raj took another piece of lamb and began to chew on it. It wasn't as tasty as the grapes or the cheese but long-term it would do him more good. And eating gave him time to think, and to get his thoughts in order.

Mahmud knew who he was. There had been no doubt, it hadn't been a question and he wasn't asking for confirmation. He knew who Raj was, but did he know everything? Raj could feel his stomach churning and it wasn't the food causing it. He had no choice; he had to continue with the lie. He had no choice because if he told the truth he'd be dead.

Mahmud sat back in his chair and folded his arms. Raj swallowed the meat, then washed it down with more of the lukewarm mint tea.

Mahmud continued to stare at Raj with featureless brown eyes, his face impassive.

Raj picked up another piece of goat's cheese.

"The food is to your liking?" asked Mahmud.

Raj nodded but said nothing.

Mahmud refilled Raj's beaker. "You know your Qur'an?" he asked softly.

Raj swallowed and nodded. "Of course," said Raj.

"Then you know what the Qur'an says about those who wage war against Allah?"

"I am not waging war against Allah," said Raj. "I am a jihadist, that's why I'm here, to train . . ."

Mahmud put up his hand to silence Raj and smiled sadly. "The Qur'an says the punishment of those who wage war against Allah and His Messenger and strive to make mischief in the land is only this, that they should be murdered or crucified or their hands and their feet should be cut off on opposite sides or they should be imprisoned." The man put his hands palms down on the table. "The punishment is harsh, but deserved," he

131

said. "Those Muslims who side with the infidel are the lowest of the low."

Raj found it difficult to swallow and he gulped down some more tea.

"But it is never too late to return to the fold, brother," said Mahmud. He leaned forward and lowered his voice. "You have made bad choices, Raj. But you have the opportunity now to put that right."

"What do you think I've done?" asked Raj. "Someone is lying to you, Mahmud. I am here to learn how to fight the infidel. I have given up everything to be here. I have left my family, I have given up my studies, I have put my life on hold to fight the good fight."

Mahmud nodded. "I understand your desire to lie, Raj," he said. "You are clinging to the hope that you can lie your way out of this. I have no doubt that your handler said that there was no way you would be caught. But he was wrong, Raj. Your handler lied to you." He poured more tea into the beaker and placed the pot on the table. "What is his name, Raj? This man who lied to you?"

Raj tried to fake a look of confusion, as if he didn't know what Mahmud was talking about. "Mahmud, there has been a mistake. I'm not what you think I am. I am here to learn, that's all." He lifted the beaker to his lips but his hand shook and tea spilled on to the table.

"He cannot help you, your handler," said Mahmud. "In fact he will have already given up on you. He will be protecting himself, that will be his first concern. He will be removing all evidence that you ever worked for

MI6. And he will be doing whatever he can to protect his other agents."

Raj took a handful of grapes and put one in his mouth.

"The one thing that he won't be doing is trying to rescue you, Raj. You must put any thoughts of rescue out of your mind. He has thrown you to the wolves. Now that you are no longer any use to him, you have been discarded."

Raj put the grapes down on the table. His stomach was churning and while he knew that he needed the nourishment, he no longer felt like eating. "Mahmud, please, you have to believe me. I don't work for MI6. I don't work for anybody. I gave up everything to come here. I am prepared to die for Allah. If you truly believe that I am a traitor to Islam, then you must kill me."

"Is that what you want, brother? You want me to kill you?"

"Of course I don't want that," said Raj. "But I don't know what else to say."

"The truth," said Mahmud. "You need to tell me the truth, because that is the only thing that will save you."

"I am telling you the truth!" protested Raj.

Mahmud shook his head sadly. "No, brother, you are not." He sighed. "And if you do not tell the truth, there is nothing I can do to help you."

"Mahmud, please, you must listen to me."

"I am listening to you, Raj. That's why I'm here. To listen."

Raj swallowed. His mouth had gone dry again and he reached for his tea. Mahmud's hand flashed out like a striking snake and gripped his wrist. His nails dug into Raj's flesh, making him wince.

"But there is no point in me listening if you are going to lie to me."

"I'm not lying," said Raj. "I'm not."

Mahmud released his grip on Raj's wrist. "Do you have any idea what they will do to you if you don't tell the truth?" he said.

Raj massaged his wrist. He looked down at the table, unable to meet the man's gaze. There was no point in protesting his innocence. Mahmud clearly knew that he was working for MI6.

"They will take off your head, Raj. While you are alive. Have you ever witnessed a beheading?"

Raj shook his head.

"What, never? You have never looked at YouTube? Curiosity never got the better of you?"

Raj closed his eyes. His chest felt tight as if it were in the grip of a vice and he could barely breathe.

"The brain continues to function after the head is severed," said Mahmud. "Sometimes for a few seconds, sometimes for as long as half a minute. The eyes can blink and move. The mouth opens and closes. The body also continues to move. The chest heaves. Arms and legs thrash about."

Raj shuddered but continued to stare at the table.

"Think how your mother and father will feel, seeing you die like that," said Mahmud. "And Jamila. Think of the effect it would have on her. You are planning to marry her, aren't you?"

134

Raj looked up, his heart racing. Mahmud was watching him with amused eyes. "You think I don't know everything there is to know about you? And your family?" He leant back in his chair. "You don't seriously want to die, do you, Raj? You want to marry Jamila and have children and you want to watch them grow up and when you've lived a full and happy life then you'd want to die peacefully in your own bed surrounded by your family." He clasped his hands together. "It is time for you to tell me everything, Raj."

Raj stared into Mahmud's brown eyes. The man was smiling but there was no warmth in his gaze. He was studying Raj as if he were a specimen on a microscope slide. Raj's mind raced. Mahmud seemed to know everything. But if he knew everything, why even bother with a conversation? What was it that he wanted from him? And whatever the information was that he wanted, what would happen if and when Raj gave it to him?

"Your handler has abandoned you, Raj. There is no ransom to be paid, you will not be exchanged for another prisoner. You are on your own. The only friend you have is the man sitting across from you. Let me be your friend, Raj. Let me help you get out of the hole you have dug for yourself."

Raj blinked back tears.

"This is your chance to help me help you. I beg you, please take it."

Raj took a deep breath, then slowly shook his head. "I'm a loyal servant of Allah, here to learn how to become a jihadist," he said. "*Allahu akbar*. God is great."

Mahmud pushed back his chair and slowly stood up, then walked around the table. He patted Raj on the shoulder and left the room. A few seconds later the two big bearded men burst in, grabbed Raj and pulled him off the chair. They began to kick him, all the time screaming insults at him. Raj curled up in a ball and begged for mercy even though he knew that there would be none forthcoming.

The Agusta Westland AW109 banked to the left and came in for a perfect landing on the square helipad to the south of the Credenhill barracks, home to the SAS. Major Allan Gannon was standing next to a green open-top Land Rover at the edge of the helipad, wearing a black tracksuit and black Nike trainers. As soon as the wheels of the helicopter touched the tarmac, Shepherd pulled open the side door and climbed out, then jogged over to the Major, bent at the waist even though he knew that the whirling rotor blades were well above his head.

He straightened up when he reached the Major, and the two men shook hands as the twin engines of the helicopter roared and it climbed back into the air.

"I'm surprised to see you being given the VIP treatment, what with all the cutbacks and all," said the Major, as he climbed into the driving seat of the Land Rover.

"There's considerable time pressure on this one," said Shepherd, getting into the front passenger seat.

136

"They didn't want me stuck in traffic and I have to get back tonight. Then out to Pakistan tomorrow."

The helicopter banked to the left and headed east. The Major started the Land Rover's engine and headed towards the armoury. Their route took them past several large featureless metal-sided buildings. They had been aircraft maintenance hangars when Credenhill was an RAF station but had been converted into offices and training facilities when the SAS took over the base in 1999. They had all been painted green at the insistence of the local council, which wanted them to blend in with their surroundings. During the short drive Shepherd filled the Major in on what was happening. He finished just as they arrived at the door to the armoury. "You would have thought they'd have sent in the Increment," said Shepherd. "That's what we train for."

"I suppose the Pakistanis want the credit," said the Major. "And you can see their point, can't you? If there was a hijacked PIA jet at Heathrow, we'd hardly be letting Pakistani special forces handle it."

The two men climbed out of the Land Rover. "Anyway, it might not be too bad," said the Major. "They do a fair bit of training with the Americans, at least they did until the Bin Laden business, and they're much better than most of the Asian SF mobs. They've had a fair few successes over the last few years. They took out more than ninety extremists at the Red Mosque in 2007 and a couple of years later they saved the day at the Lahore Police Academy and the Pakistan Military Headquarters."

The armoury door opened and a grizzled grey-haired sergeant appeared. His face broke into a grin when he saw Shepherd standing with the Major. "Bloody hell," he said, in a gruff Geordie accent. "Spider bloody Shepherd. I thought we'd got rid of you."

Shepherd grinned. Sergeant Pete Simpson was a Loggy, a member of the Royal Logistics Corps. The RLC made up almost a sixth of the British Army, and without the Loggys the army — and the SAS — wouldn't be able to function. Simpson had been in charge of the armoury when Shepherd had been in 22 SAS and by the look of it had no plans to leave. Simpson knew more about guns than anyone Shepherd had ever met. There wasn't a weapon in the armoury that the sergeant couldn't field-strip and reassemble in less than two minutes — blindfolded. The two men shook hands. "Good to see you, Pete. How's the lad?"

"Passed selection three years ago," said the sergeant, his chest puffing up with pride. "Out somewhere hot and sunny as we speak."

"Pity, I'd have liked to have said hello," said Shepherd. Simpson's son must have been about ten years old the last time he'd seen him at one of the family open days the Regiment had run at the old Stirling Lines barracks.

Simpson looked over at the Major. "I've got everything ready," he said.

"Thanks, Pete, sorry about the short notice." The SAS, officers and troopers, were unfailingly polite when it came to dealing with the Loggys, in recognition of

138

the vital role they played in the smooth running of the Regiment.

The sergeant held the door open for them and Shepherd and the Major went inside. They entered a corridor lined with wire-mesh cages where the Regiment stored the bulk of its weapons and ammunition. To their left were racks containing several dozen Heckler & Koch G3 carbines. "I've put the MP5s in there for you with the G3s," said the sergeant. He pulled open the door to the cage.

"You're a star, Pete, thanks."

"Give me a shout if you want anything," said the sergeant, and he headed back to his cubbyhole of an office. Gannon led Shepherd into the cage. "The SSG use a range of weapons, but like the SAS they're big Heckler and Koch fans," said the Major. "They produce HK G3s and MP5s locally. Snipers use the Barrett M82, the HK PSG1 and occasionally the Dragunov. So far as shorts go, they favour Hecklers and of course the Glocks."

"Am I the only one who likes the SIG Sauer?"

"The P226? You're old-school, Spider. So I'm thinking we get in some practice with the G3 and the MP5. That's what you're most likely to be given."

"Sounds good to me."

Four weapons had been laid out on a wooden trestle table, two G3s and two MP5s and several boxes of ammunition.

"We won't bother with the shorts, I'm assuming you're fine on that score."

"If we're reduced to pulling out shorts then the shit will really have hit the fan," said Shepherd.

Gannon picked up a black G3 and handed it to Shepherd. "This is the G3A4, with drum sights and a collapsible stock. It's the one they make under licence in Pakistan."

Shepherd took the rifle. The G3 had first been produced in the 1950s but had undergone many changes over the years. The one he was holding was state-of-the-art and had been designed as a modular system so components could be changed easily to produce a variety of configurations.

Gannon picked up the second G3. "They make a version of this, too. The G3A3. Drum sights and a fixed plastic stock and a plastic handguard."

They both put their G3s down and picked up MP5s. The MP5 had been developed after the G3, a 9mm sub-machine gun with almost zero recoil. It was the weapon that Shepherd was most familiar with and during his years with the SAS he had fired tens of thousands of rounds. The name MP5 came from Maschinepistole 5, and there were more than a hundred variations of the weapon. It had been the weapon of choice of the SAS since the late 1970s. Gannon slung his MP5 over his shoulder on its nylon sling. Shepherd did the same, then they both picked up their G3s again, and shared the ammunition between then.

"Any idea what they've got planned?" asked Gannon as he closed the gate and they headed down the corridor to the exit.

"No idea at all, that's the problem," said Shepherd. "He's been held under guard so probably a building. I don't know if it'll be a daytime or a night-time assault, or if it's full frontal or from helicopters." He shrugged. "I'm the ultimate mushroom at the moment, and you can imagine how happy that makes me."

"Nothing changes," said the Major with a grin. "We're off, Pete," he shouted at the sergeant's office.

"Have fun!" the sergeant called back.

They loaded the guns and ammunition into the Land Rover. "I thought we'd spend a couple of hours in the firing range and then I'll run you over to the killing house and we'll rehearse a few entry scenarios," said the Major.

"Sounds good," said Shepherd.

The climbed into the Land Rover and the Major drove them to the outdoor range. He parked by the door and produced a key to open it. "Get me the flag from the glove compartment, will you?" asked Gannon as he unlocked the door.

Shepherd opened the glove compartment and pulled out a red flag. He climbed out and handed the flag to the Major. As Shepherd began to carry in the guns and ammunition, the Major tied the flag and ran it up the flagpole, letting all and sundry know that the range was live.

Inside was a brick-built shelter open to the target area. Shepherd put the G3s and the MP5s on a wooden table, then went out to fetch the ammunition. The G3 used 7.62×51mm rounds and the MP5 took the smaller 9mm cartridges.

When he returned with the ammunition, Gannon was out on the range fixing Figure 11 targets, the standard army outline of a soldier holding a rifle with a white circle in the centre the size of a saucer. He fixed four targets at fifteen metres from the table and another four at thirty metres then walked back to the table and picked up one of the G3s. "We'll do the G3 at thirty and the MP5 at fifteen," he said.

"Sounds good," said Shepherd. The MP5 was generally used for close-quarter battle situations, while the G3 was better suited for longer distances.

The Major quickly and efficiently field-stripped the G3, then watched as Shepherd did the same. Shepherd smiled as he worked, knowing that he was much slower than the Major. "It's been a while," he said when he finally finished, a full forty-five seconds longer than it had taken Gannon.

"Let's reassemble them and do it again," said Gannon. "You don't know how good the gear is they're going to give you, so I want you familiar with both weapons."

Shepherd nodded. The Major, as always, was talking sense.

They spent a full thirty minutes stripping down and rebuilding both guns, and by the time they'd finished Shepherd was able to keep up with him on the G3 and beat him by a few seconds on the MP5.

They then moved on to the range, starting with the G3. They fired clip after clip at the targets and by the time they had finished Shepherd's eyes were burning from the cordite and his ears were ringing, but he was able to put every shot in the white circle.

The two men then loaded the clips of the MP5s and began shooting at the closer target. Shepherd was much more familiar with the MP5 and right from the start he was able to keep his grouping tight.

The Major smiled across at him. "Like riding a bike," he said.

Raj's left arm had gone numb but he was too exhausted to roll over. He could taste blood and one of his back teeth had become loose. With every breath he felt a searing pain in his chest and he was fairly sure that at least one of his ribs had fractured. He had lost track of time while they were beating him and lost count of the blows.

When they had dragged him out of the room where Mahmud had questioned him, Raj's first thought was that it was over, that they had come to kill him. He'd struggled but they were too big and too strong, they had taken an arm each and dragged him down the corridor. He'd screamed, more out of frustration than anger, sure that he was going to be beheaded, and then he'd begun to pray, in Arabic, begging Allah to help him, hoping that by hearing his prayers they would realise he was a good Muslim.

They'd stopped outside his cell and one of them had pushed open the door. Raj continued to pray. The words tumbled from his mouth on autopilot as his mind raced. He didn't want to die, and he didn't want to die like this, killed by fanatics devoted to a cause that made no sense. If Raj had to die he wanted to die for a reason, a good reason. Being beheaded by fanatics was as pointless a death as there could be. And the images painted by Mahmud kept flashing through his mind. A wicked blade cutting through his flesh, hacking through his spine. His head held high, blood pouring from the severed neck, his eyes wide in terror, dead but not completely dead.

The men had kicked Raj into the cell and he'd fallen face down on to the concrete. Before he'd had a chance to get to his feet they'd rushed him, kicking him hard in the ribs and legs. Raj had curled himself up into a ball and protected his head with his arms as he'd begged them to stop. They'd ignored his cries and he lost track of how long the kicks had continued. They'd stopped eventually, but only after they'd kicked him unconscious, and when he had eventually woken up he'd had no idea of how much time had passed.

Every muscle in his body ached, but at least the pain meant that he was still alive. The fact that they had beaten him and not taken his life meant that either he was still of use to them or he had information they had needed. Mahmud had made it seem as if he knew everything, but if that was the case then there would be no need for an interrogation or beatings. Raj had something that Mahmud wanted, and so long as that was the case he would stay alive. His survival depended on not talking, he realised. So long as he stayed silent, Mahmud would keep him alive. Raj took a deep breath but grimaced as a sharp pain lanced through his chest. The beatings would continue, he knew. He wasn't sure how much more he could stand, but he knew that he had no choice; the moment he broke, they would kill him.

Shepherd crouched low, his finger on the trigger of his MP5. The Major was to his right and there were two troopers to his left. They were facing a door and the Major was counting down on his fingers. Shepherd had no idea what was on the other side of the door but if the previous sessions were anything to go by there would be at least one hostage and a minimum of two captors. The captors could be armed with anything from a machete to an AK-47, but whatever the weapon they were the targets and had to be taken out. They were all armed with MP5s but instead of the regular ammunition the weapons had been loaded with paint bullets. The low-velocity rounds were nowhere near fatal but they could hurt soft tissue so the men all wore full protective gear and shatterproof goggles.

The killing house was away from the main Credenhill barracks on the outskirts of a village called Pontrilas, midway between Hereford and Abergavenny. It was actually a collection of buildings, hidden from the nearest road by high walls. The building they were using was two storeys high with a main door, a rear door and small windows on both floors. The roof was flat, and it was typical of the structures found throughout the Middle East. The walls inside were lined with rubber and Kevlar panels which would absorb any rounds without ricochets, and there was a projection system which meant that live rounds could be used against the virtual targets. But the Major had wanted to use live targets and paint ammunition so that Shepherd could practise close-quarter battle techniques while under fire. The projection system was fine for rehearsing entry scenarios and for tightening up target sight acquisition but projected targets couldn't take evasive action or fight back, which was what tended to happen in the real world.

The Major counted to three, drew back his right leg and kicked the door open before moving to the side. One of the troopers rushed in through the door, bent low. He headed right and almost immediately fired his weapon twice. The Major followed, moving left. Shepherd was third in through the door, followed by the last trooper.

Shepherd kept low as his eyes swept the room. The hostage was sitting on a wooden chair, dressed in an orange jumpsuit and with a sack over his head. There were two targets, one left and one right, wearing long robes and black and white keffiyeh scarves. They were wearing the same protective goggles as Shepherd and holding AK-47s in gloved hands and had on black armoured vests.

There was a doorway to the left and another doorway straight ahead. The two targets began screaming in Arabic and swung up their weapons, their fingers already inside the trigger guards.

A third target appeared in the doorway, wearing a heavy sheepskin jacket over his armoured vest. He was holding a machete in his left hand and a Glock in his right. He began screaming and waved the machete over his head.

Shepherd's mind raced. Three targets. One hostage. All targets armed, all posing an imminent threat. He mentally divided the room into four quadrants. Left, mid-left, mid-right and right. The Major had been tasked with the left quadrant, he was to cover the mid-left as his primary target area with the left and mid-right as secondary areas. The two troopers to his right were covering the right-hand side of the room.

Shepherd looked through the sight and swung his MP5 to bear on the chest of the target to the left of the hostage. All of the targets were screaming at the top of their voices. He fired two shots in quick succession and they smacked into the target's chest, leaving two red splodges on the man's armoured vest. At almost the same time two shots hit the target to the right, missing the sitting hostage by inches. Both targets slumped to the ground.

Shepherd grinned. It was a textbook rescue. As he lowered the gun a round smacked into the centre of his chest and blue paint splattered across his armoured vest. "Shit," he said. A second shot quickly followed, making a dull thump in the chest that left another blue splodge just above his heart.

He looked up at the man who'd shot him. He had moved to stand with his back against the wall and was still holding the machete high above his head while he aimed the Glock at Shepherd's chest.

"End ex!" shouted the Major, and the target lowered his Glock. The two targets who had been shot sat up and flicked on the safeties of their AK-47s.

Shepherd made his MP5 safe and turned to look at the Major. "I thought you'd take out the target on the left," he said.

"And on any other occasion I would have," said the Major. "But the guys you're going to be working with are unknown factors. With the best will in the world you can't depend on them. You must never put yourself in a situation where your safety is in their hands."

One of the targets took the hood off the hostage. He was a young trooper who had volunteered to help out and his face was bathed in sweat. Playing the hostage was never fun but it had to be done to make the scenarios as realistic as possible.

Shepherd looked down at the two blue splodges on his chest. In fact the shots wouldn't have been fatal if they had been live rounds as his armoured vest was more than capable of dealing with 9mm rounds. But in the real world the shots could well have been to his head and the Major was right. They trained hard so that when it came to a live operation they worked as a well-coordinated team. Every individual trooper knew what his role was and what his colleagues should be doing. They worked as a team. But when Shepherd was in Pakistan he'd have to think as an individual. His first priority would be to rescue Raj, but his own safety would have to come a close second.

"Remember, you never want a guy with a gun behind you," said the Major. "There's nothing friendly about friendly fire. Ideally keep your back to a wall. It's doubtful they'll have you going in first, but if you're not last make sure you get straight out of the line of fire."

148

"Got it, boss," said Shepherd.

"And never assume that someone else is going to take out an immediate threat to you. If a target is a direct threat to you, you take out that target yourself. You have to put your safety above everything. No matter what's said at the briefing, no matter what the tasking is, you protect yourself at all costs."

Shepherd nodded. That was the mental adjustment that he was having trouble with. When he'd stormed rooms in the past, each member of the team would be pre-assigned his own area. Generally the man who went left would handle any unfriendlies on the left and the man who went right would take care of the right-hand quadrant. It didn't matter where the unfriendlies were aiming their weapons; by working as a coordinated team they would be eliminated before they could return fire. But Shepherd wouldn't be able to rely on the men he was with when he was in Pakistan.

"You have to have that drilled into your head, Spider," said the Major. "If there's a guy pointing a gun at you and a guy pointing a gun at the man next to you, you have to take out the direct threat. No hesitation. Now, do you want to go again?"

Shepherd looked at his watch. It was just before five o'clock and the helicopter was due back at six to take him to London. He nodded. "Let's do it."

Raj lay curled up into a ball, his eyes closed. Every breath hurt, he was sure that at least two of his ribs were broken. They had given him an earthenware pot to use as a toilet and when he had used it there had been blood in his urine. They had damaged his kidneys, and probably his spleen. They were trying to break him, he knew that. They would beat him until he could take no more, and then Mahmud would return, smiling and offering him food and comfort. The carrot and the stick. The psychology was simple but effective and knowing what was happening didn't make it any less effective. All Raj had to do was to tell Mahmud what he wanted to hear and the beatings would stop. But once Raj had told him everything there would be no need to keep him alive. The British didn't get involved in prisoner swaps, not like in the days of the Cold War when captured agents were exchanged on the Glienicke Bridge, connecting the cities of Potsdam and Berlin. The Bridge of Spies, they used to call it. But that was then and the War against Terror had little in common with the Cold War. The West refused to negotiate with terrorists, and Hell would freeze over before the British government would approve the release of captured al-Qaeda terrorists. Raj had no value, other than the information in his head. Once he gave it up, he was as good as dead. He moaned softly. Moaning seemed to make the pain lessen, just a fraction.

His mind kept going around in circles, trying to find a way out of his predicament. Escape was impossible. There was only one way in and out of his cell and the door was always locked. There were always two men there when the door was opened, and he was too weak to even think about fighting them. Even if by some miracle he could overpower them, then what? He could barely walk and had no idea where he was. Rescue?

Rescue was impossible, even if his handler at MI6 knew where he was. And who would rescue him? Would they send in the SAS? The army? To rescue a medical student in the badlands of Pakistan? The idea was too ridiculous to consider. He was on his own and he knew he had to accept that. He moaned again. He wanted to use the earthenware pot again but he didn't have the energy to move.

He was going to die, he was sure of that. Whether or not he told them anything, they would kill him. They'd either beat him to death or put him in an orange suit and hack off his head in front of a video camera. The only way he could beat them would be to kill himself. At least then he would have some control over his destiny. He closed his eyes again and moaned. Suicide at least would put an end to the pain, but on his own terms. It was his only way out.

Shepherd climbed out of the black cab and paid the driver before heading towards the terminal. He was carrying a black holdall containing his washbag and two changes of clothes. Willoughby-Brown was standing by the entrance, smoking one of his small cigars. "How did it go in Hereford?" he asked. He was wearing a long black coat that looked as if it was probably cashmere.

"Got in plenty of practice," said Shepherd.

"The killing house?"

"Some of the time." Shepherd was reluctant to go into details. He didn't like Willoughby-Brown and he didn't trust him.

Willoughby-Brown kept his cigar in his mouth as he reached into his coat and pulled out a folder containing a plane ticket. "PIA, only business class, I'm afraid," he said. "First was full."

Shepherd took the folder. "What do I do visa-wise?"

"You'll be met off the plane by a member of the military. They'll walk you through immigration and arrange your flight to Cherat. That's where the SSG is headquartered. Your contact is a Captain Kassar."

Shepherd slid the folder into his jacket pocket. "Do they know where he is yet?"

"Captain Kassar will give you a full briefing. My understanding is that they're close."

"Why aren't you going?" asked Shepherd.

Willoughby-Brown raised his eyebrows. "Me?"

"Assuming we get Raj out of there, who's going to get him back to the UK?"

"He'll be taken care of, I'm sure."

"By the Pakistanis?"

"By our embassy out there. Don't worry, it's all in hand."

Shepherd nodded. He figured Willoughby-Brown didn't want to be in Pakistan in case the rescue attempt went wrong but he knew there would be no point in saying anything so he just turned and walked into the terminal.

"Good luck," Willoughby-Brown shouted after him.

"Bastard," muttered Shepherd under his breath.

It took just over half an hour to pass through the security check. Charlotte Button was waiting for him

152

airside, in the duty free area. "How did it go?" she asked.

"I'm as sharp as I ever was on close-quarter battle target acquisition," he said.

"Good to hear. What's Willoughby-Brown fixed up for you in Islamabad?"

"He's handing me over to the army, a captain from the SSG will take me to Cherat."

"No meeting with his man Taz?"

Shepherd shook his head. "To be honest, I think he's minimising my involvement with Six. Covering his arse in case the shit hits the fan."

Button took a small satellite phone from her pocket. It was black with a stubby aerial and not much bigger than a regular phone. She handed it to him. "Call me when you can," she said. "It's got a GPS so I'll be tracking you."

Shepherd slid it inside his jacket and then looked at his watch. "I'd better be going," he said.

Button reached out and put a hand on his arm. She gave him a gentle squeeze. "Be careful," she said.

He smiled. "Always," he said.

The PIA flight landed at Islamabad International Airport at just before ten o'clock in the morning. Shepherd had eaten a surprisingly tasty meal shortly after take-off and had then slept the whole way. As breakfast was being served, the chief purser whispered that he should prepare himself to disembark first, and as the plane taxied towards the terminal, Shepherd was ushered to the front exit door. Several of the passengers in first class frowned as he passed, clearly wondering why a business-class passenger was getting such preferential treatment. Shepherd noticed that several of the seats in first class were unoccupied and he wondered whether Willoughby-Brown had lied about the cabin being full.

When the plane door was opened, a young army captain in dark green camouflage fatigues was waiting on the jetway, flanked by two men in grey suits.

"Daniel Shepherd?" asked the captain. He was in his late twenties, short and stocky with skin the colour of milky coffee. He was wearing wraparound Oakley sunglasses and a Rolex Submariner watch, clear signs that he was Special Forces. He was wearing a maroon beret with a badge of a dagger and lightning bolts and a wing badge on the right side of his chest.

"Call me Spider," said Shepherd, holding out his hand.

The captain shook hands. He had a firm grip, his nails were neatly clipped and there was a jagged scar across the base of his thumb. "Addy Kassar," said the captain. "Can I have your passport?"

Shepherd gave the captain his passport and he passed it to the man on his left, who flicked through the pages, compared the photograph to Shepherd's face and then handed it back.

"Do you have any bags?" asked Kassar.

Shepherd held up his holdall. "I'm travelling light," he said.

"Perfect," said Kassar. "Our plane is waiting." He spoke to the men in suits in Urdu, then took Shepherd down a corridor. One of the suits followed. At the end of the corridor was a sign pointing towards Immigration but Kassar headed the other way. They reached a locked door and the suit tapped a code into a keypad and pushed the door open.

Kassar and Shepherd went through but the suit stayed behind. They walked down another corridor and another and then reached what appeared to be an emergency exit. Kassar pressed the metal bar to open it and indicated for Shepherd to go through. A metal staircase led down to the airport tarmac and as he stepped on to it Shepherd was hit by a wave of heat that took his breath away.

A grey Chinese-made Harbin Y-11 with military markings was standing on a taxiway, its two Pratt and Whitney turboprops idling.

"Where are we going?" asked Shepherd. He figured it wouldn't be far as the Short Take Off and Landing transport plane had a top speed of less than 190 m.p.h.

"Cherat," said Kassar. "It is the SSG base. Do you know much of the geography of Pakistan?"

"I've looked at maps," said Shepherd. He thought it best not to mention that his photographic memory meant that after only a few seconds he was able to recall pretty much every place and feature he'd seen. Cherat was in the Nowshera district of Khyber-Pakhtunkhwa. It was a hill station; the closest city was Peshawar.

"It was used by the British as a sanatorium for your troops."

"My troops?"

Kassar held up a hand by way of apology. "Your country's troops, of course," he said. "The British built a fort there with a hospital and a church. If soldiers suffered the effects of the heat or fell sick, they were sent there. Now it is the SSG base and an army training camp."

They walked across the tarmac to the plane. Unlike on the PIA airliner, there were no uniformed flight attendants and no in-flight entertainment or refreshments. They were the only two passengers. As soon as they had climbed in and fastened their seat belts, a pilot in green fatigues entered the cockpit and closed the door without acknowledging them. Ten minutes later they were in the air and heading west.

"You are in the SAS?" asked the captain.

"I used to be," said Shepherd.

"The best special forces in the world," said Kassar.

"That's what they say."

"But the Navy SEALs might disagree."

Shepherd smiled. "They might."

"I trained with the SEALs three years ago," said Kassar. "They are good."

"So I've heard. How do you get into the SSG?" Kassar was still wearing his shades and Shepherd found it a little disconcerting to constantly see his own reflection staring back at him.

"You can apply after you have been in the military for five years," said Kassar. "You volunteer and go to Cherat for nine months. Initially the training is all physical. You have to do a thirty-six-mile march in twelve hours and run five miles in forty minutes, both with full gear."

Shepherd raised his eyebrows. Long-distance marching was the backbone of SAS training, but five miles in forty minutes with full gear took some doing.

"There's a high drop-out rate," said Kassar. "Those that pass are trained in parachute jumping and hand-to-hand combat. More volunteers fail those stages and eventually only about one in twenty get through."

Shepherd nodded. The SAS selection course had a similar failure rate. "Seen much action?"

Kassar grinned. "Quite a bit," he said. "Did you hear about Operation Janbaz?"

Shepherd shook his head.

"Islamic terrorists attacked the Army General Headquarters in Punjab. Ten of them. This was in October 2009. They killed six soldiers including a brigadier and a lieutenant colonel and then took forty-two hostages. The SSG were sent in to resolve the situation. We stormed the building and took it room by room."

"Sounds heavy."

"It was. But we rescued all but three of the hostages with only three casualties on our side."

"Impressive," said Shepherd. "It could have been a lot worse, I guess." He looked out of the window at the inhospitable terrain thousands of feet below.

"What about you?" asked Kassar. "You've seen action?"

"Some," said Shepherd.

"Afghanistan? Iraq?"

Shepherd nodded. "Afghanistan."

"How was it?"

"Hot. And dusty."

The captain smiled. "You will feel at home in Pakistan, then." He reached over and pulled two bottles of water from a side pocket. He handed one to Shepherd. "They say SAS selection is the toughest in the world?"

"It's tough," agreed Shepherd.

"I heard about something called Escape and Evasion. The SEALs were talking about it when I was at Virginia Beach."

Shepherd grinned. "Yeah. Escape and Evasion has its moments."

"They chase you, is that right?"

"They give you a head start and then they go after you. It's a bit like hide and seek."

"Hide and seek?"

"It's a game children play. Kids go and hide and someone goes looking for them. The last one to be found, wins. But on Escape and Evasion, no one wins."

Kassar frowned. "What do you mean?"

"They call it Escape and Evasion, but everyone gets captured in the end. It doesn't matter how long you hold out, it ends with a capture and a beasting."

"Beasting?"

"You get beaten up. They have regular soldiers out looking for you, and when they get you they knock you around."

"But not for real?"

Shepherd grinned. "Oh, it's for real all right. They won't break any bones but you're battered and bruised afterwards."

"Why do they do that?"

"To make it seem real. And I can tell you, when it's happening, it feels real."

"Then what happens?"

"When they've finished beasting you? They throw you in the back of a truck and take you to an abandoned building somewhere. They tie you up and they try to break you. They knock you around and put you in stress positions. Up against a wall with most of your weight on your arms. Or just standing up. You wouldn't believe how just standing for hours can hurt like hell. Or they can be really creative. They use waterboarding or play loud music for hours. And all the time they keep firing questions at you. But you can't answer. All you can give them is your name, rank and serial number. If you tell them anything else, you get RTU'd."

"RTU'd?"

"Returned to unit. It means you've failed. You just have to take whatever they throw at you, until it's over. But the bastards try to trick you. They'll come in with a hot drink or some food and they'll tell you it's all over but it's a trap. If you say anything other than name, rank and number, you've failed."

"So how do you know when it's really over?" asked Kassar. "How do you know it's not a trick?"

"Right before the exercise starts, an officer, usually high-ranking like a major, stands in front of you. He says that the exercise isn't over until he stands in front of you and says, 'The exercise is over. Well done.' That's the only way the exercise can be ended, no matter what else they say."

"And how does it feel, when they're torturing you?"

"It's not real torture," said Shepherd. "They don't cut off your toes or use branding irons. It's more psychological pressure and making you uncomfortable. It's bad, but it's bearable. You just go into shut-down mode."

"Shut-down mode?"

"You become the grey man. You don't fight them, you don't argue, you're polite and you call them 'sir'. You don't make eye contact, you just make yourself appear as weak and as inconsequential as possible. And you wait for it to end."

Kassar sipped his water. "And you got through it?"

"Sure. Most people do. The ones that fail tend to fail because they're not fit enough, or the jungle gets to them."

"They train you in the jungle?"

"Sure, they always have done. It's probably the toughest part of selection. You can train for the hill walking and navigation and stuff, but nothing prepares you for the jungle."

"You know that the word jungle comes from Sanskrit? *Jangala*."

"I did not know that."

"A lot of English words have come out of this part of the world, mostly from the days of the British Raj," said

Kassar. "But don't worry, we won't be fighting in the jungle. The north-west of the country is desert."

"That's good to know," said Shepherd. "I was never a fan of jungles."

The door crashed open. Raj lay with his back against the far wall of his cell. He didn't open his eyes but drew his knees up to his chest and put his hands either side of his head. He'd lost track of time again. It could have been days or hours since the last beating. He remembered getting up to urinate in the bucket at some point and his urine had been red.

He heard footsteps across the rough concrete floor and he braced himself, even though he knew that it made no difference. He flinched as a hand grabbed his shoulder, then his arms were seized and he was yanked to his feet. He opened his eyes. It was the two big men. The one with the mole by his eye and the one with the pockmarked skin. Mole and Acne, he'd named them. Mole was the one who liked to kick him in the kidneys. Acne's favourite technique was to stamp on Raj's ankles.

"Just kill me," said Raj, through swollen lips. "I don't care any more."

"As you wish," said Mole.

They dragged him across the floor and down the corridor. This time they didn't go to the room where he'd previously been questioned by Mahmud. Instead they turned left. Raj tried to walk but his legs had turned to jelly and he couldn't support his weight. Mole and Acne didn't seem to care whether he walked or not and simply dragged him along between them. Raj felt the skin scraping off his toes but there was no noticeable increase in pain as his feet already felt as if they were on fire.

He was barely aware of passing three wooden doors with small barred windows at head height before they reached a barred gate. Sunlight streamed through the bars, blinding Raj. Mole unlocked the gate and pushed it open.

The two men dragged Raj into a courtyard. He blinked in the blinding sun then focused on a group of men in camouflage fatigues with grey and white keffiyeh scarves wrapped around their faces. There was a wooden chair in front of them and Raj was thrown on to it. One of the masked men gave Mole a roll of duct tape and he used it to bind Raj to the chair. He was too exhausted to resist.

Mahmud appeared from a doorway on the other side of the courtyard. He walked slowly towards Raj. He was wearing sunglasses but he removed them as he stood in front of Raj.

"Are you ready to meet your maker, Raj?"

Raj started hyperventilating, his nostrils flaring with every hasty breath.

Mahmud waved a hand at the group of masked men. "They are prepared to cut off your head, Raj. They know you are a liar and a betrayer and that you deserve to die. Is that what you want, Raj? Do you want to die? Do you want to meet your maker as a liar and a betrayer?"

162

"I just want to go home," said Raj. "I don't know anything, I can't tell you anything. I'm no use to you."

"That's not true," said Mahmud. "There is much you can tell me, and telling me will go some way to making up for the lies you have told. You know what the Qur'an says about lying?"

Raj kept staring at the ground.

"And do not cloak the truth with falsehood," said Mahmud. "Do not suppress the truth knowingly." He placed his hand under Raj's chin and gently lifted his head. "It is time to stop suppressing the truth, Raj. The truth is the only thing that will save you."

Raj tried to turn away but Mahmud gripped his chin so hard that his nails bit into his flesh. "Is this really how you want to die, Raj?" he said.

Raj stared back at him but didn't answer. Eventually Mahmud released his grip on Raj's chin. Tears were running down Raj's face and he was finding it difficult to focus.

"The members of your group here, are any of them spies for MI6?" asked Mahmud.

Raj said nothing.

"It is a simple question, brother," said Mahmud.

Raj was breathing heavily. He had been sure that he was about to be killed and was feeling light headed, as if his soul had left his body and had only partly returned. Nothing seemed real and he half expected to wake up at any moment and find himself back in his bedroom in London.

"Listen to me, Raj," said Mahmud softly. "Listen to me carefully. I have given you enough time for reflection. You need to start talking to me now. You need to tell me everything. I know that you are an agent for MI6. I need you to tell me who else in your group is working for MI6."

He folded his arms and waited. Raj looked up at him.

"We are all brothers here to learn how to fight the infidel," said Raj. "We are jihadists preparing to fight the good fight."

"The problem we have is that you are a bad apple, Raj. And a bad apple spoils the barrel. We can no longer trust the people you were training with. Perhaps they are also traitors. Or perhaps you have already betrayed them. Either way they are no use to us. Worse than that, they are liabilities. They can no longer be trusted."

He clicked his fingers and two men appeared from the doorway on the far side of the courtyard, dragging a third man. As they got closer, Raj realised it was Naseem. He was bare chested and his eyes were puffy and half closed. His hands had been tied behind his back and there were shackles binding his ankles.

"You trained with Naseem, your brother from Bradford, and now he is a liability. He is a liability because of you, Raj. So you and you alone are responsible for what is about to happen."

Raj turned his head away. Mahmud gestured at Mole and he stepped forward and grabbed Raj's hair, forcing him to face Naseem.

Naseem was mumbling incoherently. His eyes were open but he didn't seem to be aware of what was going on around him. One of the men holding him kicked

Naseem's legs from under him and he fell, hitting the ground hard. The men roughly pulled Naseem to a kneeling position.

"You can stop this, Raj," said Mahmud. "Telling the truth will set him free."

Raj tried to turn away but the man behind him kept a tight grip on his hair. Raj closed his eyes. It was a test, he told himself. They wouldn't kill Naseem. There would be no point. They were trying to scare him, that was all.

"Open your eyes, Raj," said Mahmud. "Open your eyes or they will remove your eyelids with a knife."

Raj opened his eyes and blinked away tears.

There was a tall, thin man standing behind Naseem, a long knife with a curved blade in his hand. The man's face was wrapped in a shemagh, his eyes shielded by impenetrable sunglasses. The knife glinted in the sun as he raised it above his head.

"Raj, take this opportunity to make things right," said Mahmud.

Raj stared at the knife. They wouldn't do it, he told himself. It was a test, that was all. They hadn't gone through with their threat to behead him and they wouldn't kill Naseem. They were only doing it to scare him. All he had to do was to keep protesting his innocence and they'd take him back to his cell.

"Naseem is a good Muslim," said Raj. "He was the one who persuaded me to come to Pakistan to train."

"So if you are a traitor, he is too? Is that what you're saying?"

"I am not a traitor, you have to believe me. This is a mistake. It's all a mistake."

"There has been no mistake, Raj. We know you are a traitor. And if you vouch for Naseem, then he is also a traitor."

"Mahmud, you have to believe me, I am not a traitor."

Mahmud shook his head sadly. "Very well, then," he said. He looked over at the man with the knife and raised his hand.

The man placed the curved blade against Naseem's throat and pulled. Blood spurted across the dusty courtyard and a wide red gash appeared in Naseem's throat.

"No!" shouted Raj.

The man gripped Naseem's hair with his left hand as he hacked away at the neck. Naseem's arms thrashed around for a few seconds and then stopped. The man hacked twice more and then the head came away, blood showering down on the rest of the corpse.

"*Allahu Akbar!*" screamed the man. "*Allahu Akbar!*" echoed the rest of the men. The men either side of Naseem let him go and the headless corpse pitched forward and hit the ground with a dull thump.

Raj stared at the body in horror. The man holding the head began to dance around, waving it like a trophy as he yelled "*Allahu Akbar*" over and over.

"You see what you've done, Raj?" asked Mahmud.

Raj continued to stare at the blood pooling around the shoulders of the corpse.

166

"If you had told the truth, Naseem would still be alive."

Raj said nothing. His mind was in turmoil, unable to accept that Naseem had been killed in front of him. He wanted to believe that they had somehow faked the whole thing but he knew that he was clutching at impossible straws. Naseem was dead and Mahmud was right — it was Raj's fault. Raj felt tears run down his cheeks.

Mahmud shouted something in Arabic and four of the men hurried towards a barred gate on the far side of the courtyard.

"What are you thinking, Raj?" asked Mahmud. "Do you think your handler is going to rescue you? Do you think they will send helicopters? We are in Pakistan, Raj. That is not going to happen. But even if we were in Iraq or Afghanistan, they would not come. The infidels are beaten, they are leaving with their tails between their legs. They don't care about you, Raj. You're old news. All you can do now is help yourself. You have taken a wrong turn, brother, but you can get back on the right path. Allah is a forgiving God, Raj. He understands that sometimes we fail. As it says in the Qur'an, everything in the heavens and everything in the earth belongs to Allah. He forgives whoever He wills and punishes whoever He wills. Allah is Ever-Forgiving, Most Merciful. He will forgive you, Raj. It is not too late."

The four men returned with two more men. It was Sami and Labib. They were both managing to walk, just about. Sami's right eye was closed and his lips had swollen to twice their normal size. His shirt was torn and his belly was hanging over his trousers. Labib's face was also bruised and bloody. His mouth was wide open and Raj could see that two of his front teeth were broken.

"You can't," said Raj, shaking his head. "You're a human being, how can you do this?"

"The kafir is no better than an animal," said Mahmud. "And those Muslims who betray Allah are worse than the kafir."

"They haven't betrayed anyone," said Raj. "They're good Muslims. They've done nothing wrong."

"But how can I believe anything you tell me, Raj? Every word that comes out of your mouth is a lie. You know what it says in the Qur'an, brother? 'The signs of the hypocrite are three: when he speaks, he lies; when he makes a promise, he breaks it; and when he is entrusted with something, he betrays that trust.' That is what you are, Raj. You are a hypocrite. So I cannot believe anything you tell me. You tell me that Sami and Labib are good Muslims, that they are not betrayers, but you are a liar and a hypocrite, so how can I believe you?"

"They are good men, Mahmud. They are true to jihad. They are true to your cause."

Mahmud held out his hands, palms upward. "And you, brother, are a proven liar."

The man who had beheaded Naseem went to stand behind Sami. The curved blade was still dripping with blood. Sami began to struggle but the men on either side of him tightened their grip and held him fast. The man with the knife looked over at Mahmud, waiting for the signal. Sami's whole body was trembling as if he was having an epileptic fit. Labib was struggling but was so weak that his captors had no trouble holding him.

"Stop!" Raj yelled. "For the love of Allah, stop!"

"They are tainted, so they are of no further use to us," said Mahmud. "You have tainted them with your lies, Raj. Your lies are condemning them to death."

"I'm not lying, they're good Muslims. This is nothing to do with them."

"What is nothing to do with them, Raj?" asked Mahmud quietly.

"This. All this. The things you're accusing me of. It has nothing to do with me, you know that."

"I know nothing of the sort," said Mahmud. "The one thing I know for sure is that you are lying to me. So when you tell me that they are good Muslims . . ." He shrugged carelessly. "How can I believe you?"

He looked over at the man with the knife and began to raise his hand.

"Wait!" shouted Raj.

Mahmud stopped and lowered his hand.

There was a large wet patch on the front of Sami's pants.

"I am telling you the truth, may Allah strike me down if I lie," said Raj. "They are good men. They have not betrayed you."

"And what about you, Raj? Have you betrayed me?"

Raj said nothing.

Labib screamed something but his accent made it impossible for Raj to work out what he was saying.

"You need to tell the truth, about everything," said Mahmud. "Only then can you be believed."

"Please don't kill them," said Raj. "I beg you. In the name of Allah the Merciful."

"You will be truthful?" asked Mahmud.

"Yes, I will!" shouted Raj. "Now let them go!"

"Have you betrayed us?" asked Mahmud.

Raj closed his eyes. "Yes," he said, his voice barely audible.

"You have been working for MI6?"

Raj took a deep breath, then exhaled and nodded slowly. "Yes," he said.

Mahmud smiled as he walked towards Raj. He patted him gently on the shoulder. "Well done, brother," he said. "You have done the right thing. You have saved your friends. Now together we can save your soul."

The pilot made full use of the plane's short take-off and landing characteristics and came to a stop a few seconds after touching down. There was a single runway at the Cherat army base and a parking area where there was a line of a dozen assorted planes in army livery.

The pilot came out of the cockpit and opened the door, just as a Land Rover Defender pulled up. The desert heat hit Shepherd like a hot shower and he felt sweat beading on his face as he pulled open the rear door of the Land Rover and threw in his holdall. Kassar climbed in next to him. "We have a briefing with Brigadier Khan this evening at seven," he said.

"Can't you bring me up to speed?" asked Shepherd.

"Only the brigadier has information on the mission. We haven't been told anything other than that we are to go in early tomorrow."

"Tomorrow? We're going in tomorrow? Are you sure?"

"Is there a problem?"

"Hell, yes, there's a problem. We need to rehearse. Practise. I haven't even got a weapon."

"I'm going to take you to the quartermaster now," said Kassar. "We'll get you everything you need."

"Addy, we can't go in cold. We need to train first."

They drove past a line of hangars where mechanics in green overalls were working on three Russian-built Mil Mi-17 transport helicopters.

"We train all the time," said the captain. "We have done building entries a thousand times."

"Not with me, you haven't."

"But you are well trained. You're with the SAS."

Shepherd didn't want to contradict the captain about being a member of the Regiment, but even if he had still been in the Regiment, he would have been insisting on a full rehearsal with live rounds. "Addy, I need to speak with the brigadier now."

"That's not possible," said the captain. "He's in Islamabad briefing the prime minister. He is not expected to be here until this afternoon."

"You mean the man who is leading the mission isn't even on site?"

"Brigadier Khan won't be leading the attack, that'll be Colonel Jamali."

"So what will the brigadier be doing?"

"He'll be monitoring from the base," said Kassar.

"Typical REMF," said Shepherd.

"What is a REMF?" asked the captain.

Shepherd realised that it was probably best not to tell him that he'd called the brigadier a Rear Echelon Mother Fucker, even though the description seemed to be appropriate.

"It's what we call a soldier who stays away from the front line. What can you tell me about the colonel?"

"He is a good man. He was also at Operation Janbaz. He has been in the SSG for more than twenty years."

"Can I talk to him?"

"Of course. Once we have got you your equipment, I will take you to see him."

"I could do with a shower," said Shepherd.

"I have arranged a room for you in the officers' mess," said the captain.

Shepherd looked out of the window. Most of the troopers he saw were wearing the US woodland-pattern camouflage fatigues though only the SSG commandos were wearing maroon berets. "How many people know what's going on?" asked Shepherd.

"Six teams of four have been put on stand-by," said Kassar. "Then there are three captains, including myself. And the colonel, of course."

"What about regular army?" asked Shepherd. "Will they be moving in to secure the area afterwards?"

Kassar looked uncomfortable. "It is a difficult area to secure," he said. "It is controlled by the Taliban, and

172

has been for as long as I can remember. Troops are sent in from time to time, but they always leave."

"So what are you saying? We go in, get the hostage, and leave?"

"I don't have the operational details. We'll get those from the brigadier."

Shepherd laughed. "Sounds like you're being treated like a mushroom," said Shepherd. "Happens to me all the time in my job."

The captain frowned. "Mushroom? I don't understand."

"They keep you in the dark and feed you bullshit," said Shepherd. "That's what they do with mushrooms."

The captain's frown deepened, then he laughed. "That's good," he said. "That's very good."

"It's also very true, unfortunately," Shepherd said. "Our masters often operate on the basis that we are told only what they think we need to know. But you and I will be the ones going in with guns."

"While they carry on being REMFs?"

"Exactly," said Shepherd.

The Land Rover pulled up in front of a large featureless building. Kassar climbed out and Shepherd followed him.

"You'll need everything, all the gear?" asked the captain, as he pushed open a pair of double doors. Ahead of them was a counter some ten metres wide behind which stood three men in white overalls and behind them stretched rows and rows of clothing and equipment in metal racks that reached up to the roof.

"I bought my own boots with me," said Shepherd.

Kassar nodded. "Boots are important," he said.

"So are guns, but I don't think they would let me on a plane with an MP5," said Shepherd.

One of the men in white overalls walked over and spoke to Kassar in Urdu. Kassar replied and then turned to Shepherd. "He needs your measurements."

"Thirty-eight chest, thirty-inch waist. Five feet eleven."

The quartermaster obviously spoke English because he scribbled on a clipboard and then disappeared among the racks.

"I saw the helicopters back there," said Shepherd. "Is that how we're going in?"

"We haven't been told, but they are all being readied so we're assuming we'll be using them."

"I can't get over the fact that no one talks to you before a mission," said Shepherd.

"It's different in the SAS?"

"Chalk and cheese," said Shepherd. "We're all asked for our input, and everyone is listened to. We call it a Chinese parliament."

"In the SSG, the senior officer makes the decisions," said Kassar.

"Officers make the decisions in the SAS, too, but more often than not the troopers have more experience so only an idiot would ignore his men," said Shepherd.

The quartermaster returned with fatigues, Kevlar gloves, a black Kevlar helmet, and black Kevlar knee and elbow protectors. "Underwear? Socks?" he asked Shepherd.

Shepherd shook his head. "I'm good. Boots too. I could do with a decent vest with ceramic plates front, back and groin."

174

The quartermaster grunted and headed back among the racks.

Shepherd grinned at Kassar. "Better safe than sorry. What about radios and headsets?"

"I'll get one for you just before we leave," said the captain.

The quartermaster returned with the Kevlar vest. The plates were already in place. Shepherd tapped them with his knuckles though there was no way of knowing for sure whether they would stop a bullet. "We buy them from America," said Kassar, as if reading his mind.

"Just so long as they work," said Shepherd.

"Have you ever been shot?"

Shepherd nodded. "My shoulder, a while back," he said. "In Afghanistan."

"AK-47?" The quartermaster handed his clipboard and pen to Kassar and the captain signed with a flourish.

"AK-74. What about you?"

"I've been lucky."

"Luck's important," said Shepherd. "Luck and ceramic plates."

The captain took the jacket while Shepherd picked up the rest of the equipment. They took it out to the Land Rover, loaded it into the back, and climbed in. The SSG officers' mess was in a separate compound, a two-storey building with bedrooms on the top floor and a recreation room, dining room, gym and administration centre on the ground floor. There were a dozen or so officers in fatigues sprawled on sofas watching football on a large flatscreen television. They all turned to watch as Shepherd and Kassar carried the gear upstairs. His room was the size of a prison cell and about as welcoming. There was a single bed, a cheap wooden wardrobe and a table and chair. There were marks on the wall where there had once been posters, and cobwebs in the corners that suggested that cleaning wasn't a regular occurrence. Kassar dropped the vest on the bed. "I'll wait downstairs while you get ready," he said. "Do you need to sleep?"

"I'm fine," said Shepherd. "What I need is a gun and the opportunity to fire a few rounds."

"Soon as you're ready, I'll take you to the armoury," said Kassar.

He went downstairs. Shepherd shaved and showered and changed into the fatigues, then sat on the bed, laced up his boots and switched on the sat phone. He called Button and she answered on the third ring. "I'm here, at the SSG base in Cherat," he said.

"Any problems?"

"One big one," said Shepherd. "They're all geared up to go in tomorrow morning."

"That seems a bit sudden."

"You're telling me," said Shepherd. "And the guy in charge isn't even here. There doesn't seem to be a game plan, or if there is he isn't telling anyone."

"When will you know what they're going to do?"

"There's a briefing from some Brigadier Khan later tonight. Have you heard of him?"

"No, but I'll see what I can find out. Do you have any idea what's planned?"

"They're going to use helicopters. And they have already earmarked the guys. Six strike teams of four men, which is fair enough. But there's to be no army back-up, it's a straightforward in and out."

"It's Taliban-controlled territory, right?"

"Sounds like it. I think they're scared of a full-on battle."

"Understandable," said Button.

"I'll know after the briefing, I'll call you then," said Shepherd. He ended the call and went downstairs. Kassar was watching the football. He had acquired a transceiver that was clipped to his belt, and he had a Glock in a leather holster. He stood up and introduced Shepherd to his companions. They were all under thirty, lean and fit, and almost all were wearing impenetrable sunglasses and sporting Rolex Submariner watches.

Shepherd could tell from the way they were looking at him they had questions but none of them said anything other than to tell him their names. Introductions done, Kassar took him outside, where the Land Rover was waiting.

The armoury was outside the SSG compound, a single-storey windowless building surrounded by a chain-link fence topped with razor wire. Two guards cradling MP5s saluted and opened a gate for the Land Rover to drive up to the building. Two more armed guards stood aside to allow them inside.

"What weapon are you most comfortable with?" asked the captain, as they approached a counter behind which stood two uniformed armourers, both men in their forties.

"Addy, no offence, but that depends on what we're going to be doing, doesn't it? If it's a close-quarter battle situation then I'd be happy with an MP5, but if we're outside blasting away then a G3 or even a heavy machine gun."

"I like the G3," said the captain.

"So do I, but if we're inside, the round is a bit on the large side, you get less of a ricochet with the nine-mill."

"So which do you prefer?"

Shepherd sighed. The choice of weapon came down to horses for courses but clearly no one was going to tell him what the course was. The one thing he did know was that it was a hostage rescue so the MP5 made more sense. "I'll take an MP5," he said.

"And as a sidearm. We have Glocks, the Beretta 92F and the SIG Sauer P226."

Shepherd's face brightened. The SIG was his favourite handgun. "The P226 will do fine," he said.

Kassar spoke to one of the armourers and he went over to a cage full of MP5s on racks. He took a carbine and gave it to the captain, who in turn passed it to Shepherd. Shepherd quickly field-stripped, reassembled and dry-fired it. It appeared to be almost new and he nodded his approval. The quartermaster returned with a P226 in a nylon holster. Shepherd checked the weapon. Like the MP5, it was pristine.

"OK?" asked Kassar.

"All good," said Shepherd. "Can I get in some target practice, get the sights sorted?"

"Sure," said the captain. He said something to the quartermaster, who disappeared into the back of the armoury and reappeared with two boxes of 9mm cartridges. Kassar signed for the guns and ammunition and they went back outside to the Land Rover. The shooting range was a short drive away, an outdoor area surrounded by another chain-link fence. There were free-standing targets in front of a mound of earth and a line of wooden tables from where the guns could be fired. Kassar watched as Shepherd loaded the clips and fired away, calibrating the sights until his grouping was as tight as it had been in Credenhill. "You have a good eye," said Kassar, nodding approvingly.

"It's always easy to hit targets when they're not shooting back," said Shepherd, making both the weapons safe.

The radio on Kassar's hip crackled and he put it to his ear. He listened and then nodded at Shepherd. "The brigadier's here and the briefing's in ten minutes."

Brigadier Khan was in his fifties, a barrel-chested man with swept-back hair that was greying at the temples. He had a line of multicoloured medals on his chest and an ebony swagger stick that looked as if it belonged in colonial times. His uniform was spotless and neatly pressed and his boots gleamed. From the look of the man's immaculately manicured nails he hadn't polished the boots himself.

The briefing was in a long windowless room close to the officers' mess. There were a dozen rows of plastic chairs facing a small podium on which there was a lectern decorated with the Pakistan flag. On the wall behind the lectern was a whiteboard and to the left of it was a large-scale map of the north-west of Pakistan.

There were fifteen men already sitting in the room when the brigadier walked in and made his way to the podium, an aide-de-camp hard on his heels carrying two metal briefcases. The seated men sprang to their feet and saluted. The brigadier threw them back a half-hearted salute but avoided eye contact.

The aide-de-camp opened one of the briefcases and began attaching photographs to the whiteboard, including pictures of a desert fort along with a head-and-shoulder shot of Raj and another of an Arab man that Shepherd didn't recognise.

Kassar nodded at Shepherd and took him up to the podium, where he introduced him to the brigadier. "This is Dan Shepherd, from England," said Kassar. Shepherd wasn't sure how to acknowledge the brigadier but decided to go with a salute and not a handshake. The brigadier returned the salute, again half-heartedly. Shepherd could smell the man's cologne, sickly sweet with an orangey undertone.

"You are SAS, I gather," said the brigadier. He had a clipped upper-class accent that suggested a spell at Sandhurst, the Royal Military Academy.

"Former SAS," said Shepherd. He pointed at the photograph of Raj. "I worked with Manraj Chaudhry two years ago."

"Well, I hope we can get him back for you," said the brigadier. "You are familiar with the area where he is being held?"

180

"I have looked at the geography but I have never been there," said Shepherd. "I was in Afghanistan for several tours."

The brigadier pointed his swagger stick at the map. "Waziristan," he said, in clipped tones. "Just under twelve thousand square kilometres consisting of the area west and south-west of Peshawar between the Tochi river to the north and the Gomal river to the south. I don't know how aware you are of the political situation in the area but it is an area within what we call FATA, the Federally Administered Tribal Areas."

"I've heard of FATA, of course," said Shepherd. He had also heard that the Taliban pretty much controlled the territory and that the Pakistan army pretty much treated it as a no-go area.

The brigadier tapped the point of his swagger stick at a place called Parachinar, which was at the apex of a triangle of Pakistani territory sticking into Afghanistan. "There is a fort here, very close to the border," he said.

"What sort of assault is planned?" asked Shepherd.

The brigadier's eyes narrowed. "I will explain that during the briefing," he said, and turned his back on Shepherd to watch his aide-de-camp affix more photographs to the whiteboard.

Kassar nodded for Shepherd to move away and they went to sit down in the front row. More troopers were filing into the room and sitting down. "He seems a bit prickly," said Shepherd.

"Officers are not used to being questioned by their men," said Kassar. "There are no Chinese parliaments

181

here. Any discussion would sound like criticism and soldiers are not allowed to be critical of officers."

"I wasn't being critical, Addy, I was just asking for information."

"I understand that, but he probably won't see it that way," whispered Kassar.

There was a rumble as chairs were pushed back and men got to their feet again. Shepherd turned around to see that a colonel had entered the room, flanked by two captains.

"Colonel Jamali," whispered Kassar.

The colonel was a short man, a good two inches shorter than the captains either side of him. All three were wearing desert camouflage fatigues with the sleeves rolled up, had Oakley sunglasses and had their maroon berets at the same jaunty angle. The colonel had a thick rope-like scar running from his right elbow down to his wrist. Shepherd noticed a big difference between the way the men in the room were saluting the colonel compared with the reception they had given Brigadier Khan. The salutes for the brigadier had been perfunctory at best, but for the colonel they snapped to attention and made eye contact, holding their position with ramrod-straight backs until he returned the salute. The men stayed standing while the colonel and the two captains took their seats at the front, just along from where Shepherd and Kassar were sitting.

The brigadier continued to watch his aide-de-camp place photographs on the whiteboard. Shepherd had the feeling that the brigadier had deliberately ignored the arrival of the colonel. Eventually the brigadier turned and walked to the podium, tapping it with his swagger stick to get everyone's attention.

"We will have six teams of four," said the brigadier. "Captain Ali will be in charge of teams Alpha and Bravo, Captain Sipra will be in charge of Charlie and Delta, and Captain Kassar will be in charge of Echo and Foxtrot. Colonel Jamali will be officer in command on the ground. The situation at the moment is that we have an al-Qaeda cell holding at least one hostage in a fort on the outskirts of Parachinar, close to the border with Afghanistan. We will be leaving at first light on three helicopters, designated Red, Blue and Green. Alpha and Bravo will be in red, Charlie and Delta will be in Blue and Echo and Foxtrot will be in Green. The flight time from Cherat to Parachinar is just over thirty minutes. Sunrise tomorrow is at 0658 hours so we expect to be arriving at the airfield at 0730 hours." The brigadier tapped the map with his swagger stick. "From the airport to the target is just under six miles. Transport will be taken on the helicopters and the teams will drive to a range of hills behind the fort. The teams will cross the range on foot. It should take less than fifteen minutes to reach the fort, which gives us an ETA of 0745. The mission is to take control of the fort and to rescue a British citizen who is being held captive there." He tapped his swagger stick on Raj's photograph. "Manraj Chaudhry. A British citizen of Pakistani descent. He will almost certainly have been tortured and will be in weakened condition. Mr Shepherd, if you will be so good as to stand. Thank you."

Shepherd got to his feet and turned to face the assembled men.

"This is Daniel Shepherd, he has worked with Mr Chaudhry and will be a familiar face. He is also an SAS trained special forces soldier, so he will not require babysitting. He will be alongside Captain Kassar. Teams Echo and Foxtrot are tasked with bringing Mr Chaudhry back to the airport. Thank you, Mr Shepherd. You may sit down."

Shepherd did as he was told.

The brigadier tapped another photograph on the whiteboard, this one a head-and-shoulders shot of a bearded Arab man with a hooked nose and dark patches under his eyes. "This is Akram Al-Farouq, a high-ranking al-Qaeda leader. We believe he is in the building, possibly overseeing the interrogation of the British agent. Captain Sipra and teams Charlie and Delta are tasked with capturing Akram Al-Farouq."

Shepherd looked across at Kassar, wondering whether the captain had been told about Akram Al-Farouq. Kassar was staring at the photograph of the Arab as if trying to commit the features to memory. Shepherd turned to look at the colonel. He was sitting back in his chair, his legs outstretched, nodding enthusiastically.

"We believe Akram Al-Farouq was involved in a number of attacks on Pakistani soil," said the brigadier. "In 2007 he was involved in the failed assassination attempt on former prime minister Benazir Bhutto. We believe he arranged the funding for the operation. They tried again two months later and this time they were successful. Again, we were able to show that the funding came from Akram Al-Farouq. He was also the paymaster for the car bomb attack on the Danish embassy in Pakistan in June 2008 and three months later organised the truck bomb attack on the Marriott Hotel in Islamabad that killed more than fifty people."

He tapped two more photographs, surveillance shots of Akram Al-Farouq taken with a long lens. In one he was getting into a white SUV, in another he was sitting at a café drinking tea with an Arab, both men wearing pristine white ankle-length thawbs. He pointed at Al-Farouq. "I need you all to have a clear picture of this man in your head. Under no circumstances is he to be killed. He has incalculable value as an information source — no one knows more about the workings of al-Qaeda in this region."

"Is that how you found the location?" interrupted Shepherd. "You were following Al-Farouq?"

The brigadier looked at Shepherd as if he had just broken wind. "That is an operational matter that I'm afraid I can't discuss," he said, which Shepherd took as a "yes". It was starting to look as if the operation was more about catching a high-value target and less about rescuing Raj. "Your priority is to make sure that he is captured so that he can be interrogated."

"With the greatest of respect, sir, my priority is to rescue Raj," said Shepherd. "That's why I'm here."

The brigadier's eyes hardened and Shepherd realised that the officer wasn't used to being questioned. Shepherd averted his eyes, knowing that the best course of action was to avoid a confrontation. The brigadier took a deep breath, then tapped a photograph of a stone-built fort. "The building we need to take is a small two-storey fort that used to be a garrison for the Frontier Corps until it was abandoned some ten years ago. It has fallen into disrepair but is now occupied by a small group of Taliban fighters, a dozen at most. The fort is at the bottom of a small range of hills. The teams will come over the range to the rear of the fort. There are two entrances: a main wooden door at the front and at the rear is a smaller door, also made of wood. There are windows on all sides, shuttered all the time so far as we know. Animals are kept inside and taken out during the day to scavenge for food. Teams Alpha and Bravo are to use shaped charges to blow the rear doors. They will move in to secure the rear of the fort. Teams Charlie and Delta will move to the front of the fort and blow those doors immediately after the rear has been accessed. Teams Echo and Foxtrot will follow Alpha and Bravo inside. All six units will clear the ground and upper floor, locate the hostage and Akram Al-Farouq, and then head back to the airfield." He looked up and paused for effect, before continuing. "This is to be a standard rescue operation. Move in and move out. The fort is not to be held, we are interested only in the rescue of the British agent and the capture of Akram Al-Farouq. There are substantial numbers of Taliban fighters in the area and we are not in a position to take them on." He looked at his wristwatch. "I suggest you get an early night. All teams are to gather at the helicopter landing pad with their equipment at 0500 hours." Shepherd assumed the brigadier was going to ask for questions or comments but he simply nodded, then stepped off the podium and headed for the door. His aide-de-camp began hurriedly pulling the photographs off the whiteboard.

"What do you think, Addy?" asked Shepherd.

"The brigadier is correct, we need to get in and out quickly," said the captain. "We cannot fight an extended battle there. It's a difficult area to fight in. The troops of the British Raj called it Hell's Door Knocker, and if anything it's worse these days. It's controlled by the Taliban and looks set to stay that way." He smiled. "You might like to think of it as the equivalent of the Wild West, the people there are effectively a law unto themselves. It has long been that way. It was an independent tribal territory from 1893 and remained outside the control of the British Raj, and also independent of Afghanistan. Since 1947 it has been part of Pakistan but really that's in name only."

Kassar jumped to his feet. Shepherd looked up to see Colonel Jamali looking down at him with an amused smile on his face. Shepherd stood up. He realised that Kassar was saluting so he did the same. The colonel returned the salute. "So you are the SAS man?" he said. He had a slight American accent, as if he watched a lot of Hollywood movies.

"Former SAS," said Shepherd. "I'm with the Security Service these days."

The colonel nodded. "So you are a spy?"

"I wouldn't say that," said Shepherd.

"This Manraj we are going to rescue, how will he have stood up to interrogation?"

It was a good question, thought Shepherd. One that the brigadier should have asked. "He's young and strong, so physically he should be OK. But his youth also means he doesn't have much experience."

The colonel nodded. "They will play mind games with him," he said. "Al-Qaeda are good at that. When we go in, as soon as we find him you are to stick with him. Like glue."

"Understood."

The colonel studied Shepherd for several seconds. Shepherd could see his twin reflections in the lenses of the sunglasses. "So tell me, what do you think of our brigadier's strategy?" the colonel asked eventually.

Shepherd looked at the colonel, wondering what he should say. The truth could well end up with him being put on the next plane back to London.

The colonel grinned as if he sensed his confusion. "You can speak frankly," he said. Shepherd looked across at Kassar and the captain nodded encouragement.

"If it was me, I'd go in at night," he said. "Attacks on a fortified building are all about having the element of surprise, and you're more likely to get that in the middle of the night while everyone is asleep."

"Agreed," said the colonel. "But the territory is mountainous and we don't like flying our helicopters at night."

"If we leave it until after dawn, they'll be awake. What time is sunrise prayers?"

"Just before 0700 hours."

"And Fajr prayers?"

The colonel lowered his head and looked at Shepherd over the top of his sunglasses. "You are not a Muslim, are you, Mr Shepherd?"

"I'm not, Colonel. But I know the importance of praying five times a day to those who are."

The colonel pursed his lips, then nodded slowly. "Fajr prayers commence at just after five thirty."

"So they'll all be wide awake some three hours before we get there," said Shepherd. "We lose the element of surprise. When the attack starts they'll be on a level field. In fact they'll have the advantage because they'll be inside and we'll be outside. If it's night and we have night vision goggles, we have the advantage. If night flying is a problem, why don't we head off before dark? What time is sunset here?"

"Eighteen forty-five hours," said the colonel. "We wouldn't have time to get there before dark."

"So put it off one day," said Shepherd. "We could fly to the airfield just before it gets dark tomorrow and move in before first prayers. Five o'clock, say. Then back to the airfield at sunrise."

The colonel nodded slowly. "In a perfect world, that would make sense," he said. "Unfortunately, Brigadier Khan has just returned from informing the prime minister that the attack will go ahead first thing tomorrow morning. If he has to backtrack on that promise, he will lose face. And the brigadier never loses face."

"I see," said Shepherd.

"Is that not how it works in the United Kingdom?" asked the colonel.

"Decisions like that are usually taken at a pay grade well above mine," said Shepherd.

"But it is the politicians who call the shots?"

Shepherd shook his head. "In my experience, once the politicians have called in the SAS they allow the Regiment to do what has to be done. It would be a very brave politician who tried to second-guess the Regiment. The SAS are the professionals, they're best left to get on with the job."

The colonel's jaw tightened and Shepherd wondered whether the man had thought he had been critical. But then the colonel smiled. "So, assuming we are locked into the mission timetable as outlined by the brigadier, what other suggestions do you have?"

Shepherd went over to the whiteboard. The brigadier's aide-de-camp was about to take down the photographs of the fort, but Shepherd waved for him to stop. He pointed at the turret at the top of the fort. "This worries me," he said. "I don't see a guard here in the pictures, but it's the obvious place to put one. If there is a guard there and he sees us approach he'll sound the alarm. I'd suggest a sniper on at least one of the teams. If there is a guard we can take him out before we move in."

"You are a sniper?" asked the colonel.

"I used to be, but it's years since I have done any distance shooting. Again, if we were going in at night it wouldn't matter so much because unless the guard has night vision equipment he wouldn't see much."

The colonel jutted out his chin and nodded slowly. "What else?"

190

"I wouldn't go in through the doors, not even with shaped charges. It's the obvious way in, which means they are more likely to be reinforced or defended." He walked to the whiteboard and tapped a window on the upper floor. "I'd go in through this window. Throw up a ladder, you wouldn't even need a shaped charge. Throw in a couple of flash-bangs to disorientate anyone inside and then straight in. It's always easier to move down a building than up it, so I'd put most of the team through the upper windows. Downstairs, I'd go in through the windows and again I'd throw in flash-bangs first."

The colonel rubbed his chin thoughtfully. "You've done this a lot?"

"A fair amount for real, but I've practised it hundreds of times. Can I ask you why we're not rehearsing first? Even a few hours in a mock building would help."

"There isn't time," said the colonel. "The worry is that Akram Al-Farouq might well only be there temporarily. We don't want to lose him."

"Then you should put the fort under observation. Get an observation team dug in and they can report on any comings and goings."

"Again, it's too late for that, I'm afraid," said the colonel. "There's nothing we can do to change the time frame. Brigadier Khan has promised the prime minister that we will go in tomorrow, so tomorrow it is." He tilted his head on one side. "But I like the sniper idea, I will make sure that we have snipers on at least two of the teams."

"What about details of the layout inside?"

"That we don't have," said the colonel.

"Another reason for waiting," said Shepherd. "We could do with intel on the interior. Going in cold is asking for trouble."

The colonel stared at Shepherd for several seconds, then he looked at Kassar. "Make sure you take good care of our English friend," he said.

"I will, sir," said Kassar.

The colonel nodded, flashed Shepherd a tight smile, then turned and walked away, followed by his two captains.

Kassar seemed to have been holding his breath and he didn't exhale until the colonel had left the room. "I don't think I've ever seen anyone talk to the colonel like that," he said.

"I was just offering my opinion. And he did ask."

"Usually when an officer asks for an opinion, he means he just wants to hear that he's right."

"You know that I'm right, though? It would be better moving in at night."

"We don't do much with night vision gear," said Kassar.

"Why not?"

The captain shrugged. "I don't know. We just don't. I used them a few times during basic training but that was it."

"You guys have a killing house, right?"

"A what?"

"A killing house. Where you can practise entering and clearing buildings."

Kassar shook his head. "We don't have anything like that."

192

"That's what we need. That way the teams can practise going in and we get to iron out any problems before we do it for real."

"Do not worry," said Kassar. "Like the SAS, we are professionals too. We will rescue your man, I am sure of it."

Shepherd nodded and smiled, but he wished he had done more to persuade the colonel that a night assault was the way to go.

Kassar took Shepherd back to the officers' mess. "We should eat," said the captain. "Then get a few hours' sleep."

"Sounds like a plan," said Shepherd. "Let me freshen up first." Kassar went to get a table in the dining room while Shepherd headed upstairs to his room. He took his sat phone from his holdall, lay down on the bed and called Button. "We're going in tomorrow, at dawn," he said.

"Are you OK with that?"

"I'd have preferred a night-time assault but the guy in charge says first thing so first thing it is."

"You don't sound happy."

Shepherd sighed. "I'm not. They're well equipped and their intel seems spot on, but I don't think they're prepared. I raised the question of a rehearsal and they looked at me as if I'd broken wind. They seem to think that they are all highly trained professional soldiers and that they don't need to practise."

"And what's their plan?"

"Helicopters going in low to a drop-off about six miles away. Then on foot to get to the target."

"That sounds good to me."

"If it was a night assault, sure. But they're waiting for dawn before they go in. Something to do with their helicopters not being up for night flying."

"Can't you get them to change their minds?"

"The problem is that the brains behind the mission isn't actually taking part. He's a desk warrior and is more interested in the politics of it all. The colonel who'll be leading the assault seems to have his head screwed on OK but he isn't allowed to second-guess the brigadier. It just feels like it's being rushed. They have satellite photographs of the area, they know what the target building is like, it would make sense to rehearse it until everyone knows what they're doing."

"You don't have to go in with them, Spider. Not if you're not happy."

"I don't see there's a choice," said Shepherd. "I'm the only one who knows Raj, if I'm not there then there's a chance of collateral damage. Have you ever heard of an Akram Al-Farouq, by the way?"

"Al-Qaeda Akram Al-Farouq? Of course. We've been looking for him for years."

"According to the brigadier, Akram Al-Farouq is the one questioning Raj. It looks as if that's how they found Raj in the first place."

"This is the first I've heard of it," said Button. "Akram Al-Farouq is a very high-value target, possibly number three in the al-Qaeda hierarchy. I'm assuming the Americans don't know because they'd have sent drones in after him."

"Lucky for Raj they don't know, then," said Shepherd. "The thing is, it's looking to me that this is more about Akram Al-Farouq than it is about Raj."

"You might be over-thinking it," said Button. "If Raj wasn't a priority, they wouldn't have agreed to have you on board."

"Do you think Willoughby-Brown knows about this Al-Farouq?"

"It's possible, I suppose," said Button.

"I hope he's not playing the 'need-to-know' game," said Shepherd. "That's how people get hurt."

"Do you want me to ask him?"

"Nah, I just want you to be aware that Akram Al-Farouq is in the picture."

"Spider, as I said, if you have any doubts at all about this, take a back seat. You don't have to go in with them, you can take a step back and be an observer. No one will think the worse of you. I don't want you putting yourself in harm's way."

"It has to be done, Charlie," said Shepherd. "Raj has put his life on the line. The least I can do is return the favour."

"OK, but call me as soon as it's over."

"I will," he said.

"And I know I'm always saying this, but be careful."

"You can count on it," said Shepherd. He ended the call and lay back on his bed, staring at the ceiling.

Shepherd opened his eyes at four o'clock on the dot. He took a deep breath, rolled off the bed and grabbed a plastic bottle of water. He drank, then wiped his mouth with the back of his hand. He decided against showering, but cleaned his teeth and shaved. There was a knock on his door and he opened it to find Captain Kassar standing there in his Kevlar helmet and armoured vest, a Heckler & Koch G3 on a sling. "Just wanted to check you were up," said Kassar. "Our transport is outside when you're ready."

Shepherd thanked him and finished dressing. Boots, vest, helmet, gloves. He slotted his SIG Sauer into its holster and swung the sling of his MP5 over his right shoulder. He was about to leave when he remembered the sat phone. He took it out of his holdall and slipped it into a pocket on his vest.

Kassar was waiting for him in the rear of the Land Rover Defender. "OK?" asked the captain.

"All good," said Shepherd.

They drove in silence to the runway. The Mi-17 helicopters had been wheeled out of their hangars and were lined up on the ramp with blue-overalled mechanics busy making last-minute adjustments. Their five-bladed rotors drooped limply like giant hands ready to grab the fuselages.

Colonel Jamali was standing with Captain Ali next to one of the helicopters, studying what appeared to be a handheld GPS unit. The eight men in teams Alpha and Beta were checking their equipment. The first rays of the sun were starting to creep over the horizon, smearing the early morning sky with a yellow glow.

Shepherd and Kassar climbed out of the Land Rover and walked over to the helicopter on the left, where eight men were lined up waiting to board. They were the men of teams Echo and Foxtrot and Kassar introduced them before leading them up the rear ramp into the belly of the helicopter. The Mi-17 was big enough to carry thirty troopers and their equipment but using three helicopters meant they wouldn't find themselves caught short if one developed mechanical problems. A Toyota Hilux pick-up truck in desert camouflage livery was in the middle of the helicopter, tied down with webbing straps and clamped to the floor. There were folding metal seats attached to the fuselage, each with a webbing harness. Shepherd wasn't familiar with the harness and struggled with it until Kassar came over and helped him buckle up. The rear ramp slowly came up, sealing off the rear of the helicopter.

Shepherd heard the twin turboshaft engines of one of the other helicopters fire up. He looked at his watch. It was almost seven o'clock and the sun was edging higher above the horizon. There was a roar above his head and the helicopter began to vibrate and he felt as much as he heard the whoop-whoop-whoop of the rotor blades.

The helicopter that Shepherd was in was the third to rise into the air. The roar of the engines and the whooping of the blades made conversation impossible. The helicopters flew at less than a thousand feet above the ground as they headed west. Once they left the base the terrain below was inhospitable, a dry rock-strewn wasteland as alien as the moon. Where there was water there was vegetation, clumps of bushes and pale green grassy areas that looked as if they could shrivel up and die at any moment.

The helicopters began to descend at 7.20 and five minutes later they touched down at Parachinar airfield, away from the main runway and close to a line of maintenance hangars. The rear ramp slowly tilted down and a flurry of dust swirled into the cabin, making Shepherd cough. Kassar unclipped his harness and stood up. He pointed at the open door. Shepherd fumbled with his harness and followed Kassar down the ramp. Two of the troopers began releasing the clamps on the wheels of the pick-up truck.

Shepherd joined Kassar on the tarmac. They watched as the pick-up drove slowly down the ramp. The captain climbed into the front passenger seat while Shepherd got into the back with the rest of the troopers.

Once all three helicopters had disgorged their pick-up trucks they drove off the airfield, Colonel Jamali leading the way. They went along a narrow road for about a mile, passing only a goat herder and his son with a flock of twenty or so malnourished goats. They turned off on to a single track that wound through bleak featureless scrubland, the pick-up bouncing and lurching over the rough terrain.

Shepherd shifted uncomfortably. One of the troopers grinned at him. "It's better than walking," said the man.

"Only just," said Shepherd.

"This man we're going to rescue, he's very brave."

Shepherd nodded. "He risked a lot."

"And he's not a soldier?"

198

"He's just a regular guy," said Shepherd. "He was a medical student."

The trooper nodded. "My parents wanted me to be a doctor." He was in his twenties with a neatly trimmed moustache. Kassar had introduced him as Sunny.

"Yeah? What happened?"

The trooper grinned and tapped the side of his head. "I wasn't smart enough," he said. "Dropped out of university and signed up."

Shepherd nodded. "Story of my life," he said.

"No regrets?" asked Sunny.

Shepherd looked at the MP5 he was holding between his legs, the barrel pointing up at the sky. He thought about what lay ahead — storming a fort in the Pakistani wilderness to rescue an MI5 agent whose life depended on him — and smiled. "No," he said. "Not yet, anyway."

Ahead of them was a range of hills, dotted with straggly bushes at the bottom, bare rock near the summit. There was still a chill in the air though the sun was now fully above the horizon.

"Your friend is unusual, right?" said another of the troopers. His name was Naveed. Like Sunny he was in his twenties, but shorter and stockier and lighter skinned. "Seems like most Brits end up fighting for al-Qaeda, not against them."

Another of the troopers nodded in agreement. His name was Ziad and he seemed to be the oldest member of the Echo and Foxtrot teams. The left side of his face had been burned at some point in the past and had healed badly, leaving a pale splodge of scar tissue just below his cheekbone. "Why do they do that? Why would someone born in the UK think it was a good idea to become a jihadist in Syria or Iraq?"

Shepherd shrugged. "They're kids, usually. They think it's exciting."

"That's it?" said Naveed. "It's a game?"

"They're indoctrinated by the imams," said Ziad. "They're brainwashed. It happens in Pakistan too. But what I don't understand is why anyone lucky enough to be born in the UK would throw it all away."

Sunny nodded in agreement. "Especially the ones who did those bombs in London. When was that?"

"It was 2005," said Shepherd.

"That made no sense to me," said Sunny. "They were born in Britain, weren't they? Britain was their home. So why blow yourself up in your own country?"

"Like I said, they're brainwashed," said Ziad. "It can happen to anyone. It's like training a dog. And trained dogs can be the most dangerous."

The trucks came to a halt. Kassar climbed out of the cab and opened the tailgate. He helped the men out and they lined up and checked the weapons. They had stopped at the base of the hills. Colonel Jamali strode over, his G3 shouldered.

"Spread out as we go up, we'll meet together at the summit," said the colonel. He nodded at Shepherd. "Just to let you know I have added two snipers to the group. They'll stay on the ridge."

"Good to know," said Shepherd.

The colonel nodded again and then headed up the slope. His men fanned out behind him.

"Right, up we go," said Kassar. "Keep up the colonel's pace, but don't overtake him." The captain grinned at Shepherd. "He likes to lead from the front."

Shepherd lay on his stomach and peered down at the fort below them. There was a single guard in the turret atop the fort but he appeared to be asleep. Shepherd looked over to his left. One of the colonel's snipers was already in position, looking through the telescope sight of his Heckler & Koch PSG1 semi-automatic sniper rifle. It wasn't the rifle that Shepherd would have chosen for the job. Its main feature was its rapid rate of fire, it wasn't the most accurate of weapons. Heckler & Koch came up with the design following the terrorist killings at the 1972 Munich Olympics. The West German police discovered that they couldn't target the terrorists quickly enough and eleven members of the Israeli team were killed. Heckler & Koch were asked to design a semi-automatic rifle that was both accurate and had a large magazine and that same year they came up with the PSG1, mechanically based on the G3.

The colonel's second sniper had set up a few yards to Shepherd's right. He was using a more accurate Dragunov rifle with a black polymer stock. The rifle had the PSO-1 optical sight mounted on a side rail so that it didn't block the iron sight line. Shepherd had trained with the gun and the sight and was a fan of both. The gun was accurate to more than 1,300 yards and the sight came equipped with an illuminated rangefinder grid and a bullet drop compensation elevation adjustment facility.

The colonel raised his hand and motioned for the men to head down the hill. He led from the front with teams Alpha and Bravo fanning out behind him in a wedge shape. Two of the troopers were holding wooden frames on to which C4 explosive had been fixed.

Captain Sipra's Charlie and Delta teams were to the colonel's left. Two troopers were carrying the shaped charges for the main doors at the front of the fort.

Shepherd and Kassar got to their feet. The captain checked that his men were prepared and motioned for them to head down the hill.

Shepherd bent down in a crouch over his MP5, his finger outside the trigger guard, scanning the ground in front of him. It was a steep slope of stony red soil and the most efficient way of moving down was to make a series of zigzags. Stones were cascading down the slope but there wasn't much the troopers could do about that. Shepherd narrowed his eyes and focused on the guard in the turret. The man was slumped against the wall, his head back and his mouth open.

It took them just four minutes to reach the bottom of the hill and jog to the wall. It was built of local stone that had become weathered over the years from the relentless desert winds. The blocks fitted perfectly and mortar didn't seem to have been used. The colonel and Captain Sipra led Charlie and Delta teams around the side of the fort, sticking close to the wall, heading for the main door at the front of the building. Captain Ali and his Alpha and Bravo teams headed for the rear door. Shepherd and Kassar followed with teams Echo and Foxtrot. Shepherd found himself between Ziad and Sunny, both cradling G3s.

They reached the wall and stood with their backs to it. From somewhere inside the fort, a cock crowed. Captain Ali was already at the door, supervising the two troopers with the shaped charges. The charges were affixed to wooden frames about two feet square on the end of ten-foot poles. The men holding the poles stood either side of the door, placed the charges in the middle of the two wooden doors and turned their faces away. The charges were shaped so that almost all the energy went forward; there would be little in the way of a blast at the side, just noise and a flash.

Captain Ali nodded and moved to the side. As he did, a small black object thudded into the sand by his feet.

Shepherd stared at the metal object in horror. "Grenade!" he shouted. Barely had the word left his mouth when a second grenade hit the ground, this one landing in between two of Sipra's troopers. Shepherd recognised them as Soviet-made F1 grenades, nicknamed the *limonka* by the Russians because of their lemon-like shape. The weapon's statistics raced through his mind — the standard time delay for the fuse was between three and a half and four seconds, the grenade contained about sixty grams of TNT, and the explosion was deadly up to about thirty metres.

He was dimly aware of an explosion on the other side of the fort. He knew immediately it was a grenade detonating and not one of the shaped charges. The shaped charges made a dull thudding sound as all the explosive energy was aimed inwards. The sound Shepherd heard was that of a grenade exploding, sending lethal shrapnel in all directions.

Time had slowed to a crawl as it always did when Shepherd was in a combat situation. He was aware that a second had already passed since the first grenade had landed at Sipra's feet. Sipra's mouth was open and he was staring at the grenade, but not moving. Shepherd knew that there was nothing he could do to help the man. He was dead. So were the two troopers holding the shaped charges. They still had their faces turned to the side so hadn't seen the grenades.

Shepherd turned to look at Kassar. Kassar's eyes were wide and fearful but his feet were rooted to the spot. Only Ziad was moving, his left knee high in the air, his G3 in his right hand, running back along the wall. Shepherd counted off another second in his head. His mind was running the numbers. The nearest grenade was twenty metres away. The kill zone was thirty metres — if he was standing up. If he was down on the ground and his head was away from the source of the blast, twenty metres was survivable. On a good day.

He grabbed Kassar by the neck of his armoured vest and twisted him round and then thumped him in the back. Kassar dropped his weapon and started to run. Shepherd ran with him, one step, then another, then he reached the count of three in his head and knew that hitting the ground was the only option. He pushed Kassar down and fell on top of him and then the two grenades exploded, almost as one. The double blast knocked the breath from his body. He wiggled his toes to check that his legs were OK. His ears were ringing as he pushed himself up on to his knees and rolled Kassar over. Kassar's eyes were wide and staring but he was alive. His mouth opened and closed like that of a stranded fish. "It's OK, you're OK," said Shepherd. His voice sounded as if it were coming from the end of a very long tunnel but at least his eardrums didn't seem to have burst. He dragged Kassar by the scruff of his neck towards the wall.

He heard shots from up the hillside and realised that the colonel's snipers were firing at the fort. He looked up and saw a rifle barrel sticking out of one of the upstairs windows and almost immediately heard the distinctive deep pop-pop-pop of an AK-47 being fired on fully automatic.

He pulled Kassar to his feet and they both hugged the wall while they looked around. The only part of Captain Ali to be seen was his head, still in the Kevlar helmet. The rest of his body had been vaporised by the explosion. The two troopers holding the shaped charges had been ripped apart though their charges hadn't gone off. One of the troopers had lost an arm though the hand was still gripping the pole that had held the charge. Both had lost their legs and blood had pooled around the stumps.

There was another flurry of AK-47 fire above their heads. Shepherd looked up. There were now three AK-47s firing up at the hillside. He held his MP5 to his chest. From where he was standing it was impossible to get a clear shot at the men on the upper floor. But if he moved out, he'd be a sitting duck.

Two of the men in Team Echo were down, possibly dead. Ziad was down but as Shepherd watched he got to his feet and grabbed for his rifle. Shepherd opened his mouth to shout a warning but before he could say anything Ziad was cut down in a hail of bullets. Sunny was standing with his back to the wall, frozen. The shrapnel seemed to have missed him completely. His gun was at his feet. Naveed was farther along the wall. He seemed more composed than Sunny but was clearly out of his depth. There was another trooper on the floor on the other side of the door, sitting on the ground, blood streaming from a neck wound. He was reaching out with his right hand as if pleading for help. Kassar moved towards the injured man but Shepherd held him back. "We can't help him," said Shepherd. "We need to get this sorted first."

He ducked involuntarily as he heard a loud whooshing noise overhead. He looked up to see the warhead of an RPG streaking through the sky, leaving a greyish trail in the air behind it. Two seconds later there was an explosion at the summit of the hill. Shepherd hoped that the sniper, whichever one it was, had managed to get out of the way.

He heard a rapid footfall to his right and saw Colonel Jamali come around the corner, followed by three troopers. The trooper in the middle was missing the lower part of his left leg and they had a makeshift tourniquet below his knee. They placed the injured trooper on the floor by the trooper with the neck wound and one of them pulled out an emergency dressing and slapped it on the man's neck.

The colonel hurried towards them, keeping his back to the wall. He stepped over the shaped charges to get to Kassar and Shepherd. "What's your situation, Captain?"

Kassar stared at the colonel, a slight frown on his face as if he didn't understand the question.

"Captain Ali is dead," said Shepherd. "We have two troopers active plus myself from Echo and Foxtrot."

Two more of the colonel's men came around the corner. They looked as if they were about to run for the hill but Shepherd waved for them to get back to the wall.

"They've just fired an RPG and they've got AK-47s and grenades. At the moment they don't realise we're down here but as soon as they do it'll only take a couple of grenades and it'll all be over."

The colonel nodded grimly. "Captain Kassar and I will lay down covering fire so that you can get to the hill. You can lay down covering fire so that we can join you."

"That'll be suicide," said Shepherd. "We're outgunned now. Shit, we were probably outgunned the moment we got here."

"Do you have a better idea?"

Shepherd gestured at the shaped charges. "We can still blow the door. Fight them from the inside."

The colonel looked at the charges and nodded. "Let's do it," he said.

Shepherd let his MP5 hang on its sling as he picked up the poles connected to one of the shaped charges. He pried the fingers of the dismembered arm off the pole and let it fall to the ground.

The colonel picked up the second shaped charge and pressed it against the door.

Shepherd looked at Kassar. "Turn your head and cover your ears," he said. "As soon as the door is blown we go in, you go to the right, I'll take the centre. Tell Sunny and Naveed to follow you. Just shoot anyone with a weapon."

The captain relayed the instructions to Sunny and Naveed as Shepherd pressed his shaped charge against his side of the door. "On three," said the colonel. Shepherd nodded and turned his head to the side, away from the door. "One, two, three."

On three, Shepherd tensed and flicked the switch. The pole jerked in his hands and he felt as much as heard the dull thud as the explosive went off. He heard the door crash inwards and he dropped the pole, grabbed his MP5 and swung it up, his finger automatically slipping inside the trigger guard. He had the weapon set for single shots; it was no time to be wasting ammunition on fully automatic.

Colonel Jamali was already stepping through what was left of the smashed and smoking door, his G3 up at his shoulder.

The doors opened into a courtyard where there were three rusting pick-up trucks parked in a line. Half a dozen chickens were sheltering under the vehicles and in the far corner of the courtyard two tethered goats were bleating in panic. There was a balcony running around the upper level, and as Shepherd stepped across the threshold two men, their faces wrapped in black-and-white chequered keffiyeh, leaned over and took aim with their AK-47s. The colonel fired twice and the shooter on the left fell back, his chest a bloody mess, his weapon tumbling from his hands and clattering down on one of the pick-up trucks. Shepherd fired once and the second man's head exploded in a shower of red.

Overhead Shepherd heard but didn't see the whoosh of an RPG warhead heading for the hills. He was aware of Kassar moving to his right and Sunny and Naveed moving behind him. One of them, Sunny or Naveed, Shepherd wasn't sure which, let loose a hail of bullets even though there was no one to shoot at.

A door opened on the far side of the courtyard and a figure in a brown salwar kameez appeared holding something in his right hand. Shepherd shot him twice and a grenade tumbled from the man's fingers as he fell to the ground. "Grenade!" shouted Shepherd and he ducked down. The colonel dropped behind one of the pick-up trucks and Kassar threw himself to the floor just as the grenade exploded. Most of the blast was absorbed by the vehicles, but several pieces of shrapnel whistled dangerously close to Shepherd. He heard the pop-pop-pop of an AK-47 and straightened up to see rounds thwacking into the door panel of the truck that the colonel was hiding behind. He looked up and saw the shooter, a giant of a man who was so big that he made the AK-47 he was holding look like a toy. Shepherd fired a double tap and caught the man just below the throat with both shots. Blood spurted over his barrel-like chest and he slumped over the balcony.

There was firing above his head and Shepherd knew that if they were going to take them out they would have to cross the courtyard to shoot back at them. He turned and waved at Naveed and Sunny to move ahead. Naveed nodded and ran forward, bent at the waist, but Sunny hesitated. "Move!" shouted Shepherd, but the man had frozen.

The colonel was up now, running towards the far end of the courtyard. He turned and began firing up at the balcony. Shepherd heard screams and almost immediately a body tumbled to the ground. Shepherd ran to join him as the colonel provided covering fire with single well-placed shots.

Kassar had found a spot behind one of the trucks that gave him a clear view of the balcony at the rear of the fort. He fired a short burst and there was a scream from overhead.

Shepherd looked around. To his left there were stone steps leading to the upper level. He waved at the colonel, then pointed at himself, then at the stairs. The colonel nodded. Shepherd ducked behind one of the pick-up trucks, using it as cover as he headed for the steps. The colonel fired a long burst, raking the balcony. Kassar crouched behind another pick-up, laying down more covering fire.

There was a gap of about twenty feet between the last pick-up truck and the steps. Shepherd looked up at the balcony before making his run, but stiffened as he saw the warhead of an RPG poking over the railing. He caught a glimpse of the man behind the RPG peering through the sights. He fired twice but the rounds ricocheted off the metal railing. "RPG!" he shouted, just as the warhead kicked into life.

Time seemed to freeze again. Shepherd could see the warhead, a plume of smoke behind it. He turned to look at the colonel. The colonel was holding his G3 in front of his chest as he stared up at the RPG. He turned and glanced at Shepherd. The sunglasses hid his eyes but there seemed to be the faintest hint of a smile on his face. He began to move, but slowly, as if he knew it was futile. The warhead was heading straight for him. He was as good as dead, and he knew it.

As Shepherd's body reacted instinctively, his mind was racing. What happened next depended on the type of warhead that had been fired. If it was a TBG-7V or an OG-7C then there was going to be one hell of an explosion as both were anti-personnel warheads. The OG-7C was a fragmentation grenade with a kill radius of seven metres. The TBG-7V was a thermobaric warhead using heat to do the damage, and it would kill anything within ten metres. The best-case scenario would be that it was a PG-7VR dual warhead, designed to destroy armoured vehicles and fortified targets, as the second warhead might well not explode.

Shepherd leapt up on to the bonnet of the nearest pick-up truck. He saw Sunny staring at him, open mouthed. "Sunny, get down!" yelled Shepherd. He jumped off the bonnet, his MP5 held out in front of him. The explosion was deafening and hit him just before his feet touched the ground, thumping him in the back like a blow from a sandbag. He roared in pain and hit the ground hard, falling on top of his weapon and then rolling over twice.

He was facing the doorway, and as he faded into unconsciousness he saw Captain Kassar, Sunny and Naveed running back towards the hill. A burst of fire from the upper level cut Naveed and the captain down. The last thing Shepherd saw was Sunny being brought down by a hail of AK-47 fire, then everything went black.

The ringing mobile woke Charlotte Button from a dreamless sleep. She blinked her eyes and focused on the bedside clock. It was three o'clock in the morning, which meant it could only be bad news. She groped for her iPhone and squinted at the screen. The caller had withheld their number. She took the call. "Yes?"

"I'm sorry to call so late, but we have a problem." It was Jeremy Willoughby-Brown.

"In what way?" asked Button, sitting up, already wide awake.

"The Pakistanis seem to have fucked up big-time," said Willoughby-Brown.

"Specifically?"

"It went bad, that's all I know so far," said Willoughby-Brown. "It looks as if the bad guys knew what was going to happen."

"It was a trap?"

"Maybe not a trap, but they were prepared. There's a lot of dead bodies out there."

Button felt her stomach turn over. "Is Spider OK?"

"I don't know," he said. "I'm sorry, I wish I did, but the Pakistanis have gone all tight lipped. They're a bit embarrassed, obviously."

"That's not good enough. Spider was in their care, if something has happened to him they have a duty to inform us."

"Taz is pressing them for information as we speak."

"I don't understand why you've let a junior be the liaison on this operation," said Button.

"He speaks the language, and not to put too fine a point on it, he's the right colour," said Willoughby-Brown. "He's doing a terrific job, under the circumstances."

"You're obviously working under some strange new definition of 'terrific' that I've never heard of," said Button. "He managed to lose Raj and now Spider is missing in action."

"That's hardly Taz's fault, though."

"Then whose fault is it?" said Button. "You should have been out there."

"I've already explained why that wasn't a good idea."

"It seems to me that you not being there was more of an arse-covering exercise," said Button. "If you're not in the field, you can avoid any shit that goes flying if and when it hits the fan."

"Oh, come now, Charlotte, that's not fair."

"Fair? Do you think it's fair what's happened to Spider? Damn you. Damn you to hell." She cut the connection, threw the phone and paced up and down, fuming. She caught sight of herself in the dressing-table mirror. Her face was red and there was a near-manic gleam in her eyes. She stared at her reflection and took several deep breaths. "Getting angry won't solve anything, Charlie," she whispered. She picked up her phone and called Willoughby-Brown back.

"Charlotte?" he said, clearly bracing himself for another verbal assault.

"I'd like to see you in my office at nine o'clock sharp for a full briefing," she said.

"No problem," said Willoughby-Brown.

"Thank you so much," said Button, before ending the call.

Shepherd groaned and opened his eyes. Everything was black. He opened and closed his eyes, wondering whether he had gone blind. He waved his hand in front of his face but saw nothing. He was lying on his side, on a stone floor. He was naked, he realised. Totally naked. He rolled on to his front and pushed himself to his knees. He was sore all over, but there were no sharp pains to suggest that he had broken anything. He moved his head, left and right, opening his eyes as wide as they would go. There was a thin line of light to his left, about three feet long, running along the floor. He crawled towards it. There was a fainter line running up at an angle to the horizontal line. It was a door. He stood up and ran his hands over it. It was rough wood. There was no keyhole and he couldn't feel any hinges.

He walked to the left, keeping his fingertips on the wall. The surface didn't feel like stone, it had a more man-made texture, like concrete or brick. There was less than three feet of wall before there was a corner. The second wall was just ten feet long. The wall opposite the door was nine feet long. Then another ten-foot wall. Then three feet to the door. His cell was nine feet wide and ten feet long. Ninety square feet. Slightly smaller than the average United Kingdom prison cell. But this was no cushy British prison cell with television, in-cell plumbing and a choice of nutritious meals. This was Pakistan and his captors were in all likelihood the Taliban or al-Qaeda. He reached up but couldn't touch the ceiling. He jumped but it was still out of reach. So the cell was at least ten feet high.

He knew there was no point in calling out. His captors knew where he was, they'd get to him when they were ready. He took a deep breath and exhaled slowly. And when they did get to him, it was pretty much guaranteed not to be a pleasant experience. He sat down with his back to the wall facing the door and drew his knees up to his chest. All he could do now was wait.

Charlotte Button didn't get up when Jeremy Willoughby-Brown was shown into her office. She was determined not to lose her temper with the MI6 man again, but that didn't mean she was going to show him anything other than polite contempt. She waved him to a chair and he sat down before carefully adjusting the creases of his made-to-measure trousers, avoiding eye contact with her. "I really can't tell you how sorry I am about all this, Charlotte," he said.

Button bit back the sarcastic comment she wanted to make and waited for him to continue. When she didn't say anything, he looked up and she saw the confusion in his eyes. He'd obviously expected her to bite his head off. "Taz has had a more in-depth briefing from the Pakistani military and I'm afraid it's not good news," he said. He paused, expecting her to say something, but she just nodded for him to continue. He took a deep breath, like a police officer on the doorstep about to break the worst possible news. "Sixteen SSG men were killed including three of the officers on the operation, a colonel and two captains. Four were injured. Two of the injured were taken prisoner." He took a deep breath. "Shepherd was captured."

"Was he injured?"

"Stunned by an explosion. An RPG, I gather. One of the snipers saw it happen. The warhead went off and . . ." He shrugged.

"An RPG?" said Button, her hand flying up to her mouth involuntarily. "He was hit by an RPG?"

"The sniper said it was behind him, and that he was some distance away. He had on an armoured vest and a Kevlar helmet, he's probably OK."

"Probably? I want more than probably."

Willoughby-Brown put up his hands. "According to the sniper, Shepherd went down but a group of the bad guys pounced on him and dragged him away. He didn't seem to be bleeding. Then the sniper left the area. He and the survivors made it back to the helicopters. They're back in Cherat now."

Button rubbed the bridge of her nose. She could feel a headache coming on. "What the hell happened?" she asked quietly.

216

"They were getting ready to go in as planned, through the doors, front and back. The bad guys seemed to have been ready and they tossed out grenades. There were armed men on the upper floor who started shooting. There were a lot of casualties but Shepherd and the colonel went ahead and blew a set of doors and went charging in. It was all very Butch and Sundance, apparently." He averted his eyes as Button glared at him.

"So they knew they were coming."

"Possibly. Or they could have just been well prepared."

"That wasn't a question, Jeremy. They had to have known. Grenades. RPGs. They were ready for a war."

"It's the Taliban, Charlotte. They have weapons on tap."

"The Pakistanis must have done a recce, surely."

"One would assume so, yes."

"So they would presumably have known if the RPGs were on site."

Willoughby-Brown sighed. "I wasn't there, Charlotte. I'm getting my details second-hand."

"As am I," said Button. "You know when the Americans took out Bin Laden, they didn't have a single casualty? And that's despite crashing one of their helicopters. They stormed the compound in Abbottabad and didn't take a single shot."

"That was the middle of the night."

"So the Pakistanis go in a few hours later than that and they find themselves in a full-on firefight. This wasn't a few goat herders with guns, Jeremy. This was a battle and a highly trained Pakistani special forces assault group came off worst. How could have that happened?"

Willoughby-Brown shifted uncomfortably in his seat. "I'm not sure what you want me to say, Charlotte," he said. "It was a Pakistani operation. I'm not privy to the ins and outs."

She looked at him coldly. "Were you privy to Akram Al-Farouq, by any chance?" she said quietly.

Willoughby-Brown frowned. "What?"

"You know who Akram Al-Farouq is?"

"I wasn't born yesterday. Of course I do."

"And you didn't know he was there, with Raj?"

Willoughby-Brown's frown deepened. "I did not. And if you don't mind me asking, how do you know?"

"I got it from the horse's mouth."

"The ISI is sharing intel with Five?"

"Shepherd called me. He had been briefed that Akram Al-Farouq was there. The impression Shepherd had was that Al-Farouq had become the focus of the mission and that Raj was secondary."

Willoughby-Brown frowned. "This is the first I've heard of this, Charlotte. Trust me."

Button was tempted to tell Willoughby-Brown that she trusted him about as far as she could throw him but she just smiled. "I'm assuming the Pakistanis have been playing their cards close to their chest," she said.

"It would explain how they were so quick to locate Raj once he had been moved from the training camp," said Willoughby-Brown. "If they had Al-Farouq under surveillance, and if he went to interrogate Raj . . ." He left the thought unfinished.

"How good are Taz's contacts within ISI?" asked Button.

"Quite good," said Willoughby-Brown. "Officially and unofficially. He's had several high-level briefings and I think he has at least one unofficial contact."

"You think?"

"He talked about meeting a contact socially. He plays squash at quite a high level and he plays with an ISI guy. Why are you asking?"

"I need to see any intel they have on Al-Farouq."

"I assume there will be mountains of it," said Willoughby-Brown.

"The latest intel, obviously. How they located him, how they knew he was interrogating Raj, where they think he might be now."

"I think if they knew where he was now they'd probably be going in with guns blazing."

Button flashed him a tight smile. "I'd like that intel today," she said.

"They're five hours ahead of us."

"Then the sooner you get on to Taz, the better," said Button. "I also want to know why they didn't know what they were going to be up against. If they had surveillance, they should have known about the RPGs."

Willoughby-Brown stood up. "I'll get back to you as soon as I have it," he said.

Button waved for him to sit down. "There's something else," she said. "I need intel on anyone else who was being trained with Raj."

"I'm not sure I can share that with you," said Willoughby-Brown.

Button raised an eyebrow. "I'd be very careful about playing secret squirrel with me, Jeremy. I'm really not in the mood."

"I'll have to clear it first."

"Then clear it. Or if you'd prefer I could go through the Joint Intelligence Committee?"

Willoughby-Brown swallowed nervously. "There's no need for that, Charlotte."

"It might speed things up," said Button. "Of course, it would raise questions about the way this has been handled thus far. In particular why Five wasn't informed of the ongoing investigation. Home-grown terrorists would seem to fall more within Five's remit than yours." She smiled sweetly but her eyes were as hard as ice.

"I already explained, we were looking at overseas terrorist funding."

"Yes, you did. But once your investigation focused on British soil, you really should have started sharing your intel with us."

"That's a grey area, Charlotte."

She shook her head. "No, it's not in the least bit grey. You were running a British agent on British soil, and you can talk about overseas terrorist funding until the cows come home but what you did was outside your remit and you know it was." He opened his mouth to speak but she raised a hand to silence him. "Look, Jeremy, I'm not overkeen on involving the JIC, I just want to get Shepherd and Raj home. I need your help to do that and I'm asking for that help. If you won't help me, then this will move to a whole new level."

Willoughby-Brown nodded enthusiastically. "Charlotte, I will do whatever it takes. Believe me. I'll chase up Taz and I'll send over all the intel we have."

"Specifically I want to know who was out there with him."

"The one guy we know for sure is called Naseem Naeem," he said. "He flew out with Raj. They met in the mosque and were recruited together."

"What about the rest?"

"We were monitoring flights and we have a list of possibilities but we were waiting for Raj to get back."

"What about the location of the training camp? What intel do you have on that?"

"None, I'm afraid."

"That's not good."

"Again, we were depending on Raj for that information. But to be honest, the training can be done pretty much anywhere. I doubt they use one place for long. But the training camp was probably not too far away from the fort."

Button nodded. He was probably right. "Then I'm going to need the location of yesterday's attack."

"Taz can get that, no problem. What's your game plan?"

"I don't have one, yet," said Button. "But I'm working on it."

She waited until Willoughby-Brown had left before she picked up her Filofax and flicked through the address book. The number she wanted was written under the "Z" section. She had reversed the number and started it with two random digits. A simple code but pretty much unbreakable. She tapped out the number on her mobile. It was an American number but her call went straight through to voicemail with no introductory message. She left her name and number and ended the call. She leant back in her chair and stared at the framed map of the world on the wall opposite her. All she could do now was wait, and hope that the man she needed still checked his messages.

Shepherd stood up and stretched. He had lost all track of time and didn't even know whether it was day or night outside. It was cold, cold enough for him to be shivering, so he assumed it was night. The strip of light still outlined the door but that could have been from a lamp. From time to time he had pressed his ear against the door but heard nothing.

They hadn't fed him or given him water. If they continued to deprive him of water, he'd be dead within three or four days. He doubted that would happen, though. This wasn't about killing him. If they wanted to kill him they'd have slit his throat or put a bullet in his head. This was about breaking him. That was why they had taken his clothes before locking him up; it was the psychological phase of interrogation. They wanted him scared. Then they would move on to the physical phase. They would hurt him. Again, they wouldn't hurt him badly enough to kill him. But they would hurt him a lot. There was nothing Shepherd could do to change

222

what was going to happen. All he could do was prepare for it and get through it as best he could.

His legs and shoulders were still aching from the explosion but he didn't seem to have any broken bones or open wounds. Considering he'd been only twenty metres or so from an exploding RPG warhead, he seemed to have got off lightly. He wanted to exercise but he knew that more than anything he needed to conserve energy. Exercising would burn calories and make him sweat much-needed water out of his system. He rolled his shoulders and flicked his hands back and forth, then touched his toes a dozen times, breathing slowly and evenly. He had to stay focused if he was to get through what lay ahead. All he could do was to take it hour by hour, day by day. He sat down again and drew his knees up to his chest. He closed his eyes. He pictured himself back in Hereford, pulling on his army boots and heading out for a ten-kilometre run in the countryside, one of his favourite routes, out over the fields and through a wooded copse. He knew every inch of the route and he ran it in his mind in real time, step by step.

Willoughby-Brown cradled his Heckler & Koch G36 as he surveyed the ruined building to his left. He saw movement in one of the windows and brought his telescope sight up in a smooth motion, waited until the head was dead centre and fired a short burst. The head exploded in a shower of red and the body went down. "Nice shooting, Warlock," said the voice in his headset. Before Willoughby-Brown had the chance to reply a second figure appeared at the window. He let go another short burst and the man's face exploded.

"Got you, you bastard," Willoughby-Brown murmured under his breath. He turned and ran along the path, pulling the pin from a grenade and tossing it to his right where he was sure a gunman was hiding behind a burnt-out car. He ran faster and the car exploded behind him. Ahead of him the path branched left and right. "Left, left, left," he said.

"Roger that," said the voice in his headset. It belonged to the soldier just behind him, a Russian banker who was based in Paris. He used the name Putin, which Willoughby-Brown figured was supposed to be funny. The two others in his team were a student at Edinburgh University and a guy who claimed to be in Texas but who sounded like a Geordie.

A jeep screeched around the corner, full of gun-toting terrorists. Willoughby-Brown raked the vehicle with gunfire. The terrorists screamed and died, the jeep overturned and burst into flames. Putin raced forward, firing his M249 from the hip. "Die, you motherfuckers!" he shouted in Willoughby-Brown's headset.

"They're dead, Putin," said Willoughby-Brown. "And you're wasting ammo. We've a way to go yet."

"Aye, someone needs to put a bullet in the Ruskie," growled the Texan. He was off to Willoughby-Brown's left, carrying a Barrett .50-cal sniping rifle. He was the unit's sniper and using the call sign "Cowboy". From the way his accent was thickening, Willoughby-Brown figured he was drinking, and drinking heavily.

He heard a ringing sound and frowned, wondering where it was coming from. "What was that?" he said, into his microphone.

"What's what?" growled Cowboy in his ear.

The ringing sound was repeated and Willoughby-Brown realised it was his doorbell. He looked at his wristwatch. It was ten o'clock at night. He took off his headset, muted the sound of his television and pushed himself up out of his chair. He walked over to the window and pulled back the curtain a fraction. Whoever had rung the bell was standing at the far side of the door, out of view.

He walked into the hall and tiptoed to the front door, his heart still racing from the Xbox game. He bent down and looked through the security peephole. There didn't seem to be anyone there. He put the security chain on and opened the door. Charlotte Button was standing to the side wearing a black overcoat with the collar turned up.

"Charlotte?" he said, unable to conceal his surprise. "How did you know . . ." He left the sentence unfinished. She worked for MI5, she knew where everyone lived. He closed the door, fumbled with the security chain, and opened it again.

"I've not called at a bad time, I hope," she said.

"I was just watching television," he said. He looked down the path behind her, then up and down the road.

"Don't worry, Jeremy. I came alone."

"So who's that in the black Lexus?"

"My driver."

Willoughby-Brown looked back at her, frowning. She was holding something in her pocket, something quite large. "Please don't tell me that's a gun," he said.

She took her hand out, holding a bottle of Pinot Grigio. "We need to talk," she said. "I figure we can handle this in one of two ways. Either we sit down, open the bottle and talk like civilised adults." She hefted the bottle in her hand. "Or I beat you to a pulp with it."

Willoughby-Brown chuckled and held the door open for her. "I'll get some glasses."

Shepherd was lying on his side, trying to sleep. It was warm in the cell, but not stiflingly hot, so he figured it was either late morning or early evening. His internal body clock was no help as it had been disrupted by the flight from London to Islamabad. His mouth was bone dry and his breath rasped in his throat. The stone floor was unyielding and he was using his left arm as a pillow. Sleep wouldn't come, though he did drift in and out of consciousness. How long had he been in the cell? One day? Two? Three? He had no way of knowing. Two maybe. He hadn't needed to go to the toilet. His body was shutting down, conserving water in every way it could.

He tried to focus on home. On Liam. On Katra. He pictured Katra standing at the kitchen sink, but then she was cooking, frying him steak and onions, and then the hunger pangs kicked in, so painful that they made him grunt out loud. He forced himself to ignore the hunger. They'd feed him eventually, he was sure of that. And they'd give him water. It was just a matter of time. There was a structure to what was happening. Isolation. Darkness. Hunger. Thirst. Soon there would be sleep deprivation. Then beatings. And torture. Shepherd closed his eyes and tried to think happier thoughts; it was best not to dwell on what lay ahead.

Willoughby-Brown gave the corkscrew a twist and a tug and the cork slid out with a whisper. He poured wine into two glasses, handed one to Button and sat down. He had pushed his Xbox, controller and headset under the coffee table and switched off the television. She commandeered his favourite chair, the winged leather one that he sat on while he played video games, so he sat down on the black leather sofa that faced the fireplace. "What is it you want, Charlotte?" he asked. "I gave you the intel."

"I want my man back from Pakistan, alive and in one piece."

"Anything I can do, I will do, you have my word on that."

"Good. I'm going to hold you to that. The information you sent through to me today, it's been redacted."

"Of course. It's an ongoing investigation, we have agents at risk."

"I'm not a *Guardian* reporter, Jeremy. Anything you give me will stay in-house."

"I was following instructions, Charlotte."

"Not good enough," she said. "And you know it's not good enough. Listen, Jeremy, and listen well. I am not going to let my man suffer a second longer than is

227

necessary. I will do whatever it takes to get him out. Do you hear what I'm saying? Whatever it takes."

Willoughby-Brown nodded. "I do understand."

"I want all the data you have. All of it. I'll decide what's relevant or not."

"I can't do that, Charlotte."

"Yes you can. You just have to do it unofficially. You download the data to a thumb drive and you give that thumb drive to me."

"Have you any idea how much trouble I would be in if I was found out?"

"One, you won't be found out. You have my word on that. And two, do you have any idea how much trouble you will be in if you don't help me?"

Willoughby-Brown's eyes narrowed. "That sounds like a threat, Charlotte," he said quietly.

"Sounds like a threat?" She laughed harshly. "Jeremy, if I don't get Spider back in one piece I am going to lash out in ways that I've never lashed out in before. If I was looking for anyone to blame for this present situation I'd be looking at you. That's not a threat, that's a promise."

Willoughby-Brown swallowed and almost gagged. He took a quick drink of wine.

"I want the data, and I want it first thing tomorrow. I want everything you have on the mosque in Bradford and the Brits who you know have been over to Pakistan for training."

Willoughby-Brown nodded slowly. "OK," he said.

"And I need you to get Tazam Gill back to London so that I can talk to him."

Willoughby-Brown frowned. "He's of more use in Pakistan. He speaks the language, he can keep track of what's happening."

"Let's face it, Jeremy, he hasn't done a great job so far, has he? Raj's cover was blown on his watch and now they've got Shepherd, too."

"You can't blame him for that," said Willoughby-Brown.

"I need to talk to him."

"I don't want a witch-hunt, Charlotte."

"I left my pitchfork and torch at home," she said. "I want to sit down and talk to him. Considering what's happened, I don't think that's an unreasonable request. And that's what it is, Jeremy. A request. From me to you."

"And if I refuse your request?"

"Then, as I said, I'll take that bottle and smash it over your head." She grinned. "Not literally, of course. But that's what it'll feel like after I've finished with you. Two major operations have gone bad and you're the common factor. At the moment you appear to be flying below the radar but it wouldn't take much to change that." She sipped her wine as she let her words sink in.

"I haven't done anything wrong, Charlotte. If there's been a slip-up, it wasn't me. I wasn't even in-country."

"No, you weren't. But I'll tell you this, Jeremy. If it had been my operation, I would have been there, on the spot."

Willoughby-Brown fumbled for his pack of cigars and lit one. He blew smoke before speaking. "OK, I'll bring him back."

"Tomorrow?"

He nodded. "Tomorrow."

She smiled sweetly and raised her glass to him. "Thank you so much."

Lex Harper settled into a steady rhythm as he pounded along the walkway between the road and the beach. It was an hour after dawn had broken, his favourite time to run in Pattaya. The air was as close to cool as it ever got in the seaside resort, and the pavement was pretty much deserted, allowing him to run at a fair pace. A few foreigners were sleeping in the shade of palm trees, too drunk to make their way back to their cheap hotels, but the jet ski operators and stallholders had yet to arrive and there were none of the hookers and transsexuals who usually touted for business along the strip.

Harper ran every morning before breakfast; three miles to the start of Walking Street, the city's main entertainment area, then three miles back to his apartment, a three-bedroom penthouse with a wraparound balcony that offered stunning views of the bay. He felt a vibration in the denim hip pack around his waist. Harper always had the hip pack on him, no matter what the time of day. It contained one of his many phones, an Irish passport in the name of Brendan O'Brien, two credit cards in the same name and fifty thousand baht in cash. The pack, and the heavy gold chain he always wore around his neck, meant that he could leave the country at a moment's notice, either through the airport or overland to Laos or Cambodia if necessary.

He had a larger bug-out bag under the bed in his apartment and another in the back of his SUV, but the essentials were in the hip pack. He loved living in Thailand, the Land of Smiles, but he had made it a rule never to be so enamoured with a place that he couldn't leave at a moment's notice. He jogged on the spot and took out his phone. The text message was from a UK number that he didn't recognise. "YOU HAVE MAIL".

Harper grinned, slid the phone back into the hip pack, and started running again. He ran at full pelt and he was drenched with sweat when he reached the point where the beach road became Walking Street, home to many of Pattaya's raunchier go-go bars. At night it was neon lit and packed with drunks, sex tourists and Asian tour groups being shouted at by scantily dressed girls and overenthusiastic touts offering cheap booze and sex shows. It was a much gloomier place during the day, the sunlight exposing the shabby shopfronts, dubious electrical wiring and potholed pavements. Harper picked up a bottle of freshly squeezed orange juice from a roadside stall and drank it as he walked along a side street to a beauty parlour that doubled as an internet café. It was open twenty-four hours a day, and even at that early hour there were customers, a girl having her hair washed and two girls sitting together at one of the computer terminals. The bargirls were in the process of composing an email to one of their sponsors, a request for money to pay for an operation for an aged relative who in all likelihood didn't exist.

The lady who ran the shop was in her late fifties. Khun Bee's nut-brown face was wrinkled and her hair was starting to grey but she still had a fit body that suggested she had once made her living dancing around a chrome pole. He ordered a coffee and paid her for half an hour's internet usage before sitting down at the terminal farthest away from the two bargirls. He took a swig of orange juice and logged on to Yahoo Mail. He had committed the email address and password to memory though he had never used the account to send an email. Only he and Charlotte Button had the password and they used the Drafts folder to communicate. It was a technique first developed by al-Qaeda to ensure instantaneous communication that was pretty much surveillance free. Between them the National Security Agency in the States and GCHQ in the UK could eavesdrop on every phone call made and read every email sent, but using the Drafts folder trick meant that the email was never actually transmitted and so never became visible.

There was a single message in the folder. It had been placed there an hour earlier. "I NEED YOU IN LONDON. NOW". Harper deleted the message just as Khun Bee arrived at his elbow with his coffee. He flashed her a beaming smile. "I'll take that to go," he said.

The door was flung open and Shepherd flinched at the sudden bright light. He rolled over and sat up with his back against the wall, his hand up to protect his eyes from the glare. He heard the scuffle of sandals on concrete. He tensed, not sure what was coming. He squinted up at the light. There was a figure there, bearded and scarfed. There was a blur of movement and Shepherd flinched and then he was doused in water. He heard a voice say something in Arabic or Pashto and then the door slammed shut and he was in darkness again. Water was running down his face and chest and he used his hands to gather as much of it as he could, licking the precious liquid off his fingers. He dropped to the ground and ran his fingers along the floor. There was a small dip in the concrete and water had pooled there. He lowered his head and lapped at the liquid. It tasted foul but he forced himself to gulp it down. The fact that they had given him water was a good sign. It meant they wanted to keep him alive, for the time being at least.

Charlotte Button was sitting in her office studying a report on the Bradford mosque where Raj had been recruited for the overseas training when her mobile rang. It was Willoughby-Brown. "I'm reluctant to send this around by courier," he said.

"Do you want to meet?"

"I don't think I have much choice," he said.

Button looked at her watch. It was ten o'clock and she was due to attend a JIC meeting at 10.30. "How about lunch? On me?"

"I could do lunch," he said.

"You'll have to come across the river, I'm afraid."

"Not a problem."

"There's a Pizza Express down the road," she said. "Cheap and cheerful. Shall we say twelve?"

"I'll be there."

"Isn't there something you need to tell me?" asked Button.

"Of course," said Willoughby-Brown. "I'm really sorry about all this, Charlotte."

"That's not what I meant," said Button. "I'm talking about Taz."

"Ah, right, yes, sorry. He's arriving this evening. I'll give you the flight details when I see you."

Button shook her head and ended the call. Willoughby-Brown was an idiot but until she had the data files she had to be reasonably civil to him.

Harper smiled as he handed the passport to the overweight Garda officer. "How's it going?" he said.

The officer scowled. He clearly hadn't joined the Irish police force to end up checking passports at Dublin Airport. He took the British passport from Harper and slowly flicked through it, examining every page even though most of them were blank. The picture and the date of birth were Harper's, but the name wasn't. For the purposes of entering Ireland he was Nicholas Cohen. Harper had paid five thousand pounds for the passport to a guy in Pattaya who swore that it was genuine and that the details on the biometric chip were in the Home Office computer database. Harper could see that the passport was good, but there was no way of knowing what would happen when it was checked against the Home Office's Warning Index, which immigration officers relied on to weed out suspected terrorists, criminals and paedophiles, so instead of flying direct to London he had caught a KLM flight to Amsterdam and from there flew to Dublin. The guards who carried out the duties of immigration officers did nothing more than give the passports a visual once-over, they didn't check the details on biometric chip or run them against any databases. As a EU citizen Harper could enter Ireland without hindrance and then all he had to do was to take a taxi from Dublin Airport up to Belfast. Belfast Airport was in the UK so the only check made was that the name in the passport matched the name on his ticket. Harper always laughed when he heard British immigration officials talking about tightening up border controls as in his experience every man and his dog knew about the Irish back-door route.

The Garda reached the final page of the passport, looked at the photograph then at Harper. Harper smiled. The Garda handed the passport back and waved for Harper to move on. "You have a nice day," said Harper, though that clearly wasn't on the cards.

Charlotte Button sat back in her chair. It was ergonomically designed to make sitting for long periods as comfortable as possible, but already her back and neck were aching. Lunch with Willoughby-Brown hadn't helped the tension in her neck muscles and more than once she had had to fight to resist the urge to throw her wine in his face. He had given her the thumb drive in a folded copy of the *Daily Telegraph* and she'd asked him for a verbal briefing while they ate their pizza.

According to Willoughby-Brown, the operation had been all about Akram Al-Farouq, at least in the early stages. Al-Farouq was an al-Qaeda paymaster and a legitimate MI6 target. Somewhere along the line, Willoughby-Brown didn't seem to be exactly sure when, the name of a Bangladeshi-born British imam based in a Bradford mosque had surfaced. Mohammed Ullah was the sort of Muslim cleric the British media adored, a moderate who believed that British Muslims should be building bridges with other religions in the country. He was often quoted in the *Guardian* and the *Independent* and was a frequent guest on BBC radio panel shows such as *Any Questions?*, where his moderate views were loudly applauded. But according to the MI6 investigation, Ullah was in fact a hardline fundamentalist who was helping funnel al-Qaeda money to home-grown jihadists. Unlike many of the hardline clerics who burned poppies and called for British soldiers to be killed and demanded that sharia law be instated in the UK, Ullah just smiled and told the British what they wanted to hear. He was all sweetness and light, and was even rumoured to be in line for an MBE or CBE in the next New Year's Honours list. According to Willoughby-Brown, Ullah was playing a very clever long game, and the British were falling for it hook, line and sinker. The only way to test that theory for sure was to send in an undercover agent, and Raj had been selected for the task. Knowing how successful he'd been when working for MI5, Six had appealed to Raj's patriotic instincts and he'd agreed to help. He'd been briefed, given a watertight legend, and sent to Bradford where he'd begun to attend Ullah's mosque. Raj had portrayed himself as an angry young British-born Asian Muslim and had started hanging out with other young extremists. After six months he had been invited to evening sessions with the imam, supposedly for extra Qur'an studies, but it soon became clear that the meetings had a much more sinister purpose. Raj — or Rafiq, as he had been known in Bradford — was groomed to become a jihadist and eventually offered the opportunity to travel to Pakistan for specialised training.

What Button didn't understand — and what Willoughby-Brown seemed to be at a loss to explain — was why details of the Ullah investigation hadn't been passed on to MI5. Or why the decision had been made to run an MI6 undercover agent on British soil. And there was no justifiable reason for MI5 not being informed that one of their former agents had been reactivated. She had the feeling it was because Willoughby-Brown had been determined to keep any credit for himself, but if that were true he was a liability and deserved to be out of a job. He wouldn't admit that, though, he'd insisted that the decision to go it alone had been taken at a higher level.

Button sighed and massaged the back of her neck with her fingertips. The key to finding Shepherd and Raj was to locate Akram Al-Farouq, and the key to finding Akram Al-Farouq was to get Mohammed Ullah to talk. And that wasn't going to be easy, not when he was a British citizen with the full protection of the 1998 Human Rights Act.

Her mobile beeped to let her know that she had received a message. She didn't recognise the number but the message made her smile. "Bloody London weather. Same place as before? 4pm?"

She sent a text message back. "Sounds good to me."

There was a cold wind blowing along the Thames, and Charlotte Button turned up the collar of her coat before checking her watch for the umpteenth time. He was late. She looked across the river at the London Eye, the 135-metre tall Ferris wheel between Westminster Bridge and Hungerford Bridge.

"You ever been on it?" said a voice behind her.

The man she had been waiting for had come up behind her without her noticing, and from the grin on his face he was obviously taking pleasure in the fact. His name was Richard Yokely; former CIA, former NSA, former DIA, the intelligence agent had accumulated enough initials on his CV to play a half-decent game of Scrabble.

Button smiled and held out her gloved hand. "Richard, thank you for coming."

The American smiled. "How could I refuse a summons from my favourite MI5 operative?" he said, with a slight drawl that suggested a Southern plantation and iced tea on a terrace. He was in his very early fifties with short grey hair and thin lips. He was wearing a long black coat over a dark blue blazer, a crisp white shirt and a blue tie with pale yellow stripes. His shoes were tasselled, the black leather gleaming as if they had been freshly polished. He had a chunky gold ring on his right ring finger and an even chunkier Breitling watch on his left wrist.

"Not so much a summons as a cry for help," she said.

His smile widened. "Charlotte, my dear, as you are very well aware, I owe you one. So ask and you shall receive."

"That's lovely to hear, Richard. I hope you'll still be so generous when you've heard what my problem is."

"Tell me as we walk," said the American. "I need the exercise, I'm told."

They walked along the Thames, heading east, as Button ran the situation past him. Yokely nodded as he listened, and his jaw tensed when she told him what had happened to Shepherd. When she finished she put a hand on his elbow. "I need your help, Richard."

"You sure do," he said. He exhaled through pursed lips. "You have yourself one hell of a situation. Why did you ever agree to let the Paks handle it in the first place?"

"It's their territory," said Button. "The way you handled the Bin Laden assassination caused a lot of ill feeling, so there was no chance they'd ever allow us to send in the SAS. And they had the intel on where Raj was being held."

"This Raj, he was moved before the attack, was he?"

Button shrugged. "We don't know. It might have been a set-up, and they knew the attack was coming. Or it might just have been that they were well prepared."

Yokely nodded. "What's the position now with the Paks?"

"They've battened down the hatches. Huge embarrassment all around, obviously."

"But they're looking for Shepherd, presumably."

"That's what they say, yes."

Yokely looked pained. "Their intelligence services and their military are among the most corrupt in the world, you know that? That's why they were cut out of the Operation Neptune loop."

"We can't afford to get on their wrong side," said Button. "They're in the Commonwealth. So officially we can't do anything without their approval and cooperation."

"Well, you've seen how far that's got you. The thing is, the only way for anyone to get promoted in politics or the military is to embrace the corruption. The same goes for the police and the intelligence agencies. Anyone who rocks the boat ends up out on their ear, or dead. You're not going to get anywhere if you involve the Pakistani authorities at any level."

Button smiled tightly. "I'm all too well aware of the position I'm in, Richard. And I'm equally aware of how few options I have. MI6 screwed up in the first place by allowing Raj to be captured. Then they compounded it by letting Spider fall into their clutches."

"So no more Mister Nice Guy, is that what you're telling me?"

"I want my man back, safe and sound. And I want Raj back, too. I'm going to call in every single marker I have to make sure that happens."

Yokely nodded slowly. "As I said, I owe you and I pay my debts. But there's no way I can help you if the Paks are involved."

"They won't be," said Button.

"Off the books?"

"Totally."

"No official sanction, is that what you're saying?"

"You know exactly what I'm saying, Richard."

Yokely started walking again and Button kept pace with him. "You're asking a lot," said Yokely. "But you know that."

"I can offer you a carrot," said Button. "If one's needed."

"A carrot would be good, considering the resources that I'll be using."

Button glanced over her shoulder to check that no one was within earshot. "The intel we have is that Akram Al-Farouq was involved in Raj's interrogation."

Yokely flashed her a sideways look. "That would be the same source that led to the botched rescue mission, of course."

"The intel seems good," said Button. "They had an inside man and he reported that Al-Farouq was at the compound. Is that a good enough carrot for you?"

"It's one hell of a carrot," said Yokely. "One of the biggest darn carrots there is. He's up near the top of our ten most-wanted."

"A big enough carrot for you to get involved?"

"I'll need to see the intel," said Yokely.

"I'd rather not," said Button. "I wouldn't want it traced back to me."

"I protect my sources, Charlotte," said Yokely. "And with respect I probably do a better job than you do." He smiled tightly. "No offence."

"None taken," said Button. She reached into her inside pocket and slid out a single sheet of paper, folded in half and half again. She passed it to him. Yokely studied it for several seconds, then put it in his jacket pocket.

He saw the look of concern on her face. "Relax," he said. "I promise to swallow it when I'm done." He patted the pocket. "There is a problem, of course. A big one. We don't know where Spider is, right?"

"Not at the moment. But I'm working on it."

"Charlotte, we're talking needle in a haystack. Remember how long it took us to find Bin Laden? And that was using all the resources we have in the US of A. No offence, but all you have is GCHQ and most of their data comes from us."

"Why is it that whenever you say 'no offence' you always go on to be offensive?"

Yokely chuckled. "I don't mean to be, it's just that sometimes the truth hurts."

"Tell me, what's the situation re surveillance drones and spy satellites in that part of the world?"

"North-west Pakistan? There's a watching brief, obviously. The problem is that the bad guys know what satellites we have and when they pass over. They just go inside and wait until they've gone. We have movable sats, obviously, so if there's something in particular we need to look at, that can be arranged."

"And drones?"

"Drones are terrific if the subject doesn't know we want to look at him. But if it's a training camp, they'll post lookouts. Drones are small but a keen pair of eyes

242

and a pair of binoculars is all you need. What is it you need?"

"Ideally I want to know who was out at the training camp, but as I can't even get a location for it I'm going to have to give up on that. But I do have a location for where they were keeping Raj. It would be helpful if you'd had eyes on it at any point."

"Give me the coordinates and I'll run it by the NSA."

"Would you? That would be super." She reached into her pocket and took out a small slip of paper. She gave it to him and he glanced at it, nodded, and slipped it into his wallet. "In return, how about I tell you something you probably don't know?"

"Go for it."

"The intel for Operation Neptune Spear came from us."

"Get the hell out of here," said Yokely.

"Specifically, from Raj."

Yokely stopped in his tracks. "Are you serious?"

"It's not something I'd joke about, Richard. Raj penetrated an al-Qaeda cell in the UK and as part of that he went to Pakistan. He met Bin Laden in the compound in Abbottabad. He told us and we passed the intel on to the CIA."

"They kept very quiet about that," said Yokely.

"We didn't want the world knowing that we had an agent in place. And we didn't want the credit because if it was known that a Brit had been involved, there could have been repercussions."

"What about al-Qaeda? Did they ever know that they had been betrayed from within?"

"The CIA released a plethora of disinformation but unfortunately it wasn't enough. Yes, they found out what Raj had done. And his colleague, another British Pakistani, Harveer Malik. Harvey, we called him."

"And where is this Malik now?"

"Running a restaurant. Under a new name. He's quite safe."

Yokely nodded thoughtfully. "And who had the bright idea of sending Raj undercover after he'd been blown?"

"Six thought he had value," said Button. "They moved him to Bradford, gave him a new identity and had him penetrate a group of hardliners in a mosque there. He was asked to go for specialist training in Pakistan."

"What sort of specialist training?"

"Ground-to-air missiles. MANPADS."

"Ah," said Yokely. "Difficult to say no to that, I suppose."

"Six helped change his appearance. Gave him a couple of scars, changed his nose, had him grow a beard."

Yokely grinned. "False moustache?"

"His cover was good, Richard. I wouldn't have used Raj, but Six felt it was worth the risk."

"I know, hindsight is a wonderful thing. But sending a man back undercover after he'd already been blown . . ." He shrugged.

"You're preaching to the converted, Richard. I've already made my feelings known." She sighed. "The last thing Raj said to me was that he was going to go back to being a doctor and that he'd leave the fight against terrorism to me." She smiled at the memory. "I tried to get him to join MI5 but deep down I thought he was doing the right thing. And he'd done his bit."

"So Six went behind your back?"

Button nodded.

"Do you think his captors know about the Bin Laden connection?"

"There's no way I could know that," she said. "But I hope not."

Yokely wrinkled his nose. "They'll be torturing him, Charlotte. If he talks . . ." He left the sentence unfinished.

"I know," she said. "There's something else you don't know. Spider was also on Operation Neptune."

Yokely's jaw dropped. He opened his mouth to speak but then words failed him and he clamped his jaw shut.

"He was there as an observer as quid pro quo for the intel."

"I'm stunned," said Yokely. "It's not often I'm lost for words."

"Very few people know," said Button.

"Well, let's hope his captors don't find out," said Yokely.

"I don't think things can get much worse, can they?" asked Button.

"If they find out he was involved in the assassination of the Sheikh, God only knows what they'll do to him," said Yokely. "There are worse ways to die than beheading, Charlotte. Much worse." He shuddered and started walking again. "So how do we handle this?" he asked.

"You want Akram Al-Farouq. And this is a way of getting him alive. If I can find out where they are, you can send in a SEAL team or Delta Force or whoever, grab Akram Al-Farouq and rescue Spider and Raj."

"You make it sound so simple, Charlotte. If it's that easy, why not send in the SAS?"

"Because we'd have to tell the Pakistanis. You have a track record of keeping them out of the loop."

Yokely rubbed his chin. "Where was this attack, exactly?"

"Waziristan. A place called Parachinar. Just over the border with Afghanistan. We're thinking that they won't have moved them too far, they'll still be somewhere in that area."

"Rough terrain," said Yokely.

"Perfect for special forces."

"And jihadists."

"The advantage is that it's far from prying eyes. Nowhere near as populated as Abbottabad and virtually no Pakistani military presence. It's the badlands."

"I know it well," said Yokely. He nodded. "OK, it's close enough to the border for a team to get in and out without setting alarm bells ringing. And that whole region is a grey area as to who exactly controls it. Pakistan has claimed it since 1947 but it could just as easily be claimed to be Afghan territory. And Akram

Al-Farouq is a high-value target. You get me a location and we'll see what we can do."

"Can you be ready to go at short notice?"

"I'll get the wheels in motion. But tell me, Charlotte, how on earth do you expect to find them? It took us years to locate Bin Laden."

Button smiled. "I have a plan," she said.

Yokely grinned. "Off the books?"

"I'm afraid so," she said.

Shepherd heard footsteps outside his door and then the sound of two bolts being drawn back. He was sitting with his back to the wall and he put up his hands to shield himself against the light. It was an electric light, he realised, a soft yellowish glow. There was a figure standing in the doorway, tall and wide shouldered wearing a floor-length dishdasha and a keffiyeh around his head. Shepherd braced himself for a dousing but this time there was no water. The man said something and then stepped to the side. Two men rushed into the cell. They were shorter than the man in the dishdasha and were wearing grey shalwar kameez. They were holding canes and began to scream at Shepherd. He got to his feet but he had been sitting for so long that his legs had gone numb and he stumbled backwards against the far wall of the cell.

The man nearest Shepherd lashed out with the cane and caught him on the upper thigh. Shepherd stepped forward, punched the man in the throat and felt the cartilage splinter and break. The second man raised his cane and took a step towards Shepherd but Shepherd was too quick for him, stepping to the side, grabbing the man's wrist with his left hand, moving in close and driving his elbow into the man's chin, knocking him out cold. Shepherd moved back as the man slumped to the ground, then he stepped over him and out into the corridor.

The man in the dishdasha was backing away, his hands fluttering in front of him. The corridor behind him seemed to be a dead end. Shepherd turned his back on him and moved in the other direction. There was a wooden door to his left, and another to his right, both with large bolts top and bottom.

"Rafiq?" shouted Shepherd at the top of his voice. "Rafiq? Are you here?" He wasn't sure how Raj would react to the sound of his cover name being shouted, he just hoped that he would recognise Shepherd's voice.

He took a couple of steps. Ahead of him the corridor branched left and right. There were no windows, the only light came from bare bulbs hanging from the concrete ceiling.

"Rafiq!" he shouted.

There was the sound of footsteps and three big men in dishdashas came around the corner, holding AK-47s. The corridor was narrow so they had to stay in single file, not that numbers mattered. He was unarmed and naked and while his unarmed combat skills were second to none, there wasn't much he could do against an AK-47.

Shepherd raised his hands. "Rafiq!" he yelled again.

"Yes! I'm here!" The voice was muffled and some distance away but Shepherd recognised it.

He took a step back, his hands still in the air. The men waved their AK-47s menacingly. Their fingers were inside the trigger guards but Shepherd knew they wouldn't shoot him, not deliberately anyway. "Easy, boys," he said. "I'm going back to my kennel like a good dog."

He kept his hands high as he walked backwards until he reached the door of his cell. The man in the dishdasha had gone inside to check on his injured colleagues. He was kneeling by the side of the man that Shepherd had hit in the throat. He wasn't dead but he would have trouble eating and breathing for a few days. The man in the dishdasha stood up, glaring at Shepherd with undisguised hatred. "I've been a naughty, naughty boy," said Shepherd.

The man sprang forward and slapped Shepherd across the face, hard enough to rattle his teeth. Shepherd tasted blood in his mouth and he hawked and spat bloody phlegm on to the floor.

The man screamed at Shepherd in what sounded like Arabic. Shepherd had opened his mouth to tell the man to go screw himself when the butt of an AK-47 smashed into the back of his head. He was unconscious before he hit the floor.

Charlotte Button scanned the faces of the people walking into the arrivals area, then at her wristwatch. Tazam Bashir's flight had landed an hour earlier. "Maybe the baggage is late," said Amar Singh. "It's never great at Terminal Three." Singh was in his early thirties and one of MI5's top technical experts. Button sighed. "I just hope they didn't give us the wrong flight. It wouldn't be the first time," she said.

"I checked the flight manifest; he was definitely on board," said Singh. He adjusted the cuffs of his immaculate white shirt. Singh was overdressed for the Terminal 3 arrivals area in his black Armani suit and gleaming Bally shoes. Button was wearing a long black coat and had her hands in her pockets. To her right was a line of taxi drivers and chauffeurs holding up signs with the names of their allotted passengers. Arrivals emerged from the doors to the customs area in clumps of a dozen or so. Button scanned their faces. An Air India flight had landed an hour earlier and the majority of the passengers coming through the doors were Asian, as were most of the friends and family names gathered to meet them in the arrivals area. Every now and then there were shrieks of joy, along with shouts and waves.

"There he is," said Button. Bashir was pulling a wheeled Samsonite suitcase and had a Nike holdall over one shoulder. He was wearing dark glasses and had his head down so clearly he wasn't expecting visitors. He was heading in the direction of the taxi stand and Button moved to intercept him.

"Taz?" she said.

He looked up, frowning.

"Tazam Bashir?"

"Yes. Do I know you?" He was wearing a purple Puffa jacket over a pale blue suit, and had loosened his tie.

"My name's Charlotte Button. I'm from Five. We're here to meet you."

Bashir looked at her, then at Singh, then back to her. "What's going on?"

"There's nothing to worry about, Taz, we just need to debrief you as a matter of some urgency."

"I don't work for you, Miss . . . I'm sorry, what was your name again?"

"Button. Charlotte Button. No, I know you don't work for me but I've spoken to Jeremy Willoughby-Brown and he's in the loop."

"He didn't say anything to me."

"It's all very short notice, I'm afraid. You'd probably already left for your flight."

"You won't mind if I call him, then?"

Button smiled sweetly. "Go ahead," she said.

Bashir put down his suitcase and took an iPhone from his jacket pocket. He switched it on, then walked away to make the call. He stood looking at Button as he put the phone to his ear, then turned his back on her.

"He's not a happy bunny," said Singh.

"He's worried, isn't he?" said Button.

"Definitely."

"Good."

Bashir was clearly unhappy at whatever Willoughby-Brown was saying to him, and he began to pace up and down, waving his free hand in the air.

"Not very good at hiding his body language, either," said Singh.

Bashir ended the call and put the phone away. He forced a smile as he walked back to Button. "Seems like he's OK with it," said Bashir. "I don't understand why Five is involved."

"I'll explain once we're at the house," said Button.

"House?"

"This might take some time," said Button. "I've arranged somewhere where we'll have some privacy."

"A safe house? You're taking me to a safe house? What the hell's going on?"

Singh picked up Bashir's suitcase. "Let me give you a hand with that," he said.

Button and Bashir walked towards the entrance. Singh followed, pulling the suitcase.

"How long do you think this will take?" asked Bashir. "I was hoping to go to the office."

"Not long, hopefully," said Button. She took him outside where her black Lexus was waiting and climbed into the back with him while Singh put Bashir's case in the boot. Singh got into the front passenger seat and the driver pulled away from the kerb. Button looked out of the window, making it clear to Bashir that she didn't want any conversation in the car. He folded his arms and sat back, looking out of the other window.

They drove to a house on the outskirts of Richmond, an ivy-covered former manor house sitting in several acres and surrounded by a high wall. The gate opened electronically as the Lexus drove up and closed silently as the car parked by the front door. The door opened and a young woman in a grey suit emerged. "Hello, Laura, could you arrange for some tea?" Button said as they got out of the car. She looked around for Bashir,

252

who was already standing in the wood-panelled doorway, biting his lower lip. "Tea, Taz? Or coffee?"

Bashir forced a smile. "Coffee. Please."

Inside, Laura headed for the kitchen. Button opened the door that led to the sitting room and walked in. The radiators had been turned on full and she took off her coat and threw it across the back of a sofa.

The room was shabby chic, the leather sofas worn and the curtains faded from the sun. There was a bookcase full of leather-bound books along one wall, and a large floor-mounted globe. Button smiled at it. Her father used to have a similar one in his study. She went over to it and pulled it open to reveal a clutch of bottles, mainly whisky. She smiled as the memories flooded back. Her father would always open his globe at seven o'clock on the dot, pour himself a malt whisky, then sit and read in his armchair by the fireplace. Charlie would sit and read on the sofa, and in later years she'd do her homework there as her father read and sipped his whisky. She'd never felt safer or more secure. She heard a polite cough behind her and turned to see Bashir looking at her, clearly uncomfortable. She closed the globe.

"Have a seat, Taz," she said. "And take your coat off, we'll be here for a while."

Bashir took off his coat and placed it next to hers, then sat on a wooden chair by the French window that overlooked the garden and beyond it a clump of apple trees. Button frowned and looked around. "Now where's my briefcase?" she muttered. She stood up, went to the door and called for Laura. The woman came from the kitchen and Button asked her where her briefcase was.

"I left it in the library," she said.

Button waved at Bashir. "Let's chat in there," she said. "It's cosier."

Bashir followed her through the hallway and into a book-lined room at the side of the house. There were two winged chairs, either side of a window that overlooked an ornamental pool with a statue of a mermaid in the centre. There was a leather briefcase on a circular oak coffee table by the side of one of the chairs. Button sat down and waved for Bashir to take the other chair.

"I don't see why we couldn't have done this in the office," said Bashir.

"Your office, or mine?" said Button. "Either way, it would set tongues a-wagging, wouldn't it?"

"Is there a problem, Miss Button?"

"Oh, call me Charlotte, please," said Button. "And no, there isn't a problem. Well, aside from the fact that one of my people is being held prisoner by al-Qaeda along with a former agent of mine."

"Manraj."

"Well, we called him Raj. But yes, Raj Chaudhry was a big help to us a couple of years ago so you can imagine how upset we were when he was reported missing in the badlands of Pakistan."

"It wasn't my fault," said Bashir. He put his hands up to his face. "Shit, I can't believe I'm being blamed for this."

"No one's blaming you, Taz," said Button. "We just need to know what's happened and what options we

254

have in the way of damage limitation. We, as in Five, have come to this late. The first we knew of Raj's involvement was when he was captured so I'm well behind the curve. How long have you been running Raj?"

"Just over a year," said Bashir.

"You were his first agent specialist?" Bashir nodded. "But you didn't recruit him?"

"He was passed to me by Jeremy."

"With what by way of introduction?"

"That he had successfully penetrated an al-Qaeda cell in London and that we could use him to expose terrorism financing out in the Middle East."

"And why Bradford?"

"We'd been watching one of the imams there. He was getting cash deliveries several times a year but we weren't sure where they were coming from. We also suspected that the imam was recruiting for training camps in Pakistan."

"You were with Raj in Bradford?"

"I wasn't based there. We thought it would be too risky, so I stayed in London. If he wanted a meeting I would drive up, but he didn't need much in the way of hand-holding." He forced a smile. "Your man Shepherd did a good job training him."

Button nodded. "Yes, I know."

"I'm really sorry about what happened," said Taz, wringing his hands together. "I don't know what went wrong."

"Clearly they knew that the fort was about to be attacked," said Button.

"There was no indication of that when I was first briefed by the military," said Taz. "They told me that Raj was being held by a small number of Taliban."

"Did they have the fort under constant observation?"

Bashir shook his head. "They said it was too dangerous. I suggested we get a drone flight over but they said they didn't want that."

"Did they say why not?"

"I was told that if they saw a drone flying overhead it might spook them. That seemed reasonable so I didn't press it."

"So at some point between the Pakistanis pulling their surveillance and the SSG going in, the Taliban managed to bring in reinforcements with grenades and RPGs."

"That seems to be the situation, yes."

"And that window would have been how long?"

"Three days, I suppose. Four at the most."

"So something must have happened during that period to have tipped them off. What do you think that might have been?"

Bashir shrugged. "I wish I knew."

Button nodded and smiled sympathetically. She wasn't interested in Bashir's replies. She doubted that he had any information that would be useful. All she wanted was to keep him occupied while Amar Singh got to work on his phone.

Singh worked quickly, though he knew Button would give him plenty of time. He placed Bashir's iPhone on the desk and connected it to his laptop. It took only seconds to dump all the phone's information on to the laptop's hard drive, and another thirty seconds to download Singh's own tracking software on to the phone. The software could be found only by an expert. It turned the phone into a GPS tracker and a live microphone, even when it was switched off.

Singh disconnected the phone and reached for Bashir's Puffa jacket.

Button sipped her tea and watched Bashir over the top of her cup. He was still nervous but seemed more confident now that he realised he was being debriefed rather than interrogated.

"What's going to happen now?" he asked.

"In what way?" She put down her cup.

"With Shepherd."

Button shrugged. "There's not much we can do," she said. "He's on Pakistani territory. We have to let the Pakistanis handle it."

"What about sending in the SAS?"

"Send them in where, Taz? Do you know where he is? If we had a location then maybe, but there doesn't seem to be one forthcoming."

"So what do we do? Negotiate?"

"If there's a ransom demand, we can go down that route, though it would be difficult considering that our stated policy is to never negotiate with terrorists."

"There are ways around that," said Bashir. "Third parties."

"It's a hypothetical discussion anyway," said Button. "There's no indication that they're considering a ransom. We don't even know if he's alive. For all we know they might have killed him already."

Bashir nodded. "I guess." He picked up his teacup. His hand was steadier now. He sipped his coffee. "And what about me?"

"What do you mean?"

"Are we good? Is there anything else you want from me?"

"Is there any other information you have?"

Bashir put down his cup. "I wish there was," he said.

"Is there anyone you know who might be able to locate Shepherd? And Raj, of course. Let's not forget Raj."

Bashir shook his head. "I wish I did."

"What about sources in Pakistan? Are you running anyone there who might be able to help?"

"I have contacts, but they're mainly in the army and the civil service."

"No one in al-Qaeda?"

He shook his head again.

"Do you have any agents ready to go out for training in Pakistan?"

"We have six in place in Bradford, Leeds, Manchester and Birmingham but we're waiting for them to be approached."

"Maybe get themselves to push themselves forward a bit."

"OK, I'll run that by Jeremy. I don't see why not."

Button stood up. "Well, thanks for your time. And for your help."

"I wish there was more I could do," he said.

"I've a car ready for you. Where do you need to go?"

"My flat's in Clapham."

"Clapham it is," said Button.

She opened the study door and waved for him to go through. He looked uncomfortable having a woman hold the door open for him and he averted his eyes as he passed her.

Singh was waiting for him in the hall with his suitcase. The front door was open and there was a white Toyota with the engine running waiting outside. "My coat," said Bashir. He hurried through to the sitting room and picked up his Puffa jacket.

"Thanks again, Taz," said Button as Bashir grabbed his suitcase and pulled it towards the waiting car.

"Pleasure," said Bashir. He climbed into the back of the car. As it drove away from the house he took his iPhone out of his pocket and switched it on.

"How did it go?" asked Button as she watched the car drive through the gates.

"All good," said Singh. "We'll be able to see where he is, whether or not the phone is switched on. All his calls and text messages will be recorded. And even with the power off we'll hear everything that's said in the vicinity. And I've put a GPS tracker in his jacket, in case he ditches the phone. The battery's good for a week or so."

"What about his suitcase?"

"Nothing there out of the ordinary. No underwear, though."

"Excuse me?"

"Socks but no underwear. Obviously likes to go commando."

Button laughed. "Well, you learn something new every day," she said. "There's something else I need you to do for me, Amar. I gave Spider a sat phone." She slipped him a piece of paper on which she'd written the number of the phone. "See if you can get a location on it."

"Is it chipped?"

"Chipped?"

"If it's chipped I can get a location whether or not it's switched on."

Button shook her head. "It's just a regular sat phone. I had no inkling it was going to go tits up." She looked at her watch. "Do you want me to drop you at the office? I've got a meeting this evening."

"Any Tube station is fine," said Singh. "What about his calls? Do you want me to monitor them?"

"I've got that covered," said Button.

"Any news on Spider?"

Button shook her head.

"I hope he's OK."

"You and me both," said Button.

Shepherd groaned and opened his eyes. The back of his head was on fire. He reached up with his right hand and it came away wet. It was too dark to see anything but he knew it was blood. He got to his knees and sat down with his back to the wall. They didn't appear to have beaten him while he was unconscious but he was sure they would come back and this time there would be more of them. Fighting his attackers was never going to be anything other than a temporary victory, though he had taken some satisfaction from the damage he'd done. But at least he had managed to get a look outside his cell. And he knew that Raj was alive and close by. That information alone was worth whatever they would do to him over the coming hours.

The Lexus reversed into a space between a Sainsbury's delivery van and a Honda CRV. It was a tight squeeze but Button's driver had been driving for MI5 for two decades and made it look easy. She climbed out and looked up and down the road, her briefcase in her right hand. They were in a part of Bayswater where most of the white-painted houses had been converted into cheap hotels, and half a dozen tourists were walking single-file down the pavement, pulling their wheeled suitcases behind them.

She put her hands in her pockets and walked slowly down the road. The Goldleaf Hotel was in the middle of the row. A handwritten sign in the window promised "CLEAN ROOMS WITH BATHROOMS" and a plastic printed sign above it confirmed there were "VACANCIES". A brown and white cat was sleeping on the windowsill, though it opened one eye as Button walked up the stairs and pushed open the glass door. There was a small reception desk to the left of the stairs but there was nobody there, and Button walked slowly up to the second floor on a carpet that was threadbare in places. There was a framed picture of dogs playing poker on the landing and the floorboards squeaked as

261

Button walked softly towards the door with a silver plastic number four on it.

She knocked and the door opened almost immediately, as if he already knew she was there. "How's it going?" asked Lex Harper. He was barefoot, wearing faded Wrangler jeans and a pale blue hoodie with the hood down.

Button didn't answer. He moved aside and she walked in and looked around the room. It took all of two seconds to take it in. There was a single bed pushed up against the wall, a cheap teak dressing table with a chair in front of it and a door that opened into a small shower room. There was a teak wardrobe and next to it a shelf with a kettle on it and a tray with sachets of coffee, milk powder and tea bags in a glass beaker. "Salubrious," she said.

"It's one of the few places left where they don't insist on credit cards and I can pay in cash," said Harper. "The only downside is that hookers bring their clients here so there's a fair bit of noise throughout the night."

"More information than I needed, Lex," said Button. She pulled the chair away from the dressing table, took off her coat and hung it over the back before sitting down. She picked up her briefcase, rested it on her knees and clicked open the locks. "It's about Spider," she said. "He needs our help."

Harper sat down on the bed. "You mean us personally or MI5?"

She smiled tightly. "This is off the books, Lex. Everything you do for me is off the books. You should know that by now." She took a manila envelope from the briefcase. "What name did you use to fly over?"

"An untraceable one," he said. "And I came in through Ireland so no one knows I'm here." He nodded at the envelope in her hands. "Are you offering me a legend, because I won't say no."

She handed it to him. "Here's a passport in the name of Alex Harwood," she said. "Close enough to your own name so that you won't forget. Just in case you have to pop overseas. Also two credit cards, one Amex and one Visa. And a debit card linked to an account with five thousand pounds in it. If you need more, contact me through email."

Harper put the envelope on the bed next to him.

"I've got a receipt for the flight over."

"I'll make sure you're reimbursed."

"It was first class from Bangkok to Amsterdam. That was all they had at short notice."

Button sighed. "I won't be quibbling about the cost," she said. She took another envelope from her briefcase, several times thicker than the first one. "Here's ten thousand pounds in cash," she said.

"That's my fee, is it?"

"Expenses," she said. "For the things I don't want receipts for. Your fee will be paid into an offshore account."

"How much exactly?"

"That depends on how successful you are." She closed her briefcase and slid it on top of the dressing table. "Spider's been taken hostage in Pakistan. I need your help to get him back."

Harper's jaw dropped. "You're not expecting me to go to Paki-land," he said.

"I need your help here, in the UK," said Button. "He's been taken by al-Qaeda in Pakistan. We don't know where exactly, but I'm hoping you can come up with a location. We're pretty sure that an al-Qaeda paymaster by the name of Akram Al-Farouq is with Shepherd, and another former MI5 agent, a British-born Pakistani called Manraj Chaudhry. Manraj, Raj we call him, was undercover in a Bradford mosque. A fundamentalist imam took Raj under his wing and sent him over for training in Pakistan. The imam's name is Mohammed Ullah, he's a Bangladeshi-born Brit. It looks as if Al-Farouq has been sending money to Ullah, and Ullah has been sending out fresh jihadists for training. I've got the names of some of the men who went from the Bradford mosque. Two of them are now back home."

"Sounds like you already know everything," said Harper.

"I wish that was the case, but trust me, I've come to this very late and with Spider in jeopardy I don't have the time to play this by the book. This Ullah has avoided surveillance for years, he's an expert at flying below the radar, so conventional techniques aren't going to work."

Harper grinned. "So I fall under the heading of unconventional techniques, do I?"

"I just want the job done, Lex. I want Ullah to tell us where Al-Farouq is. Or at least a way of getting hold of him."

"No limits?"

"As I said, I just want the job done. Do whatever you have to do, just spare me the details."

Harper flipped open a pack of cigarettes and lit one. He grinned as he saw a second look of contempt flash across Button's face. He leant over and pushed the window open. "Please don't give me any health and safety crap about not smoking," he said.

"I wasn't planning to," she said.

He blew smoke through the open window. "So how much trouble is Spider in? Are they open to a deal?"

"They're not negotiating. They haven't even gone public. It's not about ransom or a prisoner swap. Not at the moment, anyway. But even if they do open negotiations, that's not going to happen."

"That's right, the only terrorists that the British government negotiates with are the IRA," said Harper. "Oh, and we happily pay off Somalis when they take our ships." He saw that Button was about to say something and he waved apologetically. "Sorry, yes, I shouldn't sound so bitter and twisted." He took another pull on his cigarette. "It's an expat thing. It's only when you leave that you see how our country is changing."

"Everything changes, Lex. Nothing stays the same."

"Yeah, well, sometimes things get better and sometimes they don't," said Harper. "The whole Middle East thing has been a bloody disaster from start to finish. Tony Blair and George Bush have a lot to answer for." He grinned and shrugged. "Sorry. Political speech over. Time-wise, how long do you think we have?"

"If we're lucky, a few weeks. But if things get heated over there, it could be a matter of days."

"Spider's been trained in surviving interrogations. He'll cope. What about this Raj character?"

"He's a civilian," said Button. "Spider gave him some training but not much."

"And what happens if and when I get a location?"

"At the moment I'm taking it one step at a time, Lex."

Harper flicked ash through the window. "Better we get started straight away," he said. "Have you got a file I can look at?"

Button shook her head. "Nothing in writing. I'll brief you verbally. Make notes if you want, but the fewer the better."

"I don't have Spider's photographic memory," said Harper. "But I'll do my best."

The Gulfstream jet turned off the runway and taxied towards the VIP section of the general aviation terminal. A black stretch limousine was parked close to the terminal. A big man in a dark suit and impenetrable sunglasses was standing by the side of the car, his hands clasped in front of him. There was an earpiece in his left ear and a thin black wire disappeared into the collar of his gleaming white shirt. A black sedan was parked some distance away and two equally large men stood by it, their eyes scanning the terminal building. The occupant of the limousine was the Secretary of State for Defense and he never went anywhere without at least half a dozen Secret Service agents. Another two agents emerged from the terminal building. One stayed by the door, the other jogged over to the limousine.

The jet came to a halt and the twin engines powered down as a set of steps unfolded from the fuselage.

A Secret Service agent appeared from the rear of the limousine, followed closely by the Secretary. He was wearing plaid golfing trousers and a canary-yellow sweater. His trousers flapped around his ankles as he strode across the tarmac, flanked by the Secret Service agents. One jogged up the steps first and disappeared inside. He reappeared after a few seconds and nodded at his companion, who then followed the Secretary up the stairs.

Richard Yokely was already on his feet and he grinned when he saw the Secretary's attire. The Secretary of Defense returned the smile. "Generally Mohammed comes to the mountain, Richard. I'm assuming this is important."

"Would I pull you away from the golf course if it wasn't?" said Yokely. He shook hands with the Secretary and waved him to one of the beige leather seats, bigger than anything in the first-class cabin of a scheduled airliner. "Have you got time for a drink?" he asked.

"I'm good, Richard," said the Secretary.

"Then I'll get straight to the point," said Yokely, sitting down opposite him. There was a manila file on the table between them and Yokely flicked it open to reveal a surveillance photograph of an Arab man with a greying beard and circular spectacles. "Akram Al-Farouq is a high-value target," said Yokely. "One of the highest.

Number three or four in the al-Qaeda leadership, depending on how you draw the flow chart. Between 2007 and 2009 he was behind a series of bombings that took hundreds of lives. His speciality has been truck and car bombings."

The Secretary picked up the photograph and studied it. "I've heard of him, of course. But I don't recall him being a bomb-maker."

Yokely shook his head. "He isn't. He's an organiser. A facilitator. A planner. He puts people together to carry out the attacks and arranges the financing. One of his truck bombs killed a hundred and thirty-five people in the main Baghdad market in 2007. In April the same year we believe he was behind a series of coordinated car bombs that killed two hundred people across Baghdad. In August he organised four suicide bomb attacks in the Kurdish towns of Kahtaniya and Jazeera that killed almost eight hundred people. He was still at it in 2011; we have photographic evidence that he was behind three consecutive car bombings that killed a hundred and thirty-three people."

"And I presume you know where he is?"

"I hope to have a precise location in the very near future."

"Where exactly? Iraq?"

Yokely shook his head. "No, not Iraq." He took a deep breath. "I think he's on the border between Afghanistan and Pakistan."

"The border?"

"Well, I suspect it will be on what the Paks will claim is their territory."

268

The Secretary looked pained. He removed his spectacles and polished them with a pristine white handkerchief. "That's awkward, as you know."

"Not as awkward as Abbottabad. The area is one of those movable feasts. Afghanistan has as much a claim over it as the Paks, it's just the Paks seized it back in 1947 and as there's nothing of any value there nobody kicked up a fuss. To be honest, the Paks don't even control the territory. It's run by the Taliban. The border is a mountain range but that's it. There's no border guards, no line in the sand. You'd walk across it and never know."

"It's clear you've never worked for the Diplomatic Corps," said the Secretary. "I think you'll find that countries are always keen to defend their borders, whether or not there are lines in the sand."

"The point I'm trying to make in my clumsy way is that if we were to mount a cross-border operation, we'd only be dealing with the Taliban, not the Pakistani military. If anything, we'd be doing them a favour."

"I doubt that they would see it that way." The Secretary put the photograph back in the file. "What sort of cross-border operation are you suggesting?"

"A small snatch squad. Navy SEALs. In and out with a minimum of fuss."

"Not helicopters, I hope."

"I'm not a big fan of helicopters," said Yokely. "They have a nasty habit of crashing."

"And you want me to take this to the President, is that it?"

Yokely shook his head. "I don't want the President informed," he said.

The Secretary frowned. "I'm not sure that's a good idea."

"He needs plausible deniability," said Yokely.

"In case something goes wrong?"

"I'm not planning for that eventuality, but yes."

The Secretary sighed. "So you want me to give you the go-ahead for an operation that if it goes wrong will mean us going toe to toe with the Paks again?"

"Do we care what the Paks think? Half the al-Qaeda leaders are on their territory. And do either of us really believe that they didn't know Bin Laden was holed up in Abbottabad? They're not our friends. Never have been and probably never will be. Let's not forget they've already agreed to sell nukes to Saudi Arabia."

The Secretary held up his hands. "I hear you, Richard."

"All I need is your approval so that I can take this to Virginia Beach. I don't see it'll need any extra funding, it can all be done within their budget."

"And if it's successful, what do we do with him?"

"I'm not suggesting a trial, obviously. Interrogation followed by a deal if he cooperates. No one knows more about the workings of al-Qaeda than Al-Farouq. He'd be a gold mine. With his cooperation we could set the organisation back years."

The Secretary stared at Yokely with unblinking pale blue eyes. "Are you telling me everything, Richard?" he asked eventually.

"How long have you known me?"

"Long enough to know that sometimes you have more than one iron in the fire."

"And have I ever let you down?"

"Not once."

"So you know you can trust me?"

"Now that is a non sequitur if ever I heard one." The Secretary leaned across the table towards Yokely. "Let me just ask you this, Richard. Are you putting me in a position where I will have plausible deniability?"

Yokely smiled. "Would you want that, rather than being told something which might come back and bite you on the arse?"

"That's a good question," said the Secretary, sitting back. "One that is probably best left unanswered." He stood up and offered his hand.

Yokely shook it.

"Be lucky, Richard," said the Secretary. He turned and walked down the steps to the waiting limousine.

The cockpit door opened and the pilot appeared in a short-sleeved white shirt with epaulettes. "Everything OK, sir?" He was in his forties with greying hair and nicotine stains on the fingers of his right hand.

"Everything is just fine and dandy," said Yokely. "Could you file a flight plan to NAS Oceana?" Naval Air Station Oceana was the military airport located in Virginia Beach, home to the Navy SEALs. Yokely fastened his seat belt as the pilot returned to the cockpit.

Button's driver dropped her outside her front door and waited until she had let herself in before driving off. It was almost midnight and she was dog-tired but she still had work to do. She opened her laptop on the kitchen counter and made herself a cup of tea while it booted up. She put three Jaffa cakes on a plate and sat down on a stool with her tea and launched the browser. The website that logged all the calls and messages to Taz Bashir's phone was password protected and also required her to press her index finger on to a fingerprint reader that she had plugged into her USB slot. For a few seconds the page seemed to hang but then it cleared and she was looking at a spreadsheet showing all the activity on the phone since Singh had installed the surveillance software.

There had been a text message sent from a Pakistan mobile shortly after Bashir had left the safe house, presumably while he was in the car. "Are you OK? Did you get there? XXX". There was no name but the three kisses suggested a girlfriend.

Bashir had replied with "Will call soon. Miss you lots. XXX".

Fifteen minutes later the Pakistan number had called Bashir's phone but he hadn't answered. A few minutes later the Pakistan number sent another text message. "Where are you? XXX".

Bashir had replied with "In the car. Can't talk now. XXX".

Bashir had phoned the Pakistan number about ninety minutes later, using the iPhone's Skype app. Button clicked on the speaker icon to the right of the number and the call began. "Salma, baby, hi, it's me."

"How are you calling me, I don't recognise the number?"

"I'm on Skype. It's cheaper."

"What happened, honey? Was your plane late?" She had a Pakistani accent but Americanised, as if she had studied at an international school. Button reached for a pen and wrote down the number, and "Salma".

"It's OK, it just took a while for my bag and I didn't want to talk in the taxi."

"How long are you going to be in London?" asked the girl.

"I don't know," said Bashir. "They haven't said."

"Are you in trouble, honey?"

"Why do you ask?"

"Because of that thing going wrong? The agent you were trying to rescue."

"I don't think that's anything to do with it," said Bashir.

Button frowned. When he'd lied about the taxi she'd thought he was following protocol, but telling an outsider about an ongoing operation was a total breach of MI6 rules.

"They're not blaming you, are they?"

"Why would they blame me, baby? I was just the agent handler, I wasn't there. I was in Islamabad all the time."

"It's just not fair," said Salma. "I want my baby here with me."

"You could come to London. If I'm here for a while."

"Do you think it'll be that long?"

"I don't know, baby. Look, I'm going to sleep now, I'll call you tomorrow"

"Goodnight honey. Love you."

"Goodnight, baby."

The call ended. Shortly afterwards there was a spate of text messages declaring undying love, then silence. Button nibbled a Jaffa cake as she stared at the spreadsheet. Whoever the mysterious Salma was, she seemed to know more than she should about Taz Bashir's work for MI6.

Shepherd heard them in the corridor outside his cell, muttering between themselves, so he had time to prepare himself. There would be no point in fighting, he knew that. The first time they hadn't expected him to lash out so he'd managed to hurt two of them. They wouldn't make that mistake again. His survival now depended on playing weakness. They clearly weren't planning to kill him, at least not in the short term. They would hurt him until he passed out or until it looked as if he couldn't take any more, so he had to convince them he was at death's door. Suffering in silence was supposedly what heroes did, but when it came to surviving torture the best strategy was to scream your lungs out.

The bolts drew back and Shepherd tensed. The door opened and his eyes instinctively closed. He squinted up through his fingers. A bearded man waved a Kalashnikov at him then stepped to the side. Two big men rushed in and grabbed an arm each. Shepherd didn't resist as they pulled him to his feet.

They dragged him out of the cell. The big man had moved down the corridor and was pointing the barrel

274

of his AK-47 at Shepherd's chest. It was a stupid thing to do because at that range the bullet would probably go right through Shepherd and hit one of his colleagues who was standing at the other end of the corridor.

They frogmarched him down the corridor and then turned left. Then along another corridor and through an open door that led down into a dusty basement. It was a big room, twenty times the size of his cell. There was a cage at the far end, about four feet square and four feet high. There were several chairs and tables stacked against a wall and a pair of what looked like stocks with holes cut out for legs or arms. Shepherd gritted his teeth. It was a torture chamber, there was no doubt about that. They'd done the isolation thing, they'd stripped him of his clothes and deprived him of food and water. Now they were moving on to the next stage. The pain.

He took a deep breath and exhaled slowly. He'd get through it. He knew he'd get through it. This wasn't about killing him, it was about hurting him. The pain would go eventually.

There were several metal hooks in the ceiling and in the middle of the floor a coil of rope. More men came into the room. Two of them wore long dishdashas and were carrying AK-47s, one was holding a machete and three were holding canes. The men he'd hit earlier were nowhere to be seen so he figured they were still out of commission. That gave him some small comfort, though he knew it was a pyrrhic victory at best. It didn't matter how many of them he punched or kicked, there'd always be more to take their places.

One of the men tucked his cane under his arm and picked up the rope. He grabbed a chair and stood on it before threading the rope through a hook. The men holding Shepherd grabbed the free end of the rope and used it to tie his wrists behind his back. They were talking to each other in Pashto, and laughing. The man with the other end of the rope yanked it savagely and Shepherd was forced forward. He grunted but then screamed as it was yanked again. Red-hot bolts of pain seared through his shoulders. The men laughed even more and the rope was pulled again, lifting his feet off the floor. Shepherd roared. There was nothing he could do to alleviate the pain, all he could do was hang there and scream.

Charlotte Button's phone rang. It was Yokely. "I have some good news for you," he said. There was a buzz on the line as if he was calling from overseas, or from a plane. She rolled over and looked at the digital clock on her bedside table. It was just after six o'clock in the morning and as it was a Saturday she had been hoping for a lie-in.

"I'm all ears," she said, sitting up and running a hand through her hair.

"The NSA had a synchronous satellite taking photographs and video of the area in the days before the attack. And the CIA had two drones pass over."

"Can I see the footage, Richard?"

"That's why I'm calling. I can arrange a feed for you this afternoon, if that suits."

"Perfect," she said. "What do you need from me?"

"I'll give you a number to call, talk to a guy named Eric. Put him in touch with your technical people and you should be able to watch it from the comfort of Thames House."

"You're a star, Richard. Have you had a chance to look at the footage?"

"No, but Eric tells me there's some coming and going that might be helpful."

Button remembered the call that she had listened to the previous night. She asked the American to stay on the line while she ran downstairs to her kitchen and picked up her notebook. "Can you check a Pakistan number for me?" she said. She gave Yokely the number, and he repeated it back to her. "It's a girl, Pakistani but with good English, I think her name is Salma. The MI6 guy who was running Raj looks like he might have been talking out of school."

"And that's how the operation was blown?"

"It's possible. Let me know what you find out about her."

"And how are you getting on with nailing a location for Spider?"

"I'm on the case," said Button.

"I've put out a few feelers but haven't come up with anything," said Yokely. "I hope he's hanging in there."

"Me too," said Button.

Shepherd came to, coughing and spluttering. He was lying on the basement floor in a pool of water. He realised that he must have passed out again and they'd thrown a bucket of water over him. He tried to roll over but he had lost the use of his arms so he lay where he was and tried to suck up some of the water off the floor. He had no idea how long he'd been unconscious, or how long he'd been down in the basement.

The pain was unbearable, but he had no option other than to bear it. The only saving grace was that the pain stayed the same. It didn't get worse, it didn't come and go in waves, it was simply searing, unrelenting pain and all he could do was to scream and wait for it to stop. It was usually unconsciousness that saved him. Sometimes he passed out after a few minutes, once he lasted as long as an hour by his reckoning, but when he did slip into unconsciousness they would let him down, throw water over him and wait for him to recover. There were no questions, there was nothing they seemed to want from him, so there was nothing he could say that would stop them. It was part of the process; that was what kept running through his mind like a mantra. It wasn't personal. It was going to happen no matter what he did or said. And at some point it would stop. All he had to do was to take one breath at a time and eventually they would take him back to his cell.

Hands grabbed him and dragged him to his feet. The rope was pulled through the hook, his arms went up behind his back, and the screams started again. He had been screaming for so long that it no longer felt as if the screams were coming from him. It was just noise, part of the process, and nothing to do with him.

Chief Petty Officer Adam Croft was deep in thought, walking across the DEVGRU compound, a cluster of

278

brick buildings around a car park that was part of the Dam Neck Fleet Training Centre in Virginia Beach. The military loved initials as much as any bureaucracy, and DEVGRU was itself short for NAVSPECWARDEVGRU, which was in itself a shortened version of the United States Naval Special Warfare Development Group. But to the outside world, DEVGRU was known as the Navy SEALs, the best of the best. Croft was due to give a presentation about decision making in combat to a group of new recruits and was starting to regret not having made some sort of PowerPoint presentation.

"Adam!" The shout stopped him in his tracks. It was Shaun Allen, another chief petty officer and a close friend. The two men were often mistaken as brothers — they had the same square jaw, piercing blue eyes and close-cropped blond hair. Croft waited until Allen caught up with him. "Adam, Gold commander wants you in his office, stat."

"What's up?"

"He didn't say. But it looks like someone's lit a fire under his arse." Lieutenant Commander Dick Blanchard was in charge of Gold squadron, nicknamed the Knights. The Knights were the best of the best and Blanchard was one of the most experienced commanders in DEVGRU, a veteran of Afghanistan and Iraq, both in Desert Storm in 1991 and in the Iraqi War of 2003.

"I'm on my way to deliver a talk to the new intake."

"He says right now."

Allen slapped him on the back and headed off. Croft jogged over to Blanchard's offices. A man in his fifties was just leaving. He was grey haired and had thin lips. He was wearing civilian clothes — a dark blue blazer and light brown chinos, black shoes with tassels on them — but Croft found himself saluting the man as he walked by him. He knocked on the open door. "Sir?"

"Croft, yes, come in." Blanchard gestured at a chair in front of his desk. "Take a load off." Croft sat down. "How are your HALO skills?" asked Blanchard.

Croft ran a hand through the stubble on his head. It had been over a year since he'd done a High Altitude, Low Opening jump. "I've done more than a dozen free-falls this year but none over five seconds, sir," he said.

"But it's like riding a bike, right?"

Croft smiled. Sure, he thought, if you were riding a bike vertically downwards at more than a hundred and twenty miles an hour. "Pretty much, sir."

"I've got a job that needs doing and I need you on board, Croft."

"Yes, sir."

"It means you going back to Pakistan. Bit of déjà vu, it turns out. Do you remember Dan Shepherd, of the British SAS?"

Croft nodded slowly. "Yes, sir."

"He was with you on Operation Neptune Spear."

"I remember, sir."

"Well, Mr Shepherd has managed to get himself into a bit of a situation and I've been tasked with getting him out of it. I'm putting together a team from Gold but you've met the man so I want you along. Are you up for that?"

280

Croft didn't have particularly fond memories of Dan Shepherd, but he'd been stuck as an instructor for going on eighteen months and was keen to get back into action, so he nodded enthusiastically. "Hell yes, sir."

"That's what I thought you'd say," said the commander. "I'm planning on an eight-man team, two groups of four. I'm tasking Lieutenant Jake Drake with the mission but on each group I want a man who knows this Shepherd."

He leaned over and tapped at an intercom. "Send Lieutenant Drake in," he said.

A few seconds later, the door opened. The lieutenant was in desert camouflage fatigues. He was a few inches shorter than Croft with broad shoulders and a steely grey crew cut. The fact that his skin was dark from the sun and he was sporting a bushy beard suggested he was just back from Iraq or Afghanistan.

"Jake, this is Adam Croft, he'll be with you on the Pakistan mission."

Drake nodded and shook hands with Croft. The lieutenant had big hands and a strong grip. "Good to have you on board," he growled.

The commander motioned for Drake to sit down. "Jake and I have already done a lot of the pre-mission planning," he said. "We're looking at an eight-man team. Jake's already briefed five men from Gold squadron, you bring the number up to seven and we're looking for one more, specifically someone who's met Shepherd and who's still serving."

"Guy Henderson," said Croft without hesitation. "He was on Operation Neptune Spear and he was tasked with hand-holding Shepherd. Did a good job, too."

"Where is he?"

"Here, Virginia Beach," said Croft. "He's with the Pirates." The Pirates was the nickname of Black Squadron, which specialised in reconnaissance and surveillance.

DEVGRU was split into four assault squadrons code-named Gold, Silver, Blue and Red. Each squadron contained fifty men, split into three troops. The troops were further divided into teams of fighters and snipers. The fifty men in Black squadron were reconnaissance and surveillance and Grey squadron was tasked with maritime missions.

"Which troop?"

"I'm not sure, sir."

Blanchard scribbled a note on the pad in front of him. "Outstanding," he said. "I'll talk to the Pirates commander and get him attached to our unit." He put down his pen and sat back in his chair. "Jake will bring you up to speed operation-wise. This is going to be way different from Operation Neptune Spear. No low-level helicopter flying, not after the Charlie Foxtrot we had last time."

Croft smiled at the commander's use of the acronym. Charlie Foxtrot, Cluster Fuck. And while Operation Neptune Spear had been touted as a success, it had come close to complete failure when one of the two helicopters had crashed.

"We're still waiting for a definitive location from the Brits," said the commander. "All we know is that it'll be close to the border with Afghanistan. Once we have the location we'll be utilising a HALO jump to effect the rescue. And once we have the targets in safe-keeping and close to the border, we'll send in birds to evac."

"Understood, sir," said Croft. "Any idea when we'll have a location?"

"They're saying they hope to have it within the next few days. So I need you to work with Jake to make sure that you're up to a thirty-thousand-feet HALO. He'll check your marksmanship, too. The bad guys won't be giving up their hostages without a fight."

"Hostages plural?" said Croft.

"Shepherd is being held with another Brit, a Pakistani, who is an MI6 asset. MI6 is the British equivalent of the CIA. He's been in captivity for considerably longer than Shepherd so we're not sure what state he's in." He nodded at Drake. "Right, I'll let you get Croft settled in and you need to start training tomorrow. But remember, no gossip, no chit-chat. No one needs to know what you're training for. I'll get Henderson over to you as soon as I can."

The two men stood up and headed out of the office.

"Oh, one thing, Jake. The beard's going to have to go. You'll be jumping with oxygen. That goes for all the guys just back from the sandpit — no facial hair."

"Not a problem, sir. The damn thing itches anyway."

"That must have been one hell of a thing, Operation Neptune Spear," Drake said to Croft as they walked along the corridor.

Croft had been the leader of the mission and the ranking non-commissioned officer. At the time he'd been a ten-year veteran of the Navy SEALs and had spent half of those years serving in Iraq and Afghanistan. "It was awesome," said Croft. "I don't see anything will ever come close."

"It was ballsy, right from the get-go," said Drake. "Flying in without telling the Pakistanis, storming the compound and taking out the target without a single casualty."

"We lost a bird," said Croft. "But yeah, no casualties."

"I was so pissed that I wasn't on the team," said Drake. "Found out like everyone else when it was on CNN. I'd have given anything to have been there."

"Luck of the draw," said Croft.

"Yeah, I know. I had an uncle die in the second tower that went down on 9/11. He was a banker. They never found his body. They didn't find the bodies of anyone on his floor." He grimaced. "Hell of a way to die. Minding your own business, just another day in the office, and some bastards you've never even thought about crash a plane into your building. Fucking cowards."

Croft nodded but didn't reply. He figured that while what the al-Qaeda terrorists did on 9/11 was pure evil, the men who had taken control of the planes hadn't been cowards. Evil, certainly, but cowards rarely went on suicide missions. It took a particular sort of bravery to carry out a mission knowing that it would end in certain death. It wasn't anything that Croft had ever been asked to do, and he wasn't sure what his reaction would be if it was ever asked of him. Undertaking dangerous missions went with the turf for Navy SEALs, but there was always the expectation that while there might be casualties, generally missions were survivable.

"Never heard that a Brit was on the mission," said Drake. He pushed open the door that led to the parade ground.

"It was secret squirrel," said Croft, following the lieutenant outside. "He was a spook but he'd been with the SAS back in the day. He carried a weapon but he was there more as an observer."

"They're good, the SAS," said Drake. "Damn good."

"Damn good," said Croft. "He was as hard as nails. We had him in at the rehearsals at Camp Alpha. We practised the operation a hundred times at a mock-up of the Bin Laden compound and Shepherd was tireless. Good shot, too. As good as anyone on Team Six. But man, he whined like a little girl."

"Say what?"

"On the day, when we took out Bin Laden. He goes all teary eyed and starts asking me why we didn't take him prisoner."

"Bin Laden? What did he want, a trial?"

Croft shrugged. "Said we shot him when he was unarmed."

"Yeah? Well, boo-hoo. I don't remember anyone in the Twin Towers carrying guns. What was his name again, this guy?"

"Shepherd. Dan Shepherd."

"So what was a Brit doing on the mission anyway?"

"The commander didn't tell you?"

"All he told me was that we're bailing out two Brits, one white and one a Pakistani. He's not over-chatty, the commander."

"Well, the intel about Bin Laden. It came from the Brits."

Drake's jaw dropped. "You're shitting me."

"Nah, they had intel. There were rumours that the Brits had an inside man within al-Qaeda. They gave the intel to us and that's why we put the compound under the microscope."

"They kept quiet about that, all right."

"Yeah, the CIA was happy enough to take the credit and the British spooks wanted to protect their source so it worked out well for everyone. They even made that movie about it, remember? *Zero Dark Thirty*. The one that skated over why our bird crashed. Made it look like one woman was responsible for tracking him down. So no one ever knew the truth." He grinned. "Now that Navy SEALs movie with Charlie Sheen. That was a movie!"

Drake clapped him on the back. "We've taken over an empty building for our quarters," he said. "There's a room each for sleeping and a kitchen and two shared bathrooms. We're to stay out of general circulation until the operation is over."

"I heard that the guy who killed him is unemployed and lives on disability benefits," said Drake.

"Yeah, I heard that," said Croft.

"Is it true, do you think?"

Croft shrugged. He knew exactly what had happened to the SEAL who had fired the shots that killed the world's most wanted man on 2 May 2011. Croft had led the mission and Croft had pulled the trigger. But his name had never been made public and the CIA had pumped out disinformation to make sure that no one ever would know. Al-Qaeda was composed of thousands of fanatics who would happily sacrifice themselves to avenge Bin Laden's death, so Croft was quite happy that his identity was a closely kept secret. "Who knows?" he said. "Anyway, you get to run this operation, right?"

"Damn right," said Drake.

Lex Harper wound down the window of his white Transit van and blew a tight plume of smoke as he watched the BMW turn into the supermarket car park. He was on the outskirts of Manchester. It was early evening and there were only half a dozen cars parked up. He flashed his lights, just once. The BMW stopped, then headed in his direction and pulled up next to the van. Jony Hasan climbed out. He was a British-born Bangladeshi, in his mid-twenties with skin the colour of mahogany and slicked-back hair that glistened with gel. He was wearing a black leather jacket and black jeans, and pointed black boots with silver tips.

He pulled open the passenger door and climbed in. He looked over his shoulder at the empty van. "So when did you become a white van man, bruv?"

"They're invisible," said Harper. "There's so many of them on the road that nobody gives them a second look. How are you doing anyway, mate? Long time no fucking see." He reached over and hugged Jony, slapping him on the back, hard.

"All good, bruv," said Jony, pulling away. He flipped down the sunshade and used the mirror there to check his hair. "Dicking and diving, you know how it is?"

"You mean ducking?" said Harper.

"I know what I mean, bruv," said Jony, punching Harper on the shoulder. "I'm getting more white pussy than I know what to do with."

"Thanks for sharing that, mate," said Harper. "You still having problems with the Yardies?"

Jony rubbed the back of his nose. "Nothing I can't handle. Providing they stay in their areas, there's no problem. Each to his own, right?"

Harper flicked the remains of his cigarette out of the window and wound it up.

"The big problem we've got is Romanians," said Jony. "They're everywhere. Now we've got muggings, cash machine fiddles, shoplifting, the works."

"Yeah?"

Jony nodded. "It got so bad my uncle put up a note in the window of his shop. 'No Romanians, No Gypsies'. Council made him take it down, said it was racist."

Harper grinned. "Yeah, well, strictly speaking it is," he said.

"They were robbing him blind, what was he supposed to do? It's the government's fault for letting them in."

"They'll assimilate. Immigrants always do eventually."

"Not this lot. And who told you immigrants assimilate?"

"Look at you, mate." Harper laughed. "You even talk with a Brummie accent."

"Yeah, well, I was born here, bruv."

"But your parents assimilated, right?"

Jony laughed. "Assimilated my brown arse," he said. "My mum still can't speak more than fifty words of English and my dad still dresses like he's just walked in off the desert."

"But they gave you an English name."

"Jony? That's Bangladeshi, bruv. It means lovely."

Harper grinned. "Lovely?"

"Don't go there, bruv. And my sisters are Jaiyasha and Laboni. My folks live here and they're proud enough to be British but they're Bangladeshis at heart. Whenever the Bangladesh cricket team is here my old man's straight down to Lord's, doesn't matter what else is happening." Jony scratched his chin. "Anyway, enough chit-chat. What do you want from me?"

"What makes you think I want something?"

Jony laughed and slapped Harper's leg. "Because you ring me up out of the blue and ask me to meet you in a van parked in the middle of nowhere. I figured if it was social you'd see me in the pub."

"I tend not to go into pubs too much these days, mate."

"Why's that? Given up the booze?" He laughed. "Don't tell me you've gone all Muslim on me. Should I start calling you Mohammed?"

"CCTV, mate," said Harper. "They've got them everywhere. And the government has access to them. It's all about facial recognition."

"Yeah, well, your ugly mug is hard to miss, innit?"

"I'm serious, Jony. They've got everyone sewn up, pretty much. Between facial recognition and GPS phones they know where everyone is and what they're doing."

"And keeping a hoodie up and your head down keeps you below the radar, does it?"

"That and not using credit cards in my name. And using different IDs. And paying in cash whenever I can. Yeah, at the moment that does it. Until the day we all get chipped."

"Chipped? What the hell are you talking about, bruv?"

Harper lit a cigarette and then offered the pack to Jony. Jony took one and Harper lit it for him. The two men blew smoke before Harper spoke. "Long-term they want us all chipped. A small chip, probably in your forearm, that'll contain everything there is to know about you. Your name, your date of birth, your DNA code, your picture, your fingerprints, your bank balance. Initially they'll sell it to us as a more efficient credit card and ID card, they'll tell us it means no more immigration queues, no more lost children, no more crime. But eventually they'll make it compulsory. We'll all have them." He blew smoke again. "Then all our freedom will be gone. They'll know where you are and what you're doing. And the moment you stop being a well-behaved little citizen they'll remotely deactivate your chip and then you'll be a total non-person. You won't be able to travel, you won't be able to buy anything, you won't be able to do anything."

"That's sci-fi, bruv," said Jony scornfully.

"Everything's sci-fi until it happens," said Harper. "Space flights were sci-fi. Satellites were sci-fi. Flatscreen TVs were sci-fi. Now we've got them all." He shrugged. "It'll happen, mate. Sure as eggs are eggs."

"Nah, people won't stand for it," said Jony.

"People? Sheeple, mate. They do as they're told. Can't you see what's happening with all this terrorism stuff? They want people scared because scared people will do as they're told." He grinned. "I ever tell you I was a blagger? An armed robber?"

Jony shook his head.

"Yeah, me and a group of former squaddies did it for a while, before I got into commodity trading. It was all about shock and awe. You go in hard and you go in noisy, slap people around and they'd piss themselves. When people are scared, they follow orders. They stand meekly in queues for an hour and then allow some sweaty security guard on minimum wage to run their hands over them. Don't worry, mate, when the sheeple are told they need chipping they'll do it. They're programmed to obey instructions."

Jony laughed. "You always were a glass-is-half-empty bastard."

"Mate, why do you think mobile phones are so cheap?"

"Competition," said Jony. "It keeps prices down."

"Doesn't seem to work with electricity, does it? Or food? Lots of competition there but prices keep going up. But look at phones. Dirt cheap to buy and dirt cheap to use. Do you know why that is?"

"I'm sure you're going to tell me, bruv."

Harper ignored the sarcasm. "Because the cops now solve half their crimes with phone records. The GPS shows them where people are. They can see who people are talking to. And they can read the texts that they send. Mate, they would pay people to carry phones if they had to. They want everyone in the country to use a mobile. That's why they're getting rid of all the phone boxes."

Jony laughed. "Bloody hell, I'm starting to regret coming to see you now. We start a conversation about CCTV and now you're on a rant about Big Brother."

"Mate, if you got any sense you'll be hiding your money now because when it happens it'll be too late. Once the chip's in they'll know everything you have and everything you earn." He held up his hands and chuckled. "Rant over. I need a gun. Something untraceable. Revolver, ideally a .22."

"Price range?"

"Fuck me, Jony, when have I ever haggled about price? I want something clean and something that won't let me down. A Smith 17 or 18 would do just fine."

Jony nodded. "Rounds?"

"Ten, twenty, maybe. I'm not planning to fight a war."

"When?"

Harper grinned. "I've got the cash on me, mate."

"So you want it now?"

"You read my mind. And I want a stun gun. Not a taser, I don't need to use it at a distance, something handheld but with a lot of power. I want to totally immobilise someone with one stab."

"Bruv, a baseball bat does the job and it doesn't need batteries."

"Can you get me one?"

"A baseball bat? Sure."

"Twat. A stun gun."

"Of course, bruv. I'm only messing with you." Jony chuckled and let himself out of the van. He took his mobile phone out of his pocket and he talked into it as he paced up and down. After a couple of minutes he climbed back into the van. He saw Harper looking at the phone. "It's a throwaway," he said. "Don't worry."

"The phone or the Sim card?"

Jony frowned. "What do you mean?"

"These days they can pull info off the phone no matter what Sim card is in it," said Harper. "The days of just being able to put a new Sim card in are long gone. You have to ditch the whole phone."

"Good job they're so cheap," said Jony. "But I hear what you're saying, bruv."

They sat and smoked and chatted for twenty minutes, until a black VW Golf with alloy wheels turned into the car park. It stopped near the entrance. Its headlights were on main beam so Harper couldn't see who was in the car. Jony patted him on the leg. "Don't worry, bruv. They're with me." He climbed out of the van, slammed the door and jogged over to the Golf. He pulled open the rear door and climbed in.

Harper took a long pull on his cigarette and looked at his watch. He needed a bed for the night and figured that Manchester was as good a place to crash as any. He had just taken a final drag on the cigarette as Jony reappeared. Harper wound down the window and flicked the butt out across the car park. It hit the tarmac, sparked, and went out. Jony handed a large Tupperware container through the window. Harper put it in his lap and opened it. Inside was a Smith and Wesson and a Ziploc bag containing two dozen rounds. "Looks good, mate, thanks." He took the gun out of the container and sniffed it. It didn't seem to have been fired, not recently anyway.

"I've had it for six months, a Yank managed to get a dozen over from the States."

"It's not new."

"Not new, but he used them for target shooting."

"Bloody hell, mate, if you're that simple there's a bridge over the Thames I can sell you for a good price."

Jony reached for the gun. "If you don't want it . . ." he said.

Harper moved it out of his reach. "Don't get shitty, I'll take it. I'm just saying that you don't want to believe everything you hear, that's all. The main thing is, they've not been fired in this country, right?"

"Cross my heart, bruv."

Harper nodded. He was happy enough with the gun and Jony had always been as good as his word in the past.

"I'm thinking three hundred," said Harper. He put the gun back in the Tupperware container.

"Yeah? I was thinking six," said Jony.

"So we'll settle for four?"

Jony handed over a stun gun in a Ziploc bag. Harper took it out of the bag, examined it, then pressed the switch on the side. Blue sparks crackled between the two prongs. "Two million volts, bruv," said Jony. "It'll do the job."

"You know as well as I do that the voltage means nothing," said Harper. "It's the amperage that does the damage."

"Four milliamps," said Jony. "It'll go right through pretty much all clothing and you're out like a light."

"You ever used one?"

Jony grinned and nodded. "It's brilliant, bruv, a real tasty piece of kit."

Harper put the stun gun back in the bag then slid it and the Tupperware container under his seat. "So a monkey for everything? Five hundred?"

"We'll settle for six, bruv, because it's after hours and you wanted it here and now."

Harper laughed, reached inside his jacket and took out an envelope. It was filled with twenty-pound notes. He flicked through the notes, pulled out a handful, and gave the envelope to Jony. He slipped the rest of the money into his jacket pocket.

"You were gonna pay me more?" said Jony. "Shit."

"You got a fair price, Jony," he said. "Be lucky."

"You take care, bruv," said Jony. He hugged Harper and headed back to his own car. The Golf was already driving out of the car park.

Croft was unpacking his gear when his mobile phone rang. He grabbed it. It was Guy Henderson. "So the top team is back together, huh?" said Henderson.

"You're on board?"

"My LC's happy, I'm packing my bag as we speak."

"What have they told you?"

"Just it's a secret squirrel mission and that I'm teaming up with you. To be honest I don't think my LC knows what's going on."

"Remember that Brit you babysat on Neptune Spear?"

"Never likely to forget," said Henderson. "Dan Shepherd."

"Well, Mr Shepherd is being held by al-Qaeda ragheads in the tribal lands of Pakistan. And guess who's been tasked with rescuing his sorry ass?"

"That would be us?"

"That would indeed be us. How ironic is that?"

"What, they want us to fly into Pakistan for a shoot-out with al-Qaeda to rescue a Brit who hates the US of A?" He grinned. "Hell, yeah, that's the dictionary definition of ironic. I can't wait to see the look on his face when the cavalry arrives."

Charlotte Button tapped on the door to Amar Singh's office and pushed it open. Singh was sitting in his shirtsleeves, his Armani jacket draped over the back of his chair. He was facing three monitors all showing overhead views of desert areas. She was carrying a cup of Starbucks coffee and she put it down in front of him. He thanked her but she shook her head. "I'm the one who should be thanking you," she said. "Coming in on a Saturday like this. I hope Mishti's not too upset."

"She's not happy; it was my turn to take Neeta and Gita to ballet class today but I promised her I'd take her out to dinner on her birthday next week."

"I'll pick up the tab for that," said Button. "Make it somewhere nice." She pulled up a chair and sat behind Singh. "So these are the feeds that came through from the States?" she asked.

Singh nodded. "That guy Eric is a genius," he said. "We're getting feeds direct from the CIA in Langley but I can mix and match in real time. It's as if my terminal is in Langley. I had no idea they could do this."

The monitor on the left showed what looked like a satellite picture of a square fort, built around a courtyard. There were three vehicles parked in the courtyard but Button couldn't see any people. There was a time code running along the bottom that showed the picture had been taken three days earlier.

The monitor on the right was showing a similar satellite view of the area but it was in real time and the time code at the bottom of the screen was counting off the seconds. Singh pointed at it. "Your man was able to move a satellite on position to get me a live feed of the area now," he said. "Have you any idea how much that costs?"

"The CIA and the NSA have got budgets that dwarf ours," said Button. "The CIA spends almost seventy billion dollars a year and there's another ten billion dollars for the NSA." She smiled. "You could buy a lot of designer suits with that."

Singh grinned. He pointed at the live satellite feed. "Nothing's happening there now; other than a goat herder going in with his animals now and again, it seems to be deserted."

"They'll be long gone," said Button. She pointed at the right-hand monitor. "Do any of the pictures show anything of interest?"

Singh clicked his mouse and the screen divided up into twenty segments, each an individual picture. He clicked on one and it showed the fort, apparently empty. "This was Sunday, three days before the Pakistanis went in. No vehicles, as you can see. Then on Tuesday, the three pick-up trucks, and presumably the fighters, are in place."

"Any sign of people?"

Singh shook his head. "The satellite had a huge area to cover. There are long gaps between photographs and of course for a third of the time the place was in darkness."

"Infrared?"

"No, their sensors aren't that sensitive, not yet anyway."

"So to the best of your knowledge, when did the trucks arrive at the fort?"

"Four or five days ago. Monday or Tuesday."

"Which is about the time that Spider was heading out to Pakistan."

Singh looked at her sideways. "You think that's significant?"

"Clearly something happened. First there were no pick-up trucks. Then there were three. They sent in men with weapons, so they knew something was going to happen."

"The Pakistani military is full of al-Qaeda sympathisers, isn't it? That's why they have so many training camps on their soil. And when they found Bin Laden he'd spent five years living down the road from the country's main military academy."

"It's possible. It's also possible that the leak came from within their intelligence services, which also leak like a sieve. But this all seems very last minute, doesn't it? Just as the SSG are about to go in, Raj is pulled out and RPGs move in."

"I do have some pictures of the pick-up trucks arriving," said Singh. He nodded at the centre monitor and a video filled the screen, again with a time code across the bottom. "This is from a surveillance drone that was passing overhead at about twenty thousand feet. It was taking video non-stop." He clicked his mouse and the video fast-forwarded. A white pick-up truck appeared. Singh clicked the mouse again and the picture slowed to real time. Then he paused it. "This was the day before the Pakistanis went in," he said. "Monday afternoon." There were five figures squatting in the back of the truck, cradling rifles, their heads swathed in keffiyeh headscarves.

"What are they, Taliban?"

"Taliban or al-Qaeda," said Singh. "Or both."

"And the truck, is it one of those in the courtyard of the fort?"

"I can't tell, unfortunately. The satellite is an overhead shot so there's not enough to go on. But there isn't much else out in that part of the world."

He clicked on the mouse, then clicked again, and fast-forwarded. According to the time code on the bottom of the screen, five hours had passed. Another pick-up truck appeared on the road. Singh clicked the mouse again. Button peered at the truck. This one was red and there were seven armed fighters in the back.

"There was a red pick-up truck in the courtyard," said Button.

"Red's not an uncommon colour, but I'd say it's a fair assumption that they were heading to the fort," said Singh. He sat back in his chair. "It doesn't help us with an ID, though, there are no registration numbers to check and all the fighters have their faces covered."

"The important thing is that we know they rushed to reinforce the fort at short notice."

"They knew the Pakistanis were coming," said Singh. "Somebody tipped them off."

"They were looking for a fight." She rubbed her chin. "They could have just run off, but instead they sent in reinforcements."

"Someone in the SSG talked, then?"

"Possibly," said Button. "But whoever leaked, it was obviously at the last minute." She leaned back in her chair. "Can you call up Bashir's phone for me?"

"Sure," said Singh. He cleared the centre screen and went to the secure website. He tapped in the password, pressed his index finger on the computer's fingerprint reader, then sat back as the spreadsheet loaded.

300

"I saw the texts from last night and listened to the evening call," said Button. She gestured at the spreadsheet. "Looks like he was on Skype again this morning."

Singh clicked on the speaker icon. "Hi, baby, what's up?"

"Missing you, honey," she said. "This bed is way too big without you in it."

"What are you doing today, baby?"

"Shopping," she said. "Then dinner with girlfriends."

"I wish I was there with you, baby."

"Me too, honey," she said. "Please get them to send you back soon. I hate being away from you."

"Me too," said Bashir.

"When will you know?"

"It's Saturday so I can't do anything until after the weekend. I'll go in and see my boss on Monday."

"Do you think it's about what happened at Parachinar?"

"I don't know, baby."

"That wasn't your fault, they have to know that."

"I'm sure they do, baby, but I'll have a better idea where I stand after the weekend."

"What about the military? What are they saying?"

"They're keeping quiet. I think they're embarrassed more than anything. It shows they don't control that whole area. They send in their best-trained soldiers and almost all of them were killed."

"I'm just glad you're safe, honey."

"I am, baby, nothing's going to happen to me here."

"Stay safe and come back to me soon, honey."

"I will, baby. Kiss, kiss."

"Kiss, kiss," she said back to him, and ended the call.

"Does she work for Six?" Singh asked. Button shook her head and Singh grimaced. "That's awkward."

"Isn't it just?" said Button.

"Pillow talk?"

"I have a horrible feeling that might be the case," she said.

There were several text messages back and forth between Salma and Bashir, mainly of the "I love you, I miss you" variety.

There were two other calls, both to UK numbers. The first one was to Bashir's parents, a five-minute call basically asking about his extended family and telling them he would be up to see them the following week. The second call was to a plumber asking for someone to come out and deal with a leaking tap.

Singh tapped away at the keyboard as he checked out both numbers. The first was a house in Coventry, the second the main switchboard number of Pimlico Plumbers.

"What do you think?" asked Singh.

"I think we need to know a bit more about Taz Bashir," said Button. "What do you think? Can you pull info on him without raising red flags?"

"Of course, I'll get right on it," he said. "I ran a check on Spider's sat phone."

"And?"

"He made a call to you from Cherat. Then it was off. It was switched on shortly after the attack. Just for thirty seconds. Then it went off and has been off ever since."

302

"Any calls or texts made?"

Singh shook his head. "Not after the call to you. I think they were just checking it. They probably realise that if it's on we can track it."

"Can you keep a watching brief on it?" asked Button.

"Already in hand," said Singh.

Shepherd lay facing the wall as the bolts to his cell door were drawn back. He heard the door open and footsteps. He tensed, expecting a beating, but then he heard the scrape of plastic against the floor and then footsteps and the door being closed and bolted. He sat up, wincing at the pain that lanced through his shoulders. He groped around and felt a plastic bowl. He probed inside it and his fingers touched water. He lifted the bowl to his lips and sipped slowly. He had to fight the urge to gulp the water down as he didn't know how long it would have to last him. He put the bowl down and realised that there was a second bowl there. He probed it with his fingers and felt something soft. He picked up the bowl and sniffed the contents. It was rice and chicken. He sat with his back against the wall and ate slowly. The food and water were a good sign. They wanted to keep him alive. He doubted that the beatings had stopped, but at least the food and water would give him a chance to build up his strength. He chewed slowly. The first few swallows were physically painful but it got easier. He sipped some more water and then ate some more rice. He didn't know how long it had been since he had last eaten, but the rice and chicken were possibly the tastiest meal he had ever eaten.

He wondered what the next stage of his interrogation would be. They'd used isolation, they'd beaten him and tortured him. Now they were feeding him. First the stick, and then the carrot. Soon they would talk to him. They would ask him questions and he would have to decide how much to tell them.

Back when he was on the Escape and Evasion section of SAS Selection he'd been told to say nothing other than to give his name, rank and number. To give any other information meant being immediately RTU'd. But this wasn't SAS Selection, this was the real world. On the Escape and Evasion course, an officer would eventually appear and announce that the exercise was over. That wasn't going to happen to Shepherd this time. His captors would continue to torture and interrogate him until they got what they wanted and refusing to talk would only make them torture him even more. In the real world, when you were tortured you talked. And you begged. And you screamed.

Shepherd chewed slowly as he considered his options, though he knew the truth was that they were very limited. There was no way of escape that he could see. He doubted that anyone was going to come to his rescue. All he could do was to take it one minute at a time. Every minute he was alive was a victory.

"OK?" shouted Drake above the noise of the engines of the C-23 Sherpa transport aircraft.

"All good!" shouted Croft.

Drake looked over at Henderson. "Guy?"

"Rock and roll," said Henderson. They were fifteen thousand feet above the Virginia countryside and about to jump out of a "perfectly serviceable plane", a phrase that always seemed to be on the lips of the US National Guard aircrewmen who were doing the flying for them. There were just the three of them jumping, with Drake serving as jump-master. He knew the jumping abilities of the SEALs from Gold Squadron but Croft and Henderson were unknown qualities and he needed to check them out.

If all went to plan they'd make four jumps during the day, possibly five. They would be packing their own chutes between jumps. SEALs always jumped with chutes they'd packed themselves, that way there was no one to blame if a chute malfunctioned. They'd be pulling their own ripcords for the first jump, and there was no need for oxygen. Drake just wanted to be sure that the two men could maintain a stable position in free-fall. Assuming the basics were good they'd move up to thirty thousand feet and start jumping with oxygen.

"From fifteen down to nine I want you both in the stable position," shouted Drake. "From ten down to three you can have a bit of fun but stay close. At three you pull your mains. Got it?"

"Got it," said Croft.

"Got it," said Henderson.

The co-pilot twisted around in his seat. "Approaching the jump zone," he shouted.

The three SEALs pulled their goggles down over their eyes. They were wearing pale green jumpsuits and black backpacks containing their main chutes. On their chests were their reserve chutes, each fitted with an automatic opening device that used a small computer that would step in and open the reserve automatically in the event of an emergency.

The side door began to open inwards and upwards, revealing the green fields far below. There were a few wisps of cloud between nine thousand and ten thousand feet, otherwise the visibility was perfect.

The co-pilot began counting down with his fingers. Five. Four. Three. Two. One.

"Go!" shouted Drake.

Croft jumped first, throwing himself headlong into the slipstream and immediately adopting a perfect stable position, head back, arms and legs outstretched, his hips the lowest point of his body.

Henderson followed almost immediately and Drake was right behind him.

Drake wheeled to the left to put some distance between himself and the other two men, then he turned back to the right. Croft was in a near-perfect stable position about fifty feet away, his arms and legs barely moving in the wind. Henderson's left leg was bent awkwardly and his toes weren't pointed up enough so he was tilting to the left. As Croft watched, Henderson began to turn clockwise but then he corrected himself. The leg straightened and the turning stopped.

Drake took a quick look at the altimeter on his right wrist. In ten seconds they had fallen a thousand feet and were already close to terminal velocity — 120 miles per hour. From now on they would drop a thousand feet every five and a half seconds.

Croft maintained his perfect stable position. He began a slow clockwise turn but quickly corrected it.

Drake moved his arms back and lowered his head and went into a faster dive, taking him closer to Henderson, then snapped back into a stable position. He was about twenty feet away from Henderson, whose legs had begun to move up and down, buffeted by the wind. Drake crabbed around so that he was facing Henderson. "Legs!" he mouthed.

Henderson nodded and tensed his legs. The shaking stopped and his position stabilised. Drake flashed him the OK sign — a circle formed by the thumb and first finger of his right hand — and then crabbed away.

Drake took another look at his altimeter. Twelve thousand feet. He pushed his arms and legs out further, slowing his descent slightly, so that Croft and Henderson appeared to fall away from him. By the time they reached ten thousand feet he was about fifty feet above them.

Croft moved his arms to his side, bent at the waist, and did two quick forward somersaults and then snapped back into the stable position. Drake was impressed. He was even more impressed when Croft did a double back flip.

Henderson was less creative but he managed some very respectable sideways crabbing and a full three-sixty turn before they reached three thousand feet. Drake waited until he saw both men's chutes open before he pulled his own ripcord.

He saw both men land — Croft hit the ground running and took four or five steps before stopping, and Henderson managed to flare his chute perfectly so that he landed on both feet and stood where he was. It was the perfect landing, but Drake wasn't sure whether it had happened through luck or judgement. His own landing was somewhere in between; he hit the ground with his left foot slightly ahead of the right and took just one step before he stopped. The parachute dropped behind him and tugged at his harness. Drake quickly ran downwind of the chute to collapse it, then gathered up the rigging and chute in his arms. Croft and Henderson did the same.

A National Guard Humvee was heading their way across the grass while overhead the plane was descending towards the airfield, some twenty miles away.

"Well done, both of you," said Drake as he walked over to Croft and Henderson. "Guy, you were a bit loose on exit but you got it together. And your landing was A1." He nodded at the approaching Humvee. "We'll head back to the airfield, pick up the automatic-opening chutes and go straight back up."

"I always feel happier pulling my own ripcord," said Croft.

"I hear you," said Drake, "but we'll be opening at nine hundred feet and at terminal velocity there's no room for error."

"Yeah, but what if the automatic opening fails?" asked Croft.

"It won't," said Drake. "Never has, never will."

"Hypothetically, then?"

Drake laughed. "Hypothetically, if you get to five hundred and it hasn't opened, you can still pull the ripcord. But it won't fail, you can count on that. There's much more chance of you pulling too soon or too late if you do it manually, and if that happens then the landing could be compromised."

Croft nodded, but Drake could see that the man wasn't convinced.

"I need you focused on tracking the equipment pods we're dropping," he said. "The danger is that you lose the pods because you're too focused on your altitude, or you're so busy concentrating on the pods that you mistime the opening."

"Understood," said Croft.

Drake slapped him on the back. The Humvee pulled up in front of them and they climbed on board. "You'll enjoy it, trust me," said Drake as the Humvee moved off.

Lex Harper smiled down at the man tied to the chair, then drew back his hand and slapped him. The man groaned and his eyelids flickered. The stun gun had been as effective as Jony had promised; one burst to the man's neck and he had gone out like a light. Shakeel Usmani had remained unconscious in the back of the Transit van all the way back to the industrial unit on the outskirts of Bradford that Harper had rented for cash. Just to be on the safe side, Harper had used duct tape to bind Usmani's arms and legs and to hold a piece of cloth between his teeth. The unit was big enough to drive into and with the metal shutter door down no one would know what was going on inside.

Harper had tied Usmani to a chair and taken the gag out of his mouth before slapping him awake.

Usmani groaned and tried to focus on Harper's face.

"Wakey, wakey," said Harper.

Usmani looked around. He tried to move his arms but they were securely taped to the chair. "What the hell is this?" he asked.

"It's question time," said Harper.

"Who are you? EDL?" asked Usmani.

Harper laughed. "English Defence League? You think I'm a racist, do you?"

"You hate Muslims, is that it?"

"I hate people who try to do down my country," said Harper. "There's a name for people like that. Traitor. And that's what you are. A traitor."

"Bullshit," said Usmani.

"I know who you are and I know what you are, mate," said Harper. "I know you were in Pakistan being trained by al-Qaeda."

"Bull-fucking-shit."

"Who was it who sent you?"

"You're dreaming, man. I ain't never been to Pakistan."

"See now, I know that's a lie," said Harper. "And if there's one thing I hate as much as a traitor, it's a bare-faced liar." He walked over to the Transit, opened the rear door and took out a red petrol can. He walked back to the bound man, unscrewing the top. "You need to start telling the truth, mate. Telling the truth will set you free."

"You ain't my mate, man. I don't know what you are, but you ain't my mate."

"Tell me something. When you were out in Pakistan, did you ever meet a guy called Al-Farouq?"

"I was never in Pakistan."

"There you go, lying again." Harper splashed petrol over Usmani's legs.

"What are you doing, man? What's this about?"

"You know what this is about. I'm going to burn you." He splashed more petrol over his chest and then put the can down and took out his cigarette lighter.

"You can't do this, man," said Usmani.

"Clearly I can," said Harper. "Who's going to stop me? Allah? Do you want to pray to Allah and get him to stop me? Maybe he could send a few of your al-Qaeda mates to rescue you."

"You're sick in the head, man."

"Yeah? I'm sick? You're the one who went to Pakistan to learn how to kill people. Did they teach you to make bombs? Shoot guns? Turned you into a good jihadist, did they?"

"Who the fuck are you, man?"

Harper thrust his face close to Usmani's. "I'm your worst fucking nightmare, mate. I'm the guy who can kill you without a second thought. I'm the guy who can set fire to you and walk away with a smile on my face, because I don't give a fuck." He waved the lighter under the man's nose. He flicked the wheel with his thumb and the lighter sparked.

"OK, OK, what do you want?" said Usmani, staring at the lighter.

"Ullah sent you to Pakistan, right?"

Usmani nodded.

"For training?"

"You know he did."

Harper smiled. "That's right. Now I want you to tell me everything you know about Ullah. Every little thing."

"Then you'll let me go?"

"Sure. I don't give a shit about you, mate. You're just a cog in the machine."

"On five," said Drake, holding up his hand, fingers splayed. His seven-man team was split into two. To his right were Calvin Wood, Salvador Garcia and Lars Peterson. To his left were Adam Croft, Guy Henderson, Julio Morales and Franklin Sanders. They were standing in front of a mock-up of a two-storey building, typical of the homes found in Afghanistan and Iraq. There was a front door that led into a small room with another room behind it and beyond that a lean-to toilet and bathroom. There was a small staircase that led up to a single room that ran the full length of the building.

The building was one of fifty in the Navy's $12 million state-of-the-art training facility in Virginia Beach. It was the size of a football field and among the training buildings were houses, shops, a bank, a school, a mosque, a train and a plane. There was enough space for four units to train simultaneously using live ammunition. The walls were covered in layers of Styrofoam and rubber over steel to prevent ricochets, as were the human-shaped targets that were computer controlled and could move around on tracks.

Drake counted down with his fingers. On five, Croft kicked in the door and then immediately moved to the left. Henderson, Morales and Sanders moved into the building in single file, so close that they were touching. They all moved to the right like some three-headed six-legged animal, the barrels of their carbines covering the room. It was empty.

Croft followed them, covering the staircase, then Drake led in the rest, moving to the left.

A target appeared at the top of the stairs and Croft shot it twice, in the chest.

Henderson, Morales and Sanders moved into the next room and Drake heard all three men fire, taking out the targets at the rear of the house, followed a few seconds later by shouts of "clear!"

Drake stepped to the side, covering the stairs with Croft, and waved for Wood, Garcia and Peterson to go ahead. They moved as a well-coordinated unit, slightly crouched and their carbines constantly moving. As they entered the room at the top of the stairs there were several bursts of fire and a shout of "Clear! Hostage rescued!"

"Well done, guys, that was textbook!" shouted Drake. "We'll reset and go again in five minutes."

There were choruses of "hooyah" from the team as they headed outside. Drake stretched and looked up at

313

the roof, where a network of metal catwalks criss-crossed the mock rooms. Officers often observed from the gantries and there were facilities for recording practice sessions so that they could be analysed later. There were two figures standing looking down at them. Lieutenant Commander Villiers was casually dressed in a blue polo shirt and black jeans, leaning forward with his elbows on the railing. He nodded at Drake and Drake nodded back. Standing next to the LC was a civilian, a grey-haired man in his fifties who had been watching all the rehearsals. The LC hadn't introduced the man but from his bearing and quiet air of confidence, Drake assumed he was former military now working for the CIA or DIA or any one of the plethora of initials that made up the country's intelligence services.

The LC had asked Drake to run through a series of close-quarter battle scenarios to give the team a chance to get to know each other. They still didn't know what environment they would be operating in when they got to Pakistan, but at some point they would almost certainly be charging into a building occupied by al-Qaeda fighters.

Croft appeared at Drake's shoulder. "Nice work," said Drake.

"It's good to be doing it rather than instructing," said Croft. "You know Tiger Woods was here, a few years ago?"

"You're shitting me," said Drake.

"Nah, it was in the old House of Horrors, before they allowed live rounds. He always wanted to be a

SEAL — his dad was a Green Beret, remember? Anyway, one of the commanders was a big golfing fan so he had him in here a few times."

"Taking part?" They walked together back to the door.

"Hell, yeah. Back then it was pop-up targets and rubber bullets so it was safe enough. Except he got shot in the leg. There was hell to pay. He was lucky it was rubber rounds back then, could have ended his whole career right there."

"That's what they get for taking tourists around," said Drake. He looked at his watch. "We've got time for one more run-through," he said. "Then we're off to Kabul."

"Do we have a target yet?" asked Croft. He followed Drake through the door. The rest of the team were gathered some distance away, checking their weapons.

"They're working on it," said Drake.

"It's all a bit rushed, isn't it?"

"They want us primed and ready to go," said Drake. "That way as soon as they get a location we can be in the air." He called the rest of the SEALs over and they gathered around him. "Right, guys, just so you know, we're looking to pull two hostages out. I'll have photographs for you after this session and I need you to familiarise yourself with them. They're both Brits. One is white, and Guy and Adam are familiar with him. Just under six feet, brown hair. The other guy is also a Brit but of Pakistani heritage so we're going to have to be very careful about who we shoot. Any friendly fire is going to be more than embarrassing. We're going to have to be very, very careful out there because Raj will look like one of the bad guys. That's his name, Raj or Manraj, and he lives in London. He supports Arsenal so that's a good check question to ask him for confirmation."

"Arsenal?" asked Morales frowning. "What's an Arsenal?"

"It's a London soccer team," said Drake. "Seriously, guys, the whole point of this mission is to get these guys out in one piece so no SNAFUs." He checked to see that his message had been received and understood.

"And there's one other thing. I'll be giving you a photograph of an Arab by the name of Akram Al-Farouq. He's an al-Qaeda heavy hitter believed to be on the premises. Our ancillary mission is to bring him back alive. If not, he's a valid target. He is a major intel source so we'll look good if we can turn him in."

The men nodded.

"Right, let's go to it," said Drake.

There was another chorus of "hooyah" from the SEALs before they moved into position for the next assault.

Usmani closed his eyes and shook his head. "That's everything, man," he said. "That's all I know."

"Let me ask you a question, mate," said Harper. "You were born here, right? You're British. You're not a Pakistani, right?"

"What's that got to do with anything?"

"Because I don't understand why you're doing what you're doing. This is your country. It's your home. Why are you so hell bent on destroying it?"

316

Usmani looked up at him, blinking. "Are you stupid, man? I'm a Muslim. They want to kill us. It's a war."

"Who wants to kill you?"

"The government. They invaded Afghanistan, they invaded Iraq. They're killing our brothers and sisters around the world. Someone has to make a stand."

"By doing what? Blowing up Tube trains? Shooting down planes? You've been training to attack civilians. If you went off to try to assassinate Blair or Bush then maybe I'd say good luck to you, but killing civilians is just plain evil."

Usmani spat at the floor. "Evil? The kafirs are evil, not us." He cleared his throat and spat again. "I'm a Muslim first. That's all that matters to me."

"And that's fine, mate. You're free to believe whatever you want. That's the beauty of living in Britain, right? You want to believe the world is flat or the moon is made of green cheese, that's up to you. Nobody forces you to believe something you don't want to."

"You don't understand," said Usmani.

Harper walked slowly around the man. "I do understand, that's the problem," he said. "You don't want people to make their own choices. You want to force your religion down the throat of every man, woman and child in the country."

"Islam is the only true religion," said Usmani. "*Allahu akbar*. God is great."

"*Allahu akbar*," said Harper, taking his gun out. He pointed the barrel at the back of Usmani's head. "God is great." He turned the gun around in his hand and brought the butt smashing down on the back of Usmani's head.

Shepherd woke as soon as he heard the bolts being drawn back and he was sitting up as the door was flung open. Hands grabbed him and dragged him out into the corridor. Two big men with AK-47s kept their distance and watched him with sullen eyes. They took him to the end of the corridor and through a door into a large room with a window overlooking a small courtyard where water sprayed from a small fountain. There was a man standing looking out of the window and he turned to look at Shepherd as he was pushed into the room. He had a beaked nose and dark patches under his eyes and was wearing a long grey dishdasha robe and a small woollen skullcap atop a mop of curly hair. "My name is Mahmud," said the man. "May I know your name?" He stroked his beard as he waited for Shepherd to answer.

Shepherd looked at the man but said nothing. He knew his name wasn't Mahmud. Shepherd's memory was near-infallible at the best of times but he had seen the man's photographs only a few days earlier. It was Akram Al-Farouq. The al-Qaeda paymaster.

"You can tell me your name, surely?" said Al-Farouq. "If you tell me your name and where you are from, we can contact your embassy."

Shepherd stared at him in silence.

Al-Farouq smiled. "Never mind," he said. He pointed at a chair. "There are clothes there you can wear," he said. There was a grey cotton tunic and a pair of beige cotton pants. Shepherd pulled on the pants and tied them with a drawstring, then he pulled on the tunic. "It's not a perfect fit, but I suppose it is better than nothing," said Al-Farouq. "Now please sit."

Shepherd sat down on a wooden chair facing a small table on which there was a brass teapot and two cups. Al-Farouq said something to the two men in a language that he didn't recognise. It wasn't Arabic or Urdu so he figured it was probably Pashto, one of the two official languages of Afghanistan that was also widely spoken in north-western Pakistan. The men went to stand by the door and folded their arms.

Al-Farouq sat down and steepled his fingers under his chin. "You're not helping yourself with your silence, you realise that? You are clearly not a Pakistani so I doubt that they will help you. If you don't tell us where you are from, you will stay here and rot. Is that what you want? To die far from home, surrounded by strangers?"

Shepherd said nothing.

"Do you have a wife? Children? Don't you want them to know that you are safe?" He smiled. "Yes, you have a family, I think. You look like a family man. Think how they must be feeling, not knowing if you are alive or dead."

Shepherd felt his jaw tense involuntarily. He saw a small smile of satisfaction flit across the man's face and knew that he had seen the muscle twitch. He continued to sit in silence.

"You are American?" asked Al-Farouq. He shook his head slowly. "No. Not American. Americans are bigger, with squarer jaws. You are not American." He frowned.

"British? Are you British? But why would a Brit be with Pakistani Special Forces?"

Shepherd fought to keep his face blank as he stared at Al-Farouq.

"Are you hungry?" asked Al-Farouq. "Thirsty? All you have to do is ask." He smiled and waited, then waved at the teapot. "There is tea. Would you like tea?"

Shepherd looked down at the table.

"I can get you some water. Or some fruit. Would you like some fruit?"

Shepherd said nothing.

"You have nothing to say to me?"

Shepherd kept his eyes averted.

"I know you are British, of course. So if you are refusing to speak because you are worried that I will recognise your accent, you are wasting your time." Al-Farouq folded his arms. "The satellite phone you were carrying. You had called a London number on it. Who did you call?"

Shepherd tensed but he didn't look up. Had they brought the phone with them? If they had, and he could switch it on, it would notify Button of his location. He had to find out where the sat phone was.

"You are here for Rafiq, aren't you? This is also how I know you are British. He is your man, isn't he?"

Shepherd folded his arms and stared at the teapot. It was too soon to be talking. He had to make the man work for it.

"You shouted his name. Remember?"

Shepherd stayed silent.

"Would you like to see him? That could easily be arranged."

Shepherd said nothing.

Al-Farouq sighed. "Very well, then." He clicked his fingers and made a flicking motion with his two hands. The two men standing by the door walked towards Shepherd. Al-Farouq spoke to them in Pashto and they grabbed Shepherd by the arms and hauled him out of the chair. "Next time you are back in this room, you will be more forthcoming, I'm sure," he said. "The pain you are about to experience is the result of your own intransigence, remember that."

The two men hauled Shepherd out of the room. The men with Kalashnikovs were waiting for him in the corridor.

Charlotte Button's mobile rang as she was opening a bottle of Pinot Grigio in the kitchen. She put down the bottle and took the call. The number was blocked but she recognised Richard Yokely as soon as he spoke. "Not calling at a bad time, am I?" he said. "I can never get the hang of time differences."

"It's nine o'clock in the evening," she said. "I'm just opening a bottle of wine. Where are you?"

"I'm just leaving Virginia Beach," said Yokely. "Heading for the sandbox. I just wanted to touch base with you about the lovely Salma. Have you seen a photograph, by the way?"

"I haven't, no."

"Well, I'm looking at her photograph right now and I can tell you she's a little cutie. Long black hair, almond eyes, soft silky skin, fit body, I can see how she managed to entrance your agent."

"He's not an agent, he's an officer, and he's not mine, he's MI6."

"Well, her name is Salma Jawanda, and a cursory look suggests that she's a typical young Pakistani girl, middle-class family, university educated, Muslim but not fundamentalist, covers her head on family occasions but happy to knock back the odd glass of wine. But when I dug a little deeper all sorts of alarm bells started to ring, especially that phone number you gave me. I've checked the phone records and over the past year she's talked to a lot of people on our watch list. When she was at university she was a leading light in the student wing of Jamiat Ulema Islam and the Imamia Students Organisation. When she left university she went very quiet politically. She works for a public relations company with some big American clients. I'm told she's gotten quite close to some of those clients, too."

"So what do you think?"

"I think someone is using her. Someone who spotted her potential at university and who taught her how to stay below the radar. Do you know how she met your man?"

"I'll find out," said Button.

"One of the numbers she called belongs to a guy we're definitely interested in. A Saudi by the name of Saeed al-Haznawi who's been on our no-fly list for the last five years. And she was calling him several times a day just before the SSG went in."

"That's interesting."

"Isn't it?"

"So what do you think?"

"I think you know what I think, Charlotte. The question is, what we're going to do next."

The technique had many names, including bastinado, *falanga* and *falak*. The Germans used to call it *Sohlenstreich*. It was one of the most efficient — and painful — torture techniques, with the added advantage that it left few physical marks. Most people knew it as foot-whipping.

They had tied Shepherd to a wooden chair and fixed his legs in a set of stocks. There were two of them administering the punishment. They were either Afghans or Pakistanis — Shepherd didn't know for sure because they never spoke. The taller of the two administered the blows with a long, flexible cane. The shorter man's weapon of choice was a short flexible club made of hard rubber.

The pain was intense, and after the first few blows Shepherd had screamed at the top of his voice. The reason foot-whipping was so effective was because of the cluster of nerve endings in the foot, along with lots of small bones that were easily fractured. The excruciating pain was temporary; Shepherd could bear it because he knew it would pass, but what worried him was the damage that they were doing, short-term and long-term.

The pain wasn't as bad as when they had suspended him from the ceiling. The suspension torture had been unrelenting, and every movement had sent searing bolts of agony through his arms and shoulders, but at least he had kept passing out, which meant there had been a break until he recovered. With foot-whipping there was no passing out. Just pain. And screaming.

The two men took it in turns to beat the soles of his feet. They said nothing to him, but every now and again they spoke to each other in their own language. The one with the cane had taken his shirt off and his upper body was bathed in sweat from the exertion. He had a large gut that wobbled with every blow, and flabby bits of skin under his arms that swung to and fro. When he tired he had leant against the wall, breathing heavily, while his colleague continued the torture.

The cane and the rubber club produced completely different sensations. The cane was like an electric shock, it stung rather than burned. The club produced a duller pain that affected the whole foot.

The men weren't there to question him, they were there only to inflict pain. It wasn't personal, they weren't doing it because they hated him or because they took pleasure from his suffering. They did it because they were following orders. It was part of the process, and eventually it would end. So Shepherd screamed and shouted and tried to get free, even though he knew everything he did was futile. They would stop when they stopped and not before.

In between the blows and the pain, Shepherd tried to get his thoughts together. They must have switched the sat phone on to have known that he had called a UK number. The crucial question was where the phone had been when it was switched on, because if Charlie had been looking for it she would have seen its location. And Al-Farouq knew that Shepherd knew Raj. It had been a risk shouting out for Raj but he'd had no choice. Now he knew that Raj was in the building. But when Al-Farouq started asking questions again, Raj would be high up on his list. Shepherd had to make sure that he had his story straight. He wouldn't be able to stay silent for ever. At some point he would have to talk, and that meant he would have to lie.

Lex Harper lit a cigarette and blew smoke out through the open window of his van. His mobile phone rang and he answered it. It was Charlotte Button. "How are you getting on?" she asked.

"I'm in Bradford," he said. "I'm looking at the mosque as we speak."

"I need something soon, Lex," she said.

"I know that," said Harper. "But he's a hard man to pin down. You know he's got three families?"

"I didn't know that."

"It wasn't in the file you gave me, I got the details from one of his jihadists. Three wives, three families, three houses. He's got four kids with one wife, two with another and his latest wife — she's a teenager by the look of her — is pregnant. He moves between all three homes so you can never be sure where he is."

"So what's your plan?"

"If I can nail down which house he's staying in tonight, I can pick him up first thing when he leaves for pre-dawn prayers. Any news from Paki-land?"

"I've a few irons in the fire, but any intel you can get would be a big help."

"I should have something for you tomorrow," he said.

"Soon as you can, Lex. Spider's clock is ticking."

Shepherd touched his feet gingerly, and winced. He was sitting with his back to the wall facing the cell door. He stretched his legs out slowly and wiggled his toes. So far as he could tell there was nothing broken. His feet hurt like hell but there wasn't the searing pain of a fracture.

He'd been back in the cell for several hours. They'd dragged him all the way because his feet couldn't bear his weight. They'd let him keep his clothes and they'd given him a bowl of rancid water and a bowl of rice and some sort of vegetable. He'd eaten half the rice. At one point he'd crunched down on something hard. He had a horrible feeling it was an insect of some sort but he'd swallowed it anyway. Protein was protein, when all was said and done.

He tried to calculate how many days he'd spent in the cell. Four? Five? There was no way of telling, he didn't even know what time of day it was outside. The only point of reference he had was that when he was taken to see Al-Farouq it had been daylight, but he'd lost track of the time since then.

Charlotte Button would be looking for him, he was sure of that. But looking and finding were two very different things. He had been unconscious when they'd taken him from the fort, probably for an hour or so.

And he'd spent several more hours in the truck before they'd hauled him into his present cell. That meant he was as little as four hours' drive from the fort. Assuming the truck managed forty miles an hour on the rough roads, that would put him a hundred and sixty miles from the fort. If the trip had taken six hours then he'd be two hundred and forty miles away. That was a lot of area to cover. The only thing that would narrow the search was that the area didn't have much in the way of roads.

They'd be using satellites and drones to search for him, but he doubted that his captors would be allowing him outside any time soon. He had to do something that would help them find him. But the only thing he could think of was the sat phone and he doubted that Al-Farouq would be stupid enough to let Shepherd get his hands on it.

So far they hadn't done any permanent damage, which was good of them. He assumed that his torturers had been told by Al-Farouq not to push it too hard, to cause him pain but not to break any bones or damage any vital organs. He'd been able to tolerate the pain, albeit with a lot of shouting and screaming. He wasn't sure how brave he would be if they had threatened to cut out an eye or pull out a tooth, either of which were options available to them. There was no Human Rights Act, no rule book that al-Qaeda had to follow. They could do whatever they wanted with no comebacks. The fact that his torture had been bearable meant that they were effectively going easy on him.

He rolled up some rice into a ball and slipped it between his lips, chewing it slowly to get the maximum nutritional value from it. He tried not to think about what the next stage of the process would be. If he was lucky, they'd take him back for another chat with Al-Farouq. If he wasn't lucky . . . Shepherd shuddered and tried to think happier thoughts.

Charlotte Button made herself a cheese omelette and a green salad, poured herself a glass of wine and carried it through to the living room, where her television was already tuned to *Newsnight*. She sat and toyed with her food as Jeremy Paxman grilled a Tory politician about the failure of the government to deal with the growing problem of illiterate school leavers. She didn't have much of an appetite but knew that she had to eat to keep her strength up. She picked up the glass and smiled to herself. She hadn't lost her taste for alcohol, and there was no doubt it did help her sleep at night.

She had photographs of Saeed Al-Haznawi and Salma Jawanda on the coffee table and she stared at them as she chewed thoughtfully on a forkful of egg and cucumber. She swallowed and sipped some wine, then put down her fork and picked up her mobile. She had Yokely's number on speed-dial but the moment she heard it ring out she remembered that he wasn't in the States any more and Kabul was four and a half hours ahead of London. He answered on the fifth ring, and to her relief sounded wide awake. "Richard, I'm sorry, I'd already dialled when I remembered you're in Afghanistan."

"That's all right, Charlotte, I'm not a big one for sleeping these days. What's up?"

"I'm just looking at a photograph of the lovely Salma Jawanda."

"She is pretty, isn't she? You can see how she would have turned your man's head."

"There's no doubt, is there? She passed the info on the raid to Al-Haznawi?"

"She called him almost as soon as she'd finishing talking to your man."

"Please stop calling him that, Richard. He isn't my man, never has been and never will be."

"No offence. I meant the MI6 kid. As soon as he spilled the beans she called Al-Haznawi. That can't be a coincidence."

"Have you found out anything else about her?"

"Not much more to add, I'm afraid. She keeps a very low profile. For obvious reasons."

"What about questioning her? Either get your people to do it, or hand her over to the ISI."

"We could do that, but as soon as we move against her, Al-Haznawi will know. He'll go to ground. And probably tip off Al-Farouq."

"So why not pull in Al-Haznawi at the same time? Get them to tell us where Al-Farouq is?"

"Again, if Al-Farouq realises that we're questioning Al-Haznawi, there's a possibility that he'll just disappear. The last thing we need is him hiding in a Tora Bora cave. You sound worried, Charlotte."

"Of course I'm worried. I can only guess what hell they're putting Spider through. And Raj is a rank amateur. He hasn't been trained to withstand interrogation."

"What's your worry? That they'll kill him or that he'll talk?"

"There isn't much Raj can tell them," said Button.

"Just names, I assume. Including yours."

Button laughed. "In these days of open government, names of the MI5 big guns are easy enough to find. I just want my men home, Richard."

"How are things moving on that front?"

"Slowly."

"Then there is one thing you might consider. It'd be risky, but it would be guaranteed to get things moving."

Button picked up her wine glass. "I'm listening."

Shepherd was sleeping when they came for him, dreaming fitfully about running through a wood, branches tearing at his face and arms, dogs barking somewhere behind him. He was being hunted but he didn't know by whom or why, just that he was being chased. He wasn't aware of the bolts being drawn back or of their footsteps crossing the floor; the first he knew was when they hauled him to his feet.

They dragged him out of the cell and along the corridor. Shepherd's feet were painful but he managed to stay upright. He was bracing himself for more torture when he realised that they were taking him back to the room where he had met Al-Farouq. He relaxed a little.

Al-Farouq was standing looking out of the window at the tinkling fountain. He waited until the men had pushed Shepherd down on to the chair before turning

to look at him, a broad smile on his face. The brass teapot was on the table again, and this time there were plates of food — some chicken and what looked like lamb, some naan bread and yogurt, and fresh fruit. Shepherd couldn't see the sun through the window so other than the fact it was daytime he had no clue as to the time. The men who had brought him to the room stood either side of the door, their arms folded. A third man stood in the far corner of the room, cradling an AK-47. He had a curved knife sticking out of a thick leather belt.

Al-Farouq sat down and waved at the food. "Please, help yourself," he said. "I am sure you must be hungry."

Shepherd thought about ignoring the offer, but he knew that his body needed protein. He reached for a piece of chicken.

"Good," said Al-Farouq. "You need your strength." He poured two cups of mint tea as Shepherd chewed on the meat. He pushed one cup towards Shepherd and then sipped from the other before smacking his lips appreciatively. "You are special forces, aren't you?" asked Al-Farouq. "SAS?"

Shepherd said nothing as he continued to chew.

"Or MI6? You do not look like a spy, though." He smiled. "Real spies are nothing like they are in the movies. They are generally overweight and bald. Too much time sitting at desks. Soldiers are fit and usually have their own hair. You look like a soldier to me. And I am told you fought well at Parachinar. You stormed the building, even though you knew you were outgunned." He nodded and sipped his tea again.

Shepherd took another piece of chicken.

"You cannot stay silent for ever, you know that?" said Al-Farouq. "The pain you have suffered this far is nothing compared with what can be done to you. Have you ever had chilli rubbed into your eyes? Or your toenails removed with pliers? I know they have been beating your feet with canes, but can you imagine the pain if they were beating your testicles?" He shrugged. "My people are expert at inflicting pain. They have spent a lifetime perfecting the art."

Shepherd swallowed and took another piece of chicken.

"You are a Brit? At least tell me that."

Shepherd stared at Al-Farouq, weighing his options. He could get away without speaking only for so long. At some point they would hurt him so badly that he would have to talk, if only to stop the pain. He was on a downward slope health-wise; the chicken he was eating would give him a few hours of energy but his body was already breaking down its fat stores and before long would start work on his muscle. At least if he showed signs of cooperating, they would continue to feed him. "Yes," he said.

Al-Farouq beamed. "Excellent," he said. He nodded enthusiastically. "And why were you with the SSG?"

"I was there as an adviser," said Shepherd. "The mission was to rescue a British citizen."

"Rafiq?"

Shepherd nodded. "Yes. Rafiq Mahar."

Al-Farouq sipped his tea again. "You should try the tea," he said. "It is delicious."

"I am a prisoner of war, and I formally request that you inform the British embassy of my whereabouts," said Shepherd.

Al-Farouq chuckled softly, his eyes as hard as flint. "I would be more than happy to do that," he said. "But I will need your name, first."

Shepherd chewed on his chicken but didn't say anything.

"His name isn't Rafiq," said Al-Farouq eventually. "You know that, of course? So that was very clever of you, to call out his cover name." Al-Farouq nodded slowly. "Very clever indeed. Does he know you, I wonder? Does Manraj know you?" He smiled, like a shark going in for the kill. "Why don't we find out?"

He clicked his fingers at the man standing to the left of the door and said something to him in Pashto or Arabic. The man left the room. Al-Farouq watched Shepherd eat in silence. Shepherd swallowed his chicken, then drank some tea before grabbing a chunk of lamb. Eventually there were footsteps in the corridor and the door opened. Shepherd looked over his shoulder. He caught a glimpse of a warrior with an AK-47 peering in and then he stepped to the side and Shepherd saw Raj. He looked a lot older than the last time they'd met, even though only two years had passed. There were subtle changes in the structure of his face, the result of the plastic surgery he'd undergone, and he had a straggly, unkempt beard. But it was his eyes that worried Shepherd the most. They were blank, almost dead, as if all the life had been sucked from him.

He walked with his shoulders slumped, his arms by his side, his plastic sandals scuffing across the floor. His escort closed the door and Raj stood there, swaying from side to side.

"Tell me, Manraj," said Al-Farouk, waving a hand at Shepherd. "Do you know this man?"

Raj looked up, his face a blank mask. He stared at Shepherd and tilted his head on one side.

"He has come from England to see you," said Al-Farouq. "Do you know him?"

Raj shook his head. "No," he whispered.

Richard Yokely sat in the operations room at Basra airfield, twenty-five miles to the north of Kabul. He had his feet up on the table as he munched on a club sandwich. By his side was a carton of Tropicana orange juice. He was wearing a headset and had three cellphones lined up by his feet. On the other side of the airfield, the Navy SEALs were all primed and ready to go. All they needed was a location.

A call came in through his headset. Charlotte Button. "Are you good to go, Richard?" she asked.

"Locked and loaded," said Yokely. "I have her number being monitored. You'll get a feed of her calls and text messages. I have two teams on foot and two teams in vehicles close to her as we speak."

"And the eye in the sky?"

"Taking off at this very moment," said Yokely. "Should be over Islamabad in a little over two hours." He looked across at one of the blank screens and then looked at his wrist-watch, a multi-dialled Breitling. He was expecting a live video feed from the RQ-170 Sentinel within the next ten minutes as it made its way to Islamabad. Yokely swung his feet off the table, stood up and looked out of the window. In the distance he could see the pristine white drone waiting for take-off.

The Sentinel was one of the most secret airplanes in the world. It had never been photographed close up and its manufacturer, Lockheed Martin, remained tight lipped about its specifications. It was a tailless flying wing, some twenty metres across, with the upper surface of the wing kitted out with pods packed with sensors and communication equipment, and it had full motion video capability. It was powered by a single General Electric turbofan engine producing more than nine thousand pounds of thrust. Unlike the better-known Reapers and Predators, the Sentinel didn't carry weapons. The Sentinel was all about surveillance and stealth. It was pretty much invisible to radar, which meant it could operate at a lower height than most drones, with a working altitude of about fifteen thousand metres.

The Sentinel was being launched from Basra but once it had reached operation altitude control would be handed over to a three-man team from the 30th Reconnaissance Squadron, some 7,500 miles away in Nevada's Tonopah Test Range Airport. Three years earlier a Sentinel flown by a team at Tonopah had beamed back live footage of the Navy SEAL attack that had led to the death of Bin Laden. Since then the Sentinels had made regular flights into Pakistan airspace, leading to protests by the Pakistan government and calls for the US to stop its spy flights. As always, the protests were ignored. Once the Nevada team had control of the drone they would fly it just under a hundred miles to the Pakistan border, and another hundred miles or so to Islamabad, where it would start beaming live video to Yokely's operations room and to Charlotte Button in London. Yokely had set up lines of direct communication with the piloting team in Nevada, with Charlotte Button in Thames House in London, with Lieutenant Commander Dick Blanchard in Virginia Beach, and with his CIA technical expert, Eric Feinstein, in Langley, Virginia.

"And the SEALs?" asked Button.

"Getting some shut-eye. Their plane is fuelled and all their gear is on board. They can be in the air in thirty minutes."

"What plane are they using?"

"They were thinking about using a converted Boeing 727 in case they get picked up on Pakistan's radar, but they're going to be so close to the border they've decided to stick with the Hercules C-130. The plane will be staying at thirty thousand feet so if they do get spotted they'll just assume it's an airliner that's drifted across the border. How are things at your end?"

"Getting all my ducks in a row," she said. "Two hours sounds about right. I'll call you once we're ready."

"I'll be waiting," said Yokely, swinging his feet back up on to the table and reaching for his orange juice.

Lex Harper opened the rear doors of the Transit van and stretched. Mohammed Ullah had just shut his front door and was walking along the pavement, fingering a set of prayer beads in his right hand. He was wearing a dark green quilted jacket over a long flowing shirt and baggy trousers, and sandals over thick grey socks.

Harper was wearing a parka with the hood down so that the imam couldn't fail to notice the white-knitted Muslim skullcap he was wearing. "Good morning, brother," said Harper as the imam drew level with him.

"Good morning," said Ullah.

"Are you by any chance Mohammed Ullah?"

"I am," said Ullah. "Do I know you?"

"I'm your neighbour," said Harper. "I live at number fifty-four. Some of your mail was put into my letterbox by mistake." He took his left hand out of his coat pocket and held out three brown envelopes. "I was going to pop them round later."

"Thank you brother, that is good of you," said Ullah. He held out his hand for the letters.

Harper took a step closer to the imam. As Ullah took the letters, Harper's right hand emerged from his parka, holding the stun gun. He jammed the prongs against Ullah's chest and pressed the trigger. There was a loud cracking sound and Ullah stiffened. His eyes bulged and his mouth opened wide and then he dropped to the ground. Harper caught him and dragged him to the rear of the Transit and rolled him inside. He looked around to reassure himself that no one was looking before jumping into the back and pulling the doors shut behind him. He used a roll of duct tape to bind the imam's wrists and ankles, then shoved a piece of rag into the man's mouth and used duct tape to hold it in place. Ullah was still unconscious when Harper slid into the driving seat and started the engine.

Charlotte Button showed Willoughby-Brown and Bashir into the meeting room. It was one of the smaller rooms, windowless with a framed oil painting of the River Thames on one wall and a long beech table with six chrome and leather chairs around it. She sat down first, taking a seat at the head of the table. "Thank you both for coming in," she said.

"No problem," said Willoughby-Brown, though he was well aware that Button had given him no choice in the matter. He took the seat at the far end of the table and Bashir sat down next to him.

Button had brought a cup of tea with her but she pointedly didn't offer them a beverage.

"Any news from Pakistan?" Button asked Willoughby-Brown.

The MI6 man shook his head. "The military have gone very quiet."

Button nodded. She smiled over at Bashir. "So, Taz, what can you tell me about Salma Jawanda?"

The look of surprise on Bashir's face was priceless, thought Button, but she kept a straight face.

"I'm sorry?" Bashir looked across at Willoughby-Brown, who looked equally perplexed by the question.

"Salma. Don't tell me you've forgotten about her already."

Bashir frowned. "I don't understand the question."

"It's simple enough. How is Salma?"

"She's fine, I suppose." He looked over at Willoughby-Brown. "Salma is a friend of mine."

Button laughed. "Come on now, Taz. She's more than a friend. A girlfriend at the very least."

Bashir looked helplessly at Willoughby-Brown.

"Charlotte, seriously, what's going on here?" asked Willoughby-Brown.

Button ignored the question and kept her gaze focused on Bashir, who seemed to be having trouble swallowing. "How did you meet her, Taz?"

"A restaurant," said Bashir. "She was eating alone and so was I and we got talking. She's from a good family, she went to the top university in Pakistan. The University of the Punjab. In Lahore."

"And what does she do for a living?"

"She works in public relations."

"And she is your lover, correct?"

Bashir sat back and put his hands down on the table. "I really don't see that's any business of yours."

Button looked over at Willoughby-Brown. He was frowning now. "You were having a relationship with a local?" he said. "Why didn't you tell me?"

"She's a friend. I went out with her a few times. What's the problem with that?"

"She's a very pretty girl, isn't she? Stunning?"

"I suppose so. Yes."

Button looked at Willoughby-Brown again. "She is very, very pretty," said Button. She opened the file and slid a head-and-shoulders photograph across the table. He picked it up, looked at it, and then put it down. "I knew nothing about this," he said.

"Clearly," said Button. "You didn't wonder why a girl as pretty as Salma would fall into your bed at the earliest opportunity?" she asked Bashir. "Especially seeing as how she's from a good family."

Bashir stared at the photograph. There were beads of sweat on his upper lip.

"A good Muslim family, too. It didn't seem strange that she had sex with you so quickly?"

Bashir opened his mouth, then closed it again. He shook his head. "I don't know what you want me to say."

"Was it because you have a British passport, do you think? She saw you as a way of getting into the UK?"

"Of course not. She's happy in Pakistan. She loves her country."

"I'm sure she does. So what do you think she sees in you, then, if not a passport?"

Bashir swallowed again but didn't speak.

"Did she introduce you to her family?"

"I haven't been going out with her for long."

"What about her friends? Did she introduce you to her friends?"

He shook his head. Button took another photograph from the file and slid it over to Bashir. "What about this gentleman?" It was another head-and-shoulders shot that looked as if it had been blown up from a passport application. It was an Arab man in his forties with a close-cropped beard and deep-set, hooded eyes. "His name is Saeed al-Haznawi. Did you ever meet him?"

Willoughby-Brown reached for the photograph. "Who is he?"

"I already said. Saeed al-Haznawi. He's a Saudi. With links to Lashkar-e-Jhangvi. Have you heard of them?"

Bashir swallowed nervously. "They're a sectarian militant group." He looked up at Button. "Salma knows him?"

"They seem to be quite close," said Button. "She has been phoning him a lot lately. Especially before the SSG went in to rescue Raj."

Bashir put his head in his hands. "I don't believe this," he said.

"I think you do," said Button. "I think you know how stupid you've been."

"I thought she loved me. She said she loved me."

"Taz, you fell for the oldest trick in the book," said Button. "All you can do now is to try and make things right."

Bashir groaned and ran his hands through his hair. He looked at Willoughby-Brown. "I'm finished, aren't I?"

"Career-wise? Yes, I rather think you are."

Bashir cursed and folded his arms as he stared at the ceiling. "She told them that the SSG were going in?"

Button nodded. "Yes."

"So all those men who died. That was down to me?"

"There's no point in torturing yourself, old son," said Willoughby-Brown. "What matters now is that we try to put this right."

Bashir took a deep breath and then exhaled slowly. "What do you want me to do?" he asked Button.

"I need you to tell Salma that we know where Shepherd is and that a rescue mission is being planned."

"Do you?"

"No, but that's not the point. The point is that if Salma thinks that we do, she'll tell al-Haznawi. She'll either phone him or meet with him. We'll be listening in to her phone and we'll have them both tailed. Once Al-Haznawi is told of the rescue, he'll have to warn Al-Farouq. So all we have to do then is track Al-Haznawi to Al-Farouq."

"What will you do to Salma?"

Button frowned. "Do to her? What do you mean?"

"The bitch lied to me. And because of her, all those soldiers are dead."

"You don't need to concern yourself with that," said Button. "And you need to lose the anger. She'll pick up on it. She has to think you're still madly in love with her. You're ringing for a chat, and in between telling her how much you miss her, you let slip that we know where Spider is and the Pakistanis are about to launch a rescue. Can you do that, Taz?"

Bashir nodded. "Sure."

"Take a few minutes to compose yourself. You have to be all sweetness and light, she mustn't suspect that you're on to her."

Bashir nodded and took another deep breath. "I can do it," he said.

"Charlotte, can I have a word?" asked Willoughby-Brown. "In private?"

Button smiled at Bashir. "Taz, why don't you pop down to the canteen and get yourself a coffee."

Bashir nodded and left the office. Willoughby-Brown waited until the door had closed before turning on

Button. "I'm far from bloody happy with this, Charlotte," he said.

"I'm not best pleased myself," said Button.

"I'm talking about the way that you've handled this," said Willoughby-Brown prissily. "You practically ambushed me here."

"Things have been moving very quickly," said Button. "I haven't really had time for the niceties."

"You could have at least told me what you'd found out about Taz and this Salma woman."

"I could have done, yes. But then perhaps you should have kept a closer eye on him in the first place."

"That's not fair," said Willoughby-Brown. "I wasn't out in Islamabad."

"Exactly," said Button. "Maybe you should have been. You sent out an inexperienced officer to one of the most dangerous countries in the world. It's as if you put a target on his chest."

"That's an exaggeration and you know it."

"He's a kid, Jeremy. He probably felt out of his depth and when a pretty girl came on to him, he just acted without thinking."

"I can't believe you've made this about me," said Willoughby-Brown. "I'm not the one who fucked up."

"Taz was your man," said Button. "He fell into a honey trap and revealed operational details. And as a direct result of the information he gave to Salma, a lot of good men died and one of my best men is going through God only knows what hell. So don't you start mouthing off about an ambush. I needed Taz here without him knowing what was going on and the best way of doing that was to have you bring him in. In a perfect world I would have had time to brief you first, but I didn't and frankly I'm not going to apologise for that. This all started when you decided to run an MI6 operation on British soil without referring to MI5, then to compound that you sent out an inexperienced officer to Pakistan who then blew a rescue mission. Everything I'm doing right now is geared to clearing up the mess that you're ultimately responsible for. Anyway, you've done your bit by delivering Taz to me. You can go now."

"What?"

"Go. Just go, Jeremy."

"Are you serious?"

"Absolutely." She folded her arms and glared at him.

Willoughby-Brown opened his mouth to protest but could see from the look in her eyes that there was nothing he could say that was going to change her mind, so he got up and walked out of the room, cursing under his breath.

"Good riddance," Button muttered. She sipped her tea and gave him enough time to get into the lift, then she headed down the corridor to the operations room where Amar Singh was already sitting in front of the monitors, sipping a coffee. "Everything OK?" she asked. Most of the wall opposite the monitors was taken up with a large map of Pakistan and Afghanistan.

"We're getting there," he said.

"What about the feed from the drone?"

"Eric's on the case," said Singh.

Button sat down and fitted a headset that was plugged into a digital console. "Which button is for Yokely?" she asked.

"On the left," said Singh. "I spoke to him a few minutes ago."

She pressed the button and immediately heard a static buzz over the headset. "Richard, we'll be ready to go in a few minutes. Are you prepared?"

"We've got eyes on Saeed al-Haznawi and the girl," said Yokely cheerfully. "And the Sentinel is over Islamabad as we speak. Eric here is arranging the feed for your man Amar."

"That's great, Richard. Just please don't lose them."

"I'll do my best," said Yokely.

"And the SEALs are ready?"

"They're on the plane now."

"This is going to be very tight."

Yokely chuckled. "Operations don't get much tighter," he said.

"Tell me we're doing the right thing, Richard."

"You're not having second thoughts, are you?" asked the American.

"Not second thoughts. More like first-night nerves."

"We can still pull the plug. We haven't crossed any lines yet."

Button sighed. Part of her did indeed want to pull the plug. If it went wrong and they moved Shepherd again, they might not find him a second time. Worse, they might kill him.

"Charlotte?"

"Still here, Richard. No, we need to do something now. They'll be torturing Spider, Raj too. Every hour we delay is going to be hell for them. I know it's a risk, but it's a risk worth taking."

"The SEALs are the best of the best," he said. "If anyone can get your guys out of there, it's the SEALs."

"I know that," she said.

"All they need is a location, and we'll get that by following Al-Haznawi. Either he'll phone Al-Farouq, in which case the NSA will have his location. Or he'll go there in person, in which case the Sentinel will follow him. It's a good plan, Charlotte."

"I know that, Richard. But it's good to hear you say so."

"God bless, Charlotte."

"And you, Richard. God bless."

Al-Farouq poured tea for Raj, and then topped up his own beaker and Shepherd's. Raj was eating his way through a handful of grapes. Shepherd's mind was racing as he continued to chew on a naan dipped in yogurt. He wasn't sure when he'd be fed again so he was forcing as much food into his system as he could.

"This is the man who came to rescue you, Manraj," said Al-Farouq. "You are sure you do not know him?"

Raj avoided Shepherd's gaze and stared at the floor as he shook his head.

"You have not met before?"

Raj shook his head again.

Al-Farouq looked over at Shepherd. "And what about you? Have you met Manraj before?"

"I was just attached to the SSG as an adviser," said Shepherd.

"Why you?" asked Al-Farouq. "Why would the SSG need a soldier from England? Was it because they felt it would be advantageous for Manraj to see a friendly face?"

"He doesn't know me. I don't know him. The idea was that after we rescued him, I would be responsible for his welfare until we could fly him out of the country."

"And what did they tell you his name was?"

"I told you. Rafiq. Rafiq Mahar."

"From London?"

"From Bradford."

"And they showed you a photograph, did they? So you would recognise him."

Shepherd nodded. He reached for another piece of naan bread and dipped it into the yogurt. He could feel that Al-Farouq was toying with him, but he still wasn't sure where the conversation was heading.

"And these people who sent you all this way to take care of Manraj, did they tell you that he was responsible for the killing of Osama Bin Laden? That it was Manraj who betrayed the Sheikh?"

Raj looked up as if he had been stung and Al-Farouq smiled in triumph. "Yes, Manraj. I know who you are, and I know what you did. And soon you will pay the price."

Bashir took a deep breath, exhaled, and then forced a smile. "You're going to have to relax, Taz," said Button. "She'll pick up on any signs of nervousness. It has to sound like every other chat you've ever had."

Bashir nodded. "I can do it," he said.

"I know you can," said Button. "It might be easier if you turn your back on me. Pretend that I'm not here. And keep it light. She's your girlfriend, you miss her, you want to be with her."

"Play the lovesick puppy, you mean?"

Button smiled. She thought it best not to say that she had already heard him on the phone to his beloved Salma. "The sweeter the better," she said.

They were in the meeting room, just the two of them. Amar Singh was in an operations room down the corridor from where he was monitoring the call and liaising with Richard Yokely in Kabul.

Bashir nodded and stared at his iPhone. He scrolled through the address book.

"You use Skype, don't you?" said Button.

Bashir frowned, wondering how she knew that. He nodded. "It's cheaper."

"So make sure you use Skype this time. Are you ready?"

Bashir took another deep breath. "OK," he said. He turned his back on her and called Salma's number.

"Hello, honey," she said. "Are you OK?"

"I'm fine, baby. What are you doing?"

"Working," she said. "Boring stuff. I've got to get a press release out about some new mobile phone and I'm running out of ways of describing it. It's a phone. That's it."

"Sorry, baby. How's the weather there?"

She laughed. "It's Pakistan, honey. It's hot. What about you?"

"I'm in the office. Just been debriefed."

"Are you OK? You're not in trouble?"

Bashir forced a laugh. "They're blaming the Pakistani military," he said. "But the good news is that I'll be back in Islamabad soon."

"Really? Honey, that's great."

"They're talking about sending me back as soon as Wednesday."

"Honey, that's wonderful. That's amazing, I'm so pleased. What's happened?"

"It's all very hush-hush, baby. But it looks as if they've found out where they're holding Shepherd. Remember? That SAS guy who got taken when the SSG raided the fort."

"Really? That's great news. Where is he?"

"That's classified, baby. But the army is getting ready to rescue him and this time they're not going to make any mistakes. They want me in Islamabad so that I can be there when he's released."

"Honey, I'm so happy. When will you know when your flight is? I'll come and meet you at the airport."

"I think they'll tell me later today, baby. Tomorrow at the latest."

"That's great. I'm so, so pleased. Call me as soon as you know, honey. Anyway, I've got to go, I'm on a really tight deadline with this press release."

"I will do, baby. See you soon. Kiss kiss."

Bashir ended the call and turned to look at Button. "How was that?" he asked.

Button held out her hand and Bashir gave her the iPhone. "That was perfect," she said.

"What happens now?" he asked.

"You should go and see your parents. Spend some time with your family."

"I meant about my job. What's going to happen?"

Button looked pained. "I don't think you'll have a job for much longer, Taz. Willoughby-Brown will make sure of that. He'll want to put some distance between the two of you."

"You mean he'll make me the fall guy for this?"

"Taz, you revealed details of an ongoing operation to an enemy of the state. You'll be lucky not to end up in prison."

"Are you serious?"

"At the very least you're in breach of the Official Secrets Act," she said.

"Miss Button, please, is there anything you can do?"

Button shrugged. "Five and Six are completely separate," she said. "You're just going to have to make a clean breast of it."

"You really think I'll go to prison?"

Button shook her head. "I think Six will want to draw a veil over the whole sorry episode," she said. "They'll probably ask you to resign and that'll be the end of it."

"And what about Salma? What'll happen to her?"

Button shrugged. "That's not my concern," she said. "But if I know Willoughby-Brown, he'll want his pound of flesh. If I was a betting woman I'd put money on him telling the ISI about her once this is over."

"They'll torture her," said Bashir.

"Well, that's her problem," said Button. "You need to think about yourself from now on. She's caused you enough trouble as it is."

Bashir sat down at the table and put his head in his hands as Button left the room. She walked down the corridor and pushed open the door to the operations room. Amar Singh was sitting in front of the monitors and talking into a headset. He flashed her a thumbs-up as he continued the conversation. "Got it, Eric, thanks." He pointed at the left-hand monitor, which was showing an overhead view of Islamabad. "That's the live feed from the drone," he said to Button.

"Excellent," said Button. She pulled up a chair and fitted a headset. "What about Salma?"

"She was on to al-Haznawi as soon as she hung up on Bashir," said Singh.

"Did we hear the conversation?"

Singh shook his head. "No, but it was short and sweet."

Button pressed the button on the console that connected her to Richard Yokely. "Richard, it's me. What's happening?"

"According to my team on the ground, Salma has just left her office. And al-Haznawi is in his car as we speak," said the American. "If they're not heading for a meeting then I'm a Dutchman."

"And I know you're not a great one for clogs or dykes," said Button. "What about your SEALs?"

"On the plane," said Yokely. "As soon as we get a definite location they'll be in the air. Have to go, Charlotte, I need to talk to my teams."

Yokely cut the connection. Button settled back in her chair as she watched the live feed from the Sentinel drone, high above the Pakistan capital.

Harper closed the shutter door to the industrial unit before opening the rear doors of the Transit and dragging Mohammed Ullah out. He was conscious and stared sullenly at Harper as he lay on the concrete floor.

Harper had already fed a length of chain through a pulley affixed to one of the metal beams that criss-crossed the roof space. He took one end of the chain and tied it around the imam's ankles, then used a penknife to cut the duct tape away from his mouth. Ullah spat out the rag and gasped for breath.

"How do you contact Akram Al-Farouq?" asked Harper, putting on a pair of heavy leather gloves.

"Who?"

"You know who. Don't play the arsehole. He's the guy who sends you al-Qaeda money. Don't pretend you've forgotten."

"You have me confused with someone else," said Ullah. "I am an imam. A holy man. I am not political, I have nothing to do with al-Qaeda. Somebody has been lying to you."

"How do you contact Al-Farouq?"

"I don't know anyone by that name."

"I know that you do know," said Harper. "All you're going to do by denying it is cause yourself a whole world of hurt."

Ullah shook his head. "I am an imam."

Harper pulled on the chain and it tightened. He pulled again, using his full weight, and Ullah was scraped along the concrete.

"This is madness!" shouted Ullah. "You can't do this."

"Yeah, I can," said Harper. He grunted and used all his weight to pull down on the chain. Ullah's feet lifted off the ground. Another hard pull and his legs were up in the air and Ullah was bent at the waist. "Last chance."

Ullah swore at Harper and Harper grinned savagely before pulling down on the chain. It took several hard pulls before Ullah's head left the ground and another three to get his head up to the level of Harper's knees. Harper looped the free length of the chain over a water pipe and tied it fast.

"I don't know who you are talking about," wailed the imam.

"Yeah, you said." Harper walked over to a bench and picked up a length of two-by-four. He hefted the length of wood in his hand and swung it like a cricket bat.

"Al-Farouq sends you money," said Harper. "You send him jihadists. So you have to have some way of contacting him at short notice."

"I don't know what you're talking about!"

Harper waved the piece of wood under Ullah's nose. "You can stop this right now," he said. "Just tell me how you contact Al-Farouq."

"You're crazy!" spat the imam.

"No, crazy is you preferring to be treated like a piñata instead of telling me how to contact Al-Farouq."

"I don't know!" Ullah screamed. "Believe me, I don't know!"

Harper banged the free end of the wood on the floor. "Here's the thing," he said. "I don't believe you."

Salma Jawanda checked her driving mirror again, then turned off the main road and parked. She kept looking in her driving mirror and when she was satisfied that she wasn't being followed she did a U-turn and drove back on to the main road. It was the third time she'd done the manoeuvre since she'd left her home and on all three occasions her followers had pre-empted her. There were two teams tailing her, one in front and one behind. Each time she had turned off the car ahead of her had turned first and the car behind her had continued on its way. The cars were in direct radio contact with each other and they continued to play tag with her car as it headed west out of Islamabad. It was just before five o'clock, rush hour, so the roads were busy and the traffic moved slowly. There were two CIA agents in each car, a driver and a female passenger. The passengers monitored the radio and also maintained contact with Richard Yokely in Basra, who was monitoring their progress through the stealth drone that was flying fifteen thousand metres above them.

Salma drove to the outskirts of the Pakistan capital and parked outside a small café. As she climbed out of her Honda Civic she saw Al-Haznawi's white Daihatsu Terios. There was a man sitting in the driver's seat reading a newspaper and a garland of white flowers hanging from the driver's mirror, the sign that

354

everything was OK and that the meeting was safe. She adjusted her headscarf, put on a pair of dark glasses and headed into the café.

Al-Haznawi was sitting at a corner table, a copy of the *Pakistan State Times* in front of him. That was the final check. If the paper was open, as it was, the meeting was safe. If the paper had been folded it was a sign the meeting had been compromised and she had to leave. Salma sat down opposite him. He greeted her with a smile and a nod of his head. An elderly waiter came over and she ordered a mint tea and Al-Haznawi asked for fresh ice for his fruit juice.

Al-Haznawi didn't speak until the waiter was out of earshot. "You are sure you weren't followed?"

"I was careful," she said.

He nodded. "Tell me what he said."

"He said they knew where the SAS man was being held. He said the SSG were going to go in and rescue him and that this time there would be no mistake."

"And he is still in England?"

"He was in to see his bosses this morning. He phoned me shortly after the meeting."

"How did he sound?"

"Happy," she said. "It means they are sending him back to Islamabad."

Al-Haznawi rubbed his right earlobe thoughtfully. "Did he say when, exactly?"

"No, just that it would be soon. Maybe as early as Wednesday."

"He said that? Wednesday?"

Salma nodded. "Yes. He said he might be back on Wednesday."

"So he thinks the SSG might be ready to mount a rescue the day after tomorrow?"

"That's what he said."

The waiter returned with her tea and a glass full of ice cubes. He put the tea down in front of Salma and used a pair of brass tongs to add ice to Al-Haznawi's glass of fruit juice. "Would you care for something sweet?" the waiter asked Salma. "We have a delicious semolina cake, and some freshly baked coconut cupcakes."

"No, thank you," said Salma.

The waiter smiled and walked away slowly. His left hand was shaking as if it had a mind of its own.

"Did he say where he believed the SAS man was being held?"

"No."

"Or how they know where he is?"

"No. I couldn't ask, it would have made him suspicious."

"Yes, yes, of course. I wasn't being critical, you have been superb right from the start. If it hadn't been for you, it would all have ended in Parachinar. I just want to make sure that I have the facts straight."

Salma sipped her tea. "What will you do?" she said.

"I will have to warn them, obviously."

"I can call him again," she said. "See if he has any more information."

"You must be careful not to chase him," he said.

She smiled. "He likes to be chased," she said. Her phone beeped to tell her that she had received a text message. She took her phone from her bag, looked at the screen and smiled. She held out the phone so that Al-Haznawi could read the message. "MISS YOU BABY. ALL THE TIME. XXX".

Al-Haznawi smiled and nodded. Salma put the phone back into her bag. "You have done well, my dear," said Al-Haznawi. "Better than anyone could have expected."

"Are you seeing the drone feed, Charlotte?" asked Yokely in Button's headset.

"The picture is perfect," said Button. "The level of detail is amazing." The view on the main screen was of the car park where Salma had left her Honda.

"It's because the drone can fly so low, it's virtually invisible to radar and is so small it's almost impossible to spot visually," said Yokely. "The perfect eye in the sky. You see that white SUV? That's Al-Haznawi's vehicle. I have a team in the car park."

"Can you get a tracker on his vehicle?"

"Negative. He has a driver and the driver is staying with the car."

"What about getting your people inside the café?"

"I didn't want to push it. Any stranger in there could spook them. Now the way I see this, it will go one of two ways. Following the meeting, Al-Haznawi will phone Al-Farouq to warn him. We're monitoring Al-Haznawi's phone and will be watching for any other calls made from the vicinity of the café. If he phones Al-Farouq, we'll know and we'll get a fix on it."

"Excellent," said Button.

"The Hercules took off half an hour ago and they are already close to the border. Once we get a location they'll move in for the drop."

"What if he doesn't make a call?

"Assuming he buys what Salma tells him, he'll have to warn Al-Farouq, so if he doesn't call he'll go to see him. The flight can stay in the air until we know for sure. The drone can follow him anywhere. I'm going to be pulling the surveillance teams well back once he leaves the café. He'll be ultra-cautious."

"It'll be dark in, what, two hours?"

"Just before 1900 hours, yes. But the drone is as good in the dark as it is in daylight. Best infrared going."

"What about the SEALs? Are they good to drop at night?"

"They're big boys, Charlotte. They're not scared of the dark." He laughed. "They train for this, day or night, it's the same for these guys. Relax. Just sit back and enjoy the show."

"I know we're in good hands, Richard," said Button. "I'll let you get on with it." She cut the connection and took off her headset. Bashir's mobile buzzed and she picked it up. It was a text from Salma. "MISS YOU TOO HONEY. CAN'T WAIT UNTIL YOU COME BACK. XXX".

★ ★ ★

Raj was crying. He was sitting with his arms folded and his head down and tears were falling from his cheeks and plopping on to the concrete floor. Al-Farouq was watching him with undisguised contempt. "What I don't understand is why your bosses sent you back to Pakistan," he said. "Did they think you wouldn't be recognised? Did they think that a beard and some plastic surgery would fool us?"

"How did you recognise him?" asked Shepherd. The two guards were still standing either side of the door, their arms folded, their faces impassive. The bearded man with the AK-47 was staring at Shepherd as if he wanted nothing more than to empty his magazine into Shepherd's chest.

Al-Farouq looked over at Shepherd and tilted his head on one side as he narrowed his eyes.

"Why do you ask?"

"Maybe you're wrong. Maybe you have been misinformed."

"You think that, do you? You think I have been misinformed?"

"The Americans killed Bin Laden. Everybody knows that."

Al-Farouq's eyes hardened. "They do, yes. But not everyone knows that the Americans were acting on information supplied by Manraj and his friend. They were in Pakistan in 2012 and they met the Sheikh in Abbottabad. They met him and then they betrayed him."

Raj shook his head. "That's not true," he said, wiping his eyes with the back of his hands.

"Oh, it is true, Manraj," said Al-Farouq, his eyes still on Shepherd. "But what I am now wondering is whether or not your friend here knew that." He smiled at Shepherd without warmth. "That is the question I want answering, Mr Shepherd. Did you know? Were you involved in the betrayal of Osama Bin Laden?"

Shepherd tried not to show any reaction but his mind was racing. How did Al-Farouq know his name? And what else did he know?

Salma walked out of the café, climbed into her Honda Civic, and drove back to Islamabad. Saeed Al-Haznawi watched her drive away as he sipped the last of his fruit juice. The waiter returned with his change but Al-Haznawi waved him away. A thought struck him and he called the waiter back and ordered a semolina cake and six coconut cupcakes to go. A gift of cakes might go some way to softening the bad news that he was taking to Al-Farouq. He waited by the door until the waiter came over with his order, then went outside and climbed into the front passenger seat of the SUV. He looked at his watch. If he made good time he would reach Peshawar within two hours. He nodded at the driver and the man started the engine and headed west. Some fifteen thousand metres overhead, the stealth drone followed them.

"Cat got your tongue, Mr Shepherd?" said Al-Farouq. He grinned triumphantly. "Yes, I know who you are. And I know who you work for. I know you once served with the British SAS and that you now work for the

Security Service, MI5. See, Mr Shepherd. I know everything."

Shepherd kept his face blank. It was important that Al-Farouq didn't know what he was thinking. He maintained eye contact and tried not to swallow. Had Raj told Al-Farouq who Shepherd was? That didn't seem likely, despite everything that Raj had been through. There had to be something else going on. Raj didn't know that the SSG were going to try to rescue him, or that Shepherd would be part of the rescue team. There was nothing Raj knew that could have compromised the SSG rescue attempt. That information must have come from someone inside the Pakistan military or from their intelligence services. A traitor. Had that same traitor betrayed Shepherd to Al-Farouq?

Al-Farouq's grin widened. "Do you know who I am, Mr Shepherd?"

"You said your name was Mahmud." He tried to keep his voice flat and emotionless.

"That's right. Do you believe me?"

Shepherd feigned confusion, as if he didn't understand what was happening.

Al-Farouq knew who Raj was. And Shepherd. Shepherd wasn't sure how Al-Farouq knew. Not that it mattered how he had come by the information. What mattered now was what Al-Farouq was going to do.

"Who am I, Mr Shepherd?"

Shepherd frowned. "Mahmud."

Al-Farouq walked over to Shepherd and stood looking down at him. "Why did you come to Pakistan?"

"To help with the rescue of a British citizen."

"And how did you know where he was being held? How did you know about the fort at Parachinar?"

"The Pakistani military knew where the fort was."

Al-Farouq nodded slowly. "And who briefed you on the mission? Before the attack?"

His face was so close to Shepherd's that Shepherd could smell the garlic on his breath.

"It was a brigadier," said Shepherd.

"What was his name?"

"I can't remember," lied Shepherd.

"I don't believe you," said Al-Farouq.

"It's true. Some Pakistani name, obviously. But I don't remember."

"Let's see if some physical pain will help you remember."

"It won't," said Shepherd.

"You don't know what I've got in mind," said Al-Farouq. He straightened up and said something to the men guarding the door before turning back to Shepherd. "I know you can stand pain, Mr Shepherd. You have an astonishingly high threshold, even if you do scream a lot. But I wonder how high your threshold is when it comes to your friend." He gestured at Raj.

Shepherd could feel a growing sense of panic threaten to overwhelm him but he fought to keep his voice steady. "He's not my friend."

"We shall see," said Al-Farouq. He left the room with the two guards, leaving the man with the AK-47 watching them. He had his finger on the trigger and the selector switch was set to fully automatic. Considering they were in a confined space it was an incredibly

362

dangerous way of holding the gun; he just hoped the man knew what he was doing.

Raj looked over at Shepherd. "What's going to happen?" he asked fearfully.

"It's OK," said Shepherd, though he knew the situation was far from being OK.

"What's he going to do?"

"I'm not sure," said Shepherd.

"I didn't tell him anything," said Raj.

Shepherd forced a smile. "Good man."

The white SUV remained dead centre in the middle of the screen as it powered along the road. "How does it do that?" said Button. "No matter which way the road bends, the drone keeps it dead centre."

"The camera's controlled by an AI program," said Singh. "Artificial intelligence. Once the target is locked in, the camera will keep on it no matter what. And when necessary, the program makes suggestions for course changes for the pilot. In a few more generations, they won't even need a pilot."

"I'm not sure if that's a good thing or not," she said.

"You and me both," said Singh. "The Reapers and Predators they have at the moment can carry out entire hunter-killer missions with no human involvement at all. They just program the target in, launch, and the computers do the rest."

"It's a brave new world, that's a fact," said Button.

"What they don't tell you is that the accident rate of a drone is three times that of a conventional aircraft," said Singh.

"Please don't jinx it," said Button.

At that exact moment the screen pixellated and went black.

"That's not funny, Amar," said Button.

Singh put his hands in the air. "Nothing to do with me," he said, "I swear."

Button reached for the button on the console to talk to Yokely. "Richard. What's happening?"

"I don't know," said Yokely. "It's gone blank here too."

Singh was talking to his contact Eric as he tapped on his keyboard.

Button heard a muffled conversation through her headset, culminating with the American swearing. "Charlie, we've got a technical SNAFU. It's not the first time apparently. The sensors are working but the Sentinel isn't able to upload the data."

"Can you fix it?"

Yokely sighed. "I'd be lying if I said we can," he said. "At the moment we're flying blind. The pilot has the instrument details so we can fly it, but we're not getting any visuals at all. Like I said, I think the camera is OK and the drone has the pictures, it's just they're not getting from the drone to us. We're going to continue on the same course but if we don't get the visuals sorted we're going to have to bring it back to base. I'm sorry, Charlotte. We can't afford to have it crashing in Pakistan."

"I understand, Richard," she said.

"I'm going to see what other drones are available. If we're lucky there'll be something in the air close by."

She thanked him, took off her headset and placed it on the desk. "Shit, shit, shit," she said.

Singh pushed back his chair and threw up his hands. "I told you. They can be so bloody unreliable at times."

"He's going to try and get an alternate in the air."

"What do we do?" asked Singh.

"I don't know," said Button, her mind racing. "If we can't track al-Haznawi back to wherever they're holding Spider, they'll move him and it'll be over." Her eyes widened. "What about the number Salma called? If Al-Haznawi still has the phone on, we can track his phone."

Singh nodded and his fingers played across the keyboard. "I'll call him using a Pakistan number, he'll assume the call is local." He keyed in the number and hit enter. There was a brief pause and then the call went straight through to voicemail. Singh scowled. "I'm sorry," he said. "The phone is switched off."

Harper swung the length of two-by-four hard and it thwacked against Ullah's backside. Harper had gagged the man and after each blow he'd asked the same question. "Are you ready to talk?" When the imam made it clear he had nothing to say, Harper would wallop him again. And again. He had lost count of the number of times that he had beaten the man. Thirty? Forty? He didn't know and he didn't care. He figured the Taliban would be doing worse to Spider in Pakistan.

Sweat was beading on his forehead and he wiped it away with his sleeve. He tossed the length of wood to the side and it skidded across the floor and came to rest by the wall. Harper pulled a Swiss Army knife from his pocket and flicked open the main blade. Ullah began to struggle frantically as Harper walked over to him, swishing the blade from side to side.

Harper knelt down beside the man and cut the duct tape away from his face. Ullah began to cough. "I don't know anything," he gasped, and coughed again.

Harper stood up and put his penknife away. "You seem to be good at tolerating torture," said Harper. "Have you been tortured before?"

Ullah didn't answer.

"Or have you been taught? Is there an al-Qaeda interrogation course? Are there techniques you can learn that make it easier?"

"I'm not in al-Qaeda," said the imam. "I am not a terrorist."

"Right, then," said Harper. "I should get you down, then, right?"

He walked over to where the free end of the chain was tied off and undid it, then let it slide slowly through his gloved hands until Ullah was lying on the concrete.

Harper stood over him and took out his cigarettes and lighter. "You smoke?"

"Smoke?"

Harper wiggled the pack of cigarettes. "Smoke?"

Ullah nodded. "Yes. I smoke."

Harper lit one and blew smoke. "Terrible habit."

He pulled a wooden chair over and then dragged Ullah up and sat him down. He used duct tape to bind Ullah to the chair, then slipped the cigarette between his lips. Ullah sucked on it gratefully as Harper lit another one for himself.

Ullah began to cough so Harper took out the cigarette. Ullah took a couple of deep breaths to steady himself, then he nodded and Harper put the cigarette back between his lips.

Harper paced up and down as he smoked. Ullah watched him fearfully. "I'm not happy about you making me do this, you know?" fumed Harper. "Beating the crap out of somebody isn't my thing. You can see I'm serious, I don't understand why you don't just tell me what I need to know, then I can stop doing this." He shook his head and looked up at the roof. "I have to say, if it was me being tortured and you asking the questions, I'd be spilling my guts. No question. I'd just tell you."

He dropped what was left of his cigarette on to the floor and ground it out with his heel, then did the same with the cigarette that Ullah had been smoking. Then he walked over to a bench and picked up a red plastic can with a black cap and a black spout attached to the handle. He unscrewed the cap and put it on the bench, then screwed in the spout. He lifted up the can and poured petrol over Ullah's legs, just enough to soak into the material.

Ullah screamed as he struggled, but Harper knew he wasn't going anywhere. He poured more petrol over the bound man. The imam gasped and spat to clear his mouth. Harper put the petrol can on the floor and took out his cigarette lighter. "Why do you care so much about Al-Farouq?" said the imam.

"That's none of your business," said Harper.

"He doesn't even come to this country."

Harper said nothing.

"Why are you doing this? You are not with the authorities. You would not be allowed to do this if you were."

Harper walked to stand in front of the bound man. "You think you're the only one who doesn't have to follow rules?" he said. "That's what you depend on, isn't it? The British sense of fair play. Human rights. You want us to play by the rules while you go around killing and maiming civilians."

"We are at war," said the imam.

"Then wear a uniform and carry a rifle," said Harper. "If you did that, I might have some respect for you. You're as bad as the scum we fought in Afghanistan. During the day they'd wave and smile at the troops. At night they'd plant IEDs. That's how cowards fight."

The imam glared at Harper. "We are not cowards."

"You fight like cowards. You plot and you scheme and you murder innocents, and then as soon as the authorities give you a hard time you scream 'human rights' and claim persecution."

"And what you are doing now is honourable?" spat Ullah. "How is this not cowardly?"

"I'm not the one pretending to be a religious figure," said Harper. "I don't hide in a church." He looked at his watch. "Anyway, enough chit-chat. I need to know how you talk to Al-Farouq."

"I don't know anyone called Al-Farouq."

"Really? He's an al-Qaeda paymaster. And you send young men over to Pakistan for him to train."

The imam shook his head.

"You think this is a game?" asked Harper. He waved the cigarette lighter in front of the man's face. "You think I won't do it?"

"I am an imam," said Ullah. "I serve Allah. If it is Allah's wish that I die, then so be it. *Allahu akbar.*"

"Yeah, *Allahu akbar,* blah blah blah." Harper stared at Ullah for several seconds, then put the lighter back in the pocket of his jeans and walked over to the far side of the building. There was a package there, six feet long and wrapped in polythene. Harper hefted it on to his shoulder and carried it over to Ullah. He dropped it down on the floor with a dull thud before grabbing one end of the polythene and unrolling it. The body of Shakeel Usmani flopped on to the concrete floor, swathed in duct tape. He had been gagged with a rag and more tape. "You know Shakeel, of course."

The imam stared at Usmani in horror. Usmani was in shock, his eyes were open, but he didn't seem aware of what was going on around him.

"Shakeel told me that you sent him to Pakistan for specialised training. It was Shakeel that told me about your three families. Your wives. Your kids. He was a mine of information. Very helpful."

The imam shook his head. "You can't do this. This is England."

Harper smiled thinly. "I can. And I have done. You take money from Al-Farouq. And you send young guys like Shakeel out to train with him. So I know you know how to get in touch with him."

The imam continued to shake his head as he stared at Usmani.

"You know the difference between you and me?" asked Harper. "You've got dependants. You've got family. Me, I've got nothing. I don't care if you know who I am or where I live, because there's nothing you can do to hurt me, other than to come after me with a gun. And if you do come after me, I'd lay money on my coming off best. You can kill me, sure, but you'll have a fight on your hands. But you, you've got wives. Three wives. I don't know how you manage to get away with that in a country where bigamy is illegal, but we are a tolerant country, aren't we? When all is said and done."

Harper pulled out his gun. "I need you to know what sort of person I am, Mohammed. You need to know when I say I will do something, I will do it. Do you understand me?"

The imam's face was bathed in sweat. He was staring at Usmani, his eyes wide and fearful.

Harper grabbed Ullah's chin and stared at him from just inches away. "I'm going to kill Shakeel here and now. I'm going to kill him in front of you. Then I'm going to take off your gag and I'm going to ask you one more time how you contact Al-Farouq." Ullah tried to twist out of Harper's grip but Harper tightened his fingers like talons. "Look at me, Mohammed, I need you to look at me while I talk to you." Ullah stared at Harper fearfully. There were tears in his eyes. "If you don't tell me what I want to know, I'll go and get one of your wives. Maybe the young one. Little Smita. When's the baby due? Three months? I think that's what Shakeel said." Harper looked across at Usmani. "That's what you said, Shakeel, right? She's six months pregnant?" Harper looked back at the imam. "I'll bring Smita here and I'll kill her. And I'll cut out the baby and rub your face in it. I'll bring them all, Mohammed. I'll bring every one of your wives and kids here one by one and I'll kill them in front of you. Do you understand?" Harper stared into the imam's eyes. Tears were running down the man's cheek and over the duct tape gag. "I'll take that as a yes," said Harper. He let go of Ullah's chin and walked over to Usmani. He pulled his gun from the back of his jeans, chambered the first round and shot Usmani three times, in the groin, the chest and the throat. He stood watching Ullah with a smile on his face as Usmani bled out.

Button paced up and down, staring at the blank screen. "How the hell does something like this happen?" she said.

"It's technology," said Singh. "Sometimes it just goes wrong."

"How much do those drones cost? Forty million dollars?"

"Sure, but each component is produced for the lowest possible price," said Singh. "Remember when the *Challenger* space shuttle blew up, all because an O-ring failed?"

"Talk to Eric again, find out what's happening."

"He's working on it. Best leave him to it."

Button sighed and ran a hand through her hair. "You're right. Sorry. I just feel so bloody helpless."

"You and me both," said Singh.

"There has to be something we can do. Some way we can find out where Al-Haznawi is headed."

"If they can't fix the Sentinel, the only way would be to get another drone in the area."

"They're trying that." She put her hands over her face and fought the urge to scream in frustration.

"Do you want me to get you a coffee?" asked Singh.

Button forced a smile. "I think caffeine is probably the last thing I need just now," she said. Her mobile rang and she took the call. It was Lex Harper. "Any news?" he asked.

"Plenty, but none of it good," said Button.

"I might be able to help," said Harper. "Are you near a computer?"

"Sitting opposite one. What have you got?"

"I think I have a line to Al-Farouq," said Harper. "He changes his cellphone number every day, and there's a website his contacts can go where they get the number. It's password protected so be careful because enter the wrong code twice and the website shuts down."

Button pressed the button to put the call on speaker. "I'm with a colleague, Lex. He's going to access the website."

"OK, but easy does it," said Harper. He dictated the URL and Singh typed it in. He pressed enter and the screen went blank but for a small white horizontal oblong. "I'm in," he said.

372

"OK, now the password is today's date, in numbers. Day then month then year. Eight digits in all. Followed by A and I and G."

"Allah is great?" said Singh.

"Hardly original, is it?" said Harper. "But pretty uncrackable and it changes every day. So eleven digits in all."

Singh typed in the password. He hit enter and the screen went blank. Singh frowned across at Button.

"Lex, the screen has gone blank."

"Give me a minute," said Harper. The line went dead.

Harper pointed at Ullah. "You think you can lie to me? You think I'm stupid?"

Ullah shook his head. "I don't know what you're talking about. I gave you the website. I gave you the password." Harper had cut away the duct tape gag but the imam was still bound to the chair.

"The screen went blank," said Harper. "They put the password in just as you said, and the screen went blank. You gave me the wrong password, is that what you did?" He flicked the cigarette lighter and Ullah rocked from side to side on the chair.

"Stop!" he shouted.

"You lied to me, you bastard!"

"I didn't lie! I didn't lie! That's what happens. The screen goes blank. You click on the top right-hand corner of the screen. Then you'll see the number."

"You didn't say anything about clicking in the corner."

"I forgot!" shouted Ullah. "It's hard to think, all these fumes."

Harper put the cigarette lighter away and called Button on his mobile. "He says you just click on the top right-hand corner of the screen."

"We'll try that," said Button. "Stay on the line." He heard her talking to someone and then she came back. "Brilliant, Lex. Thanks."

Harper ended the call and put the phone away. He nodded at Ullah. "Seems you were right."

"Now what?" said Ullah. "Now you can let me go, right?"

"Sure."

"That's what you said. You said you'd let me go if I helped you. I've helped you. You have to keep your word."

Harper took out his cigarette lighter.

"No, you can't burn me," said Ullah. "You promised."

Harper took out his cigarettes and lit one. He grinned, turned his back on the man and put the lighter away. "No, I'm not going to burn you."

The imam smiled hopefully. "So you'll let me go?"

"Let's not go counting chickens until we've heard back from the little lady," said Harper.

Charlotte Button put her headset back on and called Yokely. "I'm sorry, Charlotte, we're still flying blind here," he said. "There are no drones in the immediate area but I'm trying to get one launched as we speak."

"I might be able to help you locate Al-Farouq," she said. "I have a cellphone number for him."

"Doubtful he'll be using it," said Yokely.

"It's how he keeps in touch with his people in the UK," said Button. "He changes the Sim card every twelve hours, the number is only accessible through a protected website."

"Give me the number and I'll get it checked out," said Yokely.

"If the number is live and if it's in north-west Pakistan, will you send in the SEALs?"

"It's a gamble, Charlotte. You know that."

"I understand that, but it's the only hope we have right now."

"Let me check the number and I'll get back to you." The line went dead. Button stared at the central monitor. It was still blank.

Shepherd gestured at the food on the table. "Raj, you should eat," he said.

Raj shook his head. "I'm not hungry."

"That's the adrenalin," said Shepherd. "You need to ignore it and just shove as much protein and carbohydrate as you can into your system." He leant over, picked up a piece of chicken and gave it to Raj, then took another piece for himself. Raj put it to his mouth but then his stomach heaved and he bent double. He retched but nothing came out. Shepherd stood up and patted him on the back. "Take it easy," he said.

"What's going to happen?" asked Raj.

It wasn't a question that Shepherd could answer. In fact he was trying not to answer it, because he could only see their predicament ending in one way and that was with their deaths. Al-Qaeda didn't take prisoners, or at least they didn't keep them for long. They weren't like the Somalian pirates who took hostages for ransom. Al-Qaeda wasn't about money, it was about political ideology. They would keep Raj and him alive only for as long as they were extracting information from them. Once they had what they needed, Shepherd was sure that they'd be killed. And killed brutally. Probably with a blade, the words "*Allahu Akbar*" ringing in their ears.

Shepherd helped Raj sit up then fetched him a glass of tea. "Drink," he said. "You need the liquid."

Raj sipped the tea. "Where's he gone?"

"I'm not sure. But I am sure that you need to eat and drink as much as you can because I'm not sure when we'll be offered either again."

Raj took a bite of chicken and this time managed to swallow some. Shepherd grabbed a handful of lamb and began chewing on it. He had swallowed three pieces when the door opened. It was Al-Farouq. Behind him was a guard holding a Kalashnikov. The guard stepped to the side and four heavyset bearded men rushed in. They grabbed Shepherd and Raj and roughly dragged them out of the room.

The phone rang and Button put on her headset. "That number is live," said Yokely. "How good is your source that the number belongs to Al-Farouq?"

"I'd stake my life on it, Richard."

"I'm going to need specifics."

"It's the channel for an imam in Bradford to contact Al-Farouq. Rarely used but obviously when contact is necessary it has to be done quickly. The only way to get the number is through a secure website and the Sim card is changed every twelve hours. Where is the phone?"

"About ten miles to the west of Peshawar," said Yokely. "Capital of what used to be called the North-West Frontier Province."

Button went over to the map on the wall and traced the route that Salma's contact had been taking out of Islamabad. "The car was heading that way, Richard."

"Yes, I know."

"It's Al-Farouq. It has to be."

"If the contact is going to see Al-Farouq, why didn't they phone?"

"Because the cellphone is only to be used by the imam in Bradford. He's staying off the grid in Pakistan, but he probably figures any incoming call from overseas is probably OK, especially if they call on Skype." She stared at the map. "Peshawar is close to the border, Richard. Very close."

"It's still a border, Charlotte. If we go in, we have to be sure."

"I am sure, Richard. But we have to move quickly. Al-Haznawi is probably only an hour away from Peshawar. If we're going to do it, it has to be now. As soon as Al-Haznawi reaches Al-Farouq, they'll move locations again."

"I know, I know," said Yokely. He sighed, clearly weighing his options. "OK, we'll do it," he said. "What's the worst that can happen? Both our careers crash and burn?"

"It'll be fine, Richard. Trust me."

"God bless, Charlotte."

"God bless."

The line went dead. "They're going in?" asked Singh. Button nodded. "They are."

Harper was rolling Shakeel Usmani's corpse up in the plastic sheet when his mobile rang. He stood up and smiled at Ullah as he took the call. He had shoved a piece of rag into the imam's mouth and held it in place with duct tape. It was Charlotte Button. "You're a star," she said.

"It worked?"

"It worked. The SEALs are going in now."

"Fingers crossed," he said.

"Amen to that. What are your plans now?"

"I'll clear up here and get back to Thailand."

"I'll be in touch."

"I'm sure you will," said Harper. The line went dead and Harper put the phone into his back pocket.

The imam stared at Harper with fearful eyes. "So now you can let me go?" he asked hopefully.

"I'm afraid it's not as simple as that," said Harper. He smiled, took out his gun and shot the imam in the chest, three times. "*Allahu akbar*," he said as the imam bled out.

★   ★   ★

Adam Croft took long, slow breaths, trying to get his pulse rate down to a manageable level. He wasn't scared, but he was apprehensive. There was a big difference mentally but the physical symptoms were the same; a fast heart rate, rising blood pressure and increased respiration. It was coming up for 1900 hours and sunset was only minutes away.

The eight SEALs in the fuselage of the Lockheed C-130 Hercules were all dressed in black and kitted out with full high-altitude parachute life-support equipment. They each carried their own air supply but they were still fifty miles from the drop zone so were breathing from the plane's internal supply. Even just a few minutes without oxygen at thirty thousand feet would lead to hypoxia and unconsciousness. The cold was also a problem. The four-engine turboprop plane wasn't heated and the SEALs wore black thermal suits with felt liners and polypropylene knit undergarments to protect themselves against the sub-zero temperatures at high altitude. There was a digital thermometer at the cockpit end of the fuselage giving the temperature at minus forty degrees Fahrenheit. They also wore black balaclavas, gloves and insulated over-boots on top of their regular boots. On top of their heads were goggles that would protect their eyes against the freezing wind on the way down.

Jake Drake was sitting opposite Croft. Like most of the SEALs he was leaning slightly forward so that his parachute didn't rub against the fuselage. Drake was a three-tour veteran of Afghanistan, and had been wounded twice. Shrapnel from an IED had taken out a piece of the calf of his left leg, and a bullet had grazed his right shoulder. The two near-misses had earned him the nickname "Lucky Ducky" but it wasn't a nickname that Drake appreciated so it tended not to get used when he was around.

Henderson was sitting next to Drake. He caught Croft looking at him and he grinned. He was clearly looking forward to the jump. Henderson was an adrenalin junkie, no question. Croft had been with him in firefights and Henderson always seemed to come alive when the bullets were flying. The closer the bullets flew, the more Henderson seemed to enjoy it. Croft loved being a SEAL and the physical and mental challenges that came with the career, but there was no getting away from the fact that his sphincter had a tendency to tighten in combat. Maybe it was an age thing. Croft was thirty-five, which in the SEALs had him on the wrong side of middle-aged, whereas Henderson had a couple of years to go before he hit thirty. Neither man was married — few SEALs were — but Croft had a steady girlfriend that one day he hoped to settle down with, while Henderson pretty much had a girl in every port.

Croft grinned back and made an OK sign. Henderson's grin widened and he returned the gesture.

Croft looked down towards the tail of the plane, where the jumpmaster and his three loaders were making the final checks to the plastic pods that contained the six 4 x 4 All Terrain Vehicles they would be using on the ground. The jumpmaster was Jim Grant, a grizzled veteran with a quarter of a century's service under his belt. Like the three younger men assisting him he was wearing light blue fatigues and sneakers and breathing from the plane's air supply. Each of the men was linked to the fuselage by a thick green nylon strap attached to a webbing harness.

Like the SEALs, the pods were fitted with self-opening chutes using the Cybernetic Parachute Release System that would open at seven hundred feet above the ground. The pods weren't steerable so they would be jettisoned first and the SEALs would do their best to land in close proximity to them. The system's computer also had a GPS, which meant that the SEALs would be able to track the pods if they did land some distance away.

Grant looked up and flashed him the OK sign. Croft nodded. He rolled his shoulders. He had only been sitting for a couple of hours or so but the interior hadn't been designed for passenger comfort and his back and neck were already throbbing. He could see the rest of the team were just as uncomfortable. They were sitting on metal frames that were attached to the fuselage. On their laps were the black nylon operation bags containing their equipment. The bags were clipped to their harnesses but would be released just before they landed. They cradled their weapons on top of the bags, barrels pointing down. Croft favoured a Heckler & Koch 416, though several of the men preferred the FN SCAR standard assault rifle, chambered for the 7.62 x 51mm NATO-calibre round and fitted with a standard sixteen-inch barrel. All were fitted with noise suppressors.

The HK416 had been specially made for the American special forces teams. It used a gas piston system, which meant that hot gas and burnt carbon were expelled with each shot, making it less likely to foul. It was capable of firing eight hundred rounds a minute, but Croft had it set to single fire. He preferred to pick each shot carefully rather than use the "spray and pray" technique. As with most HK carbines the kick was negligible, minimised by a recoil pad in the stock.

Each of the SEALs also carried a sidearm, either a Heckler & Koch 45 or a SIG Sauer P226. Two of the SEALs also had M320 grenade launchers fixed under their weapons.

The parachute canopies they were carrying on their backs were twice the size of standard sport parachutes, attached to a specially strengthened army harness. The SEALs were not carrying reserve chutes. There was no point. Their CYPRES opening systems were set to open their main chutes at seven hundred feet. In the highly unlikely event the system failed, at terminal velocity they would hit the ground in less than six seconds, nowhere long enough for a reserve to be safely deployed. Not that there was a likelihood of a chute failure — the SEALs used the best equipment available and they all packed their own chutes.

Next to the digital thermometer were three lights, one red, one amber and one green. The red one winked on and Grant stood up. "We're approaching the drop zone," he shouted above the noise of the engines, even though the SEALs all knew what the red light signified. "Check your buddy's equipment."

The eight SEALs heaved themselves up off their metal frames and began to methodically check each other's equipment — the oxygen supply, the webbing straps, the Irvine height-finder and the device that would ensure all the chutes opened at seven hundred feet. The SEALs were more than capable of pulling their own ripcords but at terminal velocity there was zero room for error and it was best left to technology.

Croft had been paired up with the SEAL on his left, Julio Morales, a stocky Hispanic with massive forearms and a pinched waist that suggested long hours lifting weights and a carb-free diet. Croft checked that Morales was good to go, then clapped him on the shoulder. Morales then went over Croft's gear, nodded and gave him the OK sign.

Once all the checks had been completed, the SEALs turned to look at Drake.

"Comms check," said Drake. "Sound off. Sierra one."

"Sierra two," said Henderson.

"Sierra three." Julio Morales.

"Sierra four." Lars Peterson.

"Sierra five." Salvador Garcia.

"Sierra six." Franklin Sanders.

"Sierra seven OK." Calvin Wood.

"Sierra eight OK," said Croft.

"All good," said Drake.

Croft turned and looked up at the light array. Red was still showing. His heart began to race and he took slow deep breaths as he pulled the goggles down over his eyes.

Al-Farouq held open the door and the men manhandled Shepherd and Raj down the stairs to the basement. Al-Farouq said something to the men and they bundled Shepherd on to a chair and tied him with a length of rope. The men holding Raj dragged him underneath one of the hooks. One of them held both his arms while the other stood on a chair and threaded a length of rope through one of the metal hooks in the ceiling. Shepherd struggled but the men either side kept him pinned to the chair.

"Dan!" shouted Raj, as his wrists were tied together. "Dan, help me!"

Shepherd turned his face away. There was nothing he could do to help Raj.

The man finished tying Raj's wrists and the other man hauled on his end of the rope, pulling Raj's arms up. "Dan!" shouted Raj.

"You know what is going to happen?" asked Al-Farouq.

"What sort of man are you?" replied Shepherd.

"I am a man who requires the truth, that is all," said Al-Farouq. "Tell me the truth and your friend does not get hurt."

The men holding the rope pulled it harder so that Raj went up on his toes. One of the men walked over to a table and picked up a cane. He swished it back and forth. The man holding the rope tied it to another hook on the wall. If he stretched, Raj could just about manage to stand on his tiptoes.

"You can stop this, Mr Shepherd," said Al-Farouq.

"So can you," said Shepherd.

Al-Farouq nodded at the man with the cane. He took a quick run at Raj and then smacked the cane against his backside. Raj screamed.

Shepherd closed his eyes. He heard the shuffle of feet, the whistle of the cane, and a second scream, louder than the first. Shepherd put his hands over his ears but the men holding him ripped them away, forcing him to listen.

The red light on the bulkhead flicked off and the amber one went on as the pilot cut power to two of the engines, one port and one starboard. "That's amber!" shouted Drake. "Time to switch on your O_2 supplies!" The SEALs began switching from the plane's oxygen supply to their own personal oxygen cylinders which they would be using all the way to the ground. Once they had checked the oxygen was flowing as it should, they unfastened their harnesses and shuffled towards the rear of the plane, keeping close to the fuselage. The engine noise died down again as the pilot set the throttles of the remaining two engines to idle. With a metallic grinding that the SEALs felt as much as heard, the rear door began to lower. The amber light winked off and the green light went on.

Jim Grant gave his first two loaders the OK sign. They pushed the first of the pods on rails that led down the ramp. It gathered speed quickly, and when they let go of it six feet from the end of the ramp it flew off into the sky. The loaders hurried past Grant and his colleague, who were already sending the second pod on its way. In a series of well-practised manoeuvres they threw the remaining pods out so close together that they were almost touching.

Grant flashed Drake the OK sign and Drake patted Henderson on the shoulder. Henderson nodded and jogged down the ramp. Morales followed him. Then Peterson.

Henderson threw himself off the ramp, thrusting out his arms and legs in a starfish pose as he went out. As Morales and Peterson followed, Henderson, Garcia, Sanders, Wood and Croft filed down the ramp. One by one they jumped, and then Drake took a deep breath and followed. He gasped as the wind tore at him, and he had to fight to keep his arms and legs out as he fell through the slipstream. He found himself spinning to the left so he pulled his left arm in closer. He arched his back so that his centre of gravity shifted towards his stomach. The turning stopped and he concentrated on slowing his breathing as he looked around, mentally counting off the seven other jumpers below him. They had left the plane almost as one but the speed of the Hercules, even close to stalling, meant that they were already fifty feet or so apart. Down below them were the six pods. Each pod had a small drone chute popping around, keeping them from spinning as they fell.

The pods were falling at a faster rate than the SEALs and the men moved to keep close to them. Drake concentrated on keeping stable as the seconds ticked by. He snatched a quick look at the altimeter on his right wrist. He had already fallen eight thousand feet and they were less than thirty seconds into it. He did a quick count again, ticking off the seven men by name. Beyond them, the six pods seemed to be moving to the north. The men were tracking to keep in line with the pods and Drake followed suit. He arched his back to look up and he could see the brightest of the stars twinkling above him. He snatched another look at his altimeter. Eighteen thousand feet gone. Eleven thousand to go.

Even through his insulated gloves he could feel the chill in the air. At thirty thousand feet the temperature was below minus thirty-five degrees Celsius, and without the protective gear and oxygen he would have been unconscious already. As he fell, the air warmed one degree with about every two hundred feet but it was still bitterly cold.

The ground was closer now. He could see hills off to the west, the border with Afghanistan. To the north of the drop zone there were a cluster of brown buildings and what looked like farmland. He didn't see any major roads but the area was criss-crossed with tracks.

He counted off the men again, then the pods, then checked the altimeter. Twenty-five thousand feet. Not long now. He mentally prepared himself for his chute opening, even though he had no control over it. As the pods reached seven hundred feet the CYPRES computers fired the small explosive charges that cut the line holding the main parachutes in place. The spring-loaded pilot chutes on the pods broke into the slipstream and pulled the main chute with them, and one by one the massive canopies popped open like blossoming black flowers. Then Henderson's chute popped, quickly followed by those of Morales and Peterson. Drake's breath caught in his throat as Garcia's chute didn't deploy but then it popped open at the same time as Sanders'. Woody's chute opened, then Croft's, then Drake's altimeter hit seven hundred feet and his own chute automatically deployed, yanking him by the shoulders and dramatically slowing his descent. He reached up and grabbed the toggles that controlled the direction of his chute and pulled the right one so that he turned towards the pods. He looked up and gave his black canopy the once-over. The nine-cell flat ramair canopy was clean with no tangled lines. He made another adjustment to his direction and then looked down at the liquid crystal display tablet on his chest. It showed all six pods as small dots, off to the north.

"OK, guys, let me know you're all OK," said Drake. He twisted around and counted four canopies close by but he had no way of knowing who was who. "Sierra One OK."

"Sierra Two OK," said Henderson.

"Sierra Three OK." Julio Morales.

"Sierra Four OK." Lars Peterson.

"Sierra Five OK." Salvador Garcia. Sal.

"Sierra Six. As well as can be expected." Franklin Sanders. AKA Monster. He hated jumping.

"Sierra Seven OK." Calvin Wood. Woody.

"Sierra Eight OK." Adam Croft.

All good.

They were down to two hundred feet. Drake released his operations bag and it fell on a ten-foot-long cord before swinging below him. Losing the extra weight would make his landing easier and the sound of it hitting the ground would give him warning of the impact to come. Drake pulled down on the toggles, bent his knees and braced himself. The ground rushed up at him and then he heard the dull thud of the equipment bag hitting the desert floor. He pulled down hard on the toggles and felt a surge of satisfaction as he realised he'd timed it perfectly. His feet practically kissed the sand and he took two steps and stopped. A perfect landing. He pulled hard on the right-hand strap of the harness to collapse the canopy as he jogged upwind. He wound the canopy and lines around his arms, then dropped them on the ground and unclipped his harness. He stood for a few seconds, looking around him, getting his bearings. Drake felt warm — the insulation had done its job — but the surface of his black thermal suit was wet and close to freezing. He decided to keep it on; the sun was about to dip down over the horizon and the Pakistan desert could be bitterly cold at night so they would need all the insulation they had.

Guy Henderson ran over, his chute and harness in his arms. "All present and accounted for," he said.

Drake nodded. So far so good. A broken or twisted ankle would have made things much more difficult.

"Get everyone here, give me a minute to check my downloads and establish comms." Drake went down on one knee and checked his tablet. He had incoming data, downloaded from operation control in Basra. There was a map showing the terrain and a building circled in red, some three miles to the north of their position. There was also a satellite photograph of a white SUV and on it details of the driver and the registration. Saeed Al-Haznawi.

"Base, this is Sierra One," he said. "Receiving?"

"Base receiving." Lieutenant Commander Dick Blanchard was on the other side of the world but his voice was crisp and clear. Like all the SEALs, Drake had a flesh-coloured Invisio M4S earpiece which had been laser-cut to fit his ear perfectly. There was no microphone. Sound was conducted through the bone of his jaw to a sensor in the earpiece, which completely eliminated ambient noise and meant that the merest whisper would be transmitted.

"Sierra One, on the ground and ready to go."

"Base, you should have the target and coordinates. Looks like you are three miles away. And we now have a secondary target en route to the primary location. An al-Qaeda operative named Saeed Al-Haznawi. He is driving a white Daihatsu SUV. If you can intercept him, all good. He was last seen driving on the main road from Islamabad to Peshawar."

"Sierra One, roger that."

"You need to move in now, Sierra One."

"Sierra One, understood."

"Richard?" Yokely put a hand up to his headset. It was Eric Feinstein. "Are you there?"

"Hearing you loud and clear," said Yokely.

"I have some good news for you," said the CIA technician. "We have a satellite moving over the area in about fifteen minutes. I can't change its trajectory but I can get you a video feed that will give you some idea of what's going on down there."

"Outstanding," said Yokely, his soft Southern accent stretching the word out as if he was relishing the sound. "Can you send a feed to the Brits, too?"

"If you're OK with that, sure," said Eric.

"How long will we have a picture?"

"It might stretch to an hour," said Eric. "I'll keep you posted."

"You're a star, Eric."

The SEALs gathered around Drake. They had stripped off their oxygen masks and left them in a pile along with their chutes and harnesses. "OK, Monster and Guy, you two get a hole dug and bury the gear," said Drake.

"Why is it it's always the black man who gets to dig the hole?" growled Sanders.

"Because you're the biggest and strongest and you'll do it quicker than anyone else," said Drake. "And Guy's with you because he's got less experience on the quads than anyone else."

Sanders was already down on one knee pulling a collapsible shovel from one of the equipment bags. His nickname, Monster, was a result of being called Franklin, which had quickly become Frankenstein, helped by the fact that he was just over six feet six inches tall, almost a record for the SEALs, most of whom were just below average height.

Drake knelt down and placed his LCD display on the ground. The cursors identifying the six pods were clearly visible. Three were within a hundred yards of

391

their position, one was just over two hundred yards away and the remaining two were closer to four hundred yards away, and in opposite directions.

Drake knew that Garcia and Peterson were the two fastest so he told them to collect the pods that were farthest away. Garcia headed west and Peterson went east, both men jogging

"Adam, listen up." He tapped his LCD display and the photograph of the white SUV filled the screen. "This guy is on the way to the house." He tapped the pod closest to the road. "Collect this quad and set up near the road. If you see him heading this way, take him out."

Croft grunted and headed off.

Drake assigned pods to Morales and Wood and they headed east.

He pulled his night vision goggles out of his equipment bag and went off in search of the last pod. It was easy enough to find. The wind was still tugging at the parachute but the heavy pod had dug into the sand and wasn't going anywhere. He unhitched the canopy and collapsed it. He rolled it up and then undid the catches running around the middle of the pod. It opened up, revealing the quad.

The quad — also known as an All Terrain Vehicle — had been manufactured by the Polaris Defence Vehicles company specially for the SEALs and had been painted in desert camouflage pattern. It was fitted with non-pneumatic tyres that were pretty much indestructible, which meant there was no need to carry a spare. As part of the testing of the tyres the manufacturer had blasted away at them with an AK-47 and then driven the vehicle a thousand miles over rough terrain. It had passed with flying colours.

The quad had been designed to carry two hundred pounds of gear on the front rack and up to four hundred pounds on the back, but the SEALs didn't need to carry much in the way of equipment and the rear racks had been reconfigured to carry an extra rider. The quad was equipped with two fuel tanks holding a total of thirteen gallons. The powerful 850cc four-stroke engine produced 77 horsepower and gave it a top speed of 70 m.p.h, but it would be lucky to maintain 40 m.p.h over the rough Pakistan terrain. There was no ignition key, just a fuel tap to turn and a button to press. The first time Drake pressed the button there was just a muted fart and then nothing, but the second time the engine kicked into life. Drake fitted his night vision goggles and switched them on. They hummed for a second or two and then the sensors kicked in and he was looking at his surroundings bathed in a pale green glow. He climbed on to the quad, engaged the gear and edged the vehicle slowly forward off the pod. Once it was on the sand he climbed off. A short distance from the quad was a group of rocks and he dragged the pod sections over to them. The pod's camouflage pattern rendered it virtually invisible from a few yards away. He clipped the chute on to the back of the quad, climbed on and drove slowly back to where Sanders and Henderson were digging the hole. They were already three feet down.

Woody arrived back just as Drake was climbing off his quad.

"Sierra Four and Sierra Five, sitrep," said Drake.

"Sierra Five, just reached the pod," said Garcia.

"Sierra Four, I'm looking for mine," said Peterson.

"You got a problem, Sierra Four?"

"Lots of rocks," said Henderson. "Wait, no, I see it."

"Sierra Eight? Sitrep?"

"Sierra Eight, I'm on the quad now," said Croft. "Heading for the road to intercept the SUV."

Drake walked over to the hole. It was almost big enough to hold their eight personal chutes and the six chutes that had been attached to the pods.

He heard the growl of an engine behind him and turned to see Morales on his quad, bent low over the handlebars. He pulled up, dismounted, and dragged his chute over to the hole.

Sanders and Henderson were digging like machines. The natural competitiveness of the SEAL mentality had kicked in and they seemed to be trying to outdo each other.

"Sierra Five, on my way back now," said Garcia. "ETA three minutes."

"Roger that," said Drake. "What's your situation, Sierra Four?"

"Sierra Four, pod secured and the quad's working," said Peterson in Drake's earpiece. "Looking for a way through the rocks. The terrain's rough here."

"Soon as you can," said Drake.

Sanders stopped and grinned up at Drake. "What do you think, massa?" he said. "You want Mandingo to keep digging?"

394

Drake grinned. "I think we're good, Monster." He offered his arm and pulled Sanders out of the hole, then did the same for Henderson.

They all worked together to toss the chutes into the hole. They had just finished when Garcia arrived. "Right, let's bury everything, then we're off," said Drake.

Croft was a hundred or so yards from the road when the white SUV roared by, heading west. He cursed. "Sierra Eight, that vehicle has just passed."

"Sierra One, roger that," said Drake in his ear.

"Shall I chase?"

"That's a negative," said Drake. "RV with us two hundred yards south of the house. We're moving in."

"Sierra Eight, roger that," said Croft as he turned his quad to the west, keeping parallel to the road.

Al-Farouq took the cane from the man who had been beating Raj and grinned savagely at Shepherd. The men either side of Shepherd had tightened their grip on his arms, keeping him locked into the chair. "Please don't hit him again," said Shepherd.

Al-Farouq swished the cane through the air. "Then tell me the name of the brigadier who led the assault on the fort."

"He didn't lead the assault. He stayed in the barracks."

"Don't play games with me," said Al-Farouq. He smacked the cane against the back of Raj's legs and Raj screamed out loud and began struggling.

"Khan, that's all I know. Brigadier Khan."

Al-Farouq nodded. "See, that wasn't too difficult. And who led the attack on the fort?"

"He's dead," said Shepherd. "He got hit by an RPG." Al-Farouq drew back the cane. "OK, OK!" said Shepherd. "Jamali. Colonel Jamali."

Al-Farouq held the cane with both hands and flexed it. "I have heard of Colonel Jamali, of course."

"He was a brave soldier," said Shepherd.

"He died attacking my people," said Al-Farouq. "He would have killed them if he could."

"No argument here," said Shepherd. "Except of course he was wearing a uniform and representing a democratically elected government. Your people are what? Fanatics elected by no one."

"We serve Allah, the one true God."

"Yeah, well, good luck with that," muttered Shepherd. He wanted to say more but he knew that to do so would be counterproductive. If he angered Al-Farouq, he'd only take it out on Raj, so Shepherd averted his eyes and kept quiet.

"And what is your name, my friend?" asked Al-Farouq quietly.

"I'm not important," said Shepherd. "I'm nobody."

"You're too modest," said Al-Farouq. "And you've probably already realised I know exactly who you are." He said nothing for several seconds, then swished the cane through the air. "You are Dan Shepherd and you are an MI5 officer. It's time to start telling the truth."

Drake kept his quad at just below twenty miles an hour. The terrain was rough and rocky and he was keeping well clear of what few tracks there were. The night vision goggles gave him a near-perfect view of what lay ahead, albeit with a greenish tint. The standard quad came with three lights, two in the front bumper and one in the handlebar pod, but the lights, and the bumpers, had been removed to save weight.

He saw Croft off to his two o'clock. "Sierra One, I see you. Sierra Eight, stay put, we'll be with you in a minute or two." He saw Croft lean back on his quad and wave.

The terrain ahead sloped to the left but the quads had no problem remaining stable. They were fitted with on-demand all-wheel drive that automatically engaged all four tyres whenever the rear wheels began to slip and reverted back to the more fuel-efficient two-wheel drive on the flat. They were moving in a triangular formation with Drake taking point and Sanders to his right rear and Peterson to his left rear.

Garcia and Wood were at the back, giving the formation an arrow shape. Henderson was sitting on Wood's quad, facing the rear, his carbine at the ready. The SEALs matched Drake's speed and kept him as the focal point of the formation.

Drake reached Croft and drew up alongside him. As the rest of the SEALs pulled up around him, Drake checked his tablet. The target building was four hundred yards to the north. They were on a patch of rough land dotted with boulders that gave them plenty of cover. There was a narrow track ahead of them and beyond it half a dozen buildings. Three of the buildings, including the target, were surrounded by a waist-high wall. Drake switched off his engine and the other SEALs followed suit.

"That's the SUV," said Drake, pointing at the white Daihatsu parked next to the target building. "We need to move in now." He nodded at Wood and then pointed to a power line that fed an electric cable from the street, over the wall and to the houses. "Woody, I need you to cut the power to the house. If we get rid of the lights, we have the upper hand."

"Roger that," said Wood, and he headed towards the pole, bent double at the waist as he ran, cradling his carbine.

"Assuming we achieve our objective we'll be at our most vulnerable between leaving the target and getting to the quads," said Drake. "We'll be on foot, but there's very little moonlight and as far as we know the bad guys don't have night vision equipment. The one thing we don't know is the condition of the friendlies. If the two friendlies are mobile, Guy and Adam will pair up with them. They're carrying extra NVGs. If they can make it on their own two feet then we're gold. If they're not mobile, I need Monster and Lars to team up with Adam and Guy. If they need carrying we carry them, OK? We do what we have to do to get them to the quads. Any questions?"

"Just one," said Sanders. "Why does the black man always have to do the carrying? Tote that barge, lift that bale, will it never end?"

Drake grinned. "Let's move closer. As soon as Woody kills the power, we're going in. Sal, you and Julio move around to the rear. Let me know what the door situation is there." Garcia and Morales moved out, keeping low to the ground as they ran.

"Base, this is Sierra One," said Drake. "Receiving?"

"Base receiving," said the lieutenant commander in Drake's ear.

"Sierra One to base, we're getting ready to go in," said Drake. "The SUV is already there so the area might be hot."

"Base one, roger that. You guys be careful."

Al-Farouq whacked the cane against Raj's back, between the shoulder blades. Raj was sobbing and Al-Farouq hit him again, this time on the buttocks.

"Stop!" shouted Shepherd. He struggled but the men holding him held him firm.

"You are Dan Shepherd, correct?"

Shepherd nodded. "Yes."

"And you work for MI5?"

Shepherd gritted his teeth. He knew this was going to end only one way, no matter what he said. If it was just him at risk he'd deny everything but that wasn't going to work. It was clear that Al-Farouq knew who he was and who he worked for and denying it would only cause more pain for Raj. The problem was, once Shepherd opened the door the questions would come thick and fast. And if at any point he refused to answer, the torture would start again.

"How about this?" said Shepherd. "You let Raj go. He knows nothing. But if you let him go, I'll tell you everything you want to know."

Al-Farouq smiled. "Really? Everything?"

"Just let him go. Take him to the nearest city and let him loose. He knows nothing about you, and he knows nothing about ongoing operations."

"But you do?"

Shepherd nodded. "Yes."

"And if I let him go, you'll cooperate?"

Shepherd nodded again.

Al-Farouq walked towards Shepherd, swishing the cane from side to side. At the last second he drew it back and slashed it against Shepherd's shins. Shepherd screamed in pain.

"Do you think I'm stupid?" hissed Al-Farouq. "There is no deal to be made here. You will tell me everything I want to know." He whipped Shepherd's shins again. Shepherd was prepared this time and managed not to cry out.

Al-Farouq walked back over to where Raj was hanging. One of the men standing behind Raj had a machete sticking in his belt. Al-Farouq took the machete from the man, then walked around Raj, slowly drawing the blade across his stomach. "If you do not tell me everything, I will cut your friend and you will watch him bleed to death in front of you."

Shepherd tried to look away but one of the men holding him grabbed his hair and pulled it back.

"Now, why did they send you to Pakistan? Had you worked with Manraj before?"

Shepherd glared at Al-Farouq, wishing there was some way he could get his hands around the man's throat.

"You are an MI5 officer. Manraj is an agent for MI6. So why did they send you? Why not send someone from MI6? Is it because you worked with him before? Is that it? Were you involved in the assassination of the Sheikh?"

"The satellite feed is coming in now," said Singh. "It'll be on the left screen." He put his hand up to his headset. "Yes, Eric, I've got it."

Button grabbed her headset and slipped it on as she sat down. She pressed the button on the console to connect with Yokely in Basra. "Richard, everything OK at your end?"

"All good," said Yokely. "Have you got the satellite feed?"

"It's coming through now," said Button. "Your Eric is talking to Amar as we speak." The left screen flickered and there was an overhead view of a clump of buildings. The picture was a combination of greys and it was difficult to make out anything other than the buildings. She looked over at Singh. "Is that the best we can get?"

"It's thermal infrared," said Singh. "Remember it's night out there. Give me a minute." He turned away from her and spoke to Eric in CIA headquarters.

"I'm looking at a thermal infrared view, apparently, but I can't see much," said Button.

"We've focused in on the target building," said Yokely. "I have the same screen in front of me here. The SEALs are some distance away so you can't see them. And there are no guards outside so they're not visible."

"How long do we have this picture?" asked Button.

"An hour at most," said Yokely. "It's moving and we can't alter its trajectory. We can move the camera, though, so we can stay on this view."

Singh leaned over and tapped one of the buildings on the screen. "That's the one," he said.

Button nodded. "When are the SEALs going in, Richard?"

"Minutes," said Yokely in her headset. "We should have a perfect view."

A white shape moved into the screen and pulled up next to the target building. "Richard, are you seeing this?"

"I am, Charlotte. That's Al-Haznawi's SUV."

"Is that a problem?"

"Not as far as I can see. As I said, the SEALs are on their way in."

As Button stared at the screen the SUV's door opened and a figure moved towards the front of the house.

"We believe that's Al-Haznawi," said Yokely in her ear.

"Where are the SEALs?" asked Button.

"Just out of view," said Yokely. "Don't worry, they're there. They're about to go in."

"I want you to tell me how you are connected to Manraj," said Al-Farouq, holding the machete under Raj's chin. Tears were running down Raj's face. The strength seemed to have drained from his entire body and he swung back and forth, all the weight on his arms. Al-Farouq took the machete away from Raj's throat and slashed down at his left leg. Raj screamed and blood spurted across the basement floor.

"Stop!" shouted Shepherd.

"Then talk," said Al-Farouq.

Shepherd opened his mouth to speak but then they heard rapid footsteps on the stairs and the door was thrown open by a man in a long grey dishdasha carrying an AK-47. He said something to Al-Farouq in what sounded like Arabic. Al-Farouq frowned and replied. The man nodded excitedly and said something else. Al-Farouq leant the machete against the wall. He said something to the two men holding Shepherd and they nodded. The other two men followed Al-Farouq out of the room. The fighter with the AK-47 closed the door and stood with his back to it.

"What just happened?" Shepherd asked Raj.

Raj didn't reply. His head was down and sweat or tears were running down his face and dripping on to his shirt.

"Raj! Can you hear me?"

Raj mumbled something. His eyes were closed and all his weight was still on his arms.

"Raj? I need you to tell me what just happened," shouted Shepherd.

"There's a visitor," mumbled Raj. "From Islamabad."

"Did he say who?"

Raj shook his head. "Just that it's important."

The man with the AK-47 barked at Shepherd.

"He wants you to shut up," said Raj.

"Do you think?"

"Sierra Five, we're at the rear. There's a door here, and it looks open."

"Roger that," said Drake. "How close are you?" He was at the wall, looking over at the three buildings. There were lights on in the target house. The two smaller houses appeared to be unoccupied. To his left were Henderson and Sanders, to his right were Peterson and Croft.

"Sierra Five, about fifty feet. We're behind a wall. Four feet high. We can go right over it."

"See any hostiles?"

"Sierra Five, negative on that."

"Sierra Seven, I'm at the power line."

Drake looked over at Woody. He was crouched behind the wall close to one of the poles supporting the wire that carried power to the building.

"Sierra One, can you get up there and cut the wire?"

"Sierra Seven, I don't think so. I'm not even sure it'll take my weight."

"Can you blow it?"

"Sierra Seven, absolutely. A small C4 charge will bring it right down."

Drake nodded. The C4 would make noise, but it would do the job. If the pole falling didn't break the wire, Woody would be able to cut it. "Do it," he said.

Al-Farouq smiled when he saw Saeed Al-Haznawi. He walked over to him, embraced him, and kissed him on both cheeks. "*As-salaam alaykum*," he said. Peace be upon you.

"*Wa alaykum salaam*," replied Al-Haznawi. Upon you be peace. He handed Al-Farouq a carrier bag. "I brought you cakes," he said.

Al-Farouq sniffed the bag. "Coconut?"

"Coconut cupcakes. And there is a semolina cake that is especially tasty."

Al-Farouq waved his visitor to a low table surrounded by red cushions. The door opened and a man appeared, an AK-47 slung over his back, holding a brass tray on which there was a brass teapot and two beakers. The gunman put the tray down on the table and left the room. Al-Farouq waited until Al-Haznawi had sat down on one of the cushions before joining him. He poured tea, then opened up the carrier bag and set out the cakes that Al-Haznawi had brought.

"So, brother, what brings you out here at such short notice?" he asked, as he took a slice of the semolina cake.

"I have news," said Al-Haznawi. He toyed with a cupcake. "Bad news, I am afraid. You have to move. And soon."

Al-Farouq raised his eyebrows but didn't say anything.

"The sister who is close to the MI6 officer spoke to him earlier today," Al-Haznawi continued. "He is set to return to Islamabad because he has been told that a rescue operation is being planned." He sipped his tea.

Al-Farouq frowned. "Planned by whom?"

"By the SSG."

"The SSG know where I am? If that was the case, they would be here already surely." He popped a piece of semolina cake into his mouth.

"He told Salma that he was returning on Wednesday so that he would be ready to take care of the British soldier. And presumably the other hostage."

Al-Farouq steepled his fingers under his chin as he frowned. "When did she tell you this?"

"A few hours ago, immediately after she had the conversation with him. She came to see me and I drove straight here."

"Brother, are you sure you were not followed?"

Al-Haznawi smiled. "Impossible," he said. "I was checking constantly for a tail."

"What about the skies, brother?"

Al-Haznawi looked confused.

"Drones. Satellites. The eyes in the sky."

Al-Haznawi looked even more confused. "The Pakistanis do not have drones. Or satellites."

"No, but the Americans do. And we are only twenty miles from the border with Afghanistan."

"Why would the Americans be involved?" asked Al-Haznawi. "The hostages are British. The MI6 man is British. This has nothing to do with the Americans."

Al-Farouq held up his hands. "Perhaps I am worrying about nothing," he said. Al-Haznawi smiled and sipped his tea. Al-Farouq was certain he had not been tracked from Parachinar to Peshawar. Once ensconced in the house he had not been outside, nor had the hostages. All the neighbours were known sympathisers of the Taliban and none was in any way loyal to the Pakistan government. It made no sense that the Pakistanis had tracked him down already. He sipped his tea.

"Why was this MI6 man sent back to the UK?" he asked.

"He was summoned. By his bosses."

"He was a junior?"

Al-Haznawi nodded. "He is quite young."

"Do you think they blamed him for what happened at Parachinar?"

"That's what he thought, yes. He told Salma they were ordering him back to London to punish him."

"But now they are sending him back?" asked Al-Farouq.

Al-Haznawi shrugged. "Perhaps he was wrong. They summoned him back to London to brief him about what was to happen next."

Al-Farouq broke off another piece of semolina cake. He had punished people in the past. That was what leaders did. They rewarded good behaviour and they punished bad behaviour. But if the spy had been called back to London to be punished, why the change of heart? Something didn't feel right about this.

"You seem troubled, brother?"

Al-Farouq forced a smile. "I shall have to move, and quickly," he said.

"I can assist you," said Al-Haznawi. "I have friends, not far away."

"The worry is, how are they finding me so quickly?" asked Al-Farouq. "We have never used this place before. It is surrounded by friendly faces. The government has no friends in the area."

Al-Haznawi shrugged and sipped his tea. "It is a mystery to me," he said.

Al-Farouq picked up his beaker. He was just about to raise it to his lips when he heard the rat-tat-tat of automatic fire outside and he flinched. He jumped to his feet, knocking over the tea and cakes. The man at the door raised his AK-47 and turned to stare at the door. Al-Farouq had opened his mouth to speak when the light went out and the room was plunged into darkness.

Woody realised he'd been spotted only when rounds began ricocheting off the wall behind him and he heard the distinctive sound of an AK-47 being fired on fully automatic. He'd had his back to the building as he was attaching the C4 charge to the base of the pole and he was just inserting the detonator when the bullets hit the wall. He grabbed for his Heckler and as he turned he slipped his finger on to the trigger and brought the carbine up to his shoulder. The shooter was standing by the white SUV, holding his AK-47 at waist height, which is probably why he'd missed. Woody fired three shots and the man went down. He scanned the area to reassure himself that the shooter was alone and then turned and finished attaching the detonator. He activated the five-second timer on the detonator and hurried away. "Sierra Seven, fire in the hole," he said.

"Sierra One, in we go," said Drake in his earpiece. "Join us at the building, Sierra Seven."

Woody dropped behind the wall and tensed for the explosion. He heard a burst of gunfire from the rear of the building and then a dull thud as the charge exploded. The pole cracked and fell. Woody looked over the wall and saw that the power line had snapped. He stood up and ran towards the building, which was now in complete darkness.

Shepherd had recognised the first shots as coming from a Kalashnikov but the return of fire had been from a suppressed Heckler, possibly a 416, which almost certainly meant that it was Americans outside. They must have cut the power to the building so they would probably be coming in wearing night vision goggles.

The man standing to Shepherd's left released his grip on his arm, obviously disoriented by the darkness. Shepherd moved quickly. With his left hand he grabbed the wrist of the hand that was on his right arm, twisting it as he stood up. He heard the man grunt and he increased the pressure as he ran his right hand up to the man's neck. As soon as he felt the bony trachea he pulled back his hand and lashed out. The cartilage cracked and the man dropped, gasping as his throat filled with blood. Shepherd let him go, ducking down as he turned and reaching out with his hands to feel for the other man. He brushed against a leg and moved forward, straightening up and keeping his hands against the man's clothing, fingers splayed as he reached for the throat. The man struggled but it was too late; Shepherd's fingers fastened around his neck and squeezed. He felt the man claw for his nose and Shepherd twisted his face away as he increased the pressure. The man fell to the floor and Shepherd went with him, his fingers clamped around his neck like a vice.

Shepherd heard shouting from across the room, presumably the guard with the AK-47. And he heard

409

more gunfire outside, a mixture of suppressed semi-automatic fire and Kalashnikovs on fully automatic, but he was totally focused on squeezing the throat of the man underneath him. Eventually he went still. Shepherd maintained his grip for another ten seconds and then let go and stood up.

The guard shouted again. He couldn't see anything and Shepherd doubted that he'd be stupid enough to fire the Kalashnikov in the dark. Shepherd moved on tiptoe towards the door, arms outstretched. His photographic memory kicked in and he knew exactly where he was and where the man with the AK-47 was standing.

His fingertips brushed the wall and he stepped to the side. He took three short steps to his right, and then turned. He could see nothing. The man at the door started shouting in Pashto, clearly wanting to know what was happening outside. There were more shots upstairs, once more the pop-pop-pop-pop of a Kalashnikov being fired on fully automatic.

Shepherd took a breath, held it, and walked forward, slightly crouched, his hands outstretched but slightly bent, his right hand at shoulder height, his left at stomach height. He widened his eyes to maximise his night vision but there was still nothing to be seen, just blackness. He had his head cocked to the side, listening intently. He could hear the man's panting, and the scrape of his sandal against the floor. Shepherd's right hand brushed against rough material and a fraction of a second later his left hand touched metal. The AK-47. His brain performed the mental gymnastics necessary to convert the physical sensations into a mental picture

410

in a fraction of a second. The man was standing facing the door, the gun to his left, barrel up. Shepherd took another step closer, then slapped his right hand across the back of the man's head, thumb down, fingertips close to his left ear. At the same time his left hand moved from the barrel, fingers splayed, reaching for the man's bearded chin.

The man grunted and began to move but he was too late; Shepherd already had his left hand cupped around the chin and his right hand gripping the back of his head. He pulled hard, twisting the head to the left so quickly that the neck snapped with the sound of a breaking twig. The Kalashnikov fell to the floor. Shepherd held the head tightly and let the body down gently, then dragged it over to the wall and picked up the AK-47. He felt for the sling and slung it over his back.

"Raj, are you OK?" he asked.

"What's happening? Who's shooting?"

"The Americans are moving in. You need to do exactly as I say, this could get messy."

"What's happened to the guards?" asked Raj.

"I've taken care of them," said Shepherd. He moved through the dark towards the sound of Raj's voice. He reached out with his hands and touched a leg. Raj flinched. "It's OK, it's me," said Shepherd. He flashed back to when Al-Farouq had placed the machete against the wall. He'd left it leaning some six feet from the door. He moved to the wall and then moved along it until he found the machete. Then he moved back along the wall in the other direction until he found the rope tied to the hook.

"I'm going to cut you down, Raj," he warned, then used the machete to hack through the rope close to the hook. He held on to the rope with his left hand and managed to slow Raj's fall, then hurried over to him. "Are you OK?"

He felt his way up Raj's body, then rolled him over and ran his hands down to his wrists. He pulled at the ropes binding them.

"I'm OK," gasped Raj.

"What about your leg?"

"It hurts."

"I need you to stay here," said Shepherd as he worked at the knot.

"Dan, no, don't leave me!"

Shepherd could hear the terror in his voice. "You'll be safe here," he said. He pulled the rope away from Raj's wrists and helped him to sit up.

"I want to stay with you," said Raj.

Shepherd heard more gunfire upstairs. An AK-47. Then a suppressed Heckler. Then an FN SCAR. Then silence. Then running feet. He felt Raj's fingers grab his arm. "I'm so scared," said Raj, his mouth inches from Shepherd's ear.

"It's OK, we're being rescued."

"How do you know?"

"The guns. It's Navy SEALs out there."

"How can you tell?"

"I just can," said Shepherd. "OK, stay close behind me." He swung the Kalashnikov around, felt for the safety and made sure it was off, then ran his fingers along to the selector switch and put it in the lower position, putting the weapon in semi-automatic mode, allowing him to fire single shots. He didn't know how many rounds were in the magazine but no matter how many he wasn't going to waste them with fully automatic fire. "Keep one hand on my back," said Shepherd. "Stay close but don't grab, OK. Just maintain contact."

"OK," said Raj.

Shepherd ran his hand down the rough wood of the door and found the handle. He opened it and started up the stairs, with Raj close behind him.

Button's heart was pounding as she stared at the screen. White figures were moving around the building. Two had appeared at the rear and had gone inside, their shapes merging into the grey of the building. She had seen a figure appear from a side door and move towards Al-Haznawi's SUV, then the figure had fallen. Having no sound made it seem all the more surreal.

Seconds later, six figures had moved towards the front of the house, moving independently before forming a line against the wall. They had stayed there for a few seconds then the figure at the front had motioned with his hand and one by one they moved inside.

"They're in," said Yokely in Button's headset. "It'll soon be over."

Button swallowed. Her mouth had gone dry and she reached for a bottle of Evian water, unscrewed the top and drank from it, her eyes never leaving the screen.

Shepherd reached the top of the stairs. He heard running feet and a light bounced along the wall by his head. He looked to his left. There was a figure there with a flashlight. He couldn't make out the features of the man but he figured the SEALs wouldn't be using flashlights. He fired and the flashlight wobbled and he fired again and the light fell. There was a dull thud and the clatter of a weapon hitting the ground. Shepherd ran forward and picked up the torch. He played the beam over the floor and exhaled only when he saw the Taliban fighter sprawled on the ground, bleeding from the chest and throat. The dead man had a grey and white checked scarf around his neck and Shepherd pulled it from him and handed it to Raj. "Use that to bandage your leg," he said.

As Raj tended to his wound, Shepherd bent down and pulled the magazine from the dead fighter's Kalashnikov. He heard footsteps to his left and swung up the torch. The beam highlighted another robed fighter, his mouth open in surprise, an AK-47 across his chest. Shepherd fired one-handed, catching the man in the dead centre of the chest with a single shot. The man fell to the floor.

Shepherd shone the torch around, trying to get his bearings. As he turned, two men in desert camouflage fatigues with bulbous night vision goggles below their Kevlar helmets came around a corner. Shepherd dropped the Kalashnikov and shone the torch at his own face. "Friendly, friendly!" he shouted, then held up his hands.

"Shepherd?" shouted one of the men.

Shepherd felt a surge of relief wash over him. "Yes!" he shouted. He gestured at Raj. "He's a Brit too."

414

The two SEALs moved along the corridor, their weapons still aimed at Shepherd's chest. "Are you injured?" asked one.

"I'm OK. Raj has got a cut leg."

"Where were you?" asked the SEAL.

Shepherd pointed at the stairs. "Basement," he said. "There's three dead hostiles down there."

"Nice," said the SEAL, nodding his approval.

"Sierra Five, we have Shepherd and Manraj here, both hale and hearty," said the SEAL, presumably into his comms. Shepherd couldn't hear what was being said in reply, but the SEAL nodded. "Sierra Five, roger that." The SEAL nodded at Shepherd. "We're to take you out the back way," he said. "I'm Sal Garcia." He gestured at his companion. "The quiet one is Julio Morales. Stay close. And kill that flashlight."

Shepherd switched off the torch. From the front of the house they heard a Kalashnikov being fired followed by suppressed Heckler fire and then silence. Shepherd picked up the Kalashnikov, took Raj by the arm, and followed Garcia and Morales down the corridor.

They reached the end and turned left, then stepped through a wooden door and found themselves outside, under the stars.

"Sierra Five, we're outside," said Garcia.

"Did you hear that, Charlotte?" said Yokely. Button was staring at the screen, leaning forward so that her face was only inches from the four white figures that had emerged from the rear of the house. They all looked the same, though only three appeared to be carrying weapons.

"I see it, Richard," said Button.

"Home stretch now," he said. "They're OK."

"That's brilliant, Richard. Absolutely brilliant." She looked over at Singh. He was beaming and he punched the air with a clenched fist.

There was a staircase to the left and Drake pointed at it, then at Peterson and Sanders. They nodded and headed up the stairs, keeping close to the wall. A door opened and a fighter appeared with a flashlight. Drake shot him in the face, twice, and the man fell back and the flashlight fell to the ground and winked out.

Drake moved down the corridor, keeping low. Croft was behind him to the left, and Woody to the right. Henderson had stayed by the main door just in case more fighters came from outside. There was a door to the left and Drake opened it, then pushed it wide and stepped to the side, covering the left of the room, Croft covered the right, then stepped into the room in a crouch.

Drake saw two figures standing against the wall and he began to squeeze his trigger, but he realised they were standing with their hands in the air. "On your knees!" he barked. "On your knees, now!"

The two men obeyed and Drake moved closer. Croft had his weapon trained on the man on the right and Woody kept his carbine aimed at the one on the left. The man on the right was Akram Al-Farouq. Drake gestured at him with his weapon. "That's Al-Farouq, cuff him," he said to Croft. Croft pulled a set of plastic ties from his harness. Drake stepped forward and brought the butt of his carbine down on the other man's head and he dropped face forward on to the floor without a sound.

Croft finished binding Al-Farouq's wrists and hauled him to his feet.

"Right," said Drake. "Time to get the hell out of Dodge."

Garcia put a hand on Shepherd's shoulder. "We're going to RV at the front of the building," he said. "The area seems secure now but stick close to the wall."

Shepherd nodded.

"I'll go first, then you, then Raj. Julio will bring up the rear."

"All good," said Shepherd. He took a quick look at Raj. His eyes were closed and Shepherd shook him gently. "I'm OK," he said, but Shepherd could hear the uncertainty in his voice. The scarf that he'd tied around his injured leg glistened blackly with blood. "Not long now, Raj," said Shepherd. "Stick with me." Raj nodded.

Garcia took a quick look around, then started moving, crouched over his carbine. Shepherd followed, his finger outside the trigger guard of the Kalashnikov. They moved in a crouch. Small stones pressed into the soles of Shepherd's bare feet but he was barely aware of the discomfort. Adrenalin was coursing through his bloodstream and his body's endorphins were acting as natural painkillers, taking the edge off the damage that Al-Farouq had done to his shins in the basement.

A round thwacked into the wall above Shepherd's head and flecks of brick pricked his skin. There was a loud pop off to his right, coming from a window of the nearest house. Two more rounds hit the wall, slightly lower, but Shepherd had already ducked and turned and they missed him by more than a foot. Raj screamed and fell to the ground but Shepherd ignored him and stayed totally focused on the window.

"Where did that come from?" asked Garcia.

"Top right window," said Shepherd. As he spoke a figure appeared and he let loose two quick shots that thwacked into the brickwork above the window. There was just enough moonlight for him to see that he'd missed.

"Julio," shouted Garcia.

"I'm on it," said Morales. He sighted his M320 and let loose a 40mm grenade that flew off with a whoosh and headed straight for the window, a plume of grey smoke behind it. The grenade went through dead centre and a second later the room exploded in a ball of flame.

Shepherd bent down and helped Raj to his feet. Raj was shaking uncontrollably. He was in shock, but Shepherd knew there was nothing he could do just then. He squeezed Raj's arm. "Keep it together, Raj. We're going to get out of this, I swear."

They started moving again, reached the corner of the building and turned left. There was another SEAL there, standing guard at the door. He turned to look at them and raised a hand.

There was a burst of suppressed fire from inside the house and the SEAL standing guard whirled around and peered through the doorway. Garcia jogged over to join him.

Raj leaned against the wall and bent down. He was panting like a sick dog. Shepherd put a hand on his shoulder. "Slow breaths," he said. "You're hyperventilating. It's the adrenalin. Just breathe slow and easy. We're almost home."

Raj nodded. "I can't get any air," he panted. "It's like my chest is too tight."

"I understand. Just slow it down, and take long, deep breaths."

Raj nodded again and tried to do as he'd been told.

Two SEALs came out of the main door, manhandling a bearded man in a dishdasha. It was Al-Farouq, Shepherd realised. His hands were tied behind his back and he kept his head down.

Three more SEALs emerged. Garcia spoke to them and all four headed over to Shepherd. One of the SEALs lifted up his night vision goggles to reveal his face. Shepherd recognised him immediately. Adam Croft. "Bloody hell, you're a sight for sore eyes," said Shepherd. "Long time no see."

"The powers that be thought it might be helpful if you saw a friendly face," said Croft. He gestured at Henderson. "Remember Guy?"

Henderson removed his night vision goggles.

"Sure," said Shepherd. He bumped fists with Henderson. "What happens now?" he asked Croft.

"We've got quads to get us to the border," said Croft. "Then we'll be airlifted back to Basra."

Shepherd sighed. "It can't be soon enough," he said.

Croft nodded at the man to his left. "This is Lieutenant Jake Drake, he's in charge." The lieutenant was an inch or two shorter than Shepherd with a bodybuilder's shoulders.

"Thanks for this, Lieutenant," said Shepherd.

"Always happy to lend our British cousins a helping hand," said Drake.

"Or drag their nuts out of the fire," said Croft. He grinned. "Seeing as how you are no longer in the SAS, Dan, we're treating you as a Civilian Under Naval Training. Message received?"

Shepherd laughed, figuring the SEALs had earned the right to take the piss. "Adam, mate, call me what the hell you want, I'm just glad you're here."

Drake patted him on the back. "Let's move," he said. "Keep the Kalashnikov, just remember that anyone in desert fatigues is a friendly."

Croft removed a pair of night vision goggles from a pouch on his harness and helped Shepherd put them on.

Henderson had a pair for Raj. "Thank you," gasped Raj.

"Thank us when we're out of here," said Henderson. He looked over at Drake and nodded.

"Right. Back to the quads," said Drake. "Julio, Sal, Monster, you take the rear and cover us if we need it. Let's go!"

Henderson kept a hold of Raj's arm as they jogged away from the house, and Croft stayed close to Shepherd. Drake was on the left and Woody and Peterson were on the right.

They had gone about fifty feet when a Kalashnikov went off behind them but Morales let loose a short burst with his suppressed Heckler and the Kalashnikov fell silent.

They jogged across the track and over to the clump of rocks and the quads. Croft showed Shepherd to the rear-facing seat on his quad and Henderson did the same with Raj. There was a footrest that kept his feet away from the rear wheels and a small backrest. It wasn't the most comfortable of rides but it would do the job. One by one the engines burst into life, then they sped across the desert, heading west. Shepherd kept his Kalashnikov at the ready as they drove away from the buildings, but there was no activity. He began to relax, finally able to believe that he was safe.

Button stared at the screen. She'd watched as the white figures had left the house and moved out of view. She'd counted eleven figures. Eight SEALs and presumably Shepherd, Raj and Al-Farouq.

"Charlotte, are you online?" asked Yokely in her ear.

"I'm here, Richard."

"No casualties on our side, I'm happy to say," said Yokely. "And we have Al-Farouq in the bag."

"That's brilliant. Absolutely brilliant."

"There's a Chinook on the way. We'll pick them up on the Pakistan side of the border and process them at Basra before putting them on planes back to London."

"I owe you, Richard."

"No, getting Al-Farouq in the bag makes us even," said Yokely. "We're all square. I don't know how you got the location, Charlotte, and I'm guessing I don't want to know, but you saved the day back there."

"That's sweet of you to say so," said Button. "You give Spider my best."

"I'll be sure to do that."

Yokely went offline and Button sat back and took off her headset. The screen showing the buildings in Peshawar flickered and then went blank. Singh sat back in his seat and cracked his knuckles. "I don't know about you, Amar, but I need a drink," said Button. "A big one."

The Chinook touched down gently, the massive twin rotors kicking up a dust storm as it settled on the ground. The rear ramp came down and Croft helped Shepherd out of his seat. Two other SEALs were supporting Raj. "Where are we?" asked Raj.

"Basra airfield," said Shepherd. "Not far from Kabul. We can fly back from here to the UK."

"When?"

"It won't be long," said Shepherd. "Let me talk to Charlie, we can probably get on a flight later today. But you need to get a shower and some decent food down you. After they've taken a look at your leg."

Drake patted Raj on the shoulder. "We'll get a medic to check you out," he said.

"I just want to get home," said Raj.

"You and me both," said Shepherd.

He jumped down off the ramp and on to the ground, then turned and helped Raj down. The rotors slowed and the turbine noise dropped to a low whine.

"Is that what passes for operational gear in the SAS these days?" said a soft Southern drawl behind him.

Shepherd turned and grinned when he saw Richard Yokely walking towards the Chinook. "I might have known you'd be involved somehow," he said.

Yokely was wearing desert camouflage fatigues and a Kevlar vest over his regular clothes and his normally gleaming tasselled shoes were covered with a thick layer of dust. He shook hands with Shepherd, then gave him a hearty bear hug. "I promised the lovely Charlotte I'd get you back in one piece. She moved heaven and earth for you."

"I'm glad she did," Shepherd said. Two medics appeared with a stretcher. They placed it on the ground and helped Raj on to it. His eyes closed as soon he lay down and one of the medics began checking his vital signs as the other ripped his trousers open and went to work on the injured leg.

Drake and Croft both flashed salutes and Yokely returned them. "Well done, guys," he said. "Any casualties?"

"None, sir," said Drake.

"Outstanding," said Yokely.

He looked inside the Chinook and saw two SEALs manhandling a clearly disoriented Akram Al-Farouq out of his seat. "He give you any problems?"

Drake shook his head. "Good as gold," he said.

The SEALs kept a grip on Al-Farouq's arms as they stepped off the Chinook ramp. They marched him over to Yokely.

"Pleasure to meet you, Mr Al-Farouq," said Yokely. "I've got an orange jumpsuit that I hope is your size, and a whole load of questions that I'm looking forward to asking you." He gestured at a waiting Gulfstream jet. "But not here, obviously." Yokely nodded at Drake. "Load him on to the plane, will you?"

"Pleasure," said Drake.

"Hooyah," grunted Croft.

Yokely and Shepherd watched as Al-Farouq was taken over to the jet.

"What happens to him now?" asked Shepherd.

Yokely grinned. "Best you don't know," he said. "How was it?"

Shepherd shrugged. "He caused me a lot of pain, Richard."

"Do you want a few minutes with him? Mano a mano?"

Shepherd looked over at Al-Farouq. He was being taken up the stairs into the Gulfstream, his shoulders hunched, a beaten man. Shepherd could only imagine the horrors that lay ahead for him, and there would be no hope of rescue. At the very least he'd spend the rest of his life in a metal box a few metres square with only an occasional glimpse of the sky. He shook his head. "Nah," he said. "I'm good."

ISIS publish a wide range of books in large print, from fiction to biography. Any suggestions for books you would like to see in large print or audio are always welcome. Please send to the Editorial Department at:

ISIS Publishing Limited
7 Centremead
Osney Mead
Oxford OX2 0ES

A full list of titles is available free of charge from:

Ulverscroft Large Print Books Limited

(UK)
The Green
Bradgate Road, Anstey
Leicester LE7 7FU
Tel: (0116) 236 4325

(Australia)
P.O. Box 314
St Leonards
NSW 1590
Tel: (02) 9436 2622

(USA)
P.O. Box 1230
West Seneca
N.Y. 14224-1230
Tel: (716) 674 4270

(Canada)
P.O. Box 80038
Burlington
Ontario L7L 6B1
Tel: (905) 637 8734

(New Zealand)
P.O. Box 456
Feilding
Tel: (06) 323 6828

Details of **ISIS** complete and unabridged audio books are also available from these offices. Alternatively, contact your local library for details of their collection of **ISIS** large print and unabridged audio books.